/ENGE

f LEXINGTON CONNECTION

by

E. Logan

Bella
BOOKS

Other Books by M. E. Logan

Lexington Connection

Dedication

To Blondie for giving me the idea

Acknowledgments

All persons in *Revenge* are purely figments of my imagination. Walton's Corner and Linda's campground also exist purely in my imagination. Other locations, counties, cities, rivers and creeks mentioned do exist in my home state of Indiana.

I do want to thank several people who aided me in the course of this book: Roselle Graskey for lighting a candle in my darkest moment. Cheyne Curry for answering security questions. Linda Sears and Rachel Thomas for answering location questions. Vicki Combs and Gail Dixon for countless readings and feedback. Joan Denman and Sherri Hajek for listening and giving helpful comments and encouragement. Julie Klein for editing pointers and advice. Thank you all.

Last of all, I'd like to thank Cath Walker, my editor, for her kind comments and suggestions to make it better.

I appreciate all.

CHAPTER ONE

"I must be crazy," Kendra muttered as she looked over her wooden worktable scattered with electronic parts and wires.

"How so?" Linda responded from her perch on top of the four-drawer filing cabinet. She pulled her legs up and wrapped her arms around them, resting her chin on her knee. "Isn't this what you wanted? To be accepted by the militia, to be part of the group, the inside circle?"

Kendra scowled at her. "You know damn good and well what I wanted. I wanted to find Artie."

"Well, you found him, and he's not going nowhere."

Kendra gave a derisive snort. "Not until the county releases him at least." She picked up the needle-nose pliers and the computer board. "Damn fool. Just had to be showing off and firing a gun in the air."

By itself, she fumed, that wasn't bad, but he'd been busted for domestic violence and, right before that, a DUI. Those charges kept racking up and when he came up on the weapons charge, what might have been a misdemeanor got upgraded to a third-degree felony and mandatory eighteen months.

Nothing to do with her though, except she had moved back home to Walton's Corner expecting to spend only a few months here, certainly not over a year. Artie serving time for eighteen months had sentenced her as well.

"Stupid. Stupid. Stupid."

She threw the pliers down, too irritated to do the fine detail work the computer board required. What was she doing here anyway? She spent how many years focused on escaping, going to college, getting away from all the limitations of small-town Indiana rural life and now she was right back where she started. Sitting in the middle of a compound with a bunch of malcontents and misfits, half of who were convinced the world, was going to come to an end, or at least the civilized world and the other half who were entirely willing to hasten the event. She ran her fingers through her short dark hair, clenching the thick curls in frustration.

"You know," Linda pointed out, "you don't have to stay here. You had good intentions; you came here and tried. It's not your fault Artie went to jail."

"Not for his real crime," Kendra snapped. She released her hair and rubbed her face, her blunt fingers going over the broad facial features that denoted her Midwestern background. "Besides, I ran out on you once. You really expect me to do it twice?"

Linda looked out the window, to watch a light snow falling. "I told you to go—get out of here, make a life for yourself. If we couldn't both leave, at least you had a chance."

"You could have come with me!" Full of nervous energy, Kendra got to her feet, moving around the table, looking for she didn't know what to drain off her frustration.

Linda turned to give Kendra a sad smile. "Old argument, dear heart. I didn't. Too late now."

Too late, too late, too late. The words went around and around in Kendra's brain. Missed opportunities. Things she didn't do. Things she should have done. Things she could have done.

More might have been said but they were interrupted by a sharp rap on the door. A tall, broad-faced man shoved the door open with his shoulder as he carried boxes in, kicking the door shut behind him with his foot.

"You talking to yourself again, Mac?"

"You see anyone else in here to talk to, Stockton?"

Stockton deliberately looked around even as he set the boxes down on the corner of the worktable. Kendra moved around the table, taking back her seat as he looked back at her.

"No." He shook his head. "I worry about you sometimes, Mac. Something just ain't right."

"Well, that makes us even, Stockton. I worry about you, too."

She looked up at him, still half scowling. Usually she had definite feelings about someone, but Stockton, there was an uncertainty there.

He leaned against the windowsill and watched her piece the computer parts together. "You hear the news?"

"What's that?" She took in his folded arms, seemingly casual. No, he was watching for her reaction. She was so tired of having to watch every word, every response.

"It's confirmed. Jeffers is getting out early."

Her heart lurched, but she casually reached for another piece to cover any of her involuntary movement. She glanced up at Stockton in an effort to be just mildly curious. "How'd he manage that?"

"Nothing he did. Indiana Civil Liberties Union sued the county about jail overcrowding. The state had already moved him to the county because of their overcrowding. County cut a deal, had to reduce the number kept in the jail. Wasn't anywhere else to move him. So he's getting out early."

"Well, that'll put a different spin around here."

Stockton straightened up. "That's for sure." He glanced around the room again as if looking for someone. He looked back at Kendra. "He wasn't happy hearing about you being here. You know that don't you?"

"Tough titty. He wasn't here to block it. So I'm in. He can deal with it. Not my problem." Kendra dismissed the subject of Artie as she pulled the box toward her, ripped off the taped down shipping papers. "This is. And what it is this? I didn't order anything."

Stockton pushed off from the window as Kendra didn't rise to his baiting. "Sure hope it stays that way."

Kendra gave him a sharp look of puzzlement.

"That it's not your problem," Stockton amended. Then with a wave of his hand, he indicated the box. "That just came in. Didn't have a name on it, but it's electronics so I thought it was something you ordered."

Kendra shook her head. "I'll take a look at it, track it down."

When she didn't say anything else but continued to frown at the paperwork, Stockon finally turned away. "Okay. Guess I'll catch you later."

Once the door shut, Kendra put the paperwork down.

"Damn." Linda spoke this time from the top of the bookcase. "That is news." She tilted her head in question. "Why the frown? Isn't that what you wanted? Artie out?"

"Yeah," Kendra said slowly. "I'm more curious as to why Stockton wanted to make sure I knew."

"You know," Linda said in careful tones, "he's right. Artie won't be happy that you're still here, never mind in as tight as you've gotten. I won't consider it running out on me if you decide to leave before he gets back."

Kendra absently shook her head. "No. I'm not some scared twenty-two-year-old now." She felt the steely resolve. "I'm in for the duration."

Linda sat up with an alarmed expression. "Kendra, I recognize that look. You have no idea what Artie might do if you confront him. I don't want you taking that risk. You can't undo what he's done."

"No, but I can make him pay for it," Kendra said resolutely. She looked up at Linda. "A little late for second thoughts, girlfriend. You should have thought of that when I saw you at the fireworks."

The Fourth of July fireworks at Carmelfest, Carmel, Indiana. That's when it all started.

CHAPTER TWO

The projectile launched with a thunderous muffled boom and whistled high over the crowded softball diamond before it exploded in a riot of red and silver. The slightly humid air held the colors, letting them drift down slowly to the ooooohhhhs! and ahhhhhhs! of the appreciative spectators.

"Marvelous! Good start!"

The voice was so familiar Kendra McKenna didn't even think it strange, and by the time she realized it, the last colors were fading and it was dark again, too dark to identify anyone readily.

Travis, E. E. Travis, beside her, took a deep breath of controlled breathing. "Okay," she said in a deliberate voice. "That was pretty. A chrysanthemum, wasn't it?"

"Actually," Kendra said absently as she continued to look around, surveying the people surrounding them, "it was a peony. Chrysanthemums have tails, look like streamers."

"Oh." Travis quickly gulped her soft drink, grabbed a piece of ice and flinched as the next shots went off, three in quick succession. She took some deep breaths. "I–I really appreciate you coming with me tonight, Kendra."

Kendra only half noticed the blue and silver, the greens, the bright white that lit up the ball field, exposing upturned faces. She was more aware of Travis's anxiety, the excitement of the crowd, the hushed awe that fireworks generated. "No problem," she said as she decided she had been hearing things. Memories. They can trick the mind. And it had been a long time since she had attended fireworks.

"Wonder what makes the green," Travis commented. Her face was turned up toward the fireworks, but her eyes were closed.

"Barium."

Travis opened her eyes and turned to her friend in some surprise.

Kendra stood there, uncomfortable as she grew conscious of Travis's appraisal. She didn't like drawing attention to herself, tried hard to blend into the crowd, any crowd. Average height, average weight, which meant she was stocky without being athletic. Boring, she considered herself. Reserved, she'd heard friends tactfully describe her. She didn't realize that what she considered dull and certainly unexciting, her friends found steady and comforting. Someone described her brown eyes as trustworthy, steady, which Kendra considered more complimentary than being called sexy.

"Copper for a lot of the blue green, but the pure green, like that." Kendra pointed up to the bursting color above them in an effort to get Travis's attention off her. "That's barium."

"You–uh, you seem to know a lot about fireworks for someone who doesn't like them."

Kendra took a deep draw of the canned root beer and rested her head back against the tree trunk she was leaning against. "Never said I didn't like them; just don't go to them."

"Why not?"

Kendra shook her head. She didn't want to discuss old history, old times. They were best left unspoken.

"I mean," Travis said as she stepped back into the trees when the comet exploded in four different directions, a mass of crisscrossing trails of red. She swallowed and started again, "I know what they do to me." She shook her head and leaned against the tree. "Kendra, I don't think I can stay much longer."

"That's okay," Kendra reassured her. "We can leave whenever you want. I told you when you asked me to come with you that you could set the time, when to leave, everything. I'm not going to make you stay."

Travis shook her head, stepping behind the tree. "It just seems so foolish, to be so freaked out by something so popular." She flinched at another explosion. "I think we need to leave," she said breathlessly. "Before I lose it entirely."

"Okay, okay." Kendra turned to go and only took a few steps before she realized Travis wasn't with her. She looked back to see Travis leaning against the tree, her hand on her chest. "What is it?"

"Chest. Ohhh." She drew a ragged breath, reaching for Kendra. "Kendra, get me out of here."

Kendra caught her arm. "Don't panic now. We can leave. Hold on to me."

They threaded their way through the outer fringes of the crowd, along the tree line. In an effort to lessen Travis's panic, Kendra reasoned that the fireworks were less visible there, the sound more muffled.

"Do we need to go to the emergency station?" she asked as they came out of the trees and headed for the gate to the parking lot. Behind them, another rocket went off and Kendra could feel Travis start to shake.

"No." Travis shook her head, violently. "Once I'm out of here…"

Kendra looked around for the quickest route to the lot, not the shortest. She spied the camera crew and the reporter interviewing some guy dressed in camouflage and decided to detour around them. Travis would only be embarrassed if she was accosted and had to state her panic wasn't service-related.

They reached her late model Mazda without interruption. She quickly unlocked the passenger door and helped Travis in. "Head down, between your knees. We'll be out of here in a minute."

She made sure Travis was secure and belted in, closed the door, and stood up to walk around the car only to see someone standing at the front. Western shirt, dark with white piping, black jeans.

"Excuse me," she said automatically, without really looking at the woman in the dimness. "We need to leave."

"I've been waiting for you."

For a moment, Kendra thought her heart stopped. She looked up at the pale face, the half smile, the dimple. "Oh, my God!" She took a step forward, her hand out. She heard the door open behind her, and she still couldn't tear her gaze away. "I thought—"

Whatever she thought the sound of Travis throwing up made her turn around. Travis was leaning out of the car, bent over.

Kendra turned back but the woman wasn't there. Even as Kendra did a quick scan of the lot, she wasn't there. Kendra turned back to take care of Travis, looking up and around, wanting to find her, wanting to believe. But she saw no one.

* * *

"I'm sorry, I'm so sorry," Travis moaned on the hospital gurney waiting in the emergency room.

"For what?" Kendra sat back on the hard plastic chair and crossed her ankles. What with it being a holiday weekend with lots of drinking and the resulting traffic accidents, there was no room in the inn. So they were waiting in the ER for test results. The words "heart attack" had gotten them out of the waiting room immediately.

"I know when you said you'd go along with me to the fireworks, you didn't expect this."

"No, but what difference does that make?" Kendra shifted on seat. "You say it's an anxiety attack, and maybe it is. But chest pains, nausea. Classic symptoms of a heart attack."

Travis lay back and closed her eyes. "It's an anxiety attack. God knows, I've had enough of them." She stared up at the bright lights in the ceiling. "Every Fourth of July, New Year's." She closed her eyes. "Loud noises. That whistling."

"Stop it," Kendra ordered quietly. "So you freak out at loud noises. Lot of folks do. Who do you think that reporter was interviewing out at the park?"

"Serviceman. PTSD. At least he has an excuse."

"Stop it," Kendra repeated. "Phobias are triggered by lots of things or nothing, things we can't always control. Sometimes we just have to live with them."

"Yeah, just me and the dogs," Travis muttered.

Kendra sighed. Sometimes there was no reasoning when someone wanted to beat themselves up. "Why don't you get some rest?"

But even in the emergency room, they could hear the muffled boom of the fireworks. The monitor picked up Travis's agitation.

"Down girl," Kendra said softly.

"Don't call me girl!" Travis muttered and Kendra had to chuckle at the husky, boyish-looking woman. Athletic looking and muscled in spite of her lack of height, Peter Pan haircut, broad features. Jeans in spite of the heat, with the heavy leather belt, an Abatis T-shirt and a camp shirt over it. No, not too much feminine about her. "All right," Travis went on, doing her deep breathing exercises. "Talk to me."

"About what?" Kendra was never one for the small talk, and being requested to talk, about anything, drove every idea of what to talk about out of her mind. Except what she didn't want to talk about.

Travis took a deep breath. "Why have you been avoiding the fireworks?"

"Who says?" Kendra raised her eyebrows, and if she were wearing glasses, she would be looking over the rims. As it was she just gave Travis the intimidating glare.

"Peg was surprised as hell that you were coming to the fireworks with me. Said you always avoided them, even went camping to get away. So why'd you come when I asked?"

"Yeah, well." Kendra shrugged. She should have known that such information could only have come from Peg, her office manager. "Didn't want to let a friend down." She looked down the hall, wondering when the test results might be in, when they could get out of here. She glanced back at Travis who was looking at her expectantly.

She sighed. Travis was trying hard to confront her issues involving fireworks. Maybe, Kendra considered, she needed to do the same. "I let someone down once. Fireworks are a potent reminder."

"Something happen at some fireworks show? Fireworks accident? I know that happens sometimes."

Kendra still hesitated. "No, nothing like that." Travis looked at her with expectant interest. At least, Kendra thought, this will be a distraction for her. "My first lover was passionate about fireworks," Kendra said reluctantly. "Her birthday was on the third, and she told me once she was eight or nine before she really realized all those fireworks weren't just for her." She gave a rueful smile. "We spent a lot of time going around to different shows, seeing different setups." She trailed off as memories flooded back.

"So, what happened?" Travis prompted.

Kendra shifted her position on the hard plastic chair as she remembered the woman she saw in front of the car. "Things. Life. I left town, went to college. She stayed at home, taking care of her mother who had a stroke. She ended up getting married. To a neighbor guy."

"Bummer." Travis paused as if sensing there was more to the story. "I take it she's the one you let down?" she said finally.

Kendra shrugged. "Something like that."

"And you haven't seen her since then?" Travis fished a bit more.

Kendra shook her head. *Not until tonight. Or was it just something I thought I saw? Because I wanted to?*

"No way you can make amends?"

"Nope," Kendra said with finality as she spied the harried doctor heading toward them. She had the clipboard and loose papers which maybe, Kendra hoped, meant answers. Good timing, she thought as she got to her feet.

"Great news," she said when the doctor left.

"I told you. Just a panic attack." Travis was already reaching for her clothes. "Now get me out of here."

* * *

"I thought the traffic would be out of here by now," Travis said as Kendra turned off North Meridian. "We were at the ER long enough."

"Show's just breaking up." Kendra checked the rearview mirror, seeing the steady stream of lights behind her.

"Maybe we can just leave my truck there, pick it up tomorrow," Travis suggested.

"Fine by me." Kendra drove around the block to escape the heavy traffic and head across town. "You sure you're okay? You can stay at my place tonight. Got that guest room all made up."

"No, I'm fine." Travis gave a slight chuckle. "Besides, don't want anyone to see us and have anyone think I'm sleeping with the boss."

Kendra gave her a disbelieving look. "Sorry, butch, you're not my type."

Travis laughed, or at least started to as she wrapped her arm around her midsection. "Don't make me laugh. All my muscles hurt."

Traffic was heavy. Everyone going home but as they turned through the downtown area, it thinned out a little. Kendra still kept an eye on the traffic, still distracted by the thought of the woman at the fireworks. Her attention was caught by headlights far behind her, coming up too fast for the speed limit and weaving. Probably too much celebration, she decided as she slowed down. Need to be defensive. She was relieved when the full-size dark-colored pickup went around her and shot down the street.

"Idiot." Travis straightened up to watch the taillights as they swerved from one lane to the other. "Look at that!"

The truck suddenly swerved from the left to the right lane, almost hitting the car beside it. The car slammed on its brakes and jerked hard to the right to avoid being hit. It went up and over the curb and came to a stop just before hitting the building. The truck sped up, suddenly straight in its lane and disappeared over the hill.

Kendra hit her flashers as she pulled in behind the car, blocking traffic so no one would run into either one of them. Travis was already calling 911 on her cell phone. The driver opened her door and was just getting out of her vehicle.

"Are you all right?" Kendra called as she ran up to the driver's door. Another car, very similar to the one that had been hit, pulled around and parked in front, this driver also bailing out quickly.

"Robin! What happened? Are you all right?" The male driver hurried back to the damaged car.

"Some jackass clipped me!" The woman was obviously unhurt as she walked around to the front of the car, glancing at her watch, and oblivious to the line of traffic moving around them.

Kendra followed her and frowned as she saw the passenger side fender almost leaning against the brickwork. More disturbing was the way the whole car was slanted. She walked around the other side to get a closer look only to see the wheel leaning against the curb.

"Can I just back it out?"

Kendra squatted down to examine closer the forty-five degree angle of that front wheel. "I don't think so," she said as she peered up under the fender and glanced at the other driver who squatted down beside her. "Pretty banged up. Need to call a tow truck." She stood up, dusting off her hands and looked up at the slender dark-haired woman, dressed in a straight skirt and matching jacket before she recognized her as the reporter from the fireworks. Couldn't recall her name. For the first time she noticed the station's call letters on the side of the car.

"Cops are on the way," Travis announced as she walked up.

"Ohhhhh, I don't have time for this!" the woman stormed. She was already pulling items from the car and handing them off. "Brady, get this to the station. At least the tape will be there.

I've got that interview with that soldier." She turned around to look up and down the street. "Where're the cops when you need them!"

"Probably still directing traffic," Kendra said as she looked back.

"Did you get a description?" the other driver asked the woman. "I was too far back."

"No," Robin spit out with irritation. "Just saw his headlights in the mirror, then he was up beside me."

Kendra walked around the car, checking the rest of it out. "Ford, blue I think, hard to tell in these streetlights. Dark blue or black, crew cab. Sounded like a diesel. Couple of years old."

Robin turned around as if she had just realized Kendra's presence.

"He just passed me back a bit." Kendra forestalled any question just as the squad car pulled up.

Kendra noted Robin was polite, firm and in a hurry. Kendra and Travis just bided their time and gave the officer—a cute little brunette that perked up Travis's interest—all the information they had. Kendra handed over her business card and the officer nodded.

Kendra walked over to Robin to overhear Brady asking, "Do you think it was intentional?"

Interesting. "Excuse me," she interrupted. She held out a business card. "If you need a witness, here's where you can contact me."

"I'm sure your contact information will be on the accident report," Robin retorted crisply.

Kendra shrugged. "Never hurts to have duplicate information. And you might need our other services."

"Thanks." Robin stuck the card in her pocket without looking at it, and then turned back to Brady.

Kendra shook her head at the dismissal. *Lady needs a lesson in PR.* She walked back to her vehicle, where Travis was waiting. "Ready to go?" she asked as she slid in.

"Oh, yeah. I've just about had my quota of excitement for the night."

CHAPTER THREE

"Got a minute?"

Kendra looked up from the sales report. "What's up, Mike?"

Mike Scholar, co-owner and salesman extraordinaire for Abatis Security, came in, sat down in front of her desk and stretched out his legs. He still looked like the English major he had been, mustache, scraggly hair. Kendra considered partnering with Mike the best business decision she ever made. He could talk to anyone about anything, whereas Kendra was more inclined to hide in the back room. When he had come to her after her dad had died and said he was moving on to greener pastures, she had been thrown into an absolute panic. She hadn't been back in Indiana that long. She didn't have the connections and contracts necessary to keep the company running. She never had been a salesperson. She'd just lost her dad. She could see her world slipping away.

"Why?" she had asked point-blank. She'd expected all sorts of answers. He didn't like her lifestyle. He didn't like working for a woman. He thought the company would fail—which if he left, was a very good possibility. What she got was something else.

"Nowhere to go," he answered. "Company's stagnant. Has been for about a year. I know your dad was sick, but Abatis has just been drifting. I can't afford to drift. Need to go someplace where I can grow."

Kendra hadn't hesitated. "You think there're opportunities for the company to grow?"

"Oh, hell yes. Lots of them. But, to be frank, I don't think you can do it."

Kendra didn't have an argument for that. "Neither do I. Can you?"

That had taken him back a bit but he had nodded. "Yeah, I think so. But why would I?"

"Because you want growth and challenge," Kendra said even as she formulated plans. "You're a people person, but lost in tech land. I couldn't sell water in the desert. We balance." She paused, letting it sink in. "Can I interest you in a partnership?"

So they had hammered out a deal, and it had worked well. The company had grown. Mike's partnership in the company grew. Kendra worked at dealing with people, and Mike grew tech savvy. They were still a small business in the Indianapolis area, but they were a strong small business. And besides being business partners, as employees were added, as the company grew, they became family.

"Problem customer." Mike brought her back to the present. "Says her system doesn't work. She's had false alarms twice. She's raising hell."

"Send Travis out."

Mike shook his head. "We've sent people out. There's something going on. She's raising hell up one side and down the other." He gave a small smile, shook his head. "She's visible, she can give us a lot of problems. We might want to give her some individual attention."

Kendra turned to the computer, changed programs. "What's the name?"

"Robin Slusher." He said it as if Kendra should know the name.

"Battered wife?" Kendra pulled up the file and found it had been an immediate need job.

Mike shook his head. "No, quite different." He gave Kendra a quizzical look. "I would have thought you would have heard of her."

"No," she said abstractedly. "Should I?"

"You're family."

Kendra's gaze slid from the screen to Mike and then back. "So? You think the family's so small that I know everyone in town?"

Mike chuckled. "You've got to get out more, Kendra." He lifted his legs to rest his heels on the desk. "Reporter on the local station. Go-getter, up-and-comer. Word is that she'll be going places. Likes to shake things up."

"Oh, yeah. Can't imagine that there's much around here to shake up." Kendra frowned at the follow-up reports.

"Scuttlebutt says some of the big networks are watching her. They like the story she did on that missing money over at the university. Took some digging."

"So if she's spooked so easily and wants the top security system, seems like she's putting herself in the limelight more than a bit."

Mike shrugged.

"And how do you know so much?"

"I'm a news junkie, and some of the guys I went to college with went into news. She's drawn some attention." He abruptly pulled his legs down and got up. "So, look, can you check her system out, go the extra mile? If something does happen to her, I'd really rather it not be with our system failing. Wouldn't exactly be good advertising." He gave her a good-natured leer. "Besides, maybe she'll be even more interesting in person. You never know."

* * *

The next morning, bright and early, wearing her tech uniform of black pants and green and white striped shirt, and bringing Travis along for backup, Kendra rang the doorbell of the small brick-trimmed house and was totally unprepared for the door being immediately thrown open.

"I told you—just a minute," the trim, dark-haired woman was saying into the cell phone before she cut them off. She fastened dark intense eyes on the two women as if they were to blame for whatever was going on at the other end of the cell phone conversation. "Yes?" she greeted them briskly.

"Abatis Security, to check out your system." Kendra offered the business card as if the green-and-black uniforms and the green-and-black van were not identification enough. Of course, she recognized the woman immediately, wondered if the woman would recognize her. Maybe, maybe not. In accidents, some things don't get noticed.

The woman looked her up and down, pausing at her identification tag but taking in Travis more than Kendra. Travis handed over her business card. She glanced at the name and looked back at her but stepped back from the door.

"Come on in," she invited, and immediately went back to her cell phone conversation. "I'll have to call you back. The techs are here from Abatis." As soon as she got off the phone, she turned back to Travis with a pointed finger. "I know you. From somewhere."

"Women's basketball games," Travis replied. "You're Section D. I'm in E."

Robin nodded slowly and then with more certainily. "Right." She looked at the business card again. "Elvira?"

Travis squirmed uncomfortably. "What can I say? Favorite song of my mother's. I go by Travis for anything except the most formal occasions."

Robin nodded in understanding. "I would too. For that matter, Robin's my middle name. I'm not even going to tell you what my parents named me." She turned to show them into the house.

"Why couldn't you just let me use my initials?" Travis muttered as she followed Kendra through the rooms.

"Because," Kendra muttered back. It was an old argument. "You think she's just ignoring you or really doesn't remember?"

"Pretty hectic that night. Probably just didn't register. Drop it."

Kendra and Travis gave the rooms a quick glance as Robin led them through the living room, the dining room and the French doors to her workroom and office.

"Since we don't know where the problem originated, we will be going through the whole house," Kendra explained politely deciding just to play it as if they hadn't seen each other before. Some things are so casual, they really don't register. "Will that be a problem?"

"No. Except for my office. I'd rather you not be in there without me there."

"Quite all right, ma'am."

Because the problem wasn't easily solved, they had to check everything. Robin had a complete system: sensors on the windows and doors, motion detectors on the side porch, the backyard, the side of the house where there was little visibility, remote mics at the shed in the back, lot of security, Kendra noted.

"Do you think it was intentional?" She remembered the question at Robin's hit-and-run. Maybe the lady had reason to be spooked.

As they both checked the wiring, they listened to Robin pace through the house, talk on the phone, work on the computer and check the several television sets. They glanced at each other and followed the wiring to find out the problem.

"That woman must be on steroids," Travis muttered as she checked the motion detector on the side porch.

Kendra simply raised her eyebrows. Even though the woman in question was on the phone and examining the television just inside the porch, Kendra wouldn't have put it past her to be able to hear Travis's muttered comment. "High energy, that's for sure," she replied calmly but with an eyebrow raised in warning. "Wouldn't mind tapping into some of that myself."

Among other things, she thought as she watched the woman pace through the rooms, the phone to her ear, gesturing wildly. Barefoot, black slacks, white shirt that maybe should have been buttoned further up, but then she was in her own home. Dark hair, layered cut to frame her thin face, small chin, could be sharp featured if she hadn't had such an open expression. She turned abruptly, looking at Kendra. Her eyes were sharp and penetrating until she suddenly smiled. Her expression was warm and friendly, a face to be trusted. Kendra felt a small shock and without even realizing it, she had to smile back. Nonplussed, she looked back at the wiring, trying to remember exactly what she was tracing, but now she had the sudden understanding of exactly how Ms. Slusher the reporter got people to confide in her.

"It's not here," Travis was saying. "We're going to have to look outside."

"Uh-huh," Kendra agreed having no idea what Travis was talking about.

"Lady's got quite a smile," Travis said with a sly grin once they were outside in the backyard. They walked around the fence line to check outside wiring. She glanced at Kendra to see how she might respond.

"That she has," Kendra acknowledged with a nod. "Maybe she should use it more often." She pointed down the fence line. "Let's walk it."

"I don't get the feeling," Travis went on, "this lady does the job nine to five."

"No," Kendra said absently. "I'd take it she's a twenty-four-seven deal." She felt the privacy fence. "She's ambitious. She'll either make her break and go big time or burn herself out." The motion light in the corner checked out.

"Suppose she works hard, plays hard?"

They crossed the yard. "Maybe. Maybe she doesn't play."

"Oh, with looks like that, she's just got to play."

Kendra cast a speculative look at Travis, realizing Travis was a bit more familiar than maybe she should be about a client. "You speculate about the lives of all our clients?"

Travis gave Kendra a quick look as if suddenly remembering Kendra was the boss. "Just window-shopping. You know it's harmless."

"Make sure it stays that way."

Travis smiled. "But if I tripped across her outside the work area, I'd sure be tempted to give her a whirl."

Kendra had to chuckle. "Travis, I get the feeling even you would have a hard time keeping up with this one." They had reached the house. Kendra pointed off in one direction. "You go that way, check everything out. I'll take this side."

She speculated as she moved around the house. She didn't like this house as a security issue. Too irregular a shape, looked like originally a square, then at sometime in the past an extension had been added to make it an L shape, then maybe a patio or porch enclosed. There were too many doors, too many corners, too many nooks to hide in. She pulled back bushes. And too much high vegetation around the windows. Better setup if the lady was worried about security would have been a big lot, no bushes near the house, clean lines, clear views. Not as charming but easier to secure.

"Find the problem?" Robin popped out the front door, standing on the top step, leaning over the iron railing.

Kendra shook her head. "No, ma'am. Everything seems to be in good shape."

"Well, I assure you, I've had the police out here twice because the alarm went off and there was nothing."

"Yes, ma'am. I don't doubt you. I'm just saying that on the surface, everything looks shipshape. We'll have to look a little deeper to find the problem." She looked up at the lithe form, arms on the railing, leaning over to look around the corner. Kendra came over to her, afraid the woman would topple over. She rested her hand on the railing as Robin settled back on her feet. Their arms and hands were a contrast; Robin's thin, almost delicate, very lightly tanned, Kendra's stronger, broader, more heavily tanned. "I'm sure you have the same kind of situations in your line of work," Kendra suggested. "Just takes some diligence and sometimes more time to dig out the culprit."

Robin gave her a speculative look, mollified and maybe not as dismissive as she had been to start with. "You're right," she agreed in a warmer tone. "Sometimes the problem isn't in plain sight."

"And we'll find it," Kendra assured her. "We'll keep at it until we do. I don't let things go until the solution is found."

Robin gave her a long look. "No, I don't think that you do. I don't get that feeling from you." She nodded again, apparently satisfied. "I'll let you get about your business then." She went back into the house and Kendra watched her go.

Nice-looking woman, wonder if she took ballet lessons as a kid. She has that kind of firm-footed balance. Then she mentally slapped her wrists. Here she'd been chiding Travis for speculation and what was she doing? She went back to work as the squirrels in the trees scolded her for her thoughts.

* * *

She thought about her again that night after dinner, sitting in her chair with her feet up, staring at the television without seeing it. Her drink sat at her elbow.

The woman had an intensity, an energy so palpable that Kendra could feel it, almost touch it. The entire time they were there, she was moving, pacing, on the phone, one call after another. Even when they checked out her office and she was there with them, she was moving from one screen to the other, pulling pages off her printer, looking up something on the computer while standing at the keyboard on the raised platform. Maybe it was just because they were in and around the house and she was nervous about having two strangers in her personal space.

Strange the things you can learn about people from their houses. Look at her own. Years of living outside a small town where everyone knew everyone else's business, where if someone put their car in the ditch, the news beat them back to town. Kendra wanted no more of that, so when she found this house, with its high windows right under the overhang, the living room in the center of the house, and limited visibility even at the front door, she was intrigued. Intrigued enough to keep coming back even though it was out of her price range. She was patient, and the price dropped. Ladies like to show off their curtains, to let the outside in, the real estate broker explained as the price dropped yet again. Kendra nodded. She was patient. Finally the owners who had moved on to another town, another job, accepted her offer. Now when Kendra came home, she could literally shut the world out, and until she was willing to let the outside in, no one could even tell if she was there.

Robin's house, on the other hand, was rather impersonal although with a friendly feel. She had good furniture, nice arrangements, no knickknacks. Few pictures. Nothing of family or friends. Yet there was an open feeling, welcoming. Everything very neat. Until you stepped into her office. Her office was proof positive she had not gone the paperless route. She had stacks of papers and books. There were notes posted on a buried bulletin board, even pages taped to the wall, some with arrows pointing to other pages.

Kendra reasoned that this was why Robin didn't want them in there alone. There were far too many pages to take down. It would take forever to put them up in the same order, the same connection and linkage. Certainly as long as Robin stood there watching, Kendra and Travis could hardly do more than glance at them. The sheer volume had impressed Travis but Kendra was more curious as to what Robin might be working on.

Interesting woman, Kendra decided as she sipped her drink. Much more open and inviting than Kendra ever wanted to be. Usually their clients weren't so out of the ordinary. Maybe it was simply part of her job. More because of curiosity, maybe even boredom, she picked up the remote and channel surfed until she found Late Night News with Robin Slusher.

"*Should I be jealous?*"

The question, the feeling was so strong that Kendra turned around. Convinced she had actually heard a voice, she got up, did a walk around the house, checking the doors and the security system. She stood in the middle of her office, listening to the television from the other room, wondering and puzzled. She would have sworn, but no. She had to be wrong.

CHAPTER FOUR

"Hey, boss, want to go out tonight?" Travis stuck her head in Kendra's office before she left Friday night.

Kendra looked up from her schedule for the next week. "You asking me out, Travis?" Most unlikely, she knew, since neither of them dated within the company and both of them preferred to take the lead. More likely was she and Peg had put their heads together in an effort to get Kendra out of the house and back into the social scene.

"No." Travis came in and draped herself in the chair in front of the desk. "I'm asking my buddy if she wants to go barhopping with me tonight, get out in the flow of things, see what's circulating."

Kendra grimaced. Barhopping was the last thing she wanted to do. "What? You haven't fallen off the wagon, have you?" Not that she seriously considered that.

"No." Travis fished her silver dollar out of her pocket and held it up. "Four years. Ever since you threw me out of here and told me to sober up or not come back. Then hunted me down and dragged me up to that farm of yours to make sure I sobered up."

"That long ago?" Kendra pulled the weekly schedule out of the printer, slid it under her calendar. "My, how time flies when you're having fun. What happened to Rhonda?"

Travis held up her hand. "Don't even go there. Rhonda's history; I'm a free agent again."

Kendra shook her head. "I don't see—"

"And don't go there either," Travis cut in. "I do not see that you have any room to throw stones. Now I feel like going out and seeing what's happening, and I don't feel like going alone. I know it's been forever since you've shown yourself. So I thought we'd test the waters together."

Kendra was all ready to still refuse until she met the resolve in Travis's hazel eyes. She wondered if it was worth the argument she would probably lose in the end. "Oh, all right. Who's driving this time?"

Travis leaped to her feet. "I am. You drive and we'll be going home with the chickens. Not my game plan. Pick you up at eight?"

Once at home, Kendra decided to bail out at least a dozen times and each time she considered Travis's resolve. And she considered Peg's parting comment of "Have a good time!" when they left the office. Maybe it had been too long since she had gone out. Maybe she would feel better. And what would take more energy? Going along with Travis's plans or deciding not to go and arguing with Travis about it? In the end, she decided going won. Travis and Peg were hell-bent on her getting back into the social scene.

"Knock knock!" Travis called as she let herself inside the garage door. "You ready?"

"Almost. I'm in the bedroom. Come on in." She was just pulling out her boots, wondering if she should wear them. Probably not. She glanced up to see Travis in her denim along with her leather vest. She looked at her black pants, silken shirt, long vest. "I don't know," she started.

"You look great," Travis said immediately. "Wear your boots. Comfortable ones. We're going out to boogie all night long." She raised her arms and danced in front of the mirror to imaginary music. She shivered suddenly, turned toward the dresser. "Cold. You kick the AC on already?" Without waiting for an answer, she picked up the framed picture on the side of the dresser. "Who's this?"

Kendra examined her image in the mirror. Thick curly unruly dark brown hair sculptured into shape. Face free of makeup giving that solid you-can-count-on-me impression. Not fat, not lean, just solid. Not especially attractive, but not unattractive either. Not an open face but certainly friendly enough. And charming when she wanted to be. Hides her vulnerabilities well, she thought caustically as she glanced in the mirror at Travis. "Old girlfriend." She didn't know why she had dug that picture out. Linda on my mind, she thought and dismissed it.

"The one you were telling me about the night of the fireworks?"

"Yeah." Kendra kept her tone civil. Travis was a friend, but she hoped she got the idea she didn't want to discuss the subject.

"Nice looking," Travis commented as she set the picture down. "Looks like the outdoorsy type, a lot of fun." She turned back to Kendra. "Ever see her anymore?"

"Not lately," Kendra said shortly as she stood up and picked up her jacket. "You ready to go?"

"Ready, willing and able." Travis clapped her on the shoulder. "Let's get a move on. The ladies are waiting."

* * *

Well, Kendra decided as she and Travis pushed through the crowd, if the ladies were waiting, they were occupying themselves nicely. The club was crowded and noisy, the music loud enough to preclude conversation. Travis turned around, hit her on the arm to get her attention and pointed to some friends who had a table on the upper level. Kendra nodded and they began to make their way through.

What did I let myself in for? Kendra demanded of herself, and then they reached the table.

"Kendra! Great to see you—long time no see!"

"Where you been keeping yourself? Began to think that you moved out of town!"

A tall, angular woman, heavily tanned, with shoulder-length, naturally wavy hair stood up, held her hand across the table for Kendra. "Hi! I'm Dotty! I don't believe we've met—"

"Oh, Dotty, shut up," Kendra came back, good-naturedly. "We sat side by side at the football games last year."

"And I don't think I've seen you since," Dotty retorted amidst general laughter.

Someone pulled out chairs for them, someone else snagged a waitress and everyone moved closer around the table to make room for them. Kendra sat down, looking around the crowd, picking out faces she recognized. She hadn't been out for a long time, she realized.

"Why the crowd?" she questioned to the table in general. "I didn't expect a crowd like this."

"Band night. Three of them. Going to be lively all night long."

"Loud," Kendra agreed. *At least I won't be hearing things. I'll be lucky to be hearing anything by morning.*

"So what's happening?" someone asked, and Kendra found herself talking and laughing, even if she had to look at the speaker and do as much lip-reading as listening.

The music was loud, the room throbbed with the beat and the dancers on the lower floor created their own energy as they writhed, moved and jerked. For the first time in a long time, Kendra began to relax, to feel like she wanted to be with people.

There was constant movement around the table as different women got up to go to the dance floor, others joined them, some left. Kendra hadn't been this social in a long time.

"Come on, let's dance." Stella grabbed her arm. "I need to make Ellen jealous."

"And Ellen Hayworth is going to be jealous of me?" Kendra protested even as she let the lithe, sexy femme drag her down to the dance floor.

"She will be when I get done," Stella promised, plunging into the dancers and turning around to face Kendra. She grabbed her by the vest, pulled her close and began to dance, biting her lip and closing her eyes as she moved in time to the music, her hands still in contact with Kendra as if guiding her, moving with her.

Kendra never considered herself more than a fair dancer but Stella was one of those dancers who could make a bad dancer look decent and a decent dancer look great. Kendra considered herself somewhere in the middle, but with Stella moving before her, she felt fantastic.

"You know," Stella told her, almost shouting in her face. "With a little practice, you could be good. You need to get out more, Kendra." She moved suggestively close against her. "Maybe I won't care about making Ellen jealous."

Kendra laughed, beginning to enjoy herself. She could feel the music, could catch the energy that was on the dance floor. She had an attractive woman flirting with her. "I've heard that story before, Stella. Ellen always comes back."

"Maybe this time she won't."

"It's just a game you two play. Keeps everything interesting."

Stella laughed, throwing her head back, exposing skin all the way down the unbuttoned blouse to between her breasts. "Yes, it does," she admitted. She moved against Kendra again. "You're such a good sport."

Kendra felt so good she bent down, nuzzled against Stella's neck, Stella's curly light brown hair tickling her. She could feel Stella's surprise. "Yes," she purred in Stella's ear. "I am." And she laughed when Stella drew back in surprise and gave her a quick look before she laughed also and came back against her.

"That certainly looked cozy," Travis told her when she returned to the table.

"Showing myself," Kendra answered with an enigmatic smile. "Isn't that what you said I needed to do?"

She danced frequently with many partners after that. Kendra was considered a catch. Successful, attractive, attentive when she wanted to be and known for taking good care of her lovers, at least for as long as she had them. That was the problem: most of them were short-term, but everyone said it was grand while it lasted. Her depressions, however, were as black as her charm was attentive, and more than one lover or friend had expressed concern.

She came back to the table and sat down, caught the waitress and ordered a drink. She needed a breather, but she was feeling good. There were just some times, she knew, when everything clicked, and tonight was one of those nights.

Travis was grinning at her. "And I thought I'd have to blast you out of a corner. Is there anyone you haven't danced with?"

"I don't think so, but it's so crowded down there, it's a multi-partner event." She looked over the dance floor, watching, catching her breath. She began to wonder why she had been so hesitant on coming out and promised herself to get out more often. It did feel good. The waitress brought her drink during the lull while the bands changed.

"Oldies," Kendra announced as the band started up.

"Yeah, we're ancient," Travis said, laughing.

"God, I haven't heard that since high school," Kendra exclaimed. She could feel the music flow. She felt the rush of memories, good times, hopes for the future.

"Well, look who's here!" Travis stood up to see better, laid her hand on Kendra's shoulder and pointed.

"Who?" Kendra turned, searching for whomever Travis had spotted and then she saw her. The western shirt with white piping, the black Levi's, the thick auburn hair cut short, swept back. Kendra's mouth went dry as Linda turned, still moving to the music, and looked up directly at her. She gave her a one-finger salute and turned around, and still looking back over her shoulder at Kendra, she winked.

"My God!" Kendra gasped and knocked over her drink. The dark liquid and ice cubes spread across the table.

"Hey!" Travis leaped back to avoid the overflow, and Kendra jerked her gaze from the dance floor to see what she had done. She looked back even as she was reaching for napkins to mop up the spill, but Linda was gone. She searched the dancers for someone who looked like her, some mistaken identity and although she found western shirts, none had the white piping.

"Well, I didn't think it would be that much of a shock."
Travis stopped the waitress and grabbed a handful of napkins.

"What? Who?" Kendra said distractedly. She kept glancing
back at the dance floor even as she mopped up the table, looking
at Travis to follow her conversation. Then she would look back
at the dance floor expecting, expecting what?

"Kendra! Are you all right? You look like you've seen a
ghost?"

"Funny." Kendra sat back down, only to abruptly stand up.
"I need to go to the john."

"Are you all right?" Travis called after her.

Kendra shook her head. "I just got too hot. I'll be all right.
Don't worry, I'll be back."

It was just the music, the power of suggestion, she told herself as
she moved blindly through the crowd. *Linda's been on my mind a
lot lately. That song was popular when we were in high school. It was
just my imagination. Someone who looked like her. But that one-finger
salute. Just a memory, just my mind playing tricks on me. God, I've
got to get out more. I'll end up being committed.*

* * *

The restroom was blessedly uncrowded. Kendra ran cold
water over her hands and buried her face in them. She felt
heated; maybe it was just because the room was so hot, so many
dancers on the floor, and she had been dancing for the last hour.
Yes, that had to be it. She took some deep breaths and looked in
the mirror. Flushed but not alarming. She looked like a rational
being. She just wasn't sure she felt like one. She shouldn't linger.
Travis would worry.

From the corner of her eye, she was conscious of someone
else washing her hands at the sink. She turned to pull paper
towels down at the same time the other woman reached for
them. Their hands met.

"Excuse me." Kendra jerked away and looked up into the
dark eyes of Robin Slusher. "Well," she said, recovering first
somewhat. "So you do get out and play occasionally."

Robin looked quizzically at the familiar tone. She examined Kendra's face and Kendra hoped she didn't look too ravaged. "Abatis," she said, pointing a finger at Kendra. "McKinley—no, that's not it. McKenna. Kendra."

"Very good. You have a good memory naturally, or did you have to work at it?" While it might have taken two meetings, Kendra still felt flattered Robin remembered her.

"Natural, but yes, it's a very useful trait." Robin pulled down the paper towel and dried her hands. "As well as other traits," she said lightly. She gave a half smile, inviting. "You know, somehow I got the impression you were a twenty-four-seven worker, didn't go out to play much."

Kendra felt a twinge of discomfort. Travis had said something like that about Robin that day at her house. Probably her imagination also. She was becoming too sensitive. "All work and no play, you know how that goes," she parried.

"True." Robin inclined her head and Kendra noticed that her layered short hair looked blue-black in fluorescent lighting. "Get burnt-out otherwise." Robin's dark eyes danced with amusement. "My motto is work hard, play hard. What's yours?"

"Excuse me!" Another patron needed paper towels just then, so they had to move. Then they were blocking the entrance and that wouldn't do either. Kendra opened the door for Robin.

"A job worth doing is worth doing well?" she said as Robin exited in front of her.

Robin looked over her shoulder with a slight frown. She shook her head. "Need to work on that; I had another false alarm last night. Was going to call Abatis today, but I didn't have time." They paused in the hallway where the band volume was low enough they could still have a conversation.

Kendra winced and turned her head away. "Thought we had that fixed." She looked back at Robin. "I apologize. Someone will be there tomorrow."

"Tomorrow's Saturday."

"But you have a problem."

"Twenty-four-seven?" Robin supplied.

Kendra shrugged. "Comes with the territory. You understand that, don't you?" She had to have overheard us, Kendra decided as she examined Robin's amused gaze. She just used too many of the same phrases. But while it was embarrassing, Robin didn't seem to be offended.

Robin nodded. "Yes, I know." She indicated the main room. "Can I tempt you into giving it a whirl?" She had a way of lifting one eyebrow.

"You think I can keep up?"

"Only one way to find out, isn't there?"

Kendra smiled in amusement. She liked Robin's sense of humor, the way she exuded energy. She led her back to the dance floor, her hand lightly on Robin's back. Just as they started to dance, the band changed tempo to something much, much slower. Kendra hesitated. They were strangers really, but Robin merely smiled.

"I guess you're trustworthy," she said as moved into Kendra's arms. "After all, my safety and security is in your hands."

"So it is."

A dancer, Kendra decided as she felt Robin's body move. She tried to remember this was a woman she had just met, a local celebrity. And all she could think of was how her sapphire blouse matched her eyes, how her eyes sparkled, how the television image didn't do her justice.

"How'd you hear us?" she asked abruptly. She had to pull Robin closer so she could be heard.

Robin turned her head so she was speaking near Kendra's ear, not that she had to raise her voice. "You were testing all the equipment. The mics were on. There's one by the shed."

"I'm embarrassed."

"I was flattered."

"It still wasn't very professional."

"Don't worry. I won't report you."

"No—" *No one to report me to*, Kendra started to say and then caught herself. Robin thought she was merely one of the techs, didn't realize she was the owner. "No," she continued. "You wouldn't do that," she said instead.

"Have you worked for Abatis long?" Robin asked.

"From the startup," Kendra told her, which was close enough.

"Do you like it?"

"It's interesting. Get to meet a lot of people." She smiled. "Get to play with gadgets, which I like."

"Spy stuff too?"

Kendra nodded. "Sometimes. Industrial security isn't a big part of the business, but it's an important part. More risk, higher stakes."

Robin nodded. "We might have to talk."

The song ended, and Robin withdrew. Kendra reluctantly let her go. She was surprised how nicely Robin had fit against her.

"I have to rejoin my party, but I think we'll be seeing each other again, won't we?" Kendra heard the flirting, the light tone, but there was something else underneath it.

"Of course," she responded, not letting go of Robin's hand. "Tomorrow. When I check out your system."

"Oh, please," Robin protested. "It's your day off."

"Twenty-four-seven," Kendra reminded her.

Robin rolled her eyes and laughed. "Tomorrow then. Ten-ish?"

Kendra nodded, and then Robin disappeared into the crowd. Kendra moved around the edge of the dance floor and went up the stairs.

"I saw you," Travis greeted her. "I guess you made a quick recovery. And I thought you hadn't seen her."

"What?" Kendra took her seat, curious what Robin might want to talk to her about.

"When you knocked over the drink. You looked like you had seen a ghost. I didn't think that seeing Robin Slusher would jolt you that much. And then the next thing I see you dancing with her. Looked pretty cozy."

Kendra turned her attention back to Travis. "Yes, she said to tell you she does play hard, just as hard as she works. Hard to keep up with a woman like that."

Travis's jaw dropped slightly, and her eyes darted around.

"Yes, she heard us," Kendra went on. "We left the mics on when we tested them, and there was one by the shed."

Travis closed her eyes. "Oh, God. Was she mad?"

"She was flattered, or at least she said she was."

"Oh, thank God. I never thought of the mics, and I know we checked them all out. I'm so sorry, Kendra. I didn't mean anything by it."

"I know it; she knows it. She just liked raking me over the coals a bit, but she seems like a good sport." She gave Travis a warning look. "I've told you about making comments." She paused. "I know, I made some too."

"So I don't suppose—I mean, did she just dance with you to rake you over the coals?"

"No," Kendra said thoughtfully. "Actually she said we might have to talk."

"She said that? So you're going to see her, I mean again, I mean, just her?"

Kendra shook her head at Travis's enthusiasm. "Tomorrow as a matter of fact," she said just to see Travis's response.

"Fast work!" Travis exclaimed.

"Not hardly. She had another false alarm last night."

"Rats."

"Probably not," Kendra answered. She was suddenly tired. "You ready to call it a night, buddy?"

"Yeah, I think so."

* * *

Travis even declined to come in when she dropped her off. She waited long enough to see Kendra go through the house to turn off the security system and turn on the lights before she pulled off.

Kendra watched her go down the street and turn the corner. She was glad Travis had insisted she go out; it was good to see people again. The bands had been fantastic, and the dancing had been enjoyable. Then the good feeling faded when she remembered seeing Linda in the crowd.

She shook her head. She looked so real, flesh and blood, but then she had looked that way at the fireworks. Kendra shook her head. She needed to talk to someone about this. Who? But she didn't want anyone to think she was crazy, slipping into an unreal world. Or was she? Maybe she needed to reconsider Peg's suggestion about seeing someone about her depression, someone she could talk to and have it confidential.

The rest of the night had been good, and running into Robin Slusher had been—she searched for the word—interesting. And Robin had been almost flirtatious. Kendra smiled. Now, when a good woman like that flirts with you, you've got to be grounded.

Which reminded her, maybe there was a grounding wire missing on that system. Got to set my alarm, get over to her place early and check that out, she told herself. Assuming that I can sleep tonight.

She went into the bedroom to set the alarm for eight. That would give her enough time. She tossed off the evening's outfit and slipped into sleep shorts and shirt. She still needed to unwind.

She walked through the darkened house, automatically checking doors and windows, thinking of the dancing and her many partners. Stella, that little minx; she and Ellen worked at keeping the interest up, but sometimes they got awfully close to the line. She did not understand a relationship where you had to keep your partner uncertain of your fidelity and commitment. However, it worked for them.

She went through her office to check the outer door. Even if it only opened into the garage, she wanted to make sure it was locked before she hit nighttime security on her system. As she went by her desk, she noticed a light from her laptop. She had thought she might do some work before she had settled on going out, but she was reasonably sure she had shut it down.

She went over to the desk, glancing out the window over the desk and looking down as she lifted the laptop cover. The computer was on, humming quietly, the screen saver flashing the Abatis logo and pictures. She touched the keyboard, and the blue screen came up with white letters.

I know revenge is a dish best served cold, but don't you think six years is cold enough? Why are you letting him get away with murder, Sunshine?

Kendra sagged into the chair, staring at the screen. She swallowed. No one but Linda ever called her Sunshine. Linda's sense of humor because of Kendra's geekiness, her perpetual cynicism, her frequent depression. Kendra rubbed her eyes. This was not her imagination. She wasn't seeing things. She wasn't hearing things. She just didn't understand. She couldn't believe.

CHAPTER FIVE

Kendra rang Robin's doorbell at ten o'clock sharp the next morning. She looked around as she waited. She needed a morning like this, crisp and clear, warm but not yet hot. Butterfly bushes with their golden-yellow blooms were beginning to burst out to attract the bees and butterflies. She needed the grounding.

She turned around to examine the neighborhood. The winding little street must have been used as a cut-through from one heavily traveled street to the other. She had never seen so many speed bumps but it was an old area. Houses close together, and the flowerbeds of cannas, dahlias and glads were well-developed. She turned back around when she heard the lock in the door.

Robin opened the door partly, just enough for her to peer out. Kendra caught her breath. Robin was sleepy-eyed, tousled hair, wrapped in a brightly colored black-and-pink-on-white kimono that came down just enough to be decent and short enough to expose long legs. She was barefooted.

"Good morning." Kendra found enough moisture in her mouth to speak. "I'm sorry. Obviously, I got you up. Did I get the time wrong? Did I come too early?" Belatedly she wondered, *and are you alone?*

"Ohhhhhh, I forgot you were coming." Robin rubbed her eyes as she leaned against the door. Then she shook her head and stepped back to open the door. "Come on in—if you can forgive the disarray." She turned around and walked away, leaving the door open for Kendra to come in.

Kendra shut the door, followed Robin through the living room and dining room to the kitchen. No disarray she could see. She paused at the kitchen doorway. Robin filled the coffeemaker with water and then reached to the upper shelf for the coffee. Kendra watched as the kimono hiked up, and then she shut her eyes and turned away. She was going to have a hard time watching this woman on television after such a sight.

"Late night, last night," Robin explained as she turned the coffeemaker on and turned around. "Oh, that's right. You were there, too. How come you're so fresh and alert?"

"Early riser. And I didn't close the club." She didn't need to mention that she had hardly slept after the message on the computer.

Robin stretched. "Not like me." She rotated her head, flexing her neck. "You must have left, then, right after we danced."

Kendra gave a mental sigh; Robin looked so limber, so–so touchable. But she put the thought away and smiled. "What could top that event? My evening was complete."

Robin rolled her shoulders as she gave Kendra a disbelieving look. "Funny, I didn't take you for such a flirt the last time you were here."

"On the job. Today, this is my time."

Robin came wide-awake, alert. "You're not getting paid for this? No, that's not right. I didn't intend that when I saw you last night. You leave right now, none of this courtesy stuff. I'll call in Monday and make it official. Then they can send you out on the clock."

Kendra held out her hand, forestalling her. "Calm down. It's all right. Remember twenty-four-seven?"

"That's different."

"Not so much. It's my company."

"Your company?" She frowned, tilted her head to look at Kendra. "As in the company you work for?"

Kendra shook her head. "As in I own it. At least half of it."

"Ohhhhhh." Robin hit her forehead with the heel of her hand. Then she looked at Kendra again. "So what are you doing taking service calls?"

"Keeps my hand in, problem cases. And this has been a problem case. I certainly don't want unhappy clients."

"Especially highly visible ones?" Robin asked with a knowing smirk.

"Well, that too," she admitted, "but I can hardly make claims about security if the system isn't dependable, can I? Whether the clients are highly visible or not." She leaned against the counter.

Robin appeared mollified, if a bit uncertain. "So this isn't above and beyond the call of duty? Or am I getting special consideration?"

Kendra shook her head. "No more than any other difficult case. Especially when there was a risk assessment."

Robin sobered and her attitude changed.

Evidently, Kendra considered, there was a real threat and she had just reminded her of it. Tactless. "Well, I guess I'd better get started."

"And I'd better get dressed."

Kendra checked and rechecked wiring and connections, especially the grounding. She had thought maybe interference of some sort, but she couldn't find anything. She was still puzzling over the false alarms when Robin, now completely dressed in khaki pants and a bright red pullover, came out the side door with two cups of coffee.

"Come join me?" she called as she set the cups down on the small table on the shaded patio. "As long as you're on your own time now, can you break for a cup of coffee? It seems the least I can do for dragging you out on your Saturday morning."

Kendra was still puzzling over the false alarms as she came over to the table and sat down. Robin had brought out the cream and sugar as well as a small basket of stuffed pastries. Kendra eyed them curiously.

"My Saturday morning ritual," Robin explained. "During the week, I don't have time for such niceties. But I need a change of pace or I will burn out." She smiled as she said it.

"Do you like your job?" Kendra asked, trying to imagine all the background work that went into Robin's live broadcasts. Before seeing Robin's office, she had never given the slightest thought to what went on behind the scenes.

"Yes, I love it. It's all I've ever wanted to do. Well, actually I had considered newspaper journalism for a while, but newspapers are a dying breed. They are all so much alike after being sold out to just a few big conglomerates. Television, even it's changing with the immediacy of the Internet, but to dig into a story instead of just skimming the surface, find out what isn't being said, to make people accountable in some cases. Yes." She shook her head with a bemused smile on her face. "And to think that people are paying me to do this."

Kendra could see the enthusiasm in Robin's face. Not everyone, she knew, could find their niche and their job.

"What about you?" Robin in turn asked. "Do you like your job and why do you go out on service calls? Abatis isn't exactly a small company."

"No, we're not. I like to go out, keep my hand in what my techs go through. And the problems are a challenge sometimes." She looked around the yard as if acknowledging this problem. "Keeps me from getting rusty."

"So how did you start Abatis? I don't find too many women in the security business, especially on the hardware side."

"The old-fashioned way," Kendra commented lightly with a grin. "I inherited it."

"Oh, so you were brought up in it."

"Not exactly." And without intending to and almost without realizing it, Kendra began to talk about her father and his love of gadgets. She sat back, stretching out her legs, holding the coffee cup in both hands with her elbows on the chair arms.

"After my mom died and I went off to college, Dad had his own midlife crisis. He was an engineer, always played with gadgets, got more into the security and surveillance. So he went off and started his own company. We lived in a rural area, wasn't much of a market for it there so he came here, started Abatis."

"How'd he come up with the name? Not a family name, is it?"

Kendra laughed. "Hardly. Abatis is an obstacle of felled trees complete with their branches, facing the enemy. That's why our colors are green and black, leaves and tree trunks."

"Catchy, but sorta obscure."

"But it begins with A—so it's at the beginning of any listings."

"Ahhh, so there was a reason in the madness." Robin shoved the basket of pastries toward Kendra. "You joined him after college?"

"No." Kendra shook her head. "I wanted to try my wings." She frowned at the memory. "I wanted a more open community, see the sights, see the ocean. Put as much distance as I could between me and Indiana. So California here I come." She fell silent. *Get away, make a new start.*

Robin was easy to talk to, a good listener. She sat there in the chair, sitting on one leg, sipping the coffee, focused on Kendra and listening intently. She knew the proper time to ask questions and when to wait. So she waited for a bit. "So what made you come back?" she asked finally.

"My dad's health started failing," Kendra said slowly. That was where she usually left it when people asked, but she felt comfortable talking to Robin. She could understand how the woman ferreted out information. She was an attractive woman, not just physically but also in attitude. She seemed genuinely interested and had no preconceptions.

Then it occurred to Kendra that here was an opportunity. Robin was an investigative reporter. She would know how to go about these things.

"There was another reason," she said slowly.

Robin tilted her head.

"How long have you been in this area?" Kendra asked.

"About three years."

"Where were you before?"

"Ohio, Columbus."

Kendra nodded. Out of the area. She frowned, examining Robin's face. She wasn't sure she wanted to do this but—"I came back because a friend went missing."

"Went missing?"

Kendra thought if Robin had had folded ears, they would have perked up.

"Ever find her?"

Kendra shook her head. She wasn't sure if she wanted to presume Robin's help. People probably fed her all sorts of tips and hints for stories. She didn't want to fall into that category. But if she could spark Robin's interest, well, publicity wouldn't hurt. Somebody out there must know something. And Robin was establishing a reputation for digging things up.

"Foul play?"

Kendra shrugged. "Her husband was away on a hunting trip. Came back to find her gone. He said she left him, but she didn't take her car. She didn't take a bus. She didn't take the train. No plane ticket."

"Someone could have picked up her," Robin pointed out.

Kendra nodded in agreement. "But no one came forth."

Robin thought about it for a moment. "A lover?"

"Husband said so. But nothing was proven."

"Investigate the supposed lover?"

Kendra nodded.

"Anything?"

"Nothing."

"You're sure?"

"Oh, yes."

Robin turned her head in question at such certainty.

Kendra looked down at her coffee, still debating, then looked up. "Supposed lover was me."

"Ahhhh." Robin sat back and folded her arms, one hand at her chin as she looked at Kendra anew. "So why are you telling me?"

"You asked why I came back." Kendra set her coffee cup back on the table. "And you have a knack for digging up information."

"Are you wanting me to take this on?"

"No," Kendra said quickly. She straightened up in the chair. "No, I wouldn't presume so much. I guess—" She faltered there. She wasn't sure just what she was asking. "I guess I just want to know how you do it. I don't mind digging for information; I just don't know where to start."

"My best advice is to let the police handle it."

Kendra grimaced. "Probably so, but the police aren't doing much. The case is cold; it's been five years. And I'll agree, they don't have much to go on. No evidence of a crime. They're not even convinced her disappearance is foul play. There's no body. After all, there's no legal reason why a person can't just drop out of sight and start a new life somewhere. If she was getting away from an abusive husband, then—" Kendra held her hand out, palm up. "Well, more power to her. And according to their thinking, she might have good reason for not getting in touch with anyone left behind."

"Was he abusive?"

"No police reports but local gossip says so. Linda wasn't one to air her dirty linen much, but there were suspicions." She clenched her open palm into a fist. Just the thought of what Linda might have had to put up with made her stomach clench with anger. Linda wasn't a weak woman; she wasn't without resources. If she stayed, she stayed because she didn't want to lose a lifetime of work developing the campground. And if she had finally decided to leave, she would have left. She wouldn't have changed her mind.

"I don't think she got away." There, she said it.

"Why not?"

Kendra stared at the table, tense with the memory. How could she explain? Knowing was all a mixture. Knowing Linda, knowing what she could do. Knowing what was on her computer screen. "She would have contacted me."

"You're sure? But you were in California. You said you only came back after she was reported missing. Had you kept in contact?"

Kendra came back to the present, blinking at Robin in the sunlight, sitting on her patio with birds chirping, squirrels chattering at her on the line overhead. How could she explain? "Not exactly. We were—" Kendra fumbled for the word, "at odds," she settled for. "But if she left him, even if she couldn't contact me directly, she would have let me know."

Robin shook her head. "Sketchy, Kendra. No body, no evidence. If you were not exactly speaking…" She looked at Kendra intently, speculating. Kendra could almost see the mental scales weighing her words.

"You're convinced? This isn't just wishful thinking?"

Kendra gave a derisive grunt. "Wishful thinking that she's dead rather her living happily somewhere? You've got to be kidding." She eyed Robin, feeling that she wasn't convinced. And she suddenly wanted this woman to believe her. She sat up and leaned across the table. "Look," she said as the words spilled from her. "The last time I saw Linda, it wasn't a good visit. I was leaving for California and I had some crazy idea that Linda would come with me. I thought she'd see that this marriage had been one of convenience, an effort to reassure her mother that she'd be taken care of. Now her mother was gone. There was no reason to keep up with that sham. She could get it annulled or something and we could go off into California land and live happily ever after."

"She didn't love him?"

Kendra fell back into the chair as she shook her head. "Not that way. Artie had been around forever, had helped them a good deal. After Linda's mom Claudia had the stroke, he helped even more. Linda had promised she wouldn't put her in a nursing home. So she was taking care of Claudia, taking care of the campgrounds—that was their income. She was exhausted, physically and mentally. Getting married was a way to give her mother some peace."

"So what happened?"

"She gets married. Claudia dies. It seemed to me that now Linda could go off and do what she wanted to do, be together the way we had always talked about." She looked up at Robin with a depracating look. "So I was foolish, selfish. As far as I could see, he was just a detour and now she could go back to her life." She spread her hands, unsure whether it was over her youthful blindness or Linda's stubbornness. "She told me no, she just couldn't. She had made a bargain and she'd follow it through. I wasn't real happy about it but, well, it was her choice, and she wasn't ready to walk away and give everything up."

Robin's eyebrows rose slightly but otherwise, she made no comment.

"So on the way out of town, I stopped by to say goodbye. She said she was glad that I was leaving, that I needed to get away. I'd never be happy there, they were still too homophobic in those days. But she still couldn't go with me.

"We were hugging when he came in." She took a deep breath, remembering. "He pulled us apart, slammed me into the wall, yelling that no goddamn lezzie was going to touch his wife. HIS wife. Linda grabbed his arm before he hit me again, yelled at me to get out. He shook her off and she picked up the cast-iron skillet and crowned him.

"He went down and she was pushing me out the door and to my car, all the time telling me to leave, just leave, get out of there. Then she leaned in the window and kissed me goodbye, told me to get the hell out of there."

There was a long silence broken only by Saturday afternoon traffic, kids yelling down the street. Without really seeing, Kendra watched a squirrel jump from the power line to the roof, run around the chimney and disappear.

"Did you see her, talk to her after that?"

Kendra shook her head, turned back to Robin. "I put off leaving, stuck around for a day or two, hoping that might change her mind, and to hear if she was all right. Finally her cousin came by. Sue never liked me, thought I had 'contaminated' Linda, but she had a message for me. Linda was having a hard time as long as I was still there. It'd be easier all around if I just left." She stared at the table; remembered her frustration, her distrust, her feeling of helplessness.

"So I left. I never saw her again."

"Wait a minute." Robin abruptly got to her feet and went into the house through her office.

Oh, great. Now the lady thinks I'm a crackpot. Kendra absently picked up the coffee and took a swallow. Cold. She set the cup back down and got to her feet just as Robin came back out, this time carrying a pad.

"I'm not going to promise anything," she said as she sat back down, "but I'll take a look. Because of my connections, I might find some information that you haven't been able to tap." She flipped through the reporter's pad until she got to a blank page.

Kendra sat back down, almost in disbelief that Robin believed her, much less that she was going to help her.

"You said this happened when?"

"Five years ago, in November. It'll be six years this November."

Robin made quick notes. "And where?"

"Walton's Corner. It's a small community in Warren County. About an hour away, maybe an hour and a half depending on the traffic. Lafayette's the closest town, about twenty minutes away. That's where everyone does their business." She watched Robin take notes.

"You ever go back there?"

Kendra moved her head, yes, no. "Dad never sold the place. It's not big enough to be a real farm, more of a hobby farm size. I still have it. I get back there on occasion, check on it. Use it when I need to get away."

Robin nodded, accepting the information. "And Linda's name?"

"Linda Swenson—S-W-E-N-S-O-N." Then Kendra realized any records wouldn't be under Linda's maiden name. "Oh," she corrected with some distaste. "It would probably be filed under her married name. Jeffers. J-E-F-F—"

Robin looked up with sudden sharp interest. Kendra could almost see the invisible ears perk up sharply this time. "Jeffers? J-E-F-F-E-R-S? That was the husband?" Kendra nodded. "Got a first name?" Robin questioned in a different tone.

"Artie."

"Artie Jeffers," Robin repeated. She drew an explanation point after the name. "I'll see what I can find out."

For some reason, Kendra noted, she sounded more interested.

CHAPTER SIX

Good session, Kendra thought as she left her therapist's office. Maybe seeing someone and this talking bit will do some good.

Certainly she had resisted long enough. She'd always had these periods of depression, ever since high school. Linda had been able to pull her out of them then. When Linda had married, she had felt betrayed. She had tried to be reasonable about it, reality intruding on their fantasy of being together, living together. They could still be friends.

She had come to realize that she wasn't interested in "friendship." She wanted more so she backed away. She had managed that until the opportunity to go to California came up. Part of her saw this as an opportunity for herself; and from what Linda had said, maybe it would be a new opportunity for them both.

However, that was not to be. Linda said she had made the bargain. Besides that, she couldn't leave everything she had worked so hard for, and she was married. The time wasn't right, she said. And then he had come in.

Age and distance had given Kendra perspective but a younger Kendra had left feeling betrayed yet again, first when Linda married him and then when she wouldn't leave him. Kendra had resolved to put it behind her, to shut the door, to forget. That feeling lasted until her dad called a year later to tell her Linda had disappeared. Since then, her depressions had just become worse. There was the constant feeling she should have done something, at least not just shut the door. And now there was no way to apologize, to make amends, to make other choices. Maybe that's why she was now seeing Linda these days every time she turned around. She had never been able to come to terms with Linda's disappearance.

Peg was the one who had finally suggested Kendra see someone. She had started with subtle suggestions after the breakup of Kendra's last relationship and became less subtle when Kendra isolated herself. Kendra had not taken the idea at all well, but Peg had been around forever, and knew her well. Her mother's best friend, Peg had lost her husband several years before Kendra's mother had died. She was probably one of the reasons her dad had moved to Indy. Certainly she was the first employee he had hired to run the office. Sometimes Kendra wondered why he hadn't married the trim athletic blonde who ran the office and probably his life so efficiently. So she had seen Kendra through a lot—her dad's move away from Walton's Corner, her move to California, her dad's illness which caused her to move back and finally his death. Since Kendra had lost her father, Peg was about as close as anyone Kendra could consider family. If she listened to anyone, it was Peg. Finally, just as much to pacify Peg as well as realizing this was getting worse, not better, she had decided to see someone.

About that time, she heard this interview on the radio and liked the sound of the woman's voice. On a whim, she called to see if she was taking new clients. She was.

The first appointment had been surprising. The woman, who sounded so young and energetic, was tall, angular and white-haired, not quite old enough to be motherly but certainly older than Kendra. Still, she had a relaxed manner that Kendra found comfortable.

Kendra was right up front with her, saying that talking about something had never seemed like a solution to her.

Gwen was unperturbed. "So think of me as a sounding board," she suggested. "Bounce ideas off me."

"And what do I talk about?"

"Whatever you want, whatever you feel comfortable talking about."

Kendra raised an eyebrow at that. Still, she felt comfortable with the older woman and as the sessions went on, she was able to talk about issues. She didn't think the antidepressants did anything but Peg said she noticed a difference. And everything they talked about, all the issues that Kendra avoided discussing, she supposed was helping. They talked about relationships, those Kendra couldn't maintain, the lack of intimacy, the differences between real guilt and perceived guilt, the things Kendra had control over and the things she didn't, what she could have done, and what wouldn't have mattered. She had never been one to talk about issues much. She believed the way to get things accomplished was to take action.

Yet, she had to admit, nothing she had done so far had accomplished anything for Linda. Obsessed, her therapist Gwen had said. Now, she could just imagine what Gwen would have to say if Kendra had mentioned she had actually seen Linda, not just once, but twice. Hallucinations? Hearing voices? Kendra believed in ghosts about as much as she believed in therapy.

She got into the car and turned her phone back on. Immediately the harsh annoying jingle sounded, telling her she had a message.

"Kendra, call me at the office," came Peg's serious voice.

Kendra frowned. It was unusual for Peg to call. She knew where Kendra was and normally did nothing to interrupt her. "What's up?" she asked as soon as Peg answered.

"Robin Slusher called for you."

"Oh," Kendra said calmly although she felt her heart rate increase. "That's interesting. What did she want?" *News maybe? Had she found out something? Or maybe just a friendly call? That would be nice. Hold the horses, don't let your fantasies run away with you. Had to be some other reason.* "Don't tell me her alarm system went off again," she said with mixed annoyance and resignation.

"She didn't mention that," Peg said with sudden realization. "She just said she wanted to reach you. Wanted to know if you could give her a call."

"Uh-huh. I can manage that." Curious.

"Anything going on in that quarter that I'd be interested in knowing about?"

Kendra frowned at the thinly-veiled curiosity. "Like what?"

"Like, maybe, is this business or personal?"

Kendra drew a breath. Sometimes Peg as her office manager was just a bit too personal. And immediately she realized how unfair that was when she was the one who considered staff as family.

"Well, Peg, I don't know. I haven't talked to her," Kendra replied patiently. "If it's business, I'll let you know."

"So if you don't," Peg countered, "can I assume it's personal?"

Walked into that one. "Well, neither one of us will ever find out if the lady didn't leave me the information where to contact her."

"Oh."

She could envision Peg immediately reaching for the phone number. She jotted it down on the ever-present pad in her pocket as Peg read it off. Ahhh, a cell number, not the house. Mmmm, now that was interesting.

"Thanks, Peg. I'll see you in the morning."

"You're not even going to say anything, are you?"

"Now, Peg. Like I said, there's nothing to say." She chuckled as she sensed Peg's frustration. "I'll see you in the morning."

She sat in the parking lot staring at the number, thinking about Robin. Intense. Ambitious. That was clear. She had that fresh-scrubbed, girl-next-door look that probably helped open doors. Kendra thought it might be deceiving. Certainly not the physical appearance—and Robin was a nice-looking woman—but the openness. Superficial? Or was it deeper?

She wondered why Robin had offered to look into Linda's disappearance. Just an impulse thing? Something very easily done to generate Kendra's goodwill? A potential story? All possible. Linda was a cold case, and missing people are always a human interest story. And Robin was a reporter. Solve a cold case and you made news.

She wasn't going to learn anything sitting here speculating. She punched in the number and listened to it ring. One. Two. Three. Four. Five. Six.

"I'm sorry I can't take your call right now. Please leave your name and number, and I'll get back to you—"

Even before the recorded message was completed, Kendra's phone was ringing back. She broke off that connection and hit ANSWER.

"Sorry," this breathless voice said. "I couldn't catch the phone in time. This is Robin Slusher."

"Hello, Robin, this is Kendra McKenna."

"Kendra! Great. Glad you called back. I've got just a minute now, but I do have some information for you. I don't know that it will help or not, but it's what's there. Can we meet sometime?"

She found something! "Sure. What's your schedule?"

"Hectic. How about you come over to the house Sunday afternoon? I think it should be quiet then."

"Sounds good to me. What time?"

"Two-ish?"

"Fine. Two o'clock at your house."

"Great. Gotta go. See you then." And she was gone.

* * *

That night after dinner Kendra went to her home office and unlocked the file cabinet in the corner. She pulled out her journals first, then after hesitating, she pulled out the scrapbook and spread it across her desk. She hadn't looked at any of them for a long time. It was just too painful. She opened up the scrapbook first.

Local Woman Missing read the headline on the local page and below it was Linda's graduation picture. The story took up half the page, covering the campground, Claudia, the local angle, Artie too.

The stories went on for days, displayed prominently, and then fading as nothing turned up, and new stories crowded it out. They were all there in the scrapbook. Then a blank page, the one-year anniversary; the second. Then blank pages.

She sat back. The scrapbooks weren't her doing. She had been too upset, too disoriented. At first, she had thought it would be simple. Linda was with friends or just disappeared for a few days to think things over, so she had flown back from California. Linda didn't show up and the search dragged on. Kendra had to return to California, her job with a company that handled industrial security systems, her apartment. And the search still dragged out. It was driving her crazy, being so far away. On top of that, her dad's health started failing. She threw in the towel to Fate, gave up her job, her apartment, and drove back to Indiana. She had too much going on in her life to keep scrapbooks. No, the scrapbooks were Sue's doing.

She and Sue had made an uneasy truce, at least for a while. Dislike and mistrust had been there for too many years to resolve completely. Once the need to pool their resources in the search for Linda tapered off, so did their tolerance for each other. Sue's rigid attitude against Kendra's lifestyle returned, as did Kendra's intolerance of Sue's bigotry.

Finally, just two years ago, Sue had brought the boxes over.

"I know you won't destroy them," the strawberry-blonde had said with bitter acknowledgment. "But I can't stand dealing with them anymore. You're eighty miles away. You don't turn the corner and expect to see her. You don't see her in all the old familiar places." She glared at Kendra across the three file storage boxes. "You left her a long time ago, so it must not bother you that she's really gone now."

"I didn't leave willingly, Sue. You know that. You're the one who delivered the message that Linda wanted me out of the picture. And then you were the one to call to find out if she was with me."

"Don't remind me!" Sue burst out with her hands upraised, clenched into fists.

"What, Sue?" Kendra couldn't resist twisting the knife. "You mean you would have her alive and with me instead of this awful unknowing? Rather queer than dead?"

"Damn you, Kendra McKenna! If it weren't for you—" She stopped herself.

"What?" Kendra demanded. "Then Linda would never have loved women? Or rather the two of you would have married your respective spouses and then no one would think it strange that you were always together? The boys go on hunting trips and you two would be alone together? All the things that no one would wonder about, dropping in for coffee every day, going shopping? Staying overnight together because you didn't like being in that big house all alone? Who do you think you're fooling?"

Sue went red in the face, advanced a step. "There's nothing queer about that! Linda and I were cousins, we were always close."

"Yeah. Practiced kissing on each other, didn't you?"

Sue inhaled so deeply, Kendra thought the room would empty of oxygen. "I'll have you know I'm getting married in November."

"Whoopee shit! And who might be the sorry bastard?"

"Artie."

Kendra was speechless and then she let out an explosive sound. "God, if two people deserve each other, it's the two of you." She shook her head, momentarily speechless. "No wonder you want to get rid of all these files. I expect dear Artie would be a mite uncomfortable with them in the house."

"Artie had nothing to do with her disappearance!"

Kendra shook her head. "Leave, Sue. Or I'll say something I really regret. I already think you're a hypocrite and a fool. I'd hate to think that you're an idiot besides." Sue started to say something and Kendra forestalled her. "Leave. Now."

And Sue left, leaving Kendra with all the empty hopes and promises of a successful search.

Now Kendra looked at them all again. Sue, as rigid as she was, everything in its proper place, its proper role, had been just as thorough on keeping the files. Sue kept everything: newspaper articles, every poster they put out, copies of Facebook pages Sue had started. Pictures. Cards and letters people sent. Everything. Chronological order of course. Kendra's collection was more haphazard: papers, disorganized, duplicated, covered with notes, questions. Except for her journals.

Last of all, Kendra looked at the brocade-covered journals—the Linda journals she called them. She had started them when she had first gone to California; needing to vent and knowing no one, she had poured all her anger and pain onto the handwritten page, written, afraid to put them on the computer, afraid in a fit of despair or grief or anger or any mixture, she might just delete them all. The written word would take longer to destroy.

The journals had worked. Her anger faded. The entries decreased, maybe holidays, a year's update on New Year's, Linda's birthday, Fourth of July. When there was some celebration that called for fireworks. There were months when she didn't write about Linda at all.

She didn't start updating them when Linda first disappeared. She was too upset, too shattered. And then too livid when she was investigated because Artie said Linda probably left with her. After that, she started documenting everything. She'd learned to write good reports by then. Every hint, every comment, every outcome. And what did it add up to?

"Nothing, absolutely nothing." She threw the journal back onto the desk.

Oh, I wouldn't say that.

Kendra leaned back in the chair, tilted it back and examined the ceiling. She could see a faint image just to her left. "Well," she said aloud, "gotta admit. You got more than the fifteen minutes of fame."

There was a responding familiar chuckle that set her heart pounding. *"Hell of a way to get it."*

Kendra brought the chair down hard, almost slamming into the desk. Breathing rapidly when she stood up, she felt light-headed enough to put her hand on the desk to steady herself. She had told Robin that Linda would have contacted her.

Maybe it was real; maybe Linda was trying to make contact with her. That was the theory. But to make a comment and receive a response, that was something else. Her chest felt tight, and she was shaking. She closed her eyes, took a deep breath, then another.

"What do you want?" she asked in a shaking voice.

"*Justice. Vengeance.*"

Kendra swallowed. This couldn't be happening.

"*Once you said you'd do anything for me, Sunshine.*"

"Once we said a lot of things." She was trying to calm down, trying to think, trying to hold on to her sanity.

"*But now I'm asking.*"

"So why can't you do it yourself?"

"*I ain't got no body,*" Linda sang the tune with her achingly familiar dry humor.

Kendra closed her eyes. Was she losing her mind? "Why don't you go haunt him?"

"*The connection with you is stronger, Sunshine. You remember me.*" Her voice faded. "*You still love me.*"

The room felt empty again, and Kendra took a deep breath. "I can deal with this," she muttered to herself. "Really, I can. I wanted answers. I wanted to know." She took another breath. "How many people would give their right arm for an opportunity like this?" She took another breath. "God, I wish any of them were here right now."

She sat back down. She closed up the journals and the scrapbooks and tossed them back in the drawer, slammed it shut. Without looking back, without setting the alarm, without doing anything but picking up her wallet and driver's license, she walked out the door and slammed it behind her.

* * *

"Heard you tied one on last night," Peg greeted her the next morning when Kendra came in late with sunglasses—dark sunglasses—on.

Kendra went directly to her office where she first pulled the blinds to shut out the sunshine. "Hmmmmm." She really didn't want to talk about it, even though Peg followed her in with a cup of coffee that she set on Kendra's desk.

"Travis said you came over and proceeded in short order to get smashed."

Kendra shrugged off her jacket carefully, and dropped it on the chair. Any movement hurt. She couldn't remember the last time she had done this. Actually, she couldn't remember ever doing it before. She sat behind her desk and buried her face in her hands. Peg watched her from in front of the desk. She had seen Kendra through lots of drama, but Kendra had never done anything like this.

"Have some coffee, hon," she said gently.

"Take it away, Peg," she said in a hoarse voice. "Just take it away."

Peg did as requested, and Kendra closed her eyes. She did remember driving over to Travis's. And she did remember them going out. And she did remember going to a club. What she didn't remember, though, was what she told Travis. She vaguely remembered Travis taking her to Travis's place, putting her to bed.

Then going home this morning. It felt empty. A house can feel empty or it can feel like someone is there even if they're not actually in residence. The house truly felt empty.

Peg tiptoed back in. "Kendra."

"Is it important?" *Is the building on fire?*

"I don't know. Did you talk to Robin Slusher? Is something on the schedule with her?"

"No." Kendra answered immediately and then thought about what she said. "I mean, yes, I spoke with her. No, it's not business, and no, it's not today."

"Very good." Peg still stood there. "Why don't you go home? You're the boss, there's nothing on the schedule. Just take the day off."

Kendra shook her head, a mistake. She closed her eyes for a minute. The longer her eyes were closed, the better the idea sounded. "I think I will."

CHAPTER SEVEN

Running. As fast as she could. Through the trees, dodging them, lurching into them. Her heart was pounding so loudly she could hardly hear the shouting behind her. He was gaining. She slipped on wet leaves, lurched into a tree, caught herself. Afraid, but not panicked, not yet. She should be able to make it. Just through the trees, the open field. She could see the house. Safety. She pushed off from the tree. Just a little farther. Cross the fence. Running. Running. Running. Look over her shoulder. He was gaining.

* * *

Kendra came awake with a jerk, her heart pounding. She was halfway out of bed before she realized where she was. Home. In her own bed. Safe in her own house. She fell back against the pillow, breathing hard. She closed her eyes, trying to calm her terror.

Her breathing steadied. She stopped feeling her blood pressure in her ears. She opened her eyes, still trying to shake off the nightmare. Shadows from the tree outside the high window wavered across the far wall. The outlines of the dresser, the antique cabinet, the chair where she had tossed her clothing all helped bring her back to the present.

She realized she must have slept most of the day as she sat up and threw back the covers. She sat on the side of the bed for a minute, her head buried in her hands. She had no explanation for her nightmare. This one was so real. Do nightmares have reason? She'd had dreams tap into her subconscious before, give her solutions to tricky problems. Nothing like this, nothing like she had ever had before. And she had woken up just in time, just before. Before what?

With a sigh she got up and walked through the house, first to the bathroom, then to the kitchen to brew a cup of tea, get something to eat. The dream was still present, not in reality, but in her adrenaline. She could still feel the terror, but it was there, just at the edge. There was no sense going back to bed if she would just toss fitfully, pounding the pillow, chasing elusive sleep.

As she waited for the water to boil, she stared out the kitchen window at the high privacy fence around the backyard. She had been frightened before. There had been confrontations, a road accident, but nothing like this dream. Like a feeling she was going to die. She shivered as she poured the hot water into the mug with the tea bag. Normal everyday actions were helping her drive away those last panicky feelings.

Get up. Do something until the feeling goes away.

Probably the drinking last night. She'd never had a hangover like this; never wanted another one. Maybe if she sat in her brooding chair and just thought about it, the feeling would recede and she could go back to sleep. She moved to the living room, sat down in the huge overstuffed chair.

Her mind drifted back over her life. This therapy deal, it brought up a whole lot of things, all her regrets, the things she didn't do, the opportunities she let pass by. All the dreams and none of them had come through. Her life was empty. She laid her head back on the back of the chair and closed her eyes, to sleep, perhaps to dream.

Once she had had dreams. Didn't everyone? Of having a lover, someone to love, someone to love her. Someone to fill her life with happiness. Someone she could have a life with. Someone who would make life matter. All growing up, she had thought it would have been Linda.

It didn't happen. Now her only lover was in her dreams, a dream lover, who would love her as no one in reality did. Some days the only thing she looked forward to was sleeping, to escape the emptiness and join her dream lover. Sometimes she even thought about making it permanent, a life they could have together and she wouldn't have to deal with such emptiness, such nothingness.

Coward!

Kendra took a deep breath and sat up. Some people would say suicide was cowardice. Linda had. Linda thought life was to be lived, embraced. Problems were merely a challenge and Linda would never accept defeat.

Kendra could almost see Linda now, here in the dimness of the long living room, dressed in her jeans and western shirt, standing in front of the stone fireplace across the end of the room. She'd be smiling that half smile of hers, coaxing Kendra out of a depression, dreaming up some devilment to get into.

Kendra closed her eyes again and the image faded.

"Oh, Linda," she moaned. "Why did you send me away?"

* * *

"You all right?" Peg greeted her when she dragged herself into the office the next day.

"Better," she acknowledged. "Not great. What's on the agenda?"

Work, she always threw herself into work to counter her depression. A slow day, that was good, she thought in relief as she went to her desk. And as she had to focus so tightly just to keep thoughts at bay, it was a good day to go over some thorny reports that she'd been putting off. She stayed at it, right through lunch, afraid to take her mind off crime reports, sales orders, purchases, possibilities, for fear of stray thoughts floating in. Reality. That was what she needed. Feet on the ground. Concrete.

"Kendra?"

Kendra didn't look up from the screen. Not only had she managed not to think about Linda all day, she had managed to clean up a backlog of reports. Now if she could just finish this one.

"Kendra! You're going to be late." Peg's voice held that note of insistence she used when she had to boss the boss.

With a sigh, Kendra swung her office chair around to see her. "Late," she repeated as she leaned forward to pull her office planner to her. "I thought you said I didn't have anything scheduled today."

"No business appointments," Peg came back with as she came in to stand in front of the wooden desk. She tapped her appointment book impatiently. "But you have therapy at five thirty and if you don't get out of here, you'll never make it across town in time."

Kendra stared at the notation in her calendar. Five thirty— Dr. Brown.

She didn't want to go. She didn't want to leave her office, fight the traffic and go talk. To anyone. About anything. Much less about what was bothering her today. If she thought about it, she could come up with an excuse. A report due. Traffic. A last-minute phone call.

"Kendra!" Peg's voice was sharper now, mixed with efficiency and familiarity. "You've got to get going. You've made great progress on all those reports. They don't all have to be done today." Peg came around the desk. She shoved the file cabinet drawer closed, turned out the light over the credenza. "Come on, don't be difficult."

"Peg," Kendra said in a warning tone.

Peg stood before her, hands on hips, giving Kendra that no-nonsense look. "Don't Peg me. Weren't you the one who came to me and said you had finally taken some advice and were seeing a therapist? Weren't you the one who asked me to make sure that you got out the door and got to these appointments? Weren't you the one who admitted you were going to need a prod occasionally?"

"Yes," Kendra agreed in an even tone that was also a warning. She leaned forward in her chair but made no move to get up.

"Well, then, I'm only doing what you asked me to. Or have you changed your mind?"

Reluctantly, Kendra got to her feet. "I just didn't know you were going to be so damn good at it," Kendra muttered.

"And just how many times do I get to boss the boss?"

"Every day." Kendra shook her head as she picked up files and threw them in her open briefcase and shut it. "What would I do if I didn't have you to keep me on track?"

"Besides, seeing her today might just be great timing," Peg said firmly as she ignored the question. "Now, go."

Kendra picked up her briefcase and glanced over her desk. "I forgot—" She made a move to go to the still-open computer.

"I'll shut it down." Peg intercepted her. "Now go."

Kendra walked to her car in the parking lot beside the pond. She still didn't want to go but she knew if she couldn't make an excuse for Gwen for a late cancellation, she had even less energy to come up with an excuse for Peg the next morning. And Peg would ask, nothing so crass as to what they talked about but something to ascertain that Kendra had gone. Sometimes, Kendra thought, as she slid into the seat of her late model Mazda, there were times when it wasn't good to take your staff as family.

Thirty-five minutes later Kendra pulled into the parking lot beside the three-story "painted lady" Victorian monstrosity that was once a house and now was the offices of Dr. Gwendolyn Brown. She parked in the shade of the ash tree and turned off the ignition. She sat there a moment, not moving, just staring out the windshield. Finally she sighed and opened the door. She was paying for the session; she might as well go in and not just sit in her car.

"Good afternoon, Kendra. How are you doing?" Gwen greeted Kendra at the door. With a wave of her hand, she indicated the chair in front of the desk as she took the seat adjacent to it. "Have you been sleeping any better?"

Kendra shook her head. "Not really," she answered as she took the chair. "Another nightmare last night."

"Like the others you told me about?"

Kendra nodded. "Running away from something, someone. Afraid, desperate. I can hear someone chasing me, gaining on me." She shook her head.

"Did you wake up at the same point?"

Another nod. "Just before something happens," she said. "But I don't know what."

Gwen was quiet for a moment and Kendra said nothing to fill the silence. What should she say? That she was seeing things, hallucinating? Hearing voices? Kendra wasn't up on all the mental aberrations but she knew this was serious. Any diagnosis like that scared her worse than anything she had heard or seen so far.

Even with that in mind, these past two weeks had been unnerving. Voices, no, not voices, just one voice. Talking to her. Not even clearly. Faintly. Like the radio was left on in the garage or the neighbors had talk radio on while they were gardening. Not always clear but there. And sometimes she knew exactly what the voice was saying because it was in her head.

And seeing things. Just some movement detected from the corner of her eye but when she turned, there was nothing there. Besides she was the only one in the house. And that was another thing. There's the definite feeling of being alone and she didn't have that feeling in the house anymore. Sometimes if she didn't move but just shifted her eyes to look to the side, she could see a faint shimmer, an image. But what really chilled her was that the image was getting stronger.

So now she had the opportunity to say something, have some sounding board before she herself believed she was going crazy. And she was beginning to give that idea serious consideration.

"Is there anything else going on that you'd like to share?" Gwen asked gently.

Almost against her will, Kendra nodded. Then she didn't know what to say. "Do you believe in ghosts?" she said finally.

Gwen sat back in her chair, betraying no surprise. "As in spirits of someone departed? Psychic images?"

Kendra gave a quick jerky nod.

"I'm not sure I believe in them," Gwen said smoothly. "But then I'm not sure I disbelieve either. I've seen and heard some things that seemed to have no rational explanation. And people have told me things that they believed were messages from beyond. Who am I to say they were wrong? If it makes you more comfortable, I can tell you I believe I saw my father in my bathroom mirror two days after his funeral. I've always believed he came to tell me goodbye."

Kendra let out a breath she didn't realize she had been holding. Maybe she wasn't going crazy. Maybe she wasn't seeing things, or at least imagining things. She sighed with relief.

"I've always been a rational person," she said faintly. "Black and white. Reality." She looked up at Gwen. "Oh, I've read the ghost stories, listened to them. I've had people tell me stories, the hunch that paid off, the cold feeling, the person met who wasn't really there and then finding out he was long gone." She shook her head. "I believed them, I mean, I believed the person telling the story." She frowned, trying to pick out the words as to how she felt. "I mean, I believe the person believed. I'm not sure I believed." She looked up to see if Gwen understood.

Gwen nodded. "And now you've seen something to make you question?"

More relieved than she wanted to admit, Kendra nodded, even as she wondered if the woman was just humoring her and Gwen was already thinking of all the paperwork for commitment to the local psych ward. "Yes."

"Why don't you tell me about it?"

"I saw Linda."

"You saw someone who looked like Linda?"

"No." Kendra shook her head. "I saw Linda," she repeated. "It was at the fireworks. I heard her first. When the show started. It seemed so natural for her to be there, I didn't even give it a second thought." She drew a deep breath. "And then I rationalized, well, going to the first fireworks in years, I thought maybe it was just my imagination, just someone nearby who sounded like her."

"Did your friend, Travis, was it? Did she hear her?"

Kendra shrugged. "I have no idea. Travis was having her own issues. I've seen folks with phobias before. Travis was trying hard, but I didn't think even then she'd last for long."

"You said you saw her."

Kendra sat back in the chair. "When we got back to the car, got Travis buckled in, wondering if we needed to make a trip to the ER, I started around the front and this person was standing there, just standing. And I said something about we had to leave, would she move. And she looked at me and she said: 'I've been waiting for you.'"

Kendra stopped. Even now she shivered.

"You're sure it was Linda?"

Kendra nodded. "She seemed as real and as solid as this desk." She knocked on the edge of it.

"And then what happened?"

Kendra grimaced. "Travis threw up. I went back to take care of her and when I looked again, no one was there. After that, the night got a little hectic. I took Travis to the ER, then on the way home, we saw an accident." She looked up at Gwen. "But I know what I saw, and it was Linda."

"Has that been the only time?"

Relief washed over Kendra. At least Gwen sounded like she believed her. "No. There was the night at the club." She stopped there. She could still see Linda in the middle of the dance floor.

"What happened at the club?"

Kendra recounted the events, Peg and Travis in cahoots, the dancing, suddenly seeing Linda on the dance floor. God, it had been good to see her; for an instant, just an instant, Kendra had wanted to rush down and then she remembered.

"I jumped to my feet, knocked over my drink. When I looked back, she wasn't there. She wasn't anywhere." She looked up at Gwen, her perplexity overcoming her reluctance to talk about it. "I could see her so clearly, her clothes, her expression. I looked all over, no one had a similar shirt like I could have mistaken someone for her. No one moved like her; no one had that impish grin like she was jerking my chain and it just amused the hell out of her."

There was a moment's pause. "Did Travis see her? You said that Travis was pointing someone out to you."

"No, she meant someone else, who I didn't even see until later. I felt like I'd been kicked in the gut. Linda was so clear." She shook her head, still not believing.

"What happened next?"

"God, I felt almost sick. Travis said I looked like I'd seen a ghost."

A ghost. There, she had said it. And as she contemplated the ramifications of that, Gwen was doing some thinking of her own.

"Has there been anything since?"

Kendra sighed. She was going to have to tell the rest now for sure. "Not exactly."

"What does 'not exactly' mean?"

"It's more a feeling. Like when you feel someone is behind you or watching you and you turn around and there is someone there. Only I turn around and there's no one there. But if I don't turn around, you know, just look out of the corner of my eye, I can see something, some faint image. And I can hear her, like a radio in the distance, but I know what she's saying. Sometimes I think it's just what I know she would be saying, and I'm just imagining I'm hearing her, like filling in the blanks. But that doesn't explain about the computer."

"What about the computer?"

"When I came home from the dance, I was shutting things up. I went back through my office. My computer was on. I know I shut it down before I left, I don't even leave it in sleep mode. And there was writing on the screen." She pulled the folded piece of paper out of her pocket and handed it over.

Gwen opened up the folded sheet that looked like it had been wadded up more than once. She read it, glanced up at Kendra and back at the page. "Sunshine?"

"Linda's sense of humor. She always said I went around like a black cloud, that I need to smile more, be more cheerful, more optimistic."

"I don't suppose there's any chance you did this in your sleep or were playing with the computer in your half-awake state?"

Kendra shook her head. Reasonable explanations. She had considered them also. There was a long silence.

"You think Linda's trying to contact you?"

Kendra looked up. "You think I'm imagining all this?" The idea she might be deluding herself, was even more offensive than the idea of seeing a ghost.

"Then again," Gwen pointed out in her logical, reasoned voice, "there is always the possibility you're really seeing her. Or she's trying to come through to you."

Numbly, Kendra nodded. As afraid as she was of losing touch with reality, she certainly didn't understand how to deal with the actuality of seeing a ghost.

"Anything like this happen to you before?"

Kendra shook her head. "But if it were to happen, it would be Linda's ghost that I saw." She tried to reorganize her thoughts. She had thought of a lot of things, been prepared for as many different reactions from Gwen as she could think of but she discovered she really wasn't prepared for the possibility ghosts might be real.

"How so?"

Kendra tried to remember; there was so much Linda had told her about, explored. She had listened but didn't quite believe. And so she had only half listened. "She thought we had mental abilities we had forgotten how to use," she said slowly. "She thought we were tied to our bodies but the body was only the shell. The spirit was what was really 'us,' the person, the soul. She thought through learning, discipline, training, we could leave the body behind."

"A spirit."

Kendra looked up. "I suppose so. She did meditation; always talking about getting in touch with the soul, understanding that the body was temporary." She frowned. "She believed in reincarnation, thought we, she and I—not just people in general, had past lives together; we were linked, had a spiritual connection."

"But you didn't believe it?"

"Not exactly. But I didn't disbelieve it either. I mean, how do you prove something like that, whether it's reincarnation or out-of-body or—" She stopped, floundering.

"Or ghosts?"

"Yeah." Kendra thought about the ramifications. "Or disprove it for that matter," she mused in a quieter voice.

"That's a philosophical question."

The silence was comfortable this time before Gwen went back to Linda.

"Anything else strange happening? Do you only get the feeling at the house?"

"Only at the house, except that once at the dance. And the house is cold. Travis complained about it when she stopped in. And the security's been screwy. On when it should be off; off when it should be on. I've got the same thing with one of my clients." She stopped, a sudden thought, but dismissed the idea immediately. Just a coincidence.

Gwen appeared thoughtful. "Most spirits, at least what I've read, are location-bound." She looked to Kendra. "But you got this house after Linda—" She stopped.

Kendra knew what she meant. "Right. I bought this after I moved back. I've read the same thing, the emotional link." She thought about the times they shared.

"Unless it was the fireworks. That was something we shared. We spent a lot of time…And then, there is another reason," Kendra said as if were the most reasonable thing in the world.

"What's that?"

"Justice, to be avenged. To punish the guilty. To find her murderer."

Gwen gave her a long thoughtful look. "Yes," she said finally. "There is that."

Finally!

Kendra turned her head suddenly. She looked around and then back at Gwen who seemed to have noticed nothing.

"Well," Gwen said thoughtfully. She gave Kendra a tentative look. "You really think she's dead?"

Kendra nodded. If she'd had any hope before, it was gone.

"Then have her tell you where she's buried, that might be a start."

CHAPTER EIGHT

Simple enough, Kendra considered for the next two days as she went about her business, but how does one go about questioning a ghost? Hadn't she done all she could to find her, the searches, the reward notices, adding whatever pressure she could to law enforcement to keep the search up? What more could she have done? There had to be something.

Friday night she went over all the side effects of the anti-depressant, just in case this wasn't real. And when Travis called, she tried scoping her out as to what she might have said in her drunken stupor. If she had said anything strange, Travis wasn't giving any of it up.

Saturday she ran her usual weekend errands convincing herself that it was just an overactive imagination, certainly something no one had ever accused her of before. Then just to be on the safe side in preparation of the Sunday meeting with Robin, she went over the scrapbook again. She had no idea what Robin wanted to talk about but she wanted to refresh her memory. She put it so much out of her mind that she read some of the reports as if she had never seen them before. She shook her head. Not even a fresh reading gave her any more clues.

Sunday Kendra woke up early, eager for the day. When she caught herself looking at the clock again and again, she realized how much she was looking forward to seeing Robin. She even left the house early and stopped by the park near Robin's house, walking the trail, wondering whether it was the information Robin might have or whether it was just seeing her again. She found the woman attractive, congenial and easy to talk to, all the things that made her a good reporter. Finally, Kendra decided she had killed enough time, got in her car and pulled up in front of Robin's house at two o'clock on the dot.

"Right on time," Robin greeted her with a brisk tone. "Come on in."

"Like to be punctual."

Definitely not like the last time, Kendra thought as she followed Robin through the house. *First of all, she's dressed. And something else.* There was an efficiency about her this time. A chill went through Kendra. She wasn't sure she liked the something else.

"It's such a nice day, I thought we might sit on the patio. Do you mind? I spend so much time cooped up in offices that I try to spend a lot of my off-duty time outside."

"I understand perfectly." And she did, finally, belatedly. Robin was after a story. This wasn't going to be a friendly chat, although it wouldn't necessarily be unfriendly. This was going to be Robin digging. But what did that have to do with Linda?

Kendra followed Robin through the French doors and out onto the patio where there were already file folders, a notebook and a tape recorder neatly laid out on the table. A large bowl of deep purple dahlias sat in the center.

"Have a seat. Can I get you coffee or something?"

"No, thanks, I'm fine." Kendra eyed the tape recorder. She hadn't expected their conversation to be taped and didn't relish the idea. As she took the seat in the webbed chair, she debated whether she should just shut this conversation off or see what Robin was after. Her curiosity won out, that and her attraction to the woman. To the best of her knowledge, there was nothing in her life that would warrant a news story. She could listen, and maybe learn something.

Robin sat down across from her and moved the tape recorder to one side. "You were right; you were investigated." She pulled the top folder down, flipped it open, closed it, but didn't hand it over. "There probably isn't anything in here that you don't already know but I still thought I'd collect everything. I pulled the old newspaper stories, copies of the police reports." She glanced up at Kendra. "You had quite a time in California."

"I was young. It was different."

"Keep in contact with anyone?"

Kendra shook her head. California was an interlude; it seemed a long time ago. Robin handed the folder over. Kendra hadn't liked the idea of being investigated then, but accepted it was necessary. She just didn't like strangers poking around in her business. And she certainly didn't like that the information was still floating around now.

She opened the folder and found the newspaper articles neatly dated and fastened at the top with a binder clip. Most of them were the same as those Sue had put into the scrapbook. Nothing new there.

What was new was the police report on her—education, jobs, friends, the places she visited, her phone calls. A dead end as far as the police were concerned then, a vague reminder to her now of another life. And now Robin knew.

She laid the folder back on the table. "Nothing there I didn't already know."

"Like I said." Robin sat back, her fingers at her chin, her elbow on the chair arm. She watched Kendra with curiosity and speculation. "You thought about getting into law enforcement," Robin said slowly. "What made you change your mind?"

Kendra looked away, pursed her lips. Officer training had been the wrong road to take. Fortunately she learned it quickly and backed out. "I needed a job. They were hiring. Pay was good. It didn't take me long to figure out law enforcement wasn't my cup of tea. I left." She looked back at Robin, bland and closed.

Kendra leaned back in the chair. It was not in her experience that people did something for nothing, cynical she knew, but it had proved correct so many times she relied on it until proven otherwise. The stack of folders that Robin had on the table indicated to her something else was going on, but what that might be, she had no idea. She would simply have to wait until Robin made the move. So she waited, watched as Robin flipped through the folders, evidently debating.

Robin seemed to come to some decision. She looked up at Kendra, a direct look that told Kendra this was the information Robin was really after. "You think the husband killed your friend?"

Kendra wasn't ready to face it that bluntly. "The police always say to look at those closest to the victim," she answered evasively.

Robin nodded as she picked up the next folder. "Unfortunately, that is often the case. However he was away on a hunting trip, wasn't he?"

Kendra nodded as she eyed Artie's name neatly written on the file folder tab. She also noted that the file folder didn't look new. Whatever Robin's interest was in Artie, it had existed before Kendra had asked about Linda.

"You wouldn't know, by chance, where he might be these days?" Robin asked with a casualness that made Kendra immediately suspicious.

Kendra shook her head. "Not the slightest. I haven't seen him since we looked for Linda. He tossed me off the land, said I wasn't to set foot on it. That was five years ago."

"Literally or figuratively?" She still held on to the folder.

"Physically."

"He still didn't like you?"

"You could say that."

"Why not?" Robin cocked her head like a curious pup. "With Linda gone, I would think his issue would be done with."

"Probably because the last time he saw me, I stuck a gun in his face."

Robin's eyes widened in surprise. "I thought," she said slowly, "you said that Linda told you to leave and you did."

"She followed me out to the car, leaned in the window and kissed me. He came upon us, jerked her away, threw her to the ground and was reaching in for me." She could still remember, indeed, feel the turmoil of that day, all the conflicting emotions. She had been just twenty-two; she'd never had to face any violence before. Scared? Terrified had been a better term for it.

"And?" Robin finally prompted.

Kendra came back to the present. "I had a gun under the seat," Kendra said in even tones. "I pulled it out and stuck it in his face." She watched Robin recoil. "Maybe I should have killed him. Maybe if I had, Linda would still be here."

"Why'd you have the gun?" Robin asked quietly.

Kendra looked up at her and gave a small grunt. "Dad thought it'd be a good idea. Here I was, a single woman, driving across the country to California. I liked driving at night." She drew a deep breath. "It wasn't like I carried it all the time. I was all packed and ready to leave. The gun was licensed, I knew how to use it."

"Did you ever consider you could have faced criminal charges if you had shot him?"

Kendra shook her head. "It would have been self-defense."

Robin shook her head. "Maybe not. You just said you normally didn't have it. But you went over there with it; could have easily been premeditation. You wanted her to go with you. Her husband was in the way. Convictions have been made on less evidence."

Kendra shifted her position, leaned forward to fold her arms against the table. Robin's questions about what she had or hadn't done bothered her. They were too close to her own recriminations. "Well, I didn't shoot him. I wish I could say I haven't spent any time second-guessing myself, but I have. Especially for the past five years." With a wave of her hand, she indicated the stack of folders. "However, that's my connection with Artie Jeffers. If you don't mind me being blunt, what's your interest?"

Robin looked a little surprised at Kendra's directness, surprised and maybe a little taken aback. "Right to the bottom line?"

"Might save us both some time."

Robin scrutinized her for a moment, and then passed the folder over. "How well did you know him?"

"He was some years ahead of me in high school, so I didn't know him well, although he was a neighbor in Walton's Corner. His folks had a place on the other side of the creek. Linda and I both lived on one side, he on the other."

"How much older than you?"

"Four, five years, something like that. Quite a bit really."

"What did you think of him?"

"Nothing."

Robin looked at her sharply, and the look was as much of a question as if she voiced it. "I didn't have much interaction with him. By the time I was old enough to have really noticed him, he was off in the service or running around Europe somewhere. I can't remember where, or if I ever even knew. Then I went off to college, Purdue, and he came back. Lived with his folks. Claudia hired him occasionally to work at the campground, so I knew him. That is, I recognized him, would say hello to him, occasional chats when I was over there, but as to know him? No, I can't say that I did."

Robin frowned. Kendra surmised she had been hoping for something more.

"What do you know about militia units?"

"Not much. Big boys playing war games in the woods."

"Some of them are playing a little more seriously than others."

"How's that?"

"Have you ever heard of the Miami Militia Unit, the MMU?"

Kendra shook her head. "Not the militia unit. Now I've heard of the Miamis, the Indiana ones, not the Florida one. They were the predominant Indian tribe around here when Indiana was first settled. Had a big settlement up in Cass County on the Wabash. So it's a prominent place name, county, township, bunch of groups. But that's as far as it goes. Does the name come from that connection?"

Robin still frowned.

"So what's the connection? Is Artie a member or something?"

Robin slowly nodded.

Robin still seemed to debate but finally picked up another folder and passed it across the table to Kendra.

Kendra gave her a puzzled look, but she took the folder.

"I'll let you read that one in some peace. You want some coffee?" Robin was already getting to her feet.

Kendra nodded; she had already opened the folder and started reading. There was a mishmash of articles on militia from the general to the specific: *Time* magazine's cover story, an article from *Newsweek*, newspaper articles, printouts from the Internet.

The next folder was about Artie. There was a whole stack of information, all the way back to high school, local stuff, gossipy stuff out of the weekly paper that had folded many years ago. And of course, the pieces about his missing wife. No interviews, though. And nothing recent.

Kendra skimmed it, looking for anything relevant to her cause. While he was a person of interest, and the husband is always suspected, he had been cooperative. The campground, now his land, had been searched, walked by groups more than once. Metal detectors and cadaver dogs. Nothing.

Kendra hadn't known that. She was disappointed. She'd had some far-fetched idea that all it would take was a proper search and presto! All would be solved.

She flipped through the entire file, glancing up when Robin put the coffee close to her. She thanked her with a nod and went back to reading. Much of it she knew, so she could skim through it. She went back over the parts she hadn't known and also to peruse the margin notes more carefully.

She closed the folder and dropped it back in front of Robin, who immediately closed the file she had been reading and looked up expectantly.

"Interesting reading, I suppose," Kendra told her, "but I didn't see anything or at least very little that could help me."

"No, I didn't suspect it would," Robin said slowly. "That was just background."

Kendra waited, wondering if this was the way investigative reporting went. If so, it was a good thing she didn't do it. She didn't have the patience. "And the rest?"

Robin drew a breath, evidently deciding. "I think Artie's associated with the Miami Militia Unit. The local unit isn't very large, as units go, maybe twenty at the most. Maybe even less. But they have links with other units across the country."

"So what's their beef? Are we going to be invaded or is the government going to come in and take all our guns?" Kendra rolled her eyes. In the security business, she had run into most of the stories the extremists put out. She was of the mind that anyone with any common sense would see the foolishness of their ideas.

"The government's tyrannical, needs to be taken down, at least be smaller and get out of everyone's lives."

Kendra shook her head. "Malcontents. There's always a percentage of the population who wants to live in a world where no one is telling them what to do."

"Recruitment's up, training's more serious," Robin pointed out. "It's as high as it's ever been since Waco and Ruby Ridge. More threats. They're getting bolder. Did you know that Miami was openly claiming they were the first responders after the tornado outbreak in March?"

"Those tornados were massive," Kendra pointed out. "Damn near wiped two or three towns off the map."

"Right. And Miami was right there. Now the local law enforcement agencies and the local Federal Emergency Management Agency offices said they had no official standing, but they're still claiming they were right there. And they've got the locals to back them up."

Kendra put her head back, looked up at the sky, trying to find a tactful way to word this. "Sometimes," she said finally with a sigh, "FEMA leaves much to be desired." She looked at the papers again. "And twenty people can't do that much." Kendra paused as she remembered the devastation of that spring outbreak. "Although," she added thoughtfully, "if they were there first, then they could be key players."

"They're making noises."

"Like how? What are they saying?"

"The Feds are too big, too bloated, just interested in taking our money and they don't do anything except apply rules and regulations that strangle the rural areas. They don't like big corporations, the environmentalists, bankers."

Kendra nodded. Those were views she had grown up with. She might not have agreed with all of them, but they were familiar to her.

"Nothing new there," she commented. "Rural attitudes like that have been around since the nineteen thirties."

"Mix in the fears of the 'new world order,' implausible things like FEMA concentration camps, martial law and of course, the biggie—they're going to take away our guns."

Kendra paused. She'd heard references to most of these, and she knew that the militia movement had grown in the past few years. "But are they to be taken seriously? I mean, okay, there's a lot of talk, people getting upset. I see and hear that all the time. Is there anything really happening? Besides blowing off of hot air."

"Pockets here and there. You're right, most of it is hot air, but there are some who are really serious."

"And you think the MMU is?"

Robin slowly nodded. "Maybe not the whole unit but something's going on."

"And it's in Walton's Corner?"

Robin shrugged, noncommittal on that point. "Some strange stories are coming out of that area. May not be based there but there is evidence a number of members are there."

Kendra sat back. Of course, the Second Amendment was an issue, the right to bear arms. The Tea Baggers were annoying. There was that university shooting at in February. Had the shootings really gone up since Columbine or did they just get more attention? Whatever it was, she knew that it had an effect on her business. Good or bad, it couldn't be ignored. The guns versus no-guns polarization was growing.

"So what's being done?"

Robin shook her head. "Nothing. They haven't done anything. There's a lot of talk, but whether they're doing anything or not, well, nobody knows."

"And the bigwigs don't have people out there investigating?"

"What I hear, they're not getting far."

"Probably not," Kendra conceded. "It's Artie's old stomping grounds. They still don't like strangers much. Friendly but only so far."

"Sorta my grandfather knew your grandfather?"

"Sorta kinda." Kendra thought about the area. Yeah, she decided, they would be that way. A person could move into the area, live there the rest of their lives and still be known as "the new people." Sometimes it seemed like everyone was related to everyone else in some manner or another.

She thought about it. Interesting, but hardly her concern. She just wanted to find out what happened to Linda. For sure. And bring someone to justice. She sat back in the chair and made a steeple of her hands. "And Artie's part of this militia unit?"

"From what we can gather." She frowned at the file. "What I don't understand is what his beef with the government is. His service record was so-so, nothing great, nothing dangerous. He traveled in Europe, toured some exhibition that was government-sponsored. I can't see he was ever in serious trouble." She looked up at Kendra. "I guess what I'm saying is that I can't see what makes him tick."

"That I can tell you."

Robin's eyes brightened with interest.

"The government took away his high school." Then she had to laugh at the bewildered expression on Robin's face. She backed up. "You said you're from Ohio, Columbus?" Robin nodded. "Big high school?"

"Northland."

"You like basketball?"

"So-so, take it or leave it. I follow the college teams because that's about the only way to survive here."

Kendra chuckled and shook her head. "Yes, we do like our basketball." She collected her thoughts. "In the small rural areas like Walton's Corner, the school isn't just an educational center, it's the heart of the community. It touches everyone whether they have kids in school or not. It's used for community meetings and events. Ball games were the glue that held the community together. Everyone came out for high school games, went to away games, rehashed them all week until the next one. Nowadays, more people follow college ball or football, but in Artie's day, it was basketball. And there is no greater social standing in high school than to be the basketball star." She smiled at the memory. "We were too small for football. I don't think there were more than seven or eight on the full basketball roster, maybe not even that many. But Artie, he was the star. And he was good."

"I thought you didn't know him that well."

"I was in grade school but you don't understand: that was *our* school." She thought about those days, long past. "County champs. Got creamed in the state tourney when we went against the bigger schools, but we were respectable. But county champs. The only time we won." *A long time ago.* She came back to the present.

"And another thing about these small communities. People may leave, may have accomplishments but there's a lot of kids in high school who never achieve more than what they did then—basketball star, the glory. Everyone clapping you on the back, thinking you're great stuff. Hard to top that in the outside world, the real world."

"Artie couldn't?"

Kendra shook her head. "Got a basketball scholarship, but he just wasn't college material. I think that was when he joined the service, but it wasn't a great fit for him either. I heard he might have joined one of those European basketball teams, but he was just small potatoes there, too. But when he came back home, damn, he was still hot stuff. He was the basketball player the year we won the county tourney. He still had that glory."

"Then what happened?"

"School consolidations hit us. All over the state, schools had been consolidated but somehow our little area had been neglected. So we were scheduled to merge and if that wasn't bad enough, it was with our rival. The whole community resisted. I know you think it's foolish in this day and age; seems strange now but I can remember it. Took a police escort to come in and take away the school's accreditation." She paused. "My class was the first graduating class in the new school. Uncomfortable."

"So the government came in and took away his glory."

"About it. Everything else might have been what was said, but the school consolidation was the heart of it."

"That's crazy!"

Kendra raised her eyebrows and looked at Robin. "I didn't say it was reasonable." Kendra pointed to the folder on the militia units. "But are you saying all those guys are rational?"

"Well, no, but if you follow their reasoning, you can see the thread. They're wrong, mistaken, but at least you can see the thread."

Kendra paused. "I've been thinking about Artie for the past couple of weeks. I didn't see it at the time, but certainly looking back at it, I can see his progression. The snide comments about the government, but then everyone bitches about the government. The destruction of the community. Outsiders coming in. Different."

"Is that why he didn't like you?"

"Well, maybe part of it. My family hadn't been in the county as long as his so maybe we were still the 'new people.' And I wasn't impressed with basketball stars, especially ones who hadn't done anything recently. And probably most of all was a bit of sexism. If anything I'd be more impressed with the girl players than him, and I didn't follow sports of any kind that much, so jocks just didn't do anything for me."

"And you were interested in Linda."

Kendra gave a rueful smile. "Interested wasn't the word. But I think it was something else. I think it was the fact that I left to go to college, and he was there, helping out with running the campground, you know the faithful family friend. Then I came back, and there was a good chance I could just take her away from him." She shook her head. "Maybe I should have pressed harder, argued more. Maybe she would have left with me if I had been more insistent."

"Hindsight is twenty-twenty."

Kendra looked up. "I was pissed when I went to California. I'm not saying I always got my way, but I had been so sure. And she said no. With what I know now, I probably could have persuaded her." She thought about it a minute. "Well, maybe. Linda was not easily persuaded, so I don't know. But certainly I made just a token effort to contact her from California." She paused again. "It's hard to know when you're trying to do something like that. When are you being persuasive? And when are you interfering?"

"Yes, it's hard to know."

Kendra stared at the folder. She sat there a minute and Robin said nothing. Finally Kendra shook her head and shrugged. She couldn't do anything about that now. And there were things she could do in the present. "Do you have any idea of who's just talk and who's serious?"

Robin pulled out a sheet of paper from the folder she'd held back from Kendra. "No. We've got a list of possible militia members, but we can't sort them out because we can't get in." She glanced up at Kendra. "I really shouldn't share this, but I suppose if you read over my shoulder…"

Kendra got up and came around the table, leaning over Robin. Even as she read down the list of names, she was conscious of the woman's closeness, the faint scent of spice, the sight of her hands, long graceful fingers holding the page. The sharp memory of dancing with Robin, bodies pressed together, flooded her.

"Anyone you know?" Robin looked over her shoulder and up at Kendra, and for a split second, Kendra wanted to bend down, meet those soft lips and…And what? She pulled herself back sharply, wondering where that sudden sensual feeling came from.

Stop it, she told herself. This woman isn't going to be interested, and besides, she's just after a story. Don't read anything else into it. She focused on the list.

"Several," Kendra admitted. She'd be foolish to deny it since she had already said Artie was a neighbor and she went to school there. "Are these talkers or doers?"

Robin shook her head and put the paper away. "No idea. You talk to them and nobody knows anything. See nothing, hear nothing. Certainly say nothing."

Kendra could hear the frustration in Robin's voice as she moved back around to sit across from her. Evidently Robin Slusher wasn't accustomed to not getting answers.

"And Artie?" That's who Kendra was interested in.

Robin shook her head. "He disappears. If anyone knows, they're not saying. At least not to anyone who talks to me."

Kendra wasn't surprised at that. The rural community she remembered might bicker among themselves but they definitely closed ranks against outsiders. But then it occurred to her: *They might talk to me. They might tell me something about Artie. Someone must have seen something. All it would take is one person to tie him back here.*

CHAPTER NINE

Wouldn't they? she thought as she drove home. *They were people I went to high school with, neighbors.* At some level in her unconscious, she was already imagining talking to them, getting in with them, finding out where Artie might be, just what he was doing. No, she wasn't buddy-buddy with all of them, but all it would take would be one or two. She needed to plan this out. She couldn't just go charging in. Getting into this group would be like breaking into a house. The front door's secured, and usually the back door, but those side doors. They get neglected all the time. Gaining acceptance might not be easy, but the longer she thought about it, she didn't think it would be impossible.

She drove on autopilot, deep in thought. She was a block past the marquee when the words registered. She drove around the block to see it again.

"GUN SHOW. Open to the Public."

She pulled in, no charge because it was so late in the day. Vendors were already breaking down but there was still enough for her to see. Revolvers, rifles, shotguns, hunting guns. Holsters, carrying cases, conversion kits. She'd forgotten what it was like. Not that she had ever considered herself an enthusiast. She'd had the Glock because she was in the country and then on the road. But then things changed. When she caught herself in one of her more depressed moods, examining it, considering, wondering, she decided maybe she didn't need to have it in the house. In some dark mood, it might be just too tempting. She'd sold it and never replaced it.

Guns by themselves didn't bother her. They were simply tools, and it all depended on the person handling them. Respect them. Take care of them. A good many of her clients had guns. Gun safes were occasionally part of her sales. Looking around, she wondered if there might be a bigger gun market than what she had thought.

As she walked through the aisles, she looked at everything on two levels: business possibilities for Abatis and a link to the militia. She noticed the number of men and surprisingly, quite a few women dressed in camouflage. She mentally shook her head.

"Can I help you?"

Kendra hadn't realized she had stopped at one of the booths. She looked down at the table and randomly picked up the pistol. "Tell me about this."

"Sig P226. Good sidearm." He glanced at Kendra. "A lot of law enforcement uses it. Takes 9 mm, 357SIG or .40 S&W. Tritium Fiber Optic front sight, night rear sight. Polymer Maxwell grips. Four-point safety system."

Kendra hefted it. Lighter than what she thought. Heavier than the Glock. She frowned, not sure whether this was the way to go. "I don't know."

"In the market?"

"Considering it."

"Got a lot of choices. What's the purpose? Target, self-protection? Maybe you're on the road a lot?"

Kendra shook her head. "No, just thought it might be time to get one." She looked up. "You know, just in case."

He nodded. "Live in town?"

"Yeah." She gave a short laugh. "House is secure, though." She pulled out a business card and handed it over.

He read it with interest. "Pretty bad when security firms need to carry something."

"Can't live behind those walls all the time." Kendra lifted the revolver as if to fire, aiming down the empty aisle. It felt vaguely unpleasant, but she was so out of practice she wasn't sure. Another thing she would have to brush up on. "I don't know, have to think about it." She handed him back the gun. "You local?"

"Have the shop over on King." He gave her a speculative look. "Have a shooting range attached."

Kendra looked around and he supplied a business card. She nodded. "Thanks. Just might come check you out. Need to get back in practice."

She walked around a bit more. The opportunity had presented itself, the timing was right. Now if other things would just fall in place. As she sidestepped someone carrying cases out and stepped on a bright yellow flyer, she looked down.

ARE YOU PREPARED?

She picked it up and read it as she walked down the aisle.

Are you prepared for survival? If a catastrophe hit your area, whether it be nature or man-made, could you and your family survive? Military personnel are trained and conditioned beforehand for survival. Should civilians be any less? If you had to rely on yourself for your and your family's survival in the aftermath of an event, would you be surviving, or would you be one of those in line waiting for the government to take care of you?

Kendra raised her eyebrows as she skimmed the page. Good questions. And maybe an unlocked door. A possibility. Should attract the type of people she was thinking about. She made a note of the date as she folded the flyer and stuffed it in her pocket. Was this the way in? she wondered as she drove home.

She spent the next three days trying not to think of Linda, Robin or the MMU.

* * *

Linda's death was still a cold case, not even ruled as a homicide, just missing with suspected foul play. The police weren't going to do anything.

Artie? A weapons charge? Patriotic movement. MMU. Yeah, that would be about his speed. But did that mean they were planning anything more than playing military games, preparing for survival?

And then Linda. Or rather Linda's ghost. Was Linda actually reaching from the other side, asking for vengeance, for revenge, for justice? Did she believe? Or was this only her guilt manifesting in ways she didn't understand?

"I made atonements," she told herself as she drove to work the next morning. Security systems. Security checks free of charge. She supported the self-defense classes, the shelter for battered women. All in atonement for what she didn't do for Linda.

Justice. The word hung in the air.

She plunged into her work blindly, her door closed to all except the most pressing business. She started reading blogs, security reports, the conspiracy theorists, the clashes with law enforcement, the malcontents spouting off. Her business gave her some additional access to crime reports, the problem spots. None provided any answers.

"What's with Kendra?" she heard Travis ask Peg.

She didn't hear what Peg answered. All she wanted were answers. Ghosts and militia units. What a combination.

A ghost? That was truly a wild card. Yes, they existed—no, they were figments of imagination. Eyewitness accounts? A little booze involved in some of these sightings? Not always. Wishful thinking? Emotional trauma? A lot of theories and no clear answers. It boiled down to faith and what you believed and what you wanted to believe.

What did she want to believe? What was proof?

Have her tell you where she's buried. That was Gwen's suggestion.

"Nice suggestion," Kendra muttered as she poured her evening drink. Red wine. Good for the heart. If she was going to test the alcohol hypothesis, she might as well have something positive come out of it. Her heart might need it.

She set the wineglass on the table, took her normal seat. Dusk left a soft light through the windows but the living room was in the center of the house, and it was dimmer. Shadows in the corner. Let the imagination flow. She took a deep breath, and closed her eyes. She did not believe she was actually doing this.

She opened her eyes and stared at the far end of the living room, at the stone fireplace, the wingback chair at one side. This was where she had thought she had seen something before.

"I know you're there."

There was only silence. She searched the pattern of the stonework. Nothing.

"I—I can't do anything." She took a swallow of the wine. "I don't know what you want."

The silence was deafening.

She leaned back in the chair, and looked up at the ceiling. This was a stupid idea. She gave a sigh of resignation. "Justice," she said. "Is that what you want? For what? I know you're gone. I feel it. But I can't prove it. If Artie killed you, there's no proof. Can't find you. He's certainly not talking. I don't know what you want, Linda."

Justice. Retribution. Revenge.

"So you're haunting me because I didn't do anything? Didn't do enough? What do you want from me?"

"Belief. Faith."

Kendra raised her head and caught her breath. Linda stood before the fireplace like a hologram, flickering, wavering. "You're a figment of my imagination."

"No."

"So it's really you?"

Linda gave a familiar smile. "In the spirit."

Kendra reached for the wineglass and Linda laughed. "You never believed me when I told you there was something more to life. I told you I'd show you some day."

Kendra felt a profound sadness wash over her so strongly she wanted to cry. "I guess," she said with a steadiness she really didn't feel, "that means you're really gone from this life."

Linda looked at her sadly. "Yes. But you already knew that."

"I knew, but I didn't want to know." *This is surreal. I'm talking to a ghost!* She stared at Linda, expecting the image to disappear. Linda didn't.

"And where might you be buried?" She forced herself to speak in a steady voice.

Linda shook her head. "I can't tell you. I don't know." She frowned and shook her head. "Passing over was…" she hesitated. "Jumbled. Images."

"What happened?"

"He came back unexpectedly, just went berserk when he realized I was leaving. I couldn't get away." Her image wavered.

"Wait, don't go!" Kendra came half out of the chair.

"Not enough energy." And she was gone. *Later* came drifting through Kendra's mind.

Kendra sat back and absently finished the wine. She was there, actually there. And she answered questions. And if she didn't look solid, she wasn't just something to be caught out of the corner of Kendra's eye. Kendra put the empty glass down and took a deep breath. *Not enough energy. Wonder what that meant? Her energy? My energy? I don't understand.*

* * *

"You don't believe, not completely."

Kendra shot up from under the covers to see Linda sitting at the foot of the bed. In the moonlight flooding in the high windows, Linda looked substantial enough. And right now, with her heart pounding enough to break a rib, Kendra decided Linda sounded real enough.

"At least you didn't."

"God, don't do that to me!" Kendra snapped much as she had snapped at Linda in life. That more than anything convinced her. "You know I hate to be startled awake."

Linda laughed.

Kendra ran her fingers through her hair, rubbed her head in an effort to wake up. Linda looked a lot more real, less like a hologram this time. Still the black Levi's and western shirt. "You look more solid."

"Your belief is stronger now."

Kendra pulled the sheet up over her legs and sat up, cross-legged in the bed. How many times had they sat and talked like this? "Well, I have two choices: either you really are here, or I'm going just plain absolutely crazy. I don't think I'm going crazy so you must be really here."

"Oh, Sunshine, still grounded in the real and concrete."

"That's me." Kendra yawned, covering her mouth. "But why now? I haven't had a good night's sleep in months."

"Yeah, I know. You'd never relax enough. You always were stubborn."

"So all that was your fault."

"Usually the barriers are down more when people sleep. Easier to get through." She shook her head. "Might've known you'd be just as stubborn asleep as awake."

"Yeah. Well." Kendra rubbed her face. *Maybe I'm dreaming.* "So now you're here."

"Finally."

"So tell me, what's your purpose?"

"I'm bound; I want loose."

Kendra looked up with no understanding.

"It's like I'm stuck here, tethered. Until—well until I have justice, until I'm found, I can't move forward."

Kendra still wasn't sure she wasn't dreaming. Even the afterlife had rules? "So? Tell me where—" She faltered. *Your body? Your remains? How do you say what's left?* "Where do I find you?"

"I don't know. That part is dark, hidden from me. He told me if I wanted to go to you so badly, then you could have me forever."

"So I need to find you and bury you, and that will set you free?"

"Justice would be nice, too."

"Doesn't that come sooner or later?"

"I'd like to have it sooner rather than later."

"I didn't think time mattered on that side."

"For someone who never considered the 'other side' was real, you've got a lot of notions about it."

"I've had time to think."

"Oh, you're a believer now?"

"Like I said, believe this is happening or believe I'm crazy."

"You had your doubts."

"I probably still do. But I don't think I'm crazy." *I don't think.*

"No, dear heart, you're not crazy."

Kendra didn't say anything.

"I think you can find him," Linda said quietly, "but you'll have to look in the Miamis."

Kendra went blank, completely. If someone had asked her her name, she couldn't have come up with it.

"I think it will take some time, but I think you can do it."

Kendra swallowed, not sure of the ramifications of what Linda was saying. Information flowed back and fell in place. "Does that mean you can see what's going to happen?"

Linda shook her head. "No, not exactly. I just know you're the one to set me free. And that's where you have to go to find him." She paused. "Might take some time, but you can get in."

"But will I get out?"

For that Linda would only shrug. And then she was gone.

Kendra bowed her head, not sure if that was an answer or not. She buried her face in her hands. To be or not to be haunted. That was the question. To set Linda free. But whether she believed or not, she realized it was a second chance. She had failed once. She wouldn't fail the second time.

* * *

"Kendra! Wait up!"

Kendra paused on her exit from the Business and Professional Women's luncheon, her mind already on finishing up the Labor

Day holiday schedule back at the office. She turned back to see Robin break away from the group and come after her. Several of the women tried to recapture her but she gave them only passing attention as she hurried down the hallway to catch up with Kendra.

Kendra had known Robin was a member. The board had been quite pleased to have a woman so visible in the community as a member even though she could rarely attend the monthly lunch meetings. Kendra, a less-than-active member herself, understood time conflicts, but when she had read the announcement that the scheduled speaker canceled and Robin Slusher was going to substitute, she had made a point of coming. She wasn't sure why; she doubted Robin had any new information for her. She certainly didn't have any for her. She just thought it would be good to see her again.

"I'm glad you were able to come today. I haven't seen you in a while," Robin greeted when she caught up with her.

Kendra felt an unexpected pleasure at Robin's words. "Well, that's good news. You don't get to see the techs when the system works. That's the way it's supposed to happen."

"How true," Robin gave a small laugh. "I'm so glad you recommended I call pest control. Squirrels in the attic tripping the system. I never would have guessed the bad guys would look so cute and could be so annoying. But I'm so relieved not to see the cops at my door unexpectedly." She pushed open the door and walked outside. "I was wondering, how are you doing on your cold case?"

Kendra followed her out, flattered that Robin remembered. Then it dawned on her that Robin was working on the Jeffers story and anything Kendra found out about Linda would probably help Robin. "Couldn't do anything. Nothing's changed. No new evidence, law enforcement's still not convinced it was foul play, although she is still considered missing." She watched for any disappointment in Robin's face.

Robin shook her head without looking surprised. "Too bad. But you knew it was a long shot. Still, it was worth a try." She looked up expectantly but Kendra said nothing as they walked toward the cars.

"You know," Robin said slowly, "one of the big goals for the militia was to have some private land to do maneuvers. It makes it more difficult for the local sheriff to drop in when they have a private place to run a trail in camouflage carrying backpacks and rifles without making the locals nervous." She paused at her car door and looked at Kendra speculatively. "I've learned they now have some private land, up by Walton's Corner. You know anything about that?"

Kendra shook her head. "Any idea where?"

"Outside town, obviously. An old campground. I wondered, well, I wondered if it was your friend's old campground."

Bastard! He didn't!

Kendra shook off Linda's voice in her head. "I don't know, but I can find out."

She hadn't planned on going up to the farm so soon but a three-day weekend would work. She hadn't been to the farm since spring when she took Travis there for some fishing in the creek. A trip now would give her the opportunity to plant the idea of her coming back. Too many people there knew she had been bound and determined to shake their dust and have it behind her, never look back, never return. Any return would have to be done in stages with a reason that would be believable. Her interest in the survivalist movement, her dad's paranoia, tired of city life, all would be believable if done correctly. Yes, she could open up the house, just be there. Her presence would be noticed. She could walk over the land, give her an opportunity to check out the neighbors. If anyone asked, well, she could complain about city life, needing to get back in the open. Yes, that would work.

"Shouldn't be hard at all," she mused half aloud.

"Thought you might be able to do something."

Kendra looked up, realizing Robin had thought she was talking to her. Well, that was all right too. Robin had her hand on the door handle but she didn't open it, and Kendra wondered if there was something else.

"If it is, I'd like to hear about this campground." Robin gave Kendra an open, wide-eyed look which only made Kendra wonder if being an information source had been the sole purpose of talking with her.

"I suppose that could be arranged," Kendra said drily, some of the pleasure of talking with Robin evaporating. She supposed that was the way it was going to be. Robin would get information for her, but she would expect something back. And, Kendra thought, with a mental shrug, she supposed that was fair. She just wished, she realized wistfully, there was another reason for contact besides being a source of information. She was so deep in thought she almost missed Robin's next words.

"Haven't seen you around much. Are you working hard rather than playing hard these days?"

Kendra looked up in surprise at Robin's friendly, bantering tone. There was a teasing glint in her dark eyes as she waited for Kendra's response. Maybe, Kendra considered, she was mistaken about the reporter's motives. After all, she had been busy. Although Travis and Peg had been on her back about her sudden new interest in the survivalist movement and endless round of meetings, she didn't think anyone else had noticed. That Robin noticed was flattering. Her crowd was accustomed to her dropping out for months at a time. "I guess working hard," she said with some reluctance.

"Can't be all security issues."

"No." She wasn't being rude, but she didn't elaborate.

Robin gave her a knowing look as if she suspected strongly what Kendra wasn't about to discuss. She cleared her throat. "I'm having a few friends over for a cookout over Labor Day. I wondered if you'd like to join us."

Kendra was surprised, to say the least, and then her next thought was wondering what motivated this casual invitation.

Don't get paranoid. It's just a friendly invitation from someone you've met and found attractive. Interesting.

Kendra pushed her cynical suspicions aside. Even if Robin was just using her as a source of information, wasn't she doing the same to Robin? On the other hand, there was no reason this line of research couldn't be enjoyable. "That sounds great. What time?"

"Oh, about two. It's just a backyard get-together. Steaks on the grill, things like that."

"Anything I can bring?"

"Something for the table to go with steak? I don't know, do you cook?"

"Reasonably well," Kendra responded. "Anything special you need?"

"Whatever you want. I'm sure we'll have a fill of deli potato salad."

"I'll try to be different."

Robin got in the car, looking up at Kendra. "You sure you'll be there? Don't want to take you away from anything you may have already planned."

"I'll be there." As if I wouldn't change plans just to attend, she thought as she watched Robin pull away.

Robin's question about the campground nagged her all afternoon. Yes, the campground would work for a militia unit. The more she thought about it, the more she had to know. Three days, simple enough to drive up Saturday, return on Sunday. She would have plenty of time to drive back in time for Robin's cookout on Monday.

Friday night she packed an overnight bag. She wouldn't need much. Then she made a layered salad, quickly pulling cans from the pantry. Since she didn't use it often, the large glass bowl was in the most inaccessible place in the cabinet. First the layer of green beans, then corn, sliced onions, a layer of pimento, small peas and lastly the carrots. She boiled the dressing of salt, pepper, water, vinegar, oil and sugar, poured it over the vegetables, covered it with a plate and stuck it in the refrigerator. It could marinate until she got back. There, she thought with satisfaction, it didn't look like it came from the deli.

She set the alarm for a decent hour, it was not the morning to sleep until noon. She wouldn't need a real early start in order to get to the farm by midmorning, noon at the very latest if traffic was really bad. She'd have enough time to check out the property, do a walk around, look over the campground, see if anything was going on. She could either come back Saturday night or even Sunday.

* * *

"Oh, what a pretty layered salad!" Robin greeted her at the door. "Come on in. We're just getting the steaks on the grill."

"Well, I thought it'd be good to have something cold. Be healthy, get all the veggies in." She followed Robin through the house to the patio where there were lights set up for the evening if it went that late, a long table set out for the food and a big tub of ice with drinks in it.

"Everyone, this is Kendra McKenna. She's the one who keeps me safe and secure here in a home behind a security fence."

"Hey, Kendra, how much did you pay her for that plug?" someone called, and Kendra lifted the salad bowl.

"A little green." She was seeing some familiar faces, some just familiar from the television. She and Robin really ran in different circles, but she knew most of the women at least by sight. She settled down to have an enjoyable afternoon.

As she watched Robin mix with what was obviously her supportive circle, Kendra had the odd feeling she was the one who was on display. Maybe, she considered, they were just a friendly group, but it seemed like every one of them made a point to speak with her, find out something about her. She did get quizzed enough to pass out three business cards, and that was fine with her. Maybe it was just because she was new to this group.

"Doing all right?" Robin came around to ask after dinner. "No one being rude or anything to you, I hope."

"No, on the contrary, everyone's been very friendly." *If very curious.*

Robin sat down beside her in the Adirondack chair and put her feet up. "That's good. I didn't know how you felt about walking into strange groups."

"Not my favorite thing but I have to do it occasionally. Sales stuff, even presentations to some groups. Comes with the territory of being a business owner."

"Yes, I suppose so." Robin put her head back and closed her eyes.

"Rough week?"

"Lots of news." Robin paused and then casually asked, "You getting anywhere?"

Kendra turned to look at her, a slender figure stretched out casually, her arms resting on the chair arms, her ankles neatly crossed. Even lying still with her eyes closed, she emitted energy. "What do you mean?"

Robin opened her eyes and turned to her with a knowing look. "I didn't figure you'd just let it drop if the cops didn't want to reopen the case. You're doing an investigation yourself, aren't you?"

Sharp, Kendra reminded herself. *Don't underestimate this lady.* "As you pointed out, information doesn't exactly spring forth."

"Tenacity." Robin sprang to her feet, took a deep breath. She looked down at Kendra who looked up at her in some puzzlement. "Remember: It's a virtue." Then she walked away.

Kendra sipped her drink as she watched Robin join another group. No one in her circle of friends suspected what might be behind her sudden interest in survivalist groups. But then no one knew about Linda, or, she amended, Linda's ghost, except Robin and Gwen. If Gwen realized what Kendra was doing, she was keeping her suspicions to herself. Robin just casually acknowledging that she was investigating Linda's disappearance on her own denoted her approval. Or was it assistance? After all, weren't they after the same goal? Well, not the same, but so closely related and intertwined they might as well be. And was that the reason behind the invitation? Just one more source of information for her? For her ambition? Kendra felt a flicker of distrust, suspicion.

"Don't be paranoid," Linda told her that night. "You got an invitation from a woman you find interesting and attractive, and you've got to look for hidden angles." She paused. "You do find her attractive, don't you?"

"Oh, yes." Kendra took a breath. She remembered Robin that Saturday morning when she had woken her up, the half-asleep tousled look, those long legs when she stretched up for coffee, the unrealized exposure. "Very."

Linda shook her head as she gave an amused smile. "You always were attracted to those high-energy extroverts."

Like you, Kendra thought but didn't say.

"Yes, like me," Linda said with a laugh. "And besides, you don't want to turn down such a good source of information."

Kendra nodded thoughtfully. "Yes, there is that aspect."

* * *

"I didn't want to bring this up at the cookout," she told Robin when she called her later in the week to express pleasure over the cookout, "but yes, it's Linda's campground."

"Did you get a chance to see it up close?" Robin asked. And then there was some distraction. "Oh, I can't talk now. Can we set up a time to meet?"

"Sure."

"Come over Sunday afternoon. I get back from my golf game about one."

"Not a churchgoer?"

"I find God on the golf course."

Kendra considered the invitation, first, wondering why all these discussions were taking place at Robin's house then realizing that was where all Robin's information was.

"I'll provide lunch," Robin offered in a coaxing voice.

"That sounds suspiciously like a bribe. Are you a good cook?"

"Simply awful, but I pay well. I'm one of Claymore's best customers."

Even Kendra had heard of the home delivery chef business. "Beats frozen dinners," she said with a laugh. "All right. I'll be over. About two?"

"Fantastic. Gotta run. I'll see you then."

* * *

"Pretty good," Kendra commented as she finished the dinner—grillades, pieces of round steak in a rich tomato gravy served over grits. Very southern, New Orleans style. "And you can cook. I saw you pull something out of the oven."

Robin sat back. "Baked grits. Hardly a culinary masterpiece. Now the grillades." She sighed in obvious pleasure. "Claymore is wonderful, has saved me from fast food many a day."

Kendra chuckled. "I hope you never get caught in a situation where you have to cook or starve."

"Better be a jar of peanut butter." Robin frowned in concentration. "I can do eggs, scrambled."

"I guess you could live on omelets."

Robin got up to clear the table. "I try to steer away from such situations. You enjoy cooking?"

Kendra picked up her glass and helped herself to more iced tea. "Getting back in the habit. If I don't want to be filled with preservatives or have God knows how many steps between me and the picking, I need to do my own cooking. I've started picking up things at the local produce stands, buying local."

"Oh, my. I'm impressed." Robin took containers out of the cabinet to store the leftovers.

"It's healthier." Kendra took a long look at Robin's fairly empty refrigerator.

Robin stacked the last of the glasses. "And now," she said as she slid an arm around Kendra with surprising familiarity, "I've wined you and dined you. Now I get to quiz you mercilessly."

Kendra frowned. "Don't remember the wine." *And with your arm around me, I don't need it*, she considered as she let herself be led to Robin's office.

"Oh, I guess I'm holding that in reserve in case you get difficult and I have to loosen your tongue." She picked up the file and let go of Kendra.

"You do all your interviews like this?"

Robin opened the door to the patio. "Oh, I don't think this is a standard interview." She let the words hang there for a moment, leaving Kendra wondering if she was supposed to read something into them. Then Robin gave Kendra a sideways look, a half smile. "I think of this more as a mutual assistance type of thing. You have information. I have information. It seems only natural we should help each other."

Kendra felt a little dash of cold water as she took the chair Robin pulled out for her. Might have known there wouldn't be any other reason. "I must admit, you are certainly more congenial than the detective assigned to the cold cases at the police department."

"I would hope so." Robin turned on the computer and while it booted up, she opened files and pulled out folded maps. She tossed them onto the desk in front of Kendra as she went to the keyboard and opened the files she wanted.

Kendra unfolded the topographical and plat maps and spread them out. She ran her fingers along the waterways, orienting herself as Robin finished with the computer. She was examining the differences from what she remembered as Robin came over. Robin leaned against her, one hand on Kendra's shoulder. After Kendra's first intake of breath at Robin's closeness, she was able to point out landmarks she knew.

"Amazing what aerial photography does now, isn't it?" She picked off the cabins, maybe one or two missing. She couldn't remember exactly how many there had been. And there was a larger cabin there where the shed used to be. There was some construction going on at the edge. She couldn't tell what it might be. "How old are these?"

"Two years at the most. I couldn't get a date fixed," Robin said. She pointed to the construction. "The permit is for storage sheds. But there's no indication what's being stored."

Kendra noted the location. If she remembered correctly, this went right into the hillside, and it wouldn't be difficult to extend it underground.

"Looks like its pretty rough ground up there. This looks like it's at the edge of the mountains. A body could hide up there."

Kendra nodded in agreement. "There's always been the story that Capone had a hideaway in the area. Never found anything," she said absently. "For sure, Dillinger hid out there for a while. The old-timers still tell stories." She traced the campground boundaries on the topographical map, seeing it in her mind's eye. How many times had she walked it?

"So there's a history of anti-government sentiment?" Robin turned around and half sat on the desk, facing Kendra. Her leg brushed against Kendra's.

Kendra sat back in the chair, moving to escape Robin's touch. "Not exactly anti-, just self-sufficiency. For example, if you were driving some of these back roads in the middle of the night and broke down, it might be safer just to stay in the car until daylight. A stranger walking up to some of these folks' homes would likely be met with a shotgun. They'd call the sheriff later."

"Hmmmm." Robin glanced back at the maps. "And this is where you grew up?"

Without looking away from the topographical map, Kendra pulled the plat map down. She tapped the spot labeled with her name.

"No wonder you wanted to get away."

Time had mellowed Kendra's attitude to her former community. "They're good people for the most part. Just believe in doing things themselves, taking care of problems themselves. Most any of them would give you the shirt off their back." She glanced at Robin. "But God help you if you steal it."

Robin nodded as if she were beginning to get the picture. "I can see," she said slowly, "why it might be hard to be accepted."

"Yeah." Kendra ran her finger along the creek which seemed to be the border where the map stopped. She tapped the blank area across the creek. "Got a map for this area?"

Robin flipped through the papers. "No. Why? What's there?"

"Artie's place. Just across the creek from the campground." She pointed to a place in the creek. "There's a shallow ford right along here, at least it used to be. We could wade across it when we were kids. I don't know if it's still there. The Big Pine can be pretty cantankerous. Changes course. Has twice in my lifetime. Otherwise, you take the road up about a mile and use the bridge." She traced the creek road around where a bridge was indicated. "There's a big gravel pit over there. Great place for a firing range. Didn't have to worry about bullets traveling any distance, hitting anything. Or anyone. A lot of the locals used it for shooting so no one would think much about shooting around there." She ran a finger along the road back to the campground and then the turn up the hill. "Flat lands, great for a cross-country trail, then rough up and down hills and gullies. Just about everything you'd want for training." She ran her finger on up the road. "Sue's family lived up this way."

"Sue's the cousin?" Kendra nodded. "So it would be hard for someone to slip in and spy on them."

"Difficult, not impossible." She sat back and stared at the maps. "But a lot easier if you know it."

"Could you show me?" Robin asked quietly.

Kendra looked up quickly, shocked. "No," she said emphatically. She quickly looked Robin over, wondering even if Robin could do even a rough hike. She looked too fragile, but on second thought, someone fragile wouldn't have considered it.

"You'd stand out in the area like a sore thumb." She considered she might have been more tactful. "And not to be insulting, Robin, you don't look the type."

She watched as Robin's eyes narrowed, and she considered how she would have felt if someone said such words to her. But then again, she didn't look anywhere as feminine as Robin. No, she was solid, rugged.

"Appearances can be deceiving," Robin said in an even voice, but Kendra could hear the undercurrent of irritation.

"Robin, I'm not being insulting. This is an area where strangers are treated politely, but they are watched. As soon as you stepped into Walton's Corner, people would know it. And all it takes is a strange car going down some of these roads to tip them off that someone's being nosy or someone's lost. In either case, some farmer's going to just mosey over and be curious. I'm not questioning your capability," although she was, and she knew it. "It's more your adaptability."

Robin looked thoughtful, and slowly nodded. "I see your point. I don't like it, but I see the value." She gave Kendra a challenging look. "You think I'm a piece of fluff, don't you?"

"No," Kendra said quickly. "You're not fluff, Robin, and if I gave that impression, I'm sorry. You've got drive and determination and ambition. You don't get there being a shrinking violet. But there's a difference between being capable and being out of your element. You yourself told me that law enforcement people couldn't make inroads. You really think you could?"

Robin didn't look mollified as she fastened her gaze on Kendra. "No, I guess not," she said finally. "I just don't like not being able to get the information firsthand."

Neither do I, Kendra thought as she drove home. *And the only way for me to get the information is to be there. And that might be a problem.*

Later that week, Peg buzzed Kendra right after lunch. "Robin Slusher calling you. Shall I put her through?"

"Of course." She picked up the phone. "Hey, I was going to call you, thank you for lunch."

"You're very welcome," Robin responded with exaggerated courtesy. "Got a challenge for you."

"What's that?"

"Meet me at Hamilton Park seven thirty tomorrow morning. By the tennis courts."

"In the morning?" Kendra was horrified. Some mornings she was just finally able to get to sleep at that hour.

Robin chuckled. "In the morning. You're going on a run with me. We'll see who's a fluff ball."

"Really rankled you, didn't it?" Her horror was replaced by amusement.

"See you in the morning." Robin hung up with a laugh.

The next morning in the coolness of the early hour, Kendra bent over, hands on knees, trying to catch her breath. She knew she was out of shape but she didn't think she'd be this bad. Robin stood before her, still running in place, not even breathing hard.

"You okay?"

Kendra nodded, not even having the breath to answer.

"You need to walk a bit, cool down," Robin advised. "Why don't you walk up to the bench and wait there. I'll run the circuit and meet you back there."

"Sorry. I'm slowing you. Down," Kendra managed to get out.

Robin didn't quite laugh openly at her but she looked pleased. "Not bad for a piece of fluff, am I?"

Not bad at all, Kendra considered as she watched Robin drop over the hill. *Said you were high energy first time I saw you.*

"And you are terribly out of shape," Linda said, walking beside her.

"Noticed that."

"So what are you going to do about it?"

"Guess I'll have to do something." Kendra settled herself on the bench.

"Now she might be an incentive to take up running."

"She's built for running," Kendra observed as she watched Robin through the trees as she came around and then back up the slope. "I'm more of a jogger, slow and steady."

Robin slowed to a walk and came up to Kendra, sat down beside her. Kendra handed her the bottle of water.

"You do this every morning?"

"Pretty much." Robin blotted her face. "Gotta work off Clayton's good meals somehow."

"In full makeup?" Kendra was incredulous.

Robin poured water on the towel and patted her face. "Never know who I'll run into. Had a run with the governor one morning. Gotta be 'on' all the time." She flipped the towel around her neck. "Care to join me?"

"Sure I won't slow you down?"

Robin stretched out. "Oh, I suppose you'll catch up quick enough."

"I don't know."

Robin chuckled and she stood up. "Now, to work. Tomorrow?"

Kendra got to her feet and nodded reluctantly. "Tomorrow."

* * *

"You know," Peg commented after a few weeks, "you're looking really good lately."

Kendra thought about it. "Yeah. Maybe it's the exercise. I've taken up running with Robin. Different diet, more fresh foods." *And Linda lets me sleep now, doesn't have to come to me in dreams!*

"You don't seem as depressed. You're getting out more."

Kendra nodded. "Meeting different people, different ideas." She didn't know what made her say the next thing. "I've been thinking about going up to the farm more, getting out of the city."

"Oh, really?"

"Just an idea." Kendra shrugged, frowning. "Give me a different outlook." *And I'd be right at Artie's back door when he does show up.*

* * *

Attending various meetings for three months finally paid off for Kendra. First the Sustaining Earth meetings crossed over into the Be Prepared group, which morphed into Survivors/Preppies. And that was where she came across James C. Harris. Tall, weathered, deep-set eyes, steel-gray hair, he had an authoritative air that Kendra normally went out of her way to avoid. But he knew his stuff, commanded attention, had a no-nonsense approach. She wasn't surprised he was ex-military.

"See what it's like without electricity," he told the group in a drill sergeant voice. "I don't mean when an electrical storm knocks out your AC for a couple of hours. And I don't mean when an ice storm wipes out your power for thirty-six hours. Not when you know there are repair crews out there working around the clock to get your power turned on. How would you function, survive if the power went out and you didn't know *when* it was coming on, *IF* it was going to come back? How would you cook? How would you get information? Get water? In the winter, keep warm?

They were the faces she had seen at other meetings. She listened to Harris with only half an ear as she watched the group's reaction, noting those who already seemed to know what he was saying. She made a point of meeting the man after his lecture.

"You wouldn't be any relation to the Harrises up by Symore, would you?" Kendra asked after introducing herself. Symore was a wide spot in the road, only the old-timers remembered it as a community, and most of the locals now knew it only as a subdivision. But it was her backyard.

"You know Symore?" He didn't answer the question.

Kendra nodded. "Walton's Corner."

He nodded toward her in acknowledgment and she watched him try to gauge her age. "Maybe last class out of Walton's Corner?"

"A little later," she corrected with a smile. "But close."

They exchanged a little chitchat back and forth, along with another person who had come in with him.

"So you know Artie Jeffers?" he said finally in a casual tone.

"Everyone knows Artie, anyone who's old enough," Kendra came back easily. "He won us the county tourney."

Harris smiled at the memory. "Quite a shot he made, wasn't it?" Just like the game was played last week. "Winning shot."

"Was quite a shot," Kendra agreed in reminiscing. "But it wasn't the winning shot." He looked at her in question.

"What?" the other fellow said. "I always heard that Artie made the winning shot."

Harris said nothing.

"Only in a manner of speaking," Kendra said as she watched him. "Final game of the county tourney, we were down four or six, something like that. End of the third quarter, seconds to go and he stands on their foul line and gives the ball a heave-ho just as the buzzer goes off." She smiled at the memory, remembering the packed gym, the roar, the sheer excitement. She brought her hands up to imitate the throw. "Went all the way down the court and dropped through that basket perfect, didn't hit the rim, didn't hit the backboard, just woosh!" She laughed.

"And it won the game?" the fellow said.

"Yes and no. End of the third quarter, not the final. But it fired everyone up. The rest of the team had been tired, discouraged. We'd been just barely staying even the entire game. They figured if the shortest guy on the bench could do that, then they could well go out and mop the floor with Eastern. They came out of that huddle and proceeded to do so. And they awarded Artie the net." She shook her head at the memory. "Quite a game."

"You were there?" Harris asked.

Kendra openly laughed and looked him up and down. "Man, are you kidding? Everyone was there." She paused. "Or maybe I should ask: Were you?"

He shook his head. "In the service. Germany." But there was a difference in his tone, his look, and Kendra had the feeling she had passed a test.

"Well," she said, "small world and all that. A lot of water under the bridge since then." She gave him a knowing look. "Different world now. But I liked your talk. Wished more people were aware of all the limitations of these conveniences. Although I guess some folks are getting the idea more. I've had more orders for safe rooms."

"What kind of business do you have?"

"Security." And she pulled out a business card and handed it over.

He read it carefully, looked up at her and nodded. "Interesting."

Kendra came away with the feeling she had just found the door.

CHAPTER TEN

"You coming to the game tomorrow or going to the farm this weekend?" Travis draped herself over the chair in front of Kendra's desk, as was her usual habit Friday afternoons.

Kendra looked up at the football schedule on the calendar. "Game? Already?" Then she realized they were a quite a few games into the season. How had she missed that? But she knew how. She had been going to the farm about every other week since midsummer. First it was just opening up the house, then it was planting a garden, making contact again with the neighbors. Summertime was an easier time to blend back into the community, when families were on vacation, not tied to a school schedule. She hadn't thought it would be easy getting back into the community. She hadn't dreamed it would be so difficult.

There was still a distance there that she couldn't cross. The farm, as much as she owned it, didn't belong to her anymore. It was a house she visited, land she walked, garden space she plotted out, someplace to go through the motions. Former friends and neighbors, when she did see them, were friendly and polite but she knew it was just on the surface. She kept at it, doggedly, hoping that pure persistence would finally open the doors, but she began to wonder if she would cross the barrier of being one of those who left.

"I don't know."

Travis chewed at a hangnail. "You missed the last couple of games," she said matter-of-factly. There was a delay and then she went on. "Robin was asking where you were."

Kendra looked up. She hadn't seen Robin since the time change and mornings were just too dark to run. "She did—she was?"

Travis nodded, nonchalant, as if she didn't know the impact this might have. "Said she hadn't seen you since you two had stopped running."

"What'd you tell her?"

Travis buffed her nails against her shirt. "Oh, I explained you get in these moods and just sorta drop out of sight for a while." She looked up at Kendra. "You do, you know."

"I know." Kendra sighed. "But I've just been so busy." Besides going to the farm, she'd been attending all these meetings and workshops. Just creating a presence, not banging on any doors, making conversation, taking her time. But it took a lot of time.

Travis got up. "Sounds like the lady misses you." She headed for the door. "Not that I'd know about such things, you understand. Just a guess." She looked back at Kendra with that sly look of hers. "'Course I could be mistaken."

Kendra laughed, aware she was being manipulated. "I think the farm can do without me for the weekend."

Travis gave her a thumb's-up. "See you at the game. Dinner afterward at Sweeney's."

* * *

Football had been so-so, Kendra discovered, a dull game, but she was surrounded by friends at Sweeney's, the local eating establishment they frequented. Perhaps it was just in contrast to the isolation she felt at Walton's Corner, perhaps it was just a reminder of what she had sought by leaving, but she discovered she missed that contact. She rearranged her schedule to attend the games.

Robin, to her disappointment, had not been at that first game, but she was at the next and the games thereafter. Even though their seating arrangements at the games weren't anywhere close, they were both part of the larger group that met at Sweeney's after the game. And when the football season ended, the basketball season began, much of the same crowd met either before or after the game, Robin and Kendra among them.

Kendra glanced around the emptying restaurant. She and Robin were the only women left at the long table where everyone had gathered for the Sunday after-game meal. While they mixed with different crowds and might not see each other during the games, somehow they always ended up sitting together at dinner. This wasn't the first time they had been the last ones to leave. Indeed, they had been so engrossed they hardly noticed the others leaving.

"They deserted us again," she commented.

Robin quickly looked around and frowned slightly. She gave a sigh of exasperation.

"Is something wrong?" Kendra checked her wristwatch. "Were you supposed to be somewhere else?"

"No." Robin turned around, looking for her purse, pulling her jacket off the back of her chair. She searched her pockets for her gloves, wouldn't look at Kendra. "It's just annoying."

"What? Losing track of time? I was enjoying the conversation, I usually do with you." She frowned, not sure what Robin meant. Were their conversations annoying?

Robin looked up at her with a glare that caught her off guard. "You can't tell me you don't know what's going on."

"Going on?" She really was confused now. "What's going on? What are you talking about?"

"The matchmaking."

"Matchmaking?" Kendra felt herself flush. While she knew she was attracted to Robin, and probably Travis and Peg did, too, she would have sworn no one else knew. Did that mean Robin might be attracted to her?

"Yes," Robin said with finality and an angry look.

"Well, don't look at me. I didn't engineer it." She had to work then to keep a straight face as Robin looked somewhere between disbelieving and insulted. "Not that I haven't enjoyed it, if that's what they've been doing," she added, rather than have Robin think she *didn't* like her. "But I hadn't noticed anything special."

"You mean you didn't think there was anything strange the way all my friends quizzed you when I invited you over for the Labor Day cookout?"

Ohhhh, is that what it was? "Well, I thought they were curious, but it was because I was simply new to the group." She chuckled at her naiveté.

"Or the way the only seats available for us when we come in for dinner are side by side?" Robin's mouth pursed.

So that was why even when she got to the restaurant early, no one took the seat beside her. The empty seat was saved for Robin, and everyone knew it. Except her. She shook her head. "Matchmaking," she repeated in amusement. "As if we couldn't do something ourselves." She looked back at Robin, trying not to laugh.

"You didn't know?" Robin looked at her in surprise, and then suddenly covered her face with her hand. "Oh, God, now I'm so embarrassed."

"Why?" Kendra said with a laugh. "Because our friends are looking out for us? Because they think we'd make a good match?" *Even Travis,* Kendra thought, *getting me to those football games.* She watched Robin with some amusement. Robin looked so flustered. She'd never seen her like this before.

Robin looked at her suddenly, very firm, decisive. "I'm not ready for a relationship," she said as if Kendra had proposed one. "There're still things I want to do career-wise, and it wouldn't be fair to get involved with someone and only be able to give them second place."

Defensive, aren't we? Kendra propped her elbow on the table, her fingers under her chin. "Very commendable," she said lightly. "I'm not interested in a relationship either." She smiled a little at Robin's jaw, slackened in amazement. "Now that we understand each other, how do you propose we tell everyone else, since they're the ones who seem to be doing the engineering?"

Robin looked away. Evidently she didn't quite expect to be turned down. Perhaps, Kendra considered, she wasn't often rejected.

"I've tried telling them. They tell me they can see the sparks fly when we're together."

"Hmmm." Kendra considered that observation. Sparks. Such could be the explanation for Travis's expression every time she said something about Robin, sorta the smug, self-satisfied expression of *I know a secret, and when are you going to find it out!* "Well, I must admit you have greatly increased my enjoyment at these dinners." She watched Robin blush and look down at her empty plate. "And I have missed our early morning runs."

Robin looked up at her, her eyelashes dark against her skin. "I have too," she said finally. "And yes, I've enjoyed our conversations here at the dinners."

"I've been told you're attending them more regularly than you used to."

Robin tilted her head. "I suppose so. I've been trying to clear my schedule more, have some balance in my life."

"Hmmm." Kendra looked around for her jacket. "You know, it occurs to me that I've seen your house several times. Would you like to come over to my place for a nightcap?" She avoided looking at Robin as she issued the invitation.

"A nightcap? Your place?"

Kendra nodded as she looked at Robin's surprised face, working hard to keep hers bland and remain breathing normally.

Robin blinked, her face slightly flushed. "That would be nice."

* * *

Kendra pulled into her driveway, hitting the opener for the double garage door. Robin, to Kendra's surprise, well, maybe not complete surprise, pulled into the empty bay beside her.

Kendra took a deep breath as she got out of the car. She hadn't planned on this. She waited for Robin to walk around the car.

"Nice neighborhood," Robin commented.

"I like it." Kendra took Robin's hand and took her through the garage door to her office. She left Robin standing in the middle of the room as she crossed it in the darkness to shut off her security alarm and turn on the lights.

She held her hand out, and Robin came to her. "Want the tour?" She led her down the hallway to the open area, the galley kitchen on one side, the dining room separated from the living room by a low wall, adjacent to the family room visible through open framing.

"Strange house," Robin commented. "No windows." Only the family room had large windows but with a high privacy fence right outside. "Very private."

"The original owner was a nudist. The privacy fence goes all around the back. You have to be standing at the front door to see anything inside and then it's only at an angle into the dining room."

Robin gestured to the rooms down the front side of the house. "Bedrooms?"

Kendra nodded. "With very high windows." Kendra went to the kitchen. "Something to drink?"

"Please."

Kendra opened the bottle of wine, handing Robin a glass.

"So what do we do about our matchmaking friends?" Robin sipped the wine.

"Nothing."

"Nothing?"

"I would guess it's not the first time they've tried to match you up with someone."

"Well, no. You're just the latest of a long list." She glanced apologetically at Kendra. "They seem to be of the opinion it's not good for me to be alone."

"My friends too." She folded her arms, watching Robin as she paced about the large room, pausing to examine the painting over the couch, the figurines on the fireplace mantel. "Annoying, isn't it? I mean, if we convince them this match is a bust, then they'll just go on to someone else. At least mine will. What about yours?"

"Probably."

"So why don't we let them think they've succeeded?"

Robin turned back in surprise. "What?"

"We both know where our priorities are. I think anyone who would get involved with you would have to understand where your priorities are, and right now, your priorities are your career. It may not always be that way, but for now…" She shrugged and sipped her wine as she watched Robin consider what she said.

Robin nervously cleared her throat and Kendra was amused to see the cool, unflappable Robin Slusher nervous. "And yours?"

"I have my own agenda. You know that. And I have no idea how long that's going to tie me up. I don't need to be tripping over women that Travis or anyone else throws in front of me."

Robin took another breath. "Kendra, it's in my best interest at this point in my life not to be linked with anyone. I don't want my private life to be a point of gossip."

"And I feel the same way about my life." She didn't move as Robin walked toward her. They were about the same height, she noted absently, but even after all her running and weight lifting, more than a few pounds heavier than Robin. If Robin was quicksilver, she was solid.

"You know," Robin said, stepping into her personal space, so close their breasts almost touched. "If we do that, they'll expect us to do things together."

Kendra met Robin's eyes with amusement and anticipation. "I suspect we could manage that."

Robin licked her lips, watching Kendra, speculating, almost teasing. Kendra didn't move. Then Robin stepped back, one step, two steps and turned to walk down to the other end of the living room. She paced it twice, and then, in front of the fireplace, turned around to face Kendra. "You're serious."

"I am."

"And how far do you want to take this?" She came back but this time stood some distance from Kendra.

"As far as we want to take it."

"And if anyone asks you?"

"I'll neither confirm nor deny."

Robin frowned with what Kendra later came to call her thinking expression. "It could work," she mused. She gave Kendra a quick, questioning look. "No strings."

"None at all."

Robin held out her glass. "Could I get a refill?"

Kendra pushed herself away from the wall and took Robin's glass. She went around to the kitchen with Robin following.

"You have had a share of lovers in town," Robin stated.

"Some," Kendra answered noncommittally as she refilled the glass.

"What will I do if they want to compare notes?"

Kendra turned around, stopping short when Robin was right there. "I guess that's up to you." She wondered how far Robin was going to push this, and watching her, she wondered if the wine was for courage.

"I won't know what to say."

"Then you'll have to come up with something." She gave a smile. "I'm sure you can ad-lib. Isn't that your stock-in-trade?"

"Research is my specialty."

Robin didn't move so Kendra put her arm around her. Like the night at the club when they danced, she found her lithe, a warm supple body in her arms. When their lips met, she found Robin's soft and warm, the taste of wine still on them.

When they broke apart, Kendra took the wineglass from Robin's hand and set it on the counter. Robin's head was tilted back, her lips partially open. She was very still.

Kendra ran her fingers through Robin's thick hair, feeling the texture, the softness, the fullness. Her fingers continued down the side of Robin's neck, then along her jaw, as she returned to kiss her. She could feel Robin yield, triggering a jumble of emotions in Kendra—wanting, desire, guardedness and uncertainty.

"Robin," she said quietly, "are you sure you want to go this far?"

"I think so." Robin didn't open her eyes.

"No, my dear. You can't just 'think.' You need to be sure."

Robin opened her eyes, smoldering. She wrapped her arms around Kendra to pull her back. "I think I'm sure." She leaned against Kendra. "You want me, don't you?"

"That is not the question," Kendra murmured against Robin's neck.

"Yes, Kendra, I'm sure."

"Austere," Robin commented as she looked around when Kendra led her into the bedroom dimly lit by the streetlights coming in the high windows.

"Surely you didn't expect ruffles and bows." Kendra clasped Robin's hands in hers, pulled her so they were standing close together.

"No," Robin answered quietly. "I never got that impression of you."

Right now, as unexpected as this was, she stood close to this attractive woman, smelled her perfume and the scent that was her, felt her hands clasped in hers. Kendra gave a slow smile. "Dare I ask?" She was curious how Robin saw her, sometimes how anyone saw her.

"Solid. Pragmatic. Once your mind's made up, you're there for the duration." Robin closed her eyes, licked her lips, waiting to be kissed.

Kendra didn't disappoint her, not releasing their clasped hands, just pulling Robin closer to her. She felt Robin's fingers tighten and guessed that Robin approved.

"What else?" she asked as she broke away. She let go of Robin's hands. She wanted to run her fingers through Robin's hair again.

"Deliberate." Robin swallowed, relaxed to let Kendra move her head and then hold her to kiss her again, her tongue flicking over Robin's lips.

They stood there in the middle of the room, kissing, exploring, making no move to undress. Kendra was quite content for the moment, feeling Robin decide about this, the same way she had decided in the living room whether she was going to do this. Her return kisses, at first deliberate, firm, slowly relaxed as she yielded. Kendra was patient. This might be unexpected, but it wasn't as if she had never fantasized about it.

Robin broke away, shaking her head, taking a deep breath. She was holding on to Kendra, and while she stepped back, she didn't let go. She met Kendra's gaze, her face flushed. "You take your time."

"Never pays to rush your fences," Kendra said with a smile. She enjoyed Robin's slight discomfort. She had the distinct feeling this woman was always in control, and it wasn't going to be that way with her.

"You always have to be in charge?" Robin asked breathlessly.

"No. There's pleasure on both sides. Do you?"

Robin gave a chagrined little laugh. "Safer."

"Really?" With deliberate slowness, Kendra pulled Robin against her, her arm around her, holding her close. Robin leaned away from her, and Kendra unconcernedly brushed back Robin's hair, stroked her knuckle across Robin's cheek. "Ever think what you might be missing?"

"No." But her answer was a hoarse whisper.

"You sure?" Kendra kissed her, holding her tight, tongue exploring this time. There was an instant of resistance, and then Robin yielded. When Kendra let her go, she was breathless and had a dazed look.

"Jeez." Robin's head fell forward onto Kendra's shoulder.

Kendra held Robin within the circle of her arms and kissed her hair. Her fingers found the zipper of Robin's mock turtleneck at the edge of her hairline. She slowly, deliberately drew it down. The soft material fell open, exposing soft flesh, the pale blue bra band as it slid off Robin's shoulders.

Robin straightened up, still a little out of focus. "What are you doing?"

"Uncovering a beautiful gift," Kendra whispered as she pulled the sweater down. Robin wore one of those little demi-cup bras, which enhance just as much as support. Kendra reached to pull it down, and Robin caught her hands.

Kendra could read the uncertainty in her dark eyes. She easily escaped Robin's hands, and she drew Robin into her arms. She kissed her again, lightly, as she caressed Robin's arm, her shoulders, held her.

"Let me." Her voice had already turned husky as she whispered into Robin's ear. "I'll stop if you want. Just say the word. But I love unwrapping beautiful gifts. Discovering such beauty." She slid her hands through Robin's hair to hold her as she kissed her again. "Let me do this in my own time, my own way."

Robin shivered as Kendra's lips went down her neck. She made no protest, not when Kendra unsnapped her bra and drew it away to uncover her breasts, not when Kendra unzipped her pants and drew them down, catching her panties at the same time. Not when Kendra knelt before her to remove her shoes, her hose, her pants, first one leg, then the other until Robin stood there naked before her.

Kendra sat back on her legs, drinking in the sight of Robin Slusher. She looked up at her standing there, trembling, one arm across her breasts.

"You're beautiful."

As if in response, Robin dropped her arm, reaching out, and Kendra came up on her knees, her hands sliding over Robin's calves, up her thighs, over her hips, cupping her ass. She tongue-kissed across Robin's belly, from one hip to the other, just above the neatly trimmed pubic hair.

"So beautiful."

She stood up, took Robin by the hand and led her to the bed. She pulled the covers back in one swift motion, and with a spread arm, invited Robin. As Robin settled in the center of the bed, Kendra turned the bedlights on low.

"I want to see you."

"Do I get to see you?" Robin asked faintly.

"Of course."

Kendra stood at the foot of bed and undressed. Robin watched as she removed her own clothing as slowly and as deliberately as she had removed Robin's. When she unzipped her pants and pushed them down, Robin sat up, but Kendra had no intention to hide from her. She had come to terms that she would never be a well-toned, muscled woman, but she had dropped the weight and was in shape. Mostly Robin's doing, and maybe for that reason alone, she deserved to see.

Then she stood there, tentatively at first, then relieved at Robin's expression. That was enough for her to crawl onto the bed beside Robin. Her thigh slid easily between Robin's legs, her hands and arms under Robin's shoulders as she felt the gorgeous woman reach for her.

"God, you're a slow one," Robin muttered as she pulled Kendra down.

"Anticipation." Kendra settled against her, feeling flesh against flesh, a sensation of warmth down the length of her. The taste of Robin as she moved down her neck, her shoulder, to her breast, Robin pushing up against her, Robin's hands trailing up and down her arms, her shoulders, alternating between pushing her away and pulling her back.

"Oh, God," she heard Robin mutter as the woman twisted and turned beneath her.

She moved further down, finding Robin ready for her, waiting for her, wanting her.

"Please, don't tease. You're driving me—" and she broke off into a moan. She tightened her grip on Kendra's shoulder, opening more for her.

Kendra closed her eyes, lost in the sensations of Robin. She wasn't fooling herself, this was not a love-match, but that didn't mean there wasn't caring and concern, and—and— She raised her head for a breath, looking up to see Robin, her body twisted, her taut nipples upright, her face tortured. And pleasure. She returned to giving pleasure until Robin thrust up against her, crying out, her fingers entwined in Kendra's short hair.

Gentle kisses on relaxed flesh, Kendra withdrew slowly. Robin's breathing slowed as Kendra crawled up beside her.

Kendra supported herself on one elbow as she took Robin in, now totally relaxed. She bent down to kiss her, to pull her tightly against her. She leaned over her, stroked her eyebrows. "Enough research?" she asked lightly.

"You treat every lover like this?" Robin asked without opening her eyes.

"Only the beautiful ones." Kendra lightly ran her fingers down Robin's cheek, down her chin line.

Robin caught Kendra's hand, brought it to her mouth to kiss, to lick her knuckles. She stretched, catlike, still holding on as Kendra leaned back to watch the slender body stretch and retract. "And how do you treat the non-beautiful ones?"

Kendra bent down to nuzzle Robin's soft warm flesh. "Don't know. They've all been beautiful. Each in her own way."

Robin made a sound somewhere between a sigh and moan.

Kendra rose up. "Do I hear a purr?"

"Mmm, you should." Robin rolled over to face Kendra and then pushed her over onto her back. "You know, I've heard about you." She came up on her knees beside her, leaned over her.

"And what have you heard?"

Robin ran her fingers lightly over Kendra's shoulders, arms, circled her breasts. "Short timer."

Kendra made no comment, feeling Robin's caresses, such a light touch. Tantalizing. Almost but not quite ticklish. Usually her lovers didn't touch her as if she were fragile glass, but that was just what Robin was doing.

"But oh, how sweet in that time." She bent down to nuzzle Kendra's nipples, her hair falling forward to brush against Kendra even as her hands went down the length of the prone woman.

Kendra drew her breath, sucked in her stomach. "Should fit right into your schedule," she managed to say.

"Maybe." Robin's fingers teased. "Fit into yours?"

Kendra parted her legs, closed her eyes. "Whatever works." Quicksilver. Robin's light touch was even more arousing than she had imagined. Her fingers were tantalizing, chilling, warming. Kendra concentrated on the sensations Robin was calling up. She felt Robin's breasts against hers. Her legs parted more. Her nipples nipped at. Robin was lightness and teasing and pleasure. And aggressive. She pulled Robin down to kiss her even as she opened for her, yielding, knowing this was a short-term pleasure but oh, was this morsel sweet.

* * *

The phone rang just as Kendra was getting ready to leave the office to go to the gym. That had been the New Year's resolution, treadmill and weights, build up her endurance and strength.

"Feel like company tonight?" came this sweet whisper.

"That might be nice," Kendra responded with a smile. "Rough day?"

"Yes," Robin answered with a sigh. "Watch the news and you'll see why."

Kendra watched the six o'clock news as she walked the treadmill, but it was only a lead-in to a county board meeting set for eight. The eleven o'clock news really delved into the issues that ended in a shouting match and almost a brawl. Robin was right there, out in front, calm, cool and collected as she asked the proper questions, chased down the proper person.

Kendra sat in her chair and sipped her glass of wine. Robin was just the one to be working on the MMU story. Kendra was beginning to think the problem was their goals might be at cross purposes. She simply wanted to get Artie for Linda's death. The first thing to do was break his alibi of the hunting trip. Robin wanted to expose the Miami Militia and, maybe use it as a springboard for her national exposure. The gal had a streak of ambition in her. Unfortunately for both, Artie seemed to be among the missing.

Over the summer, Kendra had discovered little information that she or Robin didn't already have. If anyone really knew what Artie was doing, they weren't mentioning it to her. She was still being treated like an outsider, a familiar visitor, but she knew she still hadn't been welcomed back into the fold. Now the winter weather hampered her frequent visits to the farm and left her wondering what she was going to have to do next.

Robin continued to plow on, still working on her MMU story but at the same time finding other stories to show her investigative skills. She had a growing reputation of having a nose for corruption and rocking the boat. And being doggedly persistent. And ambitious.

"Can't fault someone because they're ambitious," Kendra commented aloud. *Doesn't mean she can't get in your way.*

She heard the garage door lift and she pushed herself up from her chair. Making her way to the kitchen, she took down a second glass and took the wine from the refrigerator. When Robin came down the hallway into the kitchen, she held the glass out.

"Oh, you're an angel." Robin took it even before she gave Kendra a quick kiss.

Robin set her briefcase on the alcove table as Kendra helped her off with her coat. "What is it about some people? You could put all the evidence in front of them and they still won't believe."

"They don't want to."

In exasperation, Robin ran her fingers through her hair. "Ughhh! I don't understand. Here I am trying to tell an unbiased story, and who the hell is listening?"

"Lots of folks," Kendra assured her. This wasn't the first time Robin had come in all wound up and needed to vent. She came up behind her and put her arms around her, pulled her back against her.

"I've got a hot bath ready for you," she whispered in her ear.

Robin rested her head against Kendra's shoulder, closed her eyes. "It just feels like such a struggle."

"And then you give the broadcast that turns the light on and everyone goes 'Aha! I didn't know that.'" She kissed the side of Robin's neck.

Robin smiled. "Ahh, Kendra, the eternal optimist."

"Not hardly, dear. I've seen you do it, even in this short time I've known you."

Robin straightened up and turned around still within Kendra's arms. "It has been a short time, hasn't it?" she asked as she put her arms around Kendra's neck.

"Pretty much. What, nine, ten weeks?"

Robin wagged her head. "Something like that." She gazed at Kendra in reflection. "You've been quite a balance wheel for me."

"What? Ms. Calm, Cool and Collected needs a balance wheel?"

Robin pulled away. "Have to let off steam somewhere, sometime." She picked up the wineglass and drained it. "When do you need a balance wheel? When do you let off steam?"

Kendra laughed and pulled Robin back to her. "I rarely need a balance wheel. I need the kick to get started." She kissed her, first teasing and then slower. She could taste the wine, taste Robin's high-energy tension. "You know what happens when all that steam meets the icy exterior?"

"Yeah," Robin said quietly. "The ice melts."

They stood in the dining room, arms wrapped around each other, kissing, slowly matching breathing and moods. Kendra's hands began to roam, feeling Robin's tension dissipate. "Still want that bath?"

"And steam up the bathroom?"

"Could be fun."

Robin gave a low laugh as she broke away. She took Kendra's hand and pulled her toward the bathroom just as headlights flashed through the room.

Kendra immediately turned toward the door as someone pulled into the driveway. Belatedly it occurred to her they had been in the only spot where anyone could see into the house. She watched as the car stopped and then backed out.

"What—who was that?" Robin asked over her shoulder.

Kendra shook her head. "A turnaround," she answered but she wasn't so certain. She was in the middle of a short block, the only drive on this side of the street. No one needed to pull into the drive to turn around.

She turned back to Robin. "Go take your bath. Let me do a walk around and turn on the security." She ran her fingers over Robin's cheek. As if to chase away her concerns, she gave Robin a quick kiss. "Go."

Kendra killed the light in the dining room, walked through the house in the darkness. While it was a good thing that no one could see in, it just meant that she couldn't see out except at the front door and from her office window. The neighborhood was quiet at this hour, which was what made the turnaround even stranger. While it could have easily been just someone lost, Kendra's cautious nature could immediately conjure up many alternatives. Was it someone testing her security? That had happened once or twice since she had moved in. Or did it have something to do with Robin?

She turned on the security, something she usually didn't set when she was home. Simply locking the doors seemed enough. Tonight though, she just felt better having an early warning system set up.

"Anything?" Robin asked when Kendra came into the bathroom. She hadn't undressed. Obviously Kendra wasn't the only one who was suspicious.

"No. Probably just someone thoroughly confused and wanting to go back the way they came rather than make any more twists and turns and really get lost."

"Ah-huh."

"Why?" Kendra looked at her sharply. "Have you been having problems?"

Robin shook her head but not in any believable manner. "Nothing I can put my finger on," she said. "Just." She shrugged and stood up, beginning to undress. "This militia bit is making me a bit paranoid."

"Take it from me, a little paranoia will help keep you safe."

Robin was able to laugh. "Your business motto?"

"Could be. Don't like to say it that bluntly, but that's what everyone is thinking when they come in my doors."

Robin shook her head as she reached for Kendra's out-stretched hand and stepped in to the tub. "I don't like living like that."

"I don't know anyone who does."

Robin settled into the slightly cooled but still hot water. "Says the woman who has more security in her house than Fort Knox."

"Now that's an exaggeration." Kendra settled down on the side of the tub. "I passed on the gun towers." As Robin leaned back in the tub, Kendra leaned against the wall to observe the length of the naked body better. "Besides, what better way to test the equipment than to live with it? And certainly a good endorsement. Want me to wash your back?"

"I suppose." Robin picked up the sponge and squeezed it out as Kendra knelt beside the tub. "Just not how I want to live."

"Then drop your investigation," Kendra said simply without any real idea that Robin would agree.

"Can't do that. If I did that, it'd mean they'd won. We live in a free and open society. A united society. Disagreements are one thing. Confrontations and what they're talking about are something else." Robin sat up, forehead resting on pulled up legs. She closed her eyes, letting Kendra lather her, rinse her.

As Kendra finished rinsing her, Robin turned her head to see her. "Would you drop your investigation?"

Kendra shook her head without a second thought.

"Even though," Robin pressed on, "you believe he killed once so he's just as likely to do it again?"

"Crime of passion is different than premeditation." Kendra stood up and grabbed the towel.

"He got away with it once." Robin stepped out of the tub and let Kendra wrap the towel around her. She turned around for Kendra to dry her back.

Instead Kendra pulled her back against her, wrapped her arms around her. "Can we change the subject? This isn't very conducive to the mood I wanted to have."

Robin wrapped her arms and the towel around her. "Me either." She laid her head back on Kendra's shoulder. "You know what I really want?"

"What's that?"

"I just want you to hold me."

Not exactly what I had in mind but…"I can do that."

When Robin stepped away, Kendra let her go. "It's not that, well, sometimes, I just get lonely." She looked up at Kendra quickly. "Now, mind you, I like living alone." She looked back down as she bent over to dry her feet. "But who was it, Margaret Mead who said one of the oldest human needs is having someone to wonder where you are when you don't come home at night?" She looked up at Kendra. "Sometimes I'm afraid of that. That no one will miss me some night." She pulled the nightshirt Kendra had laid out for her over her head, as if hiding from such an admission.

"I can understand that." Kendra picked up the towel and tossed it in the basket. She turned back to wrap her arm around Robin and draw her into the bedroom. "I think anyone who lives alone has that feeling at least occasionally."

She pulled back the covers and Robin sat down on the side of the bed. "You, my dear, would be missed."

"But when? When I didn't show up for work?" Robin mused as she lay down.

Kendra went back to the bathroom to do her nightly ablutions and turn off the light. She came back just partially undressed and sat on the corner of the bed to finish changing. "Then make a backup plan."

She crawled into bed and Robin rolled over into her arms. Kendra pulled the covers over them as Robin settled herself.

"Do you ever worry about something like that?"

"Sometimes. I've got a mother hen of an office manager who's been around forever and thinks she needs to check on me. I suppose she relieves my mind." She lifted Robin's face up to hers and she kissed her forehead. "You have people who worry about you."

"You?"

"A bit," Kendra admitted. "I remind myself I'm paranoid so I won't let those worries get ahead of me."

Robin buried her face into Kendra's shoulder. "I think I like that."

"I try to please."

"Um-humm, that you do." Robin snuggled in against Kendra, her arms around her.

Kendra lay there and felt the woman against her. There was something to be said for just sleeping together. Somehow it felt more intimate than sex. She listened to the woman's breathing, slow and steady and then relax as she fell asleep.

The turnaround still bothered her and she tried to discount it, but it wouldn't go away. She remembered Robin's hit-and-run that first night they met, the request for security and all the false alarms that she'd had. They had dropped off, and Kendra had never found the cause for them. Suppose they weren't false?

After sleepless hours and Robin relaxing enough to let her go, Kendra slipped out of bed. She roamed the house, checking everything again, more out of habit rather than any feeling of insecurity. She was often awake during the night and this time, she didn't want to disturb Robin's sleep. So she lay down on the couch in front of the television and that was where Robin found her hours later.

Always cold when she first got up, Robin was wrapped in Kendra's fleece robe, bundled as if she were going out into a blizzard. "What are you doing out here?"

"Couldn't sleep." She reached for Robin's hand. "Didn't want to keep you awake."

Robin rubbed her face. "I need to get dressed and go home."

Kendra pulled Robin down and Robin stretched out on top of her. "I don't want you going home," she said as she stroked Robin's hair.

Robin closed her eyes and gave a long sigh, wrapped around her. "I need to be in my own place," she protested, but she didn't sound like her heart was in it.

"I don't like you going out and going across town at four in the morning," Kendra said quietly. "No traffic, nothing's open. It's dangerous."

"Nothing's going to happen." Robin still settled against Kendra and then after a moment, it seemed to finally register what Kendra wasn't saying. Robin rose up to look into Kendra's face. "That turnaround really bothered you, didn't it?"

Kendra slowly nodded. "It may be nothing at all." She reached up to push Robin's hair back around her ear. "It probably *is* nothing. But I'd still rather you not be driving across town at this hour of the morning."

Robin flopped her head back down on Kendra's shoulder. "We've had this discussion before."

"And we'll probably have it again, but this time, I want you to humor me. You can wait until later, go to the gym with me, whatever. It's not like you're at the office at eight o'clock."

"I don't want anyone to see me here." But she didn't move.

"So who's going to see you?"

Robin sighed. "I'm afraid if I give in this once, it'll be easier the next time."

"That's a cheery thought."

Robin rose up again. "You know what I mean." She frowned. "We said no strings. That meant no worries."

"Strings I can deal with and ignore," Kendra said quietly. "Worries? That's another matter."

"If you were staying at my house, would you stay if I asked?"

Kendra hesitated and Robin leaped on it. "See? You're just doing it because you want to be my protector."

"Stop it, Robin." Kendra's voice sharpened with annoyance. "No one's made threats against me; no one ran me off the road." Robin raised her head at that, but Kendra forestalled anything she might say. She laid her finger across Robin's lips. "It's not strings to be concerned about a friend, and it's not strings to be aware of dangers and not ignore them."

Robin frowned, her eyes narrowing.

"Come on, Robin. No one's going to see you," Kendra coaxed. "And even if they did, what of it? Just this once?"

"You won't ask again?"

Kendra bit her lip, unable to promise that. "Be nice. Humor me."

Robin sighed and laid her head back down on Kendra's shoulder. "All right. This once. But only because it's cold out there and I loath leaving a warm bed and going out into the storm."

Kendra gave an inward sigh of relief and tightened her arm around Robin.

"This is the warmest robe," Robin's muffled voice came from against her shoulder. "I think I might steal it from you."

"Not a chance. You can only use it here."

"Unfair."

"Sue me."

CHAPTER ELEVEN

"I don't understand why you're doing this," Travis said from her seat in the corner of Kendra's home office. She eyed the pile in the middle of the floor: backpack, rifle, various boxes of dried food, survival gear.

"It's just something I feel is necessary."

Travis stretched out her legs. "You've really gotten into this survival scene, Kendra. I don't understand it. You've always been too levelheaded for the end-of-the-world scene that this Harris guy preaches."

"Oh, I don't buy that so much," Kendra said reasonably as she picked up the clipboard and went down her checklist. "I know the economy's tanked, and storms seem worse than ever before. I know that bad times have happened before. I think of catastrophic events that seemed like the end of the world at the time and people survived. I just think it wouldn't hurt to be prepared."

"Prepared?"

Kendra matched items on the floor with the items on the list as she checked them off. "We've lost our sense of self-sufficiency," she countered. "Convenience stores, ATMs, credit cards, twenty-four-hour gas stations, the interstates. Immediate gratification. And then, when disaster hits, where are we? The very next day people are lined up outside shelters looking for food, water, shelter, clothing. Can't even go for twenty-four hours."

"Why bother being prepared? Disaster hits and any supplies you have built up are going to be destroyed anyway. So what's the use?"

"Bad assumption." Kendra dropped the clipboard and went out to the garage for another box. "First of all," she said as she came back in and set the box down, "few disasters destroy everything everywhere, but they do inflict damage over a wide area. So not all the emergency stores would be destroyed. If more people were prepared, then only those in the direct path would need things. And second of all, we've become so interdependent that the disaster doesn't have to be where you're at to have a major effect. Look at the ice storm that hit last winter. Our roads were fine, but truckers couldn't get goods to us and we still had empty shelves at the grocery stores. And we're not even a big city. Look at the lines in the stores down south when hurricane warnings go up. Last-minute preparations. I just think it should be more built-in."

"So you don't think the world is going to end?"

"Someday. Probably not in my lifetime. But that doesn't preclude bad things from happening. And if it does, I'd like to be prepared."

"And that's why you're joining this group? You've never been much of a joiner on much of anything else."

"If something happens," Kendra answered with studied casualness as she stood for a moment going over the boxes, making sure she had the necessities, "I'd rather be on the inside looking out than the outside looking in, wishing I'd done something." Satisfied that everything was there, she glanced at

Travis. "Now are you going to sit there and look pretty, or are you going to help me load all this?"

"I suppose." Travis slowly got up from her chair. "So what's Robin say about all this?"

Kendra gave her the raised eyebrow. "Now, why would that matter?" she asked although Travis probably knew better or she wouldn't have asked. Robin and her seeing each other was supposed to be a secret, which, like in similar cases, meant that everyone knew it. Still, she did not acknowledge it, and to the best of her knowledge, Robin didn't mention it either.

Travis looked at her with the unspoken question and finally shrugged. "If that's the way you want it." She hefted up a box and carried it to the garage. "Is that why you've been going up to the farm so much this past year?"

"Seems reasonable to stock it up," Kendra said easily, relieved at the subject change. "Never wanted to sell it. Even when Dad moved to Indy, he needed someplace to get way, back to more open spaces. Now it just seems a better spot to survive than here." There was no reason to go into it much deeper than that and Travis seemed satisfied.

"Well, it is a good getaway spot. Got to appreciate that." Travis glanced over at the Mazda parked in the second bay while she waited for Kendra to open the back door of the older model, four-wheel drive, rugged Jeep. "Surprised you didn't get a Land Rover if you were going to get a second vehicle."

"Too ostentatious. No sense advertising what I've got."

"Pickup truck would have been better."

"Yeah, guess so. Didn't suit my purpose. There's still the old one at the farm for stuff."

The Jeep was loaded in short order. Travis stood aside as Kendra pulled the door down. "Did you have to get the gun?"

"Rifle," Kendra corrected. "Those squirrels don't take off their coats and jump into your burgoo."

Travis turned up her nose and shook her head. She'd tried Kendra's burgoo and had liked it until she asked what meat Kendra had used. The venison she could deal with. The squirrel made her put her spoon down. "Whatever." She shook her head.

"You don't really think the government's going to take all the guns."

"No idea," Kendra said noncommittally. "I don't buy into all their ideas, but I think they have some value. And if I want them to take me seriously, I need to prove I can pull my weight. So I have to take their little tests to prove it. This is level one and it demands some proficiency."

"With a gun?" Travis was still dubious.

Kendra laughed, glancing at her friend. "Gotta prove I can bring home the bacon—or the squirrel as the case might be. And there's other things. I'm not worried about the hunting. All it took was some practice. It's more this hike I'm concerned about. Two miles, forty minutes, forty-pound pack. I'm not as young as I used to be."

"Oh, yeah, the old lady!" Travis did laugh at that. "You did all that running with Robin last fall. And you've been going to the gym all winter to get in shape."

Kendra tossed the last of her gear in the passenger side. Yes, she had worked to get into shape. Not only was she going to have to talk the talk, she was going to have to walk the walk. Had to be in shape for it. "So you've got the keys, you'll pick up the mail, check everything."

Travis dangled the keys off her finger. "All set. This thing really going to take all week?"

Kendra shook her head as she walked around to the driver's side. "No. There're just some other things I need to take care of while I'm up there. See how the farm weathered the spring storms, see if there's going to be any more flooding."

Travis followed her around, standing between the two cars in the double garage. "Look, Kendra, before you go, I need to say something."

Kendra paused and turned, braced for whatever Travis might say. She had voiced her opinion more than once on the whole idea of survivalists.

"Look," Travis said as she rubbed the back of her head like she did every time she wasn't sure how to say something. "I don't understand why you've suddenly gotten into this. And

I sure don't agree with the philosophy although, I guess," she shrugged, "I guess the way you explain it, it doesn't hurt to be prepared." She looked up at Kendra directly. "I just know that since you've been involved with this, you've been less depressed and act like you have some purpose in life again. You've been more the old Kendra. You're back to being levelheaded and making decisions. This isn't my bag, but as long as it does something for you, well, I guess I'll support you."

"That's good to know," Kendra acknowledged, touched more than she expected. Travis wasn't often this serious but she was a little embarrassed by such a declaration. "And I appreciate you watching over the house for me while I'm gone. Now, on that note, let me get on the road."

She held out her hand for a handshake but Travis grabbed it. "Oh, hell, Kendra. A handshake isn't going to do." She wrapped her arms around her in a bear hug. "Just come back to us."

Kendra caught her breath. She was not a huggy person and she wasn't sure how to take this. As soon as she could, she stepped back. "I'm gone a week, not forever. You know where I'm going to be. I've got my cell phone. Stop sounding like I'm going to come back different."

"Right," Travis said with an uneasy laugh. She watched as Kendra got in and hit the remote to raise the garage door.

When Kendra turned the corner and drove down the few blocks to the main artery out of the subdivision, she could still see Travis standing in the middle of the driveway watching her.

She sighed, relieved to get on the road. Travis would take care of the house. Mike would take care of the business. Peg would take care of the office. She could focus on the coming week.

"You've got a good friend there," Linda said from the backseat.

Kendra glanced in the rearview mirror at the image. "Yes, I do."

Linda ran her hand over the cloth-covered seat. "Where'd you find old Nellybelle?"

"Behind Fred's barn in the machine shed. Remember him? He had the farm on the other side of Walton's Corner. There was a big farm sale after he died. I went over there just to see who was there and found old Nellybelle. Couldn't pass her up. Like regaining an old friend."

"I was surprised when you sold her."

Kendra shrugged. "Well, there were unexpected expenses that college year. Didn't want to ask Dad. He was sinking everything into Abatis. He even talked about selling the farm, did sell some acreage. And Nellybelle never would have made it to California."

Linda shook her head. "Looks just like the day you sold her."

"Yeah. You wouldn't believe the money it took to make her look that good." She pulled out on the highway. A lot of money, a good mechanic. But it felt good to be driving her again, just like old times.

"Gonna take the interstate?"

"No, thought I'd come in the back way, the old roads."

"That'll be nice."

Kendra drew a deep breath once she was out of town. The interstate would have been quicker but she needed time to get into the mindset and make her plans. The back roads were slower, less heavily traveled. They would give her time to think, to plan.

She still had a hard time with the militia idea. Months of listening to Harris hadn't changed her mind. Self-sufficiency like Harris preached, yes, she could go along with that. She could see the drawbacks of all the country's conveniences. And disasters like Katrina or the March tornadoes demonstrated that people were overly dependent on the government to take care of them. National disasters she could acknowledge, even far-fetched ones, like asteroids hitting the earth.

However, invasion, government breakdown, or worse, war against the government, all scenarios floated by Harris, she had a much harder time with. He was convinced America was going to hell in a handbasket; the government was being taken over by the nebulous "them." Even after six or seven months, Kendra had not been able to get a clear picture of who Harris thought "them" might be. She wasn't sure he knew.

It didn't matter, not really. Her goal was to find Artie and the MMU was the method. They were the best source of information for her. Casual chats with the neighbors hadn't gotten her any answers. She got the feeling they thought her little more than a visitor and gave her polite surface answers. Buying into the self-sufficiency idea was the best way back. She hoped that the proficiency test would demonstrate her commitment, gain her acceptance. Then she might gain more information.

Everything she had heard so far was just general griping about the government, policies and finances. Nothing unique about that. Yet dropped words occasionally hinted there might be something more. Things like "all talk, no walk," or "off the dime." Once she was inside, she might hear more. She hoped.

And dear old Artie seemed to have dropped out of sight. Casual opened-ended questions were met with a shrug and the equally casual answer that he did that periodically, his business. Closed ranks.

If that wasn't bothersome, annoying, she had the feeling Robin was holding information back. What they talked about and what she heard on Robin's news reports didn't necessarily jibe. She constantly reminded herself that Robin's goal was not hers. At some point down the road, they could conflict.

Kendra was beginning to understand that the news media was not popular with the MMU, and Robin had not escaped their attention. Harris's views of "them" taking over the government were just a little stronger than his views of "them" taking over the media. No, links to Robin would not be in her best interest, at least not in meeting her goal of getting any credibility with Harris and his bunch. Then maybe they would tell her about Artie.

For not the first time, Kendra examined the mixed emotions she had about Robin. She doubted their paths would have crossed without the investigation, and she more strongly doubted she would have sparked any interest in Robin. She was too settled, too remote for someone who lived so much in the fast lane. And that led to the question of whether Robin was using her.

Well, of course she was, Kendra told herself. The same as she was using Robin.

Somehow the thought made her more uncomfortable now than it did before she had started this affair of convenience.

She had told herself it was a fair trade. They both wanted information and could work together. They both wanted to be occupied from their friend's well-meaning if a bit inconvenient matchmaking. Certainly she found Robin attractive and charming. Her high energy balanced Kendra's low energy. Robin had a sense of humor, was knowledgeable and she was ambitious. Her ambition was what concerned Kendra. Was Robin ambitious enough to use sexual attraction and sexual wiles to get information from a source? Kendra didn't think so, or rather, she didn't want to think so. She didn't like the idea that Robin might be using her in that manner.

So she held back from sharing everything with Robin. She did pass along information she gained, which wasn't much, but she didn't talk about all the meetings she was attending. She didn't share how her feelings were changing, how she found some validity in the ideas they put forth. If Robin thought Kendra was spending so much time at the farm just to get information, Kendra said nothing to dissuade her. Sometimes Kendra wasn't sure herself just how she felt about things any more.

Kendra's justification was her own uncertainty. For Robin, this investigation was a story, a stepping-stone to bigger and better things her ambition was driving her to. For Kendra, this was personal, a vendetta, a way of seeking justice. She could see potential conflict.

Three hours later she was home, her home away from home. Weather had been good for a drive and she had taken some detours, driving down roads she hadn't driven for a long time. After weeks of rain, skies had cleared and spring breezes had dried off the land. Farmers were out plowing in the fields, making up for lost time. The back roads were quiet, gave her time to think, shift gears, slow down her pace. By the time she pulled into her driveway, she had put Abatis and city living behind her, picked up the rhythms of a quieter life. For the next week at least.

She unlocked the house, opening the windows, airing it out. The house felt stuffy, chilly, for being closed up so much. Impersonal, Kendra realized as she brought in her luggage. Like a vacation house she had rented in the mountains one time. Nice furnishings, nice setting but impersonal. She and her dad had stripped the house of the important stuff, mementoes, the good furnishings, and the personal items. Although she had been coming for almost a year now, she had done nothing to replace any of it. She had spent so little time at the house, usually just a weekend, with a list of things to do, and that mostly outside, that she hadn't the time or the inclination to add any personal touch. She realized now it gave her a very temporary feel.

The open windows created a cross ventilation, bringing in the warmer outside air. By the time Kendra had brought in her luggage, the living room was almost comfortable. The kitchen at the back side, where it was well shaded, was still a little cool but that had always been the advantage during summertime cooking. Air-conditioning had never been considered, a drain on the energy her dad always said. She had never found it uncomfortable while growing up but now she might want to consider it. Hot days seemed to be more frequent or maybe just she didn't tolerate the heat as well.

She brought herself up short. Air-conditioning? She wasn't planning on spending that much time there. And there was no way she could justify the cost just for the weekend trips she was making. Where did that idea come from?

She unloaded the Jeep, parceling out the boxes. Foodstuffs in the kitchen. Clothing to the bedroom. She put the rest in the shed beside the golf cart. She would move those as soon as it got dark. Almost a full moon tonight, that would be ideal. She might not even need to use the lights. She spent the rest of the afternoon just settling in.

* * *

The almost full moon illuminated the yard so much that night she had no need of the flashlight. She took it anyway, slipping it into the pocket of her cargo pants. She left the television on. The light would make it appear she was just laid back in her recliner if someone did happen by, not that she expected anyone. And if someone noticed and called to check, well, she could say she had fallen asleep in the chair. Wouldn't be the first time.

When she had first started staying over at the farm, she had been surprised at how dark it was and how quiet. Too many years of city living with streetlights, constant traffic, security lights had made her forget what country living was like. At first she'd had trouble sleeping in that silence. She had even welcomed the neighbor's barking dog until she'd wondered what it was barking at. She'd resolved to get the security light repaired. But she hadn't. There was nothing there to steal and she never considered anyone breaking in to do her harm. She left it dark.

She backed the electric golf cart out of the shed. A great idea of her dad's to get this when his legs began to bother him and he still wanted to get around. She loaded up the boxes on the seat beside the driver as well as behind. No one was likely to notice anything if they drove by. She didn't have to use the headlamp as she guided the cart across the pasture and dropped over the slight knoll. She'd be out of sight for everything except aerial. And, she amended, the spy satellites. She shook her head at some of Harris's ideas, and then one of her dad's favorite sayings came back at her. *Just because he's crazy, doesn't mean he's wrong.* She glanced at the empty, star-filled sky, and looked around. The trees were simply darker shapes, the sounds were those of the night. Somewhere a dog barked but it sounded like it was across the creek. Sound carried on quiet nights like this.

The springhouse was tucked away in the hillside, its stone façade blending into the dirt and winter accumulation of dead leaves. A lot of the old farms had them, the original source of water for the first owners. Most of them had fallen into disuse and owners had let the buildings collapse, and Mother Nature taken back her own. This one though, she and her dad had discovered, was special.

She pulled out her flashlight so she could see to push away the winter's accumulation of litter in order to open the door. Once inside, she flashed the light around the stone room. It had been her favorite place when she was growing up. Cool in summer, out of sight so no one would ask what she was doing and why she didn't go out and play when all she wanted to do was hide from chores and read a book. The water still spilled out of the wall into the small pool before it overflowed and went down the small spillway into the hillside and toward the creek.

She had been a curious little kid, had wanted to know where the water was coming from. A little investigation, a little shovel to dig through the dirt, and she had promptly fallen through the wooden wall as it gave way. A big dark hole gaped in front of her to her surprise, and she was convinced she'd found the doorway to another world. Even at that age, she had been reading fantasy and science fiction.

By the time she had gotten her dad there, the wall was back in place but he was a patient man. A little more digging, more investigation and the wall opened for him too. A ramp. Rooms. He had stressed on her that this was a secret, a family secret. And so it remained.

Well, of course, she had told Linda.

"You think anyone remembers this place?" Linda asked now as Kendra brought in boxes and emptied them into the storage room.

"I don't think so," Kendra answered. "Dad did some nosing around after we found it but couldn't find out anything. Of course, it fit right into his paranoia. So he did some repairs, some upgrades, made some expansion. It was really in pretty good shape when we found it, considering its age."

Linda looked around at the wooden shelving, empty now. "Wonder why it was built."

"The air force base was open then, based the long-range bombers. It was a likely target during the Cold War and we're within range, longrange, but you know, the paranoid mind."

Linda laughed. "And the apple doesn't fall far from the tree, does it?"

Kendra broke down the boxes and stored them. "Maybe not. Turned into an asset in my business."

She walked through the rooms, kitchenette, living room, two bedrooms. These rooms were alive with memories. Finding this underground bunker had changed her relationship with her dad. She and he had bonded as they made repairs and upgrades and he explained why the secrecy was necessary. Harris and the Preppers were nothing like her dad and at the same time, they shared the same kind of paranoia. Harris hadn't told her anything she hadn't been told before, just the names had changed. And maybe the technology.

She knew this was why her dad had never wanted to sell the place, and maybe it was the real reason she had held on to it. Some day, he always said. That's when it would come, would happen, "it" being undefined, ever-changing. So, she was prepared. The bunker was six feet underground, could survive anything short of a direct bomb hit and even then it would have to be massive. Spring-fed water, generator-powered, air filtering. Across the years, Kendra had made some investments in alternative power, careful to hook in the house and the shelter, separately. Sanitary units. Nothing short of ground monitoring would uncover it, and even then, someone would have to suspect. Whoever had built it had picked the site well.

Before she left, after storing the new supplies, pulling out the expired stuff, she looked around, contemplating. Her memories were here. As much as she'd hate to spend years down here and believed she would never really need it, she hedged her bets by keeping it in good repair, updated the technology. Sometimes she even stayed down here, wondering what it would be like to have to depend on these rooms, what she and her dad had built.

Never happen, she told herself, as she secured the entrance at the springhouse. Not in my lifetime at least.

* * *

Her confidence was shaken badly when she went to register for the level one test.

"Supplies?" Harris asked from his position behind the registration table.

Kendra handed over the backpack and everything was spread out across the table and checked off.

"Rifle?"

She handed it over and it checked out.

"Sponsor?"

"Sponsor?" Kendra echoed. This was the first she had heard of needing a sponsor, and quickly went down a mental checklist as to who might be available. She supposed ruefully that this was one way of keeping questionable people out. She may be shot down before she was even in the door.

"Mac? Is that you?"

Harris and Kendra both turned, Harris curious and Kendra suspicious. No one had called her "Mac" in years and years, not since California. She didn't recognize the man dressed in camouflage advancing on them. She'd seen him around from time to time. He seemed to wander in and out but they'd never been introduced. From out of state, someone said, and that was as much as she knew.

"Still go by Mac?" he asked casually as he held out his hand in greeting

"Not for a long time," Kendra answered slowly as she struggled to place him. If he knew her as Mac, he had to be someone from California because that was the only time she'd used the shortened version of her family name. She eyed him guardedly, not sure if she wanted to be sponsored by someone she didn't know, and yet at the same time, she really wanted in. She took his hand, finding it a firm and reassuring grip.

"Mac and I went through police training together. California." He looked from her to Harris. "She made an impression that first day when the Training Officer called her Mac. The more she insisted on McKenna, the more he insisted on calling her Mac. Wanted to make her Scottish." He glanced back at Kendra with a smile, as Harris looked from one to the other. "She insisted she was Irish. Called her Mac the entire time."

True story, Kendra realized, but she still couldn't place him. "All of what, six weeks?" She didn't want any false pretenses floating around that she was a cop.

"Was it even that long?" He gave her an inquiring look but Kendra didn't respond. He turned back to Harris. "Mac got the score right away. Why bother enforcing the law, arresting someone if the system was just going to let them loose before you even got the paperwork finished? Took me a couple of years to figure that one out."

"Look, Stockton," Harris started but the guy turned back to Kendra.

"Thought I recognized you a couple of times, but they told me you were a local girl."

Kendra narrowed her eyes at being called "girl" and Stockton laughed as he leaned back against the table and folded his arms across his chest.

"Ahh, I remember that face. Still got that attitude. Some things never change. Didn't know you were from around here."

Kendra still didn't recognize him but all the stories were correct. Yes, she did have that attitude, although it was more over abusive husbands and battered wives than general overall attitude. She had really discovered that she wasn't ready to wade into a male-dominated arena and deal with the sexism and the macho attitudes. She had walked away.

"Look you two," Harris cut in impatiently. "I hate to cut into such a happy reunion but I've got a schedule to keep." He looked up at Kendra. "You got a sponsor or not?"

"I'll sponsor her," Stockton said easily. He had that half smile as if they shared a secret, and Kendra wondered. She had originally thought her attempt at law enforcement would have been a deterrent to this group. After she starting meeting members, she had been amazed at the number of law enforcement members who, if not in the organization, were on the fringes. Survivalists, yes, she could understand that. More than the general population, they would have a good idea how bad it could be if the system failed. What had surprised her were the ones who thought the system was too lax and were willing to take it down in favor of a more rigid system, black and white, none of the gray areas that left lawyers arguing over the fine points.

"So." Stockton turned to Harris. "Is that enough or do I have to do something else?"

Harris looked from one to the other, a questioning look that made Kendra hold her breath. "Fine with me," he said finally, and waved Kendra on.

* * *

"Do you remember him at all?" Linda asked that night when she got back home.

Kendra stepped out of the shower and grabbed the towel off the hook. She shook her head as she toweled off. "After I quit, I tried to forget the whole damn deal."

"Can't imagine you as a cop."

Kendra examined her face in the mirror. "Neither can I. I don't know what got into me." She glanced at where she knew Linda was, but Linda didn't reflect in the mirror. She knew what had driven her. And Linda knew, too. She gave a rueful smile.

"But you're in." Linda sat on the toilet tank, her legs up on the toilet seat.

"Yeah." Kendra grabbed her robe. "Now to find Artie."

CHAPTER TWELVE

She came back to Carmel recharged and relieved with a sense of accomplishment. She had done well. Good hike, those workouts all winter had helped. The shooting. That had taken two tries, and she needed practice. Where was the local shooting range? And a pistol would be better than a rifle for what she had planned. But no Artie. She had hoped the idea of the proficiency tests would make him surface but very little had been said about him and then it was hastily covered up. She gathered he was out west. Nothing else.

"Good vacation?" Mike asked with a clap on her shoulder.

"Great," she responded.

"Good. Glad to hear it. Now about these new orders…"

And it was back to work as usual, except it wasn't back to normal.

"Everything all right?" Travis asked cautiously.

"Right as rain," Kendra passed off.

"You gonna be seeing Robin again?"

"I don't think so."

"Why not?" Travis asked in surprise. "She seemed real interested." She reconsidered. "Well, as much as she could and fit anyone into her schedule."

"Yeah. That is a problem." Kendra shook her head. "Don't think I can really compete with that job."

"I thought things were—progressing nicely, as they say."

Kendra shook her head. She'd had a week to think about it. It wasn't just the fact that Robin was a good investigative reporter. Kendra wasn't sure she would be able to keep information from her. After a week of actually living there, she realized that she would not be able to get information as long as she was treated as a visitor. And the only way not to be treated as a visitor was to move back there. But if she moved, she was making a commitment, and Robin would want to know why. Even if she didn't ask, she would know that something had changed.

"I don't know." Travis shook her head. "Seems to me like you're passing up a good thing." She brightened. "Does that mean she's available?"

Kendra gave her a sideways look. "Get back to work, Travis. Break's over." She heard Travis laugh as she went out the door.

Robin could be a problem, Kendra decided. No one who had any information she sought was going to talk to her if she were friends with a reporter, never mind having a relationship with her. She sat back at her desk. She hadn't intended to get this involved with Robin, just stifle the matchmaking, but this thing just seemed to happen. At least it had happened for her. Both of them were working on related investigations, even if they didn't share everything. They were still not openly dating, just seeming to run into each other at the games then going out afterward. Their togetherness was uncertain enough that no one assumed it and yet everyone was smirking at their matchmaking success. Sometimes, as she watched Robin flirt with someone at the club, she would clap herself on the back at their success in fooling everyone. Then when she caught her breath at Robin's unexpected call, when Robin looked across the room to meet her gaze and give her that small, secret smile, she wondered if they were simply fooling each other. Or was Robin fooling her? Or worse, was she fooling herself?

She went through her messages. Dentist appointment. Party at Yvonne's. Will was updated, come in and sign it. Battered women shelter fund-raiser, would she be available? Request for talk on security to support group. Reminder about BPW, Business and Professional Women meeting. Chamber of Commerce. Damn, did everything happen the week she went out of town?

And then there was Robin.

"Hey! Heard you were back in town. Why didn't you call? Be at the club Friday night. See you then? Gotta run. Missed you."

Kendra closed her eyes. She was going to have to do something. Robin was a complication, a sweet, oh, so sweet complication, but a terrible complication. She just couldn't... well, she was going to have to do something. Quickly. Before it went any further. She pulled out her phone book.

"Hey, Stella. Kendra here. Need a favor. I'm beginning to play your games. You and Ellen tight? Can I borrow you?"

* * *

Friday night at the club was crowded but not packed. Kendra parked the car, still wondering if this was a good idea. Probably not, but it was about the best that she could come up with for the predictable results. If she told Robin she wanted to end their supposedly nonexistent relationship, Robin would want to know why. Any reason Kendra could honestly tell her would only be a signal to the investigative reporter that she had found something. Hardly the way to get rid of her. Any other reason might be a confession as to how she felt about Robin, and she wasn't sure that was any wiser. Whether Robin returned her feelings and would protest or Robin was only using her as a source and didn't want to lose that source, the results would be the same. Robin would turn on the charm and the persuasive ways. Kendra knew herself and knew Robin. She was so afraid she would succumb to Robin's charms. She closed her eyes for a moment, feeling the vulnerability. She straightened up and pulled down the visor mirror to check her hair. No, she wasn't sure she could resist if Robin turned on the charm. She had to burn this bridge and sweep away the ashes. No other way.

Stella met Kendra at the door—pounced on her would have been the correct terminology. She immediately dragged Kendra off to a dark corner with a kiss that would have curled Kendra's toes if she had thought it was serious.

"You sure you want to do this?" Stella asked when she broke away. "It's not too late to change your mind."

"Is Ellen here yet?" Kendra took Stella's face in her hands. Such a pretty woman, but such a drama queen. How she and Ellen had survived this long, Kendra had no idea.

"Coming later." Stella slid her arms inside Kendra's jacket. "Don't understand this, Kendra, but it's your call."

"My call." Kendra slid her arms around Stella. "Shall we hit the dance floor?"

There were a couple of glances at them, but then Stella was known for her games. But Kendra? And their dancing. If Kendra hadn't been so intent on her own plan, she might have been embarrassed by Stella's gyrations.

The hour grew late, and she tried not to watch the clock. Would this be one of the nights Robin couldn't get out? Just when she thought it was a lost cause, all the effort for nothing, she saw Robin. She was standing at the edge of the dance floor with some friends, and she was looking right at Kendra and Stella. Kendra was so overwhelmed at the sight of her, her heart pounding like it did every time she saw her unexpectedly, that she was caught off guard.

She was hit, shoved back, so off balance that she staggered back against other dancers, who prevented her from falling.

"You little two-timing bitch!" Ellen grabbed Stella's arm and jerked her away from Kendra. "So this is who you were with last night!"

Stella pulled her arm away, turning to face Ellen, backing up toward Kendra. "What if it was? What difference does it make? I'm tired of your dull, boring, suburban life. I want some excitement!"

The thought of Kendra being exciting was ludicrous if anyone stopped to think about it, but right now, no one was as Ellen stared at Stella in shock. Dancers parted around them, and while everyone tried to look as if they were carrying on a conversation, everyone was listening.

"As if you don't make enough excitement of your own, taking a lover in an attempt to make me jealous? Good God, Stella. That's getting old! I'm sick of it! And it's not like I find Kendra McKenna such a threat! I'm just sick of what you're doing."

"Now, look," Kendra started, not sure whether she had been insulted or not by Ellen's comment.

"You stay out of it!" Ellen turned on her. "You want this little piece of trash who takes every opportunity—"

"If I had something at home, I wouldn't need to take the opportunity," Stella cut in, pulling Ellen around to look at her. "And I'm not a piece of trash! It just takes someone to appreciate me more than you do."

"Why you—" And Ellen raised her arm. Stella cringed back and Kendra caught Ellen's arm.

Ellen jerked away. Kendra released her. Ellen fastened a cold gaze on Kendra then back to Stella. "You want her? Then take her. You'll find her clothes on the lawn in the morning."

As if realizing she had gone too far, Stella took a step forward to reach for Ellen but Ellen evaded her, in fact, gave Stella a shove that sent her back to Kendra's waiting arms. "Better get there early. Before the trash men come. Tomorrow's garbage pick-up day." And then she turned around and left, the crowd parting to let her through and buzzing behind her.

Stella turned crying into Kendra's arms while Kendra held her protectively. "Oh, Kendra, what shall I do?"

Kendra swallowed, not sure how much of this was acting and how much was real. She had asked for a scene, but this? She saw Travis's dropped jaw. How long had she been there? And then she saw Robin's shocked look. As their eyes met, Robin's gaze turned steely and cold. She turned away, but not before Kendra had seen the hurt. She suddenly felt sick.

"Come on, baby," she murmured in Stella's ear. "Let's get out of here."

"Oh, Kendra. Take me home."

No one said anything to them as they left the club. Kendra could imagine the telephone calls filling the airways tonight and tomorrow. Her circle, Ellen and Stella's circle, Robin's circle. She cast a glance through the crowd as they left, only to see Robin disappearing into a corner. Even as she told herself it was necessary, she knew she had delivered a terrible hurt.

* * *

"Did I do good or did I do good?"

"Fantastic job, Ellen. You almost had me believing."

Stella left Kendra's side to cross the kitchen and wrap her arms around her lover. Ellen put her coffee cup down and put a protective arm around Stella. Kendra shook her head. Drama queens. Both of them. Ellen was just the less apparent one.

"I'll nominate you for Best Actress any time."

"Knew all those months in the theater group would come in handy sometime." Ellen kissed the top of Stella's head. She cast a speculative look at Kendra. "But you. I hope that scene was for a worthy cause, because if I read my looks right, your chance of being forgiven is somewhere between slim and none."

"That's probably pretty accurate," Kendra agreed.

And it was. Although she did go through the motions. Her calls weren't returned. When she did get through, Robin hung up on her and then finally her calls just didn't make it through. Robin did show up at Kendra's office though, once. She brought the flowers Kendra had sent her, stalked past an amazed Peg into Kendra's office where she was meeting with Travis, and shred them, scattering them all over the floor.

"Don't," she said in a cold voice. "Bother. Me. Again."

And she turned and stalked out, past an amazed Peg who stood at her desk open-mouthed.

Kendra looked at red rose petals all over her office floor and then at Peg who had come to the doorway and stared at Kendra, then at the floor covered with red rose petals.

"I'm so sorry, I—she just caught me flat-footed, just barged right through."

"It's all right, Peg."

"I'll–I'll get the sweeper."

"No." Kendra came around the desk. "I'll take care of these."

"Well, what did you expect?" Travis demanded as Kendra just stood there.

Kendra shook her head. Robin could be a bit of a drama queen herself, she guessed. Unexpected. God, it had been good to see her again, even with fire in her eyes, and steel. No, Kendra shouldn't expect any forgiveness, even when all of this was over.

She picked up all the petals, put them in a box. Never before a sentimental person, this time she made an exception. She dried them, put them in a bowl as a potpourri. She needed the reminder.

* * *

"I'm sorry," Linda said that night.

Kendra ran her finger about the rim of glass bowl holding the petals. "Bridges burnt can't be rebuilt. Had to be done."

CHAPTER THIRTEEN

Did it now? Kendra "Mac" McKenna asked herself that question multiple times in the last sixteen months. She asked it again this morning as she drove the old pickup into Walton's Corner to pick up chicken feed. Across the field and up the hillside, trees were turning the bright reds and oranges of Indian summer, triggering memories of early morning runs with Robin. Only Robin wasn't here, or anywhere, and Kendra wondered if she had thrown away something tangible for an illusion.

"Just like always, isn't it?"

She turned to see Linda sitting in the passenger seat, her legs stretched out and her feet fading into the floorboard.

"A few differences." They came upon the sharp turn onto the old iron bridge. The road crossed the creek, curved again up the hill, a stop sign, left turn and they went into Walton's Corner. *Just a few.* She turned back to say something else and Linda was gone.

Across the road a monster of a corn picker made its way across the flat field, a sure sign of the passing season. Tall stalks disappeared into the picker, ears dropped into the bin and chopped up stalks were spit out. Only rows of short stubble remained. Winter would be coming soon. She needed to bring more wood in from the shed. Be prepared.

For what? she asked herself as she crossed the second bridge. *For how long?* The summer was just starting last year when she presented her proposal to Mike. A sabbatical of sorts. Stepping back from the daily grind of the company. She needed to reconsider things. They worked out a plan, and she had closed up the house in Carmel and moved back to the farm. She thought it'd all be done within the year, maybe even less.

Artie's high jinks had changed everything. Kendra had been settled in maybe a month or two when Artie had come home. That was the good part. The bad part came was when he had a little drunken celebration that involved firing a gun in the air. No stupid law was going to tell him what he could and couldn't do on his own property. Well, one thing led to another, a DUI still there and a domestic abuse charge, and by the time it was over, Artie had his housing courtesy of the state for the next eighteen months.

Kendra had thought about going back home to Carmel but rejected it. She knew she'd have a hard enough time establishing credibility without flitting in and out and back in again. Like it or not, and she didn't much like it, she needed to stay.

She hadn't exactly been met with open arms, but she knew enough not to rush her fences. Patience, as Robin had told her, was a virtue, but it was also a trial. Some had been guardedly cordial. Others had been less so.

"You'd think," Sue said to her bluntly when she stopped in at the diner, "that some people would know better than to come around where they're not wanted."

Discovering that Sue was now working there had been another drawback. The Kozy Korner was diagonally across the street from the grain elevator, and was a regular hotbed of gossip.

Between the farmers and farmwives stopping in while trucks were loaded or unloaded at the elevator, the high school kids coming in because there wasn't much else to do, the old folks stopping in for a cup of coffee and sitting for hours, nothing happened in the community that wasn't dissected over the old-fashioned Formica counter and scarred wooden tables. Kendra was relieved to see that some piece of her past has survived, even though she sometimes hated going in where she was the topic of conversation. If she wanted to learn about anything that was going on in the community, this was where she could hear of it.

"Really? And who might that be?" She met Sue's challenging gaze with one of her own. Betty Lou, the diner owner, walked up then and Sue moved on.

"Trouble?" Betty Lou threw the dishtowel over her shoulder as she frowned at Sue's retreating figure. She turned to Kendra for an answer.

Kendra kept her expression bland as she shook her head. "Not from my corner." The animosity between her and Sue went back a long time and Betty Lou was aware of it as much as anybody in the community was. They had all gone to school together. Now Kendra had no desire to cause Sue any problems and even less desire to bring any problems to Betty Lou's door. What Sue wanted to do with it might be another matter.

Betty Lou had been an unexpected and very welcome ally during what had turned out to be a very cold winter, and not just in terms of weather. Months of hearing conversations stop, some folks getting up and leaving when she came in had taken their toll. The locals would close ranks against outsiders, tighter than a banker held on to his money. And she wasn't a local any more. Not really. She had the feeling they just weren't sure what to think about her.

More than once, Kendra wondered if she was ever going to get anywhere, but just like they hadn't driven her out when she was in school, she wasn't ready to leave this time either, not until she had some answers. Betty Lou had been a saving grace. She had always given Kendra a cheery greeting like she was glad to see her even as she was saying goodbye to those leaving. She always poured her coffee with the question, "You look cold, you doing okay?"

Then sometime in the spring, attitudes changed. Kendra wasn't sure why but suddenly she was included more. People were talking to her, inviting her to church, to organizational meetings. She had no idea what had changed until a late afternoon conversation happened with Betty Lou.

She was on her way back from Lafayette and just hated the idea of going home to the empty house, and cooking just for herself. So she drove through Walton's Corner on the chance the Kozy Korner diner was still open.

Betty Lou had been ready to flip the OPEN sign to CLOSED as Kendra stepped up to the door. Instead of locking up, Betty Lou opened the door. "Come on in."

Kendra held her hand up palm out. "No, really. I don't want to hold you up. I imagine after a long day, you're ready to go home and put your feet up."

Betty Lou shook her head. "Empty house. Rotten night on the television. Don't know what I've got left though, might not be something you like."

Kendra gave a low laugh. "If I don't have to cook it, I'll take it."

"That I can manage."

Betty Lou scrounged in the kitchen and brought the plate of Salsbury steak, potatoes and green beans over to Kendra. "Mind if I sit down and join you? Be great to have a conversation without having to leave in the middle."

"Be my guest."

Betty Lou pulled out two chairs, one to sit on, the other to rest her legs on. She stretched, arching her back and turning her head from one side to the other. Kendra eyed her, thinking how little she had changed since high school. She still wore her dishwater-blond hair in a ponytail, which she pulled free now for it to fall down to her shoulders. She still was a little plump, like a comfortable feather pillow someone had described her back then and she didn't look much different now. She still didn't wear makeup except for bright red lipstick, which Kendra would have bet was the same shade she wore in high school. Now she stretched, arching her back and cracking her neck the same as she did in high school. That habit alone drove some of the teachers wild.

Back then, she had always been a little too much for Kendra's comfort, her laughter too loud, her clothes a little too tight, her language a little too coarse. She had the reputation of being "fast" and Kendra had heard some adult describe her as "no better than she should be." But she was a hard worker, worked part-time at the diner, had an easy, friendly way of talking to anyone and everyone, no matter who they were, but that didn't mean she took any guff from anyone. Kendra had found her terribly intimidating.

Now, two husbands later, Betty Lou was still a hard worker, still was everyone's friend, still plainspoken and still didn't take any nonsense. She'd taken over more and more of the diner when Mrs. Peterson got sick, first ran it for her so the old lady, a widow woman, had some income, then she bought it from her. She updated it and still managed to keep it as the unofficial community center of Walton's Corner. She was probably the only person in Walton's Corner who Kendra felt comfortable with.

"So how's it feel to be back?" Betty Lou asked as she took a drink of iced tea.

Kendra gave Betty Lou a puzzled look but Betty Lou had always been straight with her. "You mean like the redheaded bastard at the family reunion?"

"Can't tell me you really expected anything different." Betty Lou paused, eyebrow cocked. "Did you?"

"No, I guess not." Kendra went back to eating. "But something's changed lately. Got an invitation to go to church." She half laughed at Betty Lou's quizzical look. "No, I begged off, but still, the invitation." She paused, her fork half raised. "And got an invitation from old Ms. Collins to one of her wing-dings."

"Oh, my, you have been accepted back into the fold, haven't you?"

"I don't know why. I haven't done anything different."

"Oh, I can tell you why."

Kendra waited and Betty Lou said nothing. She always was like that, Kendra remembered, even in high school. "Okay, spill it," she said.

"Simple." Betty Lou took another drink. "They decided you weren't a lesbian anymore."

Kendra caught her mouth before her jaw dropped. "Excuse me," was all she could get out which seemed as neutral as she could muster.

"Well, you're not sleeping with anyone. Or at least no one sees you with anyone, so." Betty Lou spread her hand. "So you're not a lesbian."

Kendra frowned. "So the logic being if I slept with a woman, I'd be a lesbian; but if I'm not sleeping with anyone, I'm not."

"Right." Betty Lou smiled like a teacher smiling at a bright pupil who had just come up with the right answer. Kendra could only imagine the stupid expression she had on her face.

"Well, following that logic, you're het if you sleep with men, and then what are you if you don't sleep with anyone?"

Betty Lou tilted her head. "Beats me. I don't follow their logic so much. My cousin visiting from San Francisco thought it was the weirdest thing he'd ever heard." She watched Kendra as if there were some significance in what she had said.

Kendra continued to eat, watching Betty Lou, not sure what to say.

Betty Lou went back to the subject at hand. "So then once Ms. Collins said you were safe, then everyone decided you were okay to talk to. Of course, there are some holdouts."

"Like Sue."

"Yeah, well, Sue's never forgiven you for taking up so much of Linda's time back then."

Kendra raised an eyebrow, suddenly alert.

"And she's not exactly a friendly, forgiving person," Betty Lou continued.

"But you hired her. I would have thought—" She stopped. It wasn't her place to tell Betty Lou how to run her business or hire her waitresses.

Betty Lou shrugged. "Sue knows everyone and everyone knows Sue. They know what she's like. Sharp-tongued little bitch sometimes. I'm just glad she holds it in while she's here. From what I hear, she doesn't when she's at home."

Kendra filed that information away.

"Besides," Betty Lou went on, "with Artie locked up this time, it ain't like he's sending money home to pay the bills like he has in the past. Girl's gotta eat, have money to pay the light bill."

"Hmmm." Kendra let the subject drop. Betty Lou always was a soft touch, even back in high school. Hiring Sue was just another way of the community taking care of itself. She glanced up at her calmly drinking the tea. She wondered how much assistance Betty Lou had put in to opening the doors for Kendra to get back into the community.

"Got some fresh peach pie left," Betty Lou coaxed. "Can I interest you in a piece?"

"Peach pie? Now I think I might be able to handle that."

Kendra watched as Betty Lou went through the swinging door to the kitchen. Betty Lou knew she had a weakness for peach pie, one of the many things she had learned about Kendra over the previous year as she had become one of her regulars. Kendra knew that in a sense she was using Betty Lou but she also knew that gossip was its own currency. Betty Lou being able to share information about Kendra more than paid her back. A bad love affair, business problems, disenchantment with city life. Betty Lou had tried all the leading statements without coming right out and asking why Kendra had moved back. A direct question would have been rude, too invasive, but Kendra could be noncommittal and still be polite. Their conversations turned into sparring games.

Kendra went along with it because, well, that's where the gossip was, but she was also grateful. During her winter of cold shoulders, Betty Lou had been the only friendly voice in town.

Having someone glad to see you instead of like you'd tromped through the pig lot and forgotten to clean your boots before you came inside went a long way, even if you didn't mind living like a hermit. Nor did it hurt, Kendra considered, as Betty Lou returned to set the good-sized slice of thick, golden crust pie with peaches and peach juice oozing across the saucer in front of her, that she was a great cook.

She had breathed a sigh of relief with Betty Lou's explanation. She had been accepted, so the natural thought that followed was that getting information would be easy, at least easier. False assumptions. Easier maybe, but still not easy. However she did begin to see the community from the inside.

Walton's Corner was a small town dying. The lumberyard was closed now, so was the hardware store. The dress shop closed last winter, old Ms. Jackson just said she was tired. The barber shop/beauty shop was still open but only Thursday, Friday and Saturday, and it wasn't the same. She pulled around the corner grocery store that used to have the best fresh meats but now was a little more than a convenience store, no butcher, no wide selection of groceries. Oh yes, there had been changes. She just wasn't sure they were for the better. Soon Walton's Corner would be only a wide spot in the road where there used to be a small town.

She carefully parked in front of the grain elevator office, out of the line of traffic. The old Chevy pickup was good enough for farm errands, hauling feed, hay. She had had to baby it to get it through last winter, and winced at the thought of getting it through another one. Anything longer was unimaginable.

"Morning, Mac." Sam hung up the phone as she came into the office. "Ready for more chicken feed?"

"Yeah. Better add some bags of oyster shell or grit too, whatever you've got. They're beginning to lay more. Shells are awfully thin."

"Got 'cha." He pointed out the window to other trucks in line, long beds filled with corn. "Maybe thirty minutes."

"Sounds good. I'll be at the diner."

She crossed the street to the Kozy Korner.

"Morning, Mac," Betty Lou greeted her as she came in the door. "Coffee?"

Kendra nodded. Coffee was the commodity of the gossip trade here so she drank it whether she liked it or not. She made her way to the counter, nodding to other patrons.

"Hey, Mac. How much more you think you're gonna get out of that old truck?" one of them needled her as she went by.

She took it good-naturedly, it was a sign of her acceptance. "Ahhhh, it's only got a hundred and eighty-nine thousand miles on it. Just getting broke in good." She took a seat at the counter as Betty Lou brought the coffeepot and mug.

"Got some fresh apple dumplings this morning," Betty Lou suggested. "Feel like living dangerously?"

Kendra sighed. "You're killing my wardrobe." She hesitated. "Of course."

Betty Lou poured the coffee. "I'll bring it right back."

"Ahhh," Kendra said with obvious pleasure as Betty Lou set the plate in front of her. "Betty Lou, have I ever told you that you're a great baker?"

"No." The woman stood there with her hand on her hip. "It'd be wasted anyhow. Sue does all the baking now."

Well, that did take some of the glow off it. Kendra took a breath. "Sue's baking?" She looked down the counter where Sue was fussing at the coffeepot. "Mighty good, Sue," she said as Sue walked down the length of the counter.

Sue nodded to acknowledge her without so much as a glance at her. Betty Lou just shook her head and rolled her eyes. "She can pretty much bake anything," she commented in a low voice. "But sometimes I'd like to stick her in the oven."

Kendra decided not to comment.

Betty Lou took the opportunity to stand there for a bit, dish out some of her own gossip. "Artie never liked her working. I guess she got used to that, doing it because she wanted to and not because she had to. But it's not like he'll be bringing back a wad of money when he comes home this time."

"Oh? Is that what usually happened?" Kendra examined the flaky pastry.

"Rolls of it. Says he makes a killing working on the pipeline out west. Stuck in the middle of nowhere, no place to spend the money so he brings it all on back. Course sometimes I think he just took those jobs to get away from her. Sometimes she gets on my nerves so much I just want to smack her. I sure can't blame him if he does."

"Where he go?" Kendra asked casually.

Betty Lou shook her head. "Different places. Dakotas, wherever there was a pipeline. Driving a flatbed. Kansas, Nevada. Be gone a couple of weeks, maybe a month or so then back with the money."

Kendra had filed the information away. She had wondered how finances were in the Jeffers family. She'd heard the bank had foreclosed on the Jeffers family farm a while back. Now all that Artie owned outright was where the farm buildings set and the bottomland along the creek, nothing great for farming. The bottomland included the gravel pit and he made some money from it. He farmed Sue's family's farm, and, of course, had the small campground that Linda had brought into the marriage. There was some speculation over that because Indiana was not a community property state and Linda wasn't officially dead, but most of the community assumed it had passed to Artie. Kendra knew better.

And she had heard about the times Sue had had bruises. Artie was becoming known for having a short temper. Not a good sign. A sharp-tongued woman and a short-tempered man could make a deadly combination.

"Hey, Mac. You get any rain over your way yesterday?"

Kendra turned to see the short, heavily tanned, gray-haired man dressed in green work pants and shirt standing at the cash register paying his bill. His straw hat rested on the counter. "Not so much to speak of. Thundered and rumbled around but not enough to lay the dust. You?"

He gave a quick abrupt shake of his head as he picked up a toothpick from the holder. "Nary a drop." He picked up his hat. "Bad summer."

Kendra went back to her dumpling. The weather was always a topic with farmers, but there was gossip too. A thin line between sharing information and plain gossip: who was sleeping with who, who was having financial problems. She heard the griping about government regulations, sandbaggers, liberal attitudes, the media. Banking problems and interest rates always hit farmers hard, with their cycle of borrowing money to sow the crops, paying debts when the crops came in. The world was smaller, a lot of the old values were being lost, at least to hear some tell it. City problems were moving into the community. Some folks were adaptable; some were merely trying to hold on.

"How ya doing, Mac?" This heavy hand clapped her on her shoulder and she slowly turned her head. J. C. Harris slid onto the stool next to her. "What's good this morning? Anything?"

"Apple dumpling's good."

"Good. I'll have me a piece." He signaled for coffee and pie. "Driving through. Thought I saw your truck at the elevator. Saved me coming over to see you." He looked up as Sue set the coffee and pastry down in front of him. "Thanks." He dove right into it. "You still have your security contacts?"

Kendra shrugged. "More or less."

"Might have a project for you." She watched him take a quick look around the room. "Think you might be available for a meeting, say, Thursday night over at the Veterans of Foreign Wars?"

"I suppose so," Kendra answered in noncommittal tones even as she considered a mental list of possible projects. She wasn't sure she liked the idea of meeting with him but on the other hand, she wasn't going to turn it down.

The door opened with another jingle. "Hey, Mac! Your feed's loaded!"

She raised her hand in acknowledgment and shoved back her empty plate, set her coffee cup on it. "What time?"

"Oh, 'bout eight."

"I'll be there."

She considered the invitation as she crossed the road to pick up the truck. The elevator was getting crowded, farmers were lined up. Guess that was why they came and got her, wanted her little truck out of the way.

A project, she considered as she drove home. What kind? On the other hand, it was the first invitation she'd received to anything more than meetings open to the general public. Might be something.

"What do you think?" Linda asked.

Kendra shook her head. "No idea. My best guess would be something with security but as to what?"

"Think it's a test?"

"No doubt. Just don't know what kind."

* * *

She still had mixed feelings when she pulled into the VFW parking lot Thursday night. Stockton was waiting for her at the door of the cement block building to sign her in with guest privileges.

"Wondered whether you'd come," he greeted her.

"Doesn't hurt to listen."

"Ahh, but the invitation into the inner sanctum." He opened the door for her and she went down the hallway into the bar. "Ever been here before?" Kendra shook her head. "Back office. Through that door, down the hall. Last on the left."

Kendra ignored the speculative glances as she walked through the bar, nodding at those who greeted her. No one seemed surprised to see her and that made her even more curious. She found the office and knocked at the closed door.

Small office, three desks. Not exactly spit and polish but serviceable. Harris was there, she'd expected that. Johnny and Clyde were there. Johnny was always the hanger-on but Clyde was somewhat of a surprise.

Harris came around the desk to greet her, pulled out a chair for her. "Glad you could make it, Mac."

Kendra nodded as she took the seat. While she'd had good dealings with Harris, Johnny was a follower without much brains and Clyde carried a chip on his shoulder.

"You said you had a project I might be interested in."

"Got a security issue at the campground."

"A security issue." She almost laughed. "At the campground? What's there to be secure there?" She looked at all three of them but interesting ideas began to form in the back of her mind.

"Well, there's supplies, foodstuffs and all," Johnny began. "And then there's the guns."

Clyde cut him off. "You know we have guns and ammunition stored there for the shooting range."

Kendra turned to him. Not for the first time, it occurred to her that it would be a great cover. "So? I thought they'd be locked up and secure."

"Well, since Artie isn't there, and Sue is working away from the house, the place is empty sometimes. And you know those cabins, tucked in the trees here and there. Wouldn't be hard for someone to slip in there and do a little pilfering."

"No, I suppose not," Kendra said slowly although she privately thought the only ones in the area who would be pilfering were already members.

"And then that reporter on the tube," Johnny started but got cut off again.

"That Slusher woman, that reporter on WMIU," Clyde cut in again. "She had that story the other night about the group in Montana. Got busted for stockpiling weapons. Sorta made everyone sit up and take notice, look at us like we got an arsenal hidden away."

Kendra nodded. She had seen Robin's report. Even though she didn't always watch her nightly reports, she had caught that one. "Yeah, I can see why it would make folks nervous."

"We don't want to be a target for some break-ins just because someone gets the crazy idea we've got stuff hidden."

"You could just tell them," Kendra offered.

"Pshaw! You know they're not going to believe us if they already have a preconceived idea."

"The fact is," Clyde leaned forward, his elbows on his knees, "there's already talk around that we've been doing military training."

"That's illegal."

"Of course it is," Harris said. "All we're doing is training to keep folks in physical shape, woods craft, being able to deal with emergencies. Hell, everyone's doing it. Boy Scouts, Girl Scouts. Even read a poster about a women's group learning woods skills for moving back to the land. But we do the same damn thing and they look at us like we're planning a revolution."

Kendra considered it. "Got a point," she conceded. "All right. What'd you have in mind?"

"Perimeter check, secure buildings. Maybe a security system. Oh, and maybe a bug sweep as long as you're doing it."

Kendra nodded, accepting it at face value but she had the deep feeling there was something more. The list had all the makings of a test maybe. And did she want to pass?

But it did give her the opportunity to go over the entire campground. Artie would have had a heart attack if he knew she was doing this. That alone gave her immense satisfaction.

* * *

"It's still pretty land."

She started at Linda's voice, glanced at the woman beside her, appearing solid enough until she looked down at their feet. Linda just sort of faded away about midcalf. Rather than matching Kendra step by step through the fallen leaves, she floated alongside of her.

"Damn, I wish you wouldn't do that," Kendra muttered.

"I thought some day to turn this into a camp for children, you know, city kids who didn't get out to the country, or disabled kids, something like that."

They walked along the fence line for Kendra to do the perimeter check, across the back side of the campground that bordered the neighbor's cornfield, now just stubs sticking up in rows.

"Or maybe a spiritual retreat," Linda went on. "I had all sorts of ideas and dreams."

Kendra didn't know what to say. She knew about unrealized dreams but how does one console the dearly departed when everything is gone.

"I hate what he's done."

They paused at a steep ravine and Kendra looked for an easier way to cross without losing sight of the fence line. "It's not all bad," she consoled Linda. "People are learning things here, how to take care of themselves, how to survive in disasters."

"And how to take care of each other?"

"Yeah, well, some are learning better than others." She made her way down one side and up the other. By the time she worked her way up the steep slope, Linda was waiting for her. She gave her a look of exasperation.

"What can I say?" Linda spread her hands. "Some things are just easier now."

"Yeah, I see." Kendra pointed back to the fence. "Erosion's gonna leave a hole under the fence, a way in." She walked over to check it out. "You know, I can see you better here than I did before. You're stronger."

"My land," Linda said simply. She looked around as if searching for something. "Maybe. Maybe I'm here. What's left of me."

Kendra grimaced at that thought even though it was the truth. "Sure would help if you could remember."

"It's not the remembering, it's being unaware. Trauma." She rubbed the back of her head. "Wish I could tell you."

"So do I."

They walked along the perimeter, like they had so many other times in the past. Kendra was acutely conscious of the leaves turning, the crunch of the fallen leaves, the squirrels chattering. Someone in the neighborhood was burning leaves. For the first time in a long while, she was conscious with all her senses, the colors, the sounds of fall. She stripped off a blade of grass just to taste, to chew on, pulled off a handful of dry burnt-orange leaves from the soft maple and crumbled them.

"Life," Linda said. "Don't take it for granted."

"I don't."

"You did. You do now."

Kendra took a deep breath of the crisp air, looked up at blue skies, almost no clouds. They needed rain but the blue was intense. "Maybe I did. Maybe I still do. Just not as much."

"Don't. Don't waste a minute. Enjoy every breath."

"Easy to say," Kendra started and turned but Linda was gone.

"Damn, I wish she'd stop that," Kendra muttered again. She stood there, absently crumbling the dry leaves in her hand. Linda had always embraced life, lived in the present. And now she was gone. Kendra dropped the leaf crumbles and watched them fall to the ground. "Ash to ash, dust to dust," she murmured then dusted off her hands and started down the fence line again.

* * *

"What's the scoop?" Linda asked when Kendra got off the phone from setting up a meeting time with Harris.

Kendra shook her head. "Something. I just don't know what. I don't know if they're setting me up, or this was a test, or something else. Any one of those yahoos could have walked the fence. They're not stupid. Do they think I am?"

"Want an honest answer?"

Kendra picked up the small devices from where she had tossed them on her coffee table. "The question was rhetorical." She frowned, examining the small square objects again. "Amateurs. Sloppy work." She picked up another one, even smaller with the small antenna. "Except for this one." She examined it thoughtfully for a minute before she looked up at Linda. "It should be an interesting meeting this afternoon."

"What are you going to tell them?"

"Basic stuff, probably stuff they already know." She tossed the piece in the air, caught it. "Then again, maybe something they don't know."

* * *

They met this time at the campground in a corner of the community room, something Kendra really wasn't crazy about now that she knew about the bugs.

"Fence line across the back isn't secure. Erosion has cut under it. A body could duck under it and walk right in. Of course, you'd have to walk across two fields to get to the spot so it's not likely but it's not impossible either. And that back gate is so far out of sight an army could come in and camp down and you'd never know it."

Harris just looked at her but Johnny almost jumped.

"Not likely with Sue's mother just up the road but it wouldn't be difficult for a single person or a couple of folks to slip in without being noticed. I suggest a security camera on it, wireless. Pick it up down here."

Clyde and Harris made no comment, their expression didn't change. Kendra began to feel like she was in a poker game.

"For security, I'd suggest that fence repair of course. Add two strands of barbed wire. I'd suggest monitoring but it'd be difficult with no clear line of sight over that kind of terrain. If you really wanted security, maybe just during training, patrols might be necessary, but I don't know if you want to go that far." Still no response.

"Then there's this." She pulled the two bugs from her pocket. "Now I don't know whether this was supposed to be a test or not. If you were testing me, piss-poor job." She tossed them on the table in front of Harris. "Amateur, sloppy. The first one was at least, just under the desk. The second one was a bit better, more creative. Found it in the vent."

No one blinked and she looked from one to the other and Johnny squirmed.

"Anyone with an ounce of imagination could have done a better job. Generally when you're planting something, you can toss the first six spots you think of because anyone with any sense is going to think of them too."

"You think we did those to test you," Clyde said defensively.

Kendra shrugged. "Don't really care. It doesn't matter. I found them. Whoever planted them, well, frankly that's not my concern. However…"

She pulled the other one from her pocket, leaned forward, her elbows on the table. "I am curious about this one." She carefully examined it, holding it at eye level with Harris.

Strange, she considered. Neither Harris nor Clyde moved and yet she knew she had their full attention. However Johnny reached for the small flat piece before he dropped his hand at Clyde's glance.

"Now this one is interesting." She turned the small object over, looking at it again. "Very up to date, more sophisticated. Harder to detect. It can still be bought online, not difficult to get so it's not like it rules anyone out. But it's definitely out of the rank amateur class."

Harris finally leaned forward to take it from her. "Where'd you find it?"

"Now that's the fascinating part." She let him examine it. "In the door frame of the small meeting room." She glanced over her shoulder at the small room she knew was used for more private meetings. "You wanted the door replaced last spring, said that records you were concerned about were stored in there. Didn't you have to take the framing down to get the table in there?"

Harris slowly nodded.

"Seems like something was added when the door frame went back up."

"Who worked on that?" Clyde asked.

"Well, I guess we all did," Johnny answered. "Framing got busted, had to be replaced. Nicked the wall, and you," he pointed to Harris, "wanted it repaired and painted. Dented the door, re-sanded it and finished it. We must have all had a hand."

Kendra shook her head. "Not me. That was the week I went back to Carmel, took care of personal business." She sat back and watched them speculate.

"Find anything else?" Harris asked finally.

Kendra shook her head, pulled out her cell phone as they heard the soft burr of the vibrator. She checked it, closed it up again, laid it on the seat of the chair beside her. "Just what are you boys into?" she asked with what she hoped was the right amount of curiosity. They all looked at her. "Not that I really care, one way or the other. Well, I take that back." She sat back and crossed her legs. "I'm not real interested in getting into anything illegal."

"We're not doing anything illegal!" Harris growled, slapping the table with his open hand. "I'm tired of hearing that crap!"

"You can say it all you want." Kendra stared at him across the table, looked from one to the other and then back to him. "Someone doesn't believe you." She sat up and leaned over the table to take the bug back from Harris. She looked at it speculatively, with some appreciation. It really was a nice piece of work. "Or someone's making sure." She glanced at them speculatively and then abruptly got to her feet. "Oh, well, not my concern." She tossed the bug back to Harris who quickly caught it. "However, if I were you, I'd turn off the cell phones in the campground."

"Why?" Johnny protested. "Half the time, there ain't no signal anyway."

"GPS tracking," Harris answered automatically.

"But how are we going to communicate?" Johnny continued. Clyde silenced him with a look.

"And I'd kill the telephone extension at the far storage shed. Find an old wired system and string wire back there. Can't be tapped then. Set up a private phone system." She pushed both chairs back under the table, leaving her cell phone, hopefully without being noticed. "But I sure as hell hope you're not into anything deeper than what you say 'cause you sure are sloppy and going about it half-assed. You can count me out." She turned to leave.

"And how do we know you didn't just plant something yourself, make yourself look good?" Clyde demanded.

She turned back at the door, spread her hands, palms up, open and defenseless. "Hey, I'm all for survival, and yeah, dark days may be coming. But I'm not ready to bring more problems down on my head than what I've already got. I've done nothing for anyone to investigate me, except maybe hang around here, and I don't intend to be in anybody's spotlight." She fastened her gaze on Harris. "No one's," she repeated. "You got problems? I don't want them to be my problems. And I don't intend for them to be. Am I clear?"

Harris slowly nodded.

"See you around." And she left.

"Do you think they believed you?" Linda asked as they walked across the fields back to Kendra's house on the farm.

"A gamble," Kendra admitted as she stuffed her hands in her pockets.

They walked a little further. "I never asked. You didn't plant it, did you?"

"No. At least not that one." She walked on a bit. "Or the other one I found and didn't take."

There was a silence. "What are they doing? Or maybe I should ask, what do you think they're doing?"

Kendra shook her head as she examined the ground in front of her. "Nothing. At least nothing that I know of. I haven't seen or heard anything but then, I'm not exactly in that inner circle."

"So why the bug?"

Kendra sighed. "Maybe nothing. Maybe someone's just watching them, keeping tabs. Maybe it's not *them* per se but some*one*. But I don't know of anything anyone's done to warrant that kind of attention."

"So what do you think?"

Kendra shook her head. Big boys playing army games, she had thought. But someone was taking them seriously.

* * *

She waited. She kept to her usual habits—feed the chickens, gather the eggs, take some over to the Senior Center for the lunches they provided. Discover a roof leak in the shed. Stop in at the diner. Make small talk. Get recommendations for a handyman in the area. All the time, she wondered who would want to bug the militia's office. There were no rivals. To the best of her knowledge, there was no illegal activity.

That was the annoying part: *to the best of her knowledge*. Not for the first time, she thought about calling Robin. Having information to trade would be a great excuse.

She shook off the temptation. She didn't need any association with Robin. Whatever was going on with the militia wasn't her concern. Her concern was nailing Artie. Since Artie wasn't here, whatever and whoever was bugging the camp wasn't her concern. The security breach was just a way for her to get into the inner circle so she would be waiting for Artie when he got out of prison. She went about her business.

She began to think her derision about their security level might not have worked when she had a visitor. She saw Harris pull in when she was letting the chickens out. She waved but continued on her way. He met her at the gate to the chicken yard.

"You left this the other day." Harris held out her the cell phone.

"So I did." She took it and shoved it in her pocket. "Thanks for bringing it over." She didn't bother claiming it was an accident. She thought it'd be just the excuse to get back there; she didn't expect him to return it to her himself.

"You know," he started. "That was rather clumsy, just leaving it there."

"About as clumsy as your security test."

He didn't bother with any denial. "Have to start somewhere."

Kendra started for the house. "I suppose so." Harris fell in step beside her. "So," she asked, "who's bugging you?"

"Good question. I thought you might have an answer."

Kendra shook her head. "No idea. Equipment like that can be bought anywhere and the stuff that's out there is just as good, sometimes better than what the government buys. And sometimes it's the same source." She reached the back door. "So I guess the question needs to be turned around. What have you been doing that's worth being bugged?"

"Nothing."

Kendra paused, her hand on the door handle. "Like I told you the other day, I don't want to be drug into any problems.

All I'm interested in is building my little corner of the world in order to survive. Nothing illegal. Nothing to bring anything down on my head."

He spread his hands. "Swear it, doing nothing illegal."

Kendra searched his face, his gaze direct as she weighed his words. Her instincts said to believe him. Admittedly he was as paranoid as anyone else in the group but as her dad used to say, just because you're paranoid, doesn't mean they're not out to get you. Even now, as she reflected on the past year here, she still wasn't sure about Harris. In some ways, she had even come to like the guy. She didn't exactly trust him but she sort of liked him. Besides, he was the one in charge.

"Time for a cup of coffee?"

"Don't mind if I do."

He followed her through the back porch into the kitchen.

"I just took a cake out of the oven. Care for a piece?"

"You know, I don't understand you," Harris said after the cup of coffee was poured and the cake sliced.

"Good."

"No, that's not good." He sat back in the chair and watched her move around the kitchen as she mixed up the glaze for the cake. "You come back here but from all I hear, you were hell-bent to get out once upon a time."

"Once upon a time I was young, thought I knew everything. Thought there had to be better places, and thought I had the answer."

"And now?"

"Now, less is more. Roots are deep. Security is an illusion."

"You had a successful business."

"Built on two things: preying on people's fears and an increasingly dangerous society."

"So?"

Kendra shrugged. "People in cities seem to have lost their ability to take care of themselves. Think food comes on grocery shelves magically. Think government or someone else is going to take care of their every little problem." She grimaced. "Think every problem can be solved if you throw enough money at it."

"Money helps."

"True, but it's the aid, not the answer."

"So you came back." He shoved the plate back. "You know, even then, I really didn't think you'd stay the distance."

"Really?" She poured him another cup of coffee. She still didn't drink the stuff by choice but she always kept the pot on. And she kept a richer blend of coffee than what the campground bought.

He pulled the sugar bowl forward to add sugar to the coffee and stir. "Most folks get into this and are real gung-ho. For a while. Then it gets expensive. Or they don't have the time. Or it's just easier to run down to the supermarket, the corner grocery store. Or Walmart."

Kendra pulled out the chair and sat down. "Lots of things happen in life. You have to prioritize."

"But, damn it, shouldn't preparing to survive be a priority?"

"It should, if you think something's going to happen. It's hard to prepare for that nebulous someday or when something might happen. You know the old adage, 'It's hard to remember the objective is to drain the swamp when you're up to your ass in alligators.'"

Harris shook his head, staring into the coffee cup. "We had a good turnout in the spring."

"We had flooding and tornadoes. Clear dangers. Concrete. We got some in who stayed."

"But a lot didn't."

Kendra laughed. "But look what they learned while they were here. That first aid course. Taught them there were lots of things they already had that could be used for survival. Sold some storm shelters. Folks put in safe rooms. We made inroads."

"Not enough, not enough."

Kendra leaned back in the painted Windsor chair. "Hell, man, you can't save everyone."

He gave her a sharp look from under thick, dark brows. "No, you're right. There's a limit to what we can do." He paused there and Kendra could almost hear what he didn't say. *Some people are expendable.*

She met his gaze squarely. "All you can do is put the message out." She shrugged. "You can't hold their hand the entire time."

"No, you can't."

With that conversation, she seemed to have stepped inside the organization, at least as far as Harris was concerned. He began to stop by more frequently, presenting argument upon persuasive argument.

"The system is failing," he argued. "Just look around you. I know you've got eyes, you can see, Mac."

Kendra shook her head, still resisting. "You've got to trust the system. There are checks and balances."

"No." He almost exploded. "The system is failing. Corporations putting big money into elections. Lobbyists holding court. The middle class just being taxed out of existence. Big money holds the influence and they use it." He glared at Kendra, his eyes dark with intensity. "Just look at the justice system. The courts are overloaded. If you can afford a rich lawyer or you know someone, you can get off. A technicality. A loophole. Doesn't matter. Everyone knows you did the crime and you still get off."

Kendra shook her head, not looking at him. He was too close to arguments she wanted to wage. Her heart rate increased. Did he suspect why she was here?

"Mac, I know you know," he said with intensity. "You know someone who's committed a crime. Dead to rights, you *know* he's done it. But is he in jail? No, he's free as a bird, walking around because of some quirk in the law that lets him get away with murder."

Kendra froze, almost afraid to look at Harris, her heart almost stopping at the idea he knew her true purpose in joining.

"We all know someone. Maybe it wasn't murder." Harris went on. "Maybe it was just drugs or robbery or something. But it was something they got away with. And if it was a corporation, well, we know they're just too big to bring down. And banks, just look at the mortgage fiasco. Did anyone go to jail over that?"

He went on and on about different things, and Kendra began to breathe again. He didn't know, it was just a generalization. A shot in the dark. But it left her heart pounding and gave her an alternative she had not considered before.

"Are you saying we need to do away with the system, become judge and jury ourselves?" she asked in an emotionless voice.

"Something needs to be done," he stated firmly. "What kind of society are we if privileged individuals can flout the law and get away with it? How can we say we have equal justice if certain ones can escape punishment?"

Kendra watched him with new detachment. He sat down, shaking his head, reaching for his coffee cup as Kendra contemplated what he had said.

"The system worked once upon a time, but it's failed us now. It's broken." He stared into the coffee cup. "It just makes me sick to think of all those victims who never get justice. Makes me ashamed."

Kendra swallowed, so many thoughts chasing each other through her mind. Artie's enraged face when she last saw him, the slow realization that Linda wasn't just missing, all the gossip about Sue's bruises, her long stay in the hospital, the quiet talk about the first wife who went missing, Artie's increasingly short temper. Where was justice for Linda, for Sue? No evidence, nothing but a ghost who wanted justice.

That night after Harris left, Kendra got out the Glock she had acquired after her proficiency test. She had avoided using it, even during the trials and gun courses they had set up over the summer season. She was still wary of having it accessible during one of her black moods. Harris's words, his argument, had hit a chord. Linda's appeal for justice, her search for Artie, Harris's arguments about a failed system. They all came together and Kendra knew what she was going to do. The system had failed Linda and how many others, but Artie wouldn't get away with it. She would confront him, challenge him. She would make sure that he paid. An eye for an eye, a death for a death. But not before she found out where he buried her.

* * *

Kendra sat at her desk in the bunker and made her plans with new purpose. She didn't have to worry about finding Artie; she knew where he was. All she had to do was be prepared when he returned. If the legal system couldn't bring him to justice, then she could. She had time to do what she needed to do.

She needed to improve her marksmanship. Okay, she could practice daily on the shooting range. She made her "to do" list as she listened to the taped conversations from the campground via the bug she had left in place. Macho bullshit, talking about what they would do, could do, what should be done in their opinion. It was a regular pattern, the macho stuff, then the farming information and then it would be basketball. She could listen to all their garbage, her ears attuned to any mention of Artie.

"You know," she thought it was Johnny. He and Steve sounded so much alike. "Indiana high schools have the biggest gyms in the country, seven thousand capacity. At least."

"Where'd you get that? Off the Internet?"

"Artie was talking about it one day. Said the only one in the top ten besides Indiana spots was Dallas."

"Sure beats the little gym we had, doesn't it?"

"God, when those big schools'd come play us!" Johnny laughed. "They do a fast break and run into a brick wall six inches outside the line. Slowed them down right fast."

"Ahh, those were the days. What did you think of Central Friday night? That Knight kid's gonna end up going pro. He's already as good as the college guys."

She absently wondered where Artie went when he wasn't here, besides in jail. He took frequent trips, a dropped comment that Sue never seemed to have an accident while Artie was gone. Betty Lou said something about working on a pipeline out west. Now that would be an interesting thing to follow up on. What she knew of the pipelines was that they took months, not weeks to build. She pulled down a calendar and began a time line.

"Finding out anything?" Linda asked.

"Not much. How computer literate is Artie?"

"Not much in my day, but who knows now? He did remark one time that it was a great way to get information without anyone looking over your shoulder. And that there was all sorts of information available."

"Love to see his browsing history." Kendra pulled down her notes and went through references as to his travel. "His hunting trip in November?"

"Like clockwork."

"So what made him come back as you were leaving?" She looked up when Linda didn't answer.

"I don't know. He was just suddenly there."

Linda faded a little. She did that, Kendra noted, when Kendra pushed. She went back to her notes. After a few minutes, she was able to ask casually. "Anyone know you were leaving?"

Linda shook her head. "No. I didn't say anything to anyone. I even canceled a repair job with Frog, afraid I'd let something slip." She rested her forehead against her drawn up knees.

"Head hurt?" Kendra asked automatically. About half the time now, she was forgetting Linda wasn't really there, at least not in a physical sense.

"Remembered pain." Linda raised her head and laughed. "One thing nice about now: no physical pain." Her smile faded. "No physical joy either. Trade-offs."

Kendra threw down her pen. "Wish I knew where he went when he wasn't here. Betty Lou says he always came back energized and had wads of money."

"Can't say." Linda shook her head.

Kendra got to her feet, went through all her shutdown procedures. One nice thing, no one knew of this bunker. At least she was gambling no one remembered. She checked the exit before she left, not that she expected anyone there. Habit.

"You coming?"

"Where are you going?"

"Shopping."

"I think I'll stay here."

* * *

She had a surprise when the handyman showed up. She saw the old battered pickup pull in and she wondered who it might be. The vehicle was about the same age as her vintage pickup and she idly wondered how many miles this truck had on it. The driver took his time getting out and when he walked around the vehicle, she understood why he had been so slow. Heavyset, yet his overalls hung on him like he had once been heavier. Even the red plaid shirt looked too big on him. He paused at the front of the vehicle to look over the buildings, probably assessing how much work there was and how much to charge. Then he saw her on the porch and started across the yard toward her, walking with a slight limp.

"Ms. McKenna?" he greeted her when he got close enough.

"Yes."

"Sam at the elevator said you was looking for a handyman, needed to do some building repairs? My name's Grayson—"

"Frog?" Kendra stepped off the porch at the sound of the deep, hoarse voice, like he had something caught in his throat and was talking around it.

He stopped. "Yes?" he drew out as he squinted at her.

Kendra was already holding her hand out. "You don't remember me? You don't remember how Linda and I were under your feet constantly as you built those cabins for her mom?"

"Kendra? You that skinny little geeky kid that Linda pulled around all the time?"

Kendra laughed as she took hold of his hand. "The very same."

"Well, I'll be." He stepped back to look at her, and shook his head. "Never would have knowed you."

"Well, except for your voice, I don't think I would have recognized you. It's been a long time." She refrained from saying that he looked like a shade of his former self. Time changed lots of things.

They spent some time getting reacquainted, and for a change, Kendra didn't feel like she was walking on eggshells as she talked to someone from the past. Now he was still doing building work. It was Frog who finally brought back the subject of work.

"Sam was saying you had some work you needed doing?"

Kendra nodded. "I've had a leak in the shed, like to get it fixed before winter."

Once she showed him the leak, the damaged wall, and outlined what she wanted done, he nodded. Always one to do the figuring in his head, Kendra was a bit surprised when he pulled out a pad and pencil to write things down but she was patient. She was more confident in having the work done by someone she knew, and if he was still getting recommendations, his work was still good.

Two days later he was back with the lumber and the tools in that rattletrap pickup. Kendra took him iced tea after about an hour, finding him sitting on the tailgate.

"Ain't as young as I used to be," he said in apology. "Need more breaks."

"No problem," Kendra joined him on the tailgate. "I don't have a timeline."

Company felt good, someone to talk to a bit, nothing serious and no one she really had to watch her words with. His wife had died some years before and while he might be old and decrepit, he was a sharp dresser when he dressed up, was thought to have a bit of money in the bank and was known to like the ladies. For his age category, he was thought to be quite a catch, and to Kendra's surprise, he was up sharp on local gossip.

"All them ladies," he said when she expressed surprise. "Bringing me something to eat, inviting me to Sunday dinner. I can't remember the last meal I had alone in my own house." He shook his head as Kendra laughed. "And talk. You wouldn't believe the things they tell me, about their kids, their grandkids. You know the real reason I still do all these little jobs?"

"What's that?"

"So I can have some time alone."

Kendra laughed. Here she had come out to join him thinking he might like the company. She hopped off the tailgate and dusted off her hands.

"Now don't you get any ideas about leaving," he said, giving her a look. "Nice to sit down and talk to someone who doesn't have any designs on me."

"Me?"

"Not in this lifetime. No, I saw how you and Linda carried on. Figured you'd never marry."

Kendra sobered as Frog shook his head. Of all the people she had thought might say something, Frog was not one of them.

"Didn't figure she would either. Don't think she would have except to make Claudia feel like she was taken care of." He looked up at Kendra. "Could never figure it out. Claudia was one strong woman, able to take care of herself, bragged she didn't need no man to take care of her. But she sure was hell-bent—excuse me, that slipped out." He stopped.

"Don't worry about it, I've heard worse," Kendra accepted his apology. She didn't want the conversation to stop. Here was someone who saw them then, knew them. "Hell-bent on what?"

"Let's say she was real determined for her Linda to get married, have someone there to take care of her." He met Kendra's gaze straight on. "Linda didn't need no one to take care of her."

"No, she didn't." Kendra wasn't sure how the conversation had turned this way.

Frog set the glass down on the tailgate, got to his feet. Break was over, he was going back to work. "A mistake. From the get-go. And she knew that pretty quick. And she was fixing to rectify that."

Kendra followed him into the shed. "What do you mean, 'rectify that'?"

He shook his head and Kendra knew from experience of long ago, he wouldn't say any more. Not today at least. But there would be other days.

* * *

Kendra hadn't forgotten the private phone system she had suggested to Harris. She wasn't about to lose the toehold she had into the group. After few weeks of searching, going from one small town to another, hunting antique and junk stores, Kendra finally found what she was looking for. Outside of Delphi, two counties over, was an old country store, weathered and with a front porch missing a few boards. In the back room, she spotted the wooden boxes with hand cranks and hooks on the side.

"Do they work?"

The wiry old man shook his head. "Don't rightly know. Bought it when the old exchange was taken down. Got a switchboard back here somewhere if you're interested." He turned and looked over the piles and stacks of boxes. He stood there for a minute, scratching his head. Finally he nodded and went off down the cluttered aisle with Kendra in tow.

She nodded as she squatted down before the small board the old man pulled from behind some boxes. "Yeah, I'll take it. The whole shebang."

* * *

"Now what do we want that for?" Johnny whined as Harris gazed speculatively at the pile of antique telephones on Kendra's worktable. "We got cell phones."

"Which can be picked up by radio frequency," Kendra said patiently. "Install these at the back gate, even at the house, the main cabin, wherever you want. Private system. On private land. Can't be tapped into."

"They work?" was all Harris asked.

"They will. You got the manpower to string the wire?"

Harris nodded. "Yeah, we'll get it done."

So that was done.

"Did you bug it?" Linda asked.

Kendra looked up in injured pride.

"Sorry I asked."

She got the security camera installed, did weekly sweeps of the buildings for any additional bugs and reported nothing new. Hers, a state-of-the-art model that transmitted in bursts, would be hard to detect but what puzzled her was the second suspicious bug she had left in place hadn't been moved. She took care not to speak in its vicinity. And she waited.

Frog continued to come over even after the shed was repaired. There was other work to be done. Kendra liked the old man, and besides he was part of her good memories with Linda.

"Not the man he used to be," Linda commented as she watched him.

"No, about half. Remember when we used to hold our breath when he went up on the roof? Said he was testing the weight."

Linda gave a small smile. "Long time ago."

Kendra had to agree. A long time and a lifetime. She wondered about the changes he had seen. She asked him that one day when they were sitting on his tailgate again, drinking iced tea.

"Remember when Linda's place was the Donaldson place," he said. "Then when her dad died, Claudia couldn't keep up with the farming. No one wanted to lease it because of the creek flooding. She read in some magazine about campgrounds and she decided that was what she was going to do." He looked off in the distance, remembering another time. "And then later Linda was going to expand, talked to me about doing some more building. Wanted a little chapel, reception hall. Thought it'd be good for country weddings. That pretty spot overlooking the valley. You know the one I mean?" He turned to Kendra.

She nodded. She knew the spot. She and Linda had sat there for many an hour, for the scenic beauty, while they talked about what they wanted to do with their lives. Oh, Linda had been full of plans.

Frog shook his head. "Something happened." He looked down at the ground. "She was just beginning to pull the plans together, you know how she did. Had to have everything nailed down."

"Yes, she was a planner."

"Then she called me up, canceled me coming out here, said it wasn't necessary anymore. She'd changed her mind. Wanted to know how much she owed me, she'd drop a check in the mail." He paused. "Got the check same day she was reported missing."

Kendra caught her breath. This was something she'd never heard.

"Told Ms. Sue that I was probably the last one to talk to her. Really upset me, it did."

"What'd Sue say?"

"Said I'd probably better not say anything. She didn't see how it was important, how it could help."

"So you didn't."

"No. Just said she wasn't there when I went to meet with her, just like we had planned."

"No one talked to you?"

"Just about the meeting, nothing about before." He looked at Kendra as if for reassurance. "I always felt bad about that, you know. It might have shed some light on what happened."

"When did you tell Sue?"

"I was working over at her mama's place, fixing a ramp after she broke her hip. Linda called me there."

Kendra frowned. This was new information. Sue might have recorded it in her notes but Kendra didn't remember it. She needed to check on that. "And Linda turned up missing the next day?"

"Well, that's what they pieced together. Wasn't really sure until her man came back two days later. Someone saw her at the station gassing up her car."

"Hmm." Something else to check on.

"You don't suppose," Frog started tentatively.

Kendra shook her head. "I don't know, Frog. Might have been important, might not. Hard to say now."

"I just feel real bad about it sometimes, wonder if it would have made a difference." He set his glass down and stood up. "You think about things like that when you're old, wonder if you should have done something different."

Kendra also got to her feet. "Sometimes you do that before you get old, Frog. My grandma always said not to look back. You can't change what's been done."

"Guess not." He shuffled off to the fencerow and Kendra watched him.

"Course I never much followed that myself," Kendra muttered to herself. She turned to go to the house. Had she kept all those notes at the house or had she stored them at the shelter? She needed to reread them.

* * *

She slowly made inroads back into the community. While some things had changed, not everything had. Most of them had acquired a live and let live attitude but there were a few holdouts, like Sue, like Ross, a guy she went to school with, one who hassled her then and sounded like he might like to continue. But she had changed, and was not intimidated.

"You know," he said to her one day when they were on the shooting range. She went there frequently now. "You just don't strike me as one who just goes against the grain."

She reloaded the Glock she was beginning to feel comfortable with and paused to examine the sighting with slow deliberation. "You mean like being a dyke in a queer-baiting community?" She frowned at the paper target; she was not improving at the rate she wanted, but she was improving. She glanced at Ross.

Ross stepped back, suddenly wary. "So why'd you move back?"

Kendra turned back to the targets, back to the job at hand. "Too crowded in the city; too many problems. Regulations every time you turn around. Can't do this; can't do that; need a permit." She frowned in concentration. "More freedom here away from the major population."

"Getting crowded around here, new people moving in all the time. All kinds of people."

"Well, if I can't find what I want here, maybe I'll go west. More space. Less hassle." She gave him a look at made him think she might be thinking he was part of the hassle. He went back to his shooting and so did she.

Her apparent change in attitude was duly noted. Harris began to depend on her efficiency as he stopped by more often for coffee and pound cake. He began to talk about the other members.

"We've got that gun course coming up and I need to get back and see what those yahoos are doing." He finished up his coffee and pushed back the cup. "Sure wish you'd been in charge of that. It'd gone much smoother."

"Put me around Johnny and a gun and I might be too tempted." Kendra got to her feet. "All he wants to do is win a pissing contest. You need to put someone else in charge."

"Yeah, it's going to come to that. Although Johnny's a good shot."

And easily influenced. And eager to believe all his failures are because someone, anyone, is out to get him. Bad combination.

Men like Johnny made her glad someone like Harris was in charge. Not that Harris was conventional by any means but he appeared more sensible and grounded than some of the others. Russians? Too unreasonable. Black? Well, there are always some who were convinced about a race war. Muslim terrorists? Kendra didn't think it likely around here. If she was going to worry about anyone, it was domestic terrorists, those who wanted to bring down the government, and let them govern themselves.

She had to give Harris credit. Kept them focused on training, on the "what-if's", on discipline. She heard muttered comments about him being about to "talk the talk but couldn't walk the walk." She wondered what would happen if he wasn't in charge.

"There's always hot-heads," he told her over one of their coffee chats. "Just need to let 'em let off steam, let them wind down. Most of the time, all they are is hot air. Like kids with too much energy."

"And the other times?" Kendra asked.

He grimaced and looked away. "Then we got a problem." He frowned and Kendra wondered if he might be thinking of Artie. She let the moment pass. Harris was opening up, confiding more and more. She'd be patient. After all, he did say "we."

She had to admit, Harris kept the group useful. They were slowly gaining respect in the community. The group had been

Johnny-on-the-spot during last spring's flooding. Those with boats rescued folks living along the creek, which had flooded to make a small river, and the river, which had overflowed its banks. Sandbagging, organizing. Yeah, they had done their bit. Helping set up roadblocks in flooded roads, assisting the county sheriff's office, although there had been some discussion as to who had really done the work and who had been there first.

Still she was impatient as she crossed days off the calendar.

"Patience, dear heart, patience," Linda counseled repeatedly.

"This waiting is terrible. I feel like I'm just spinning my wheels!"

"Look how far you've come. Harris trusts you. You have access to almost everything. You're piecing things together."

"Yeah. Sure. And every day, I worry that they're going to find me."

"You're being paranoid."

"Just because you're paranoid, doesn't mean they're not out to get you," Kendra quoted.

They both laughed as she realized it was her dad's favorite quote. Kendra tossed paperwork on her desk and shoved her chair back. She realized she hadn't laughed for a long time. Linda moved to the top of the bookcase.

"Yes, Dad was paranoid, wasn't he?" Kendra put her head back and closed her eyes. "I feel like nothing's happening and yet, something's coming."

"Probably so," Linda agreed. She paused. "Everything's likely to change when Artie returns."

"Well, that won't be for a while. Gonna be May or June before he gets out." She turned her head to look at the calendar where she had been marking the days off until Artie's release date. "I don't know if I can go through this for another winter. I knew it would be slow; I just didn't think it would be this damn slow."

"Things can change, sometimes quickly."

Kendra caught Linda's warning tone. "You know something I don't know?"

Linda shook her head. "Just a warning, dear heart. Don't get settled into any timeline. Stay flexible."

"Flexible."

At least she knew what her priority was and frankly, she didn't give a crap if the world came to an end. Hers might. She had already decided that.

* * *

Harris hated paperwork and Kendra had taken it over slowly until she realized she had it all. "When the hell did I become shipping and receiving?" Kendra growled one day in early December to Stockton when he brought her invoices.

"Since you're the only one who could find the paperwork and keep it on track."

Kendra flipped through the invoices. She still had an uneasy feeling about Stockton. Not bad, just something. He was always hanging around her workspace, not pointedly, but with a good excuse. But that was what they felt like, excuses. "I didn't join this damn group only to become the glorified secretary."

"Orderly clerk," Stockton corrected. "Besides, it puts you in the middle of everything, get to know everything. Didn't you ever see how important Radar was on *M*A*S*H*?"

"Only in reruns and that was how many wars ago?" When she looked up, he was looking past her at the television set where a promo for Robin's evening newscast was on the screen. He didn't move. Instead he took out the cigarette pack from his pocket. "Nice-looking woman, isn't she?"

Mac turned slightly to look at him, considering what he meant. She made a noncommittal sound.

"I myself prefer a little more curves," he went on, "a little more meat on the bones. What about you?"

"Too intense," Kendra said carefully.

"Artie really can't stand her," Stockton went on. He shook his head. "That man is a loose cannon." He glanced around to see if anyone was close enough to listen. "Did you know he got picked up for stalking her?"

Kendra turned to him questioningly. That was one story she hadn't heard.

"She talked about the Patriot Movement as a fringe element, so far out that the kooks didn't even claim it. Artie's real taken with the Patriot Movement, so he was pretty annoyed with her. Got so bad, she got a restraining order on him."

"What did he do?"

"Stalked her, parked outside her house. Left a note that she could be floating in the Wabash."

"When was this?" Kendra sounded bored but Artie stalking Robin sure would explain why her request for security had been so urgent, and why she had been so insistent it be dependable.

"About two years ago." Stockton leaned against the column, looked out over the compound. "Didn't go over well with him but he dropped back. Then during some special report she had on, he shot the hell out of his television." He shook his head. "Guy's got some weird ideas." He ground his cigarette out in the can of sand by the step.

"Artie's never been known for being levelheaded," Kendra replied, still watching the television. *That's the understatement*, she thought as she watched Robin on the tube. *Wonder what else happened you never mentioned?* she asked as Robin signed off. But now she understood a whole lot more. Robin had used her.

"You know," Stockton said casually, "I heard he may be getting out early."

The meaning didn't register right away with Kendra and then she looked up at Stockton to see if he was kidding. "Is that so?"

"Heard that he may be getting out for Christmas." He seemed to be watching her for a reaction.

"Guess he's been a real good boy in there. I bet Sue must be looking forward to that."

"Guess so." Stockton zipped up his coat. "Heard they're letting some out early on good behavior, something about overcrowding and a January one deadline."

"Rumor or something firm?"

"Pretty firm from what I hear. Well, got to get back."

Kendra sat back in the chair after Stockton left. If Artie got out early, her entire time frame would be speeded up.

"I'll be damned," Linda said from her perch on top of the file cabinet. "What'd you think about that?"

"Things are progressing nicely—as Travis would say."

* * *

Kendra sat in front of the woodstove with her ever-present cup of hot tea. There was this uneasy feeling in the pit of her stomach, something just beyond her grasp. Something was wrong. Artie could ignite people. Just like his action had rallied the basketball team to victory so many years ago, he could get these guys together to form a team and go where he wanted. The question was, where did he want to go?

Stockton was a puzzle. On one hand, he fit right in with the rest of the gang, and yet, there was something. He disappeared every once in a while. Harris said he had assignments. Yet, there was something. He funneled information to her, like the piece about Artie maybe getting out early. Was she being warned? Or was she being set up? So if there was a leak, she would be blamed?

God, she was tired of waiting. And it really didn't matter what any of the others were planning, if they were planning anything or just letting off hot air. Her sights were on Artie. And Christmas was coming. And then January. And with a little luck, if Stockton had heard right, so was Artie.

CHAPTER FOURTEEN

Kendra sat at her kitchen table, nursing a cup of hot tea, watching it snow. The weather had been warm, rainy, dashing everyone's hopes for a white Christmas. Then a cold front had moved in, freezing rain, sleet and now snow. Six to eight inches were predicted. Temperatures were taking a nosedive when the wind chill was factored in. A full-blown January winter storm watch.

Nothing else was happening.

Kendra had been at the farm for a year and a half. What had she accomplished? Not much. Oh, she had the farm back in order, and she had to admit, she was proud of her self-sufficiency. Just the same, she'd be glad to get back to going out to lunch at Sweeney's and maybe even have Claymore's deliver some meals.

But her objective had been to nail Artie, and she hadn't accomplished much in that. She hadn't been able to break the alibi about his hunting trip. She thought her presence might bait him into making a mistake but nothing yet. She was going to have to confront him. That might goad him into flying into a rage and giving something away.

She could tell herself that she'd had the bad luck to move back just as he went to jail but that was a small consolation. At least it had given her the time to establish her credibility with the MMU before Artie was released.

"You're getting there," Linda pointed out.

"Am I?" And even as she spoke to Linda, she wondered if she hadn't wandered over the edge.

"You could have never been in this deep if he'd been here," Linda pointed out. "He would have fought you tooth and nail, just on general principles. With him being gone…"

Kendra poured what was left of the cold tea down the sink. She had always thought she could manage living alone. Now she was having second thoughts. She wanted this quest over; she wanted her life back. She just wasn't sure what her life was any more. She wasn't sure she cared.

Christmas had been a revelation. She thought it safe enough to go back to Carmel but what was it Thomas Wolf had said: at Ellen's, everyone was there. Everyone greeted her. But she'd been gone over a year. She was the one on the outside. Again. Only this time it was from her own community.

Ellen always threw an open house at Christmas. It started out as a potluck for those who had no family, no partner and didn't want to spend Christmas alone. Over the years it had evolved into a catered buffet of food, a wet bar, people coming and going from other celebrations but wanting to stay in touch with their community. Depending on the time, it could be fairly empty or a crush of people.

The house was bright with lights, there was the huge Christmas tree in front of the picture window, garlands and decorations throughout the house. From the manner of dress, casual to almost formal, Kendra could guess who was just hanging out and who was either going to or coming from other celebrations. She guessed her dress of black pants and red shirt was Christmassy enough but she felt strangely out of touch.

Conversations didn't help when Carla complained about her street not cleared for two whole days—just because she was a couple of blocks off the main drag. And Marcie complained that they had lost power the week before. It was just for a couple of hours but so inconvenient. She listened to the talk about the newest phone upgrade, the largest television and she was uncomfortable with the materialism of Christmas this year. It had never bothered her before.

In fact, Kendra just had a hard time identifying with much anymore. The worst of it was that she knew they hadn't changed. She had.

The thing that hadn't changed was Robin.

Kendra caught sight of her at the other end of the living room when she went to the bar. She hadn't expected to see her, it had never occurred to her that Robin might be here, so when she looked up at the flash of red at the other end of the room, she was unprepared. Robin stood there, half turned away as she was talking to someone so Kendra could see her profile. The red sheath draped against her without being too snug. The cowl neckline, the long sleeves stopping just above her wrist, made it a very simple dress. And very striking. She guessed either Robin had come from some dinner or maybe going to some function. Maybe even both.

Kendra was hit with a longing that was almost physical and for the moment she just stood there rather than moving away. When Robin looked up and their eyes met, she didn't know how to respond. She ended up merely nodding in acknowledgment and then had moved out of Robin's line of sight. She wasn't sure she wanted to talk to her, wasn't sure what she could say to her after their abrupt ending. It was Robin who crossed the room to speak with her.

"Haven't seen you around," Robin greeted her with a cool politeness but she stood in front of Kendra as if to prevent her escape.

"Haven't been around," Kendra had replied as she leaned back against the wall and crossed her arms. Now if she could only calm her pounding heart. Robin still looked as good as ever, maybe even better. Or maybe it was just because Kendra hadn't seen her like this in so long. The dress was jersey, soft to touch Kendra remembered. The diamond studs in her ears denoted her jewelry to impress, the matching necklace of three stones the same. She didn't know who Robin had dressed to impress but it certainly was doing its job on her.

"You're not at Abatis anymore." It was a statement, not a question.

Kendra shook her head, unable to find words right away. "Took a sabbatical."

"Oh, yes, to get the farm on a self-sufficient level," Robin said archly. She had a gleam in her eye as if she knew what effect she was having on Kendra. Clearly she had been talking to someone and Kendra wondered whether it was Peg or Travis who had given that story. "How's it going?"

"Pretty good," Kendra had answered, relieved enough to have the focus turned to the farm. "Not completely there, but close."

Robin nodded and waited but Kendra said nothing. She didn't know what she could say as she drank in the sight of Robin. For their affair being something with no strings attached she was feeling a tug of longing that was unexpectedly strong. She hadn't seen Robin in over a year and she had to bite her tongue to keep from blurting out—I'm sorry. Can we go back?

She knew she couldn't, not without throwing away months of work, not when she was this close.

"I see you're still working on the militia story," she said in a quiet voice, having to say something.

"No reason to drop it," Robin retorted.

Kendra swirled the drink in her glass, debating with herself. "You know," she said in careful and deliberate tones, "Artie's scheduled to be released any day now." She had a strong protective feeling but she couldn't do any more than this.

Robin blinked and took a breath but said nothing. Her quickly masked expression was enough to tell Kendra she hadn't known but the arch amusement was gone.

"I thought you might be interested." Kendra took a deep swallow, wondering if she was tossing away months of work. "On several levels," she added.

"I thought…" Robin started.

"This overcrowding law takes effect one-one. Gossip says he's being released."

She knew she'd made a mistake as soon as she said "gossip," and Robin's quick look confirmed it. Kendra's steady gaze stopped anything else Robin might have wanted to ask but she could read the speculation.

"I see," Robin said quietly as she turned remote and protective.

Probably not, Kendra thought, but then again, maybe so.

Robin nodded. "It was good seeing you again. I hope you're successful in your endeavor." She lifted her glass and then she left.

Kendra closed her eyes for a moment. She wondered if she had given too much away. The last thing she needed was Robin on her tail. Although, she considered as she watched Robin move through the party, there might be some good points to that.

"You all right?" Ellen stopped by to ask her. She opened her eyes to see the flaming redhead in front of her.

"So far." She pushed off from the wall. "Nice party, Ellen. Sorry about you and Stella."

Ellen shrugged. "Too much drama. I'm getting too old for that. Now tell me what you're doing? Quiet on that little piece of farm you've hidden yourself away on?"

Kendra filled in enough to give Ellen a story, all the time wanting to ask questions herself. Her circle of friends was changing, moving on without her. While it was her choice, she still had regrets. As she watched Robin at the other end of the dinner table filled with old friends and Christmas joy, she knew what this had cost her. Maybe not a relationship but certainly the possibility of one.

* * *

So far, she thought as she stood at her own kitchen sink, watching the snow move in, this move to the country had cost her more than what it had paid—being able to warn Robin about Artie's imminent release was one payment at least. She knew that victims of crime were normally notified when the assailant was released, but Artie hadn't been arrested for any crime against Robin. There had been no more security breaches at Robin's house, so she may have become complacent.

Kendra needed to remember that herself.

She had been at the campground when Artie came back. The weather had cleared slightly although there was another storm coming it. As it was, it was a day of sunshine, and had even warmed a little. Kendra sat on the front porch of the small cabin she used for a work area. She had convinced Harris she wanted this spot as an office because it had the best lighting and it overlooked the compound. Not quite untrue but the main attraction was the proximity to the main cabin and its efficient little bug.

She had seen Artie come in the back way. She stifled her first impulse to get up and move so she remained there, waiting.

He came around the corner, back in his jeans, wearing a denim jacket. He looked like he had lost weight, now whip thin, a short little man, with sandy blondish hair that had a slight curl. His normally slightly stocky features had been thinned down. He was still quick moving, still with that curl to his lip that made it appear he was constantly sneering at you. She didn't move from her leaned-back chair, her feet up on the railing. She wanted him to know she was there.

He stopped dead when he saw her, a mixture of emotions across his face—disbelief, anger, then rage, and then maybe something else. He looked as if he had seen a ghost. Appropriate, she thought. Her only movement was to watch him change direction and head for Harris's cabin.

"What the fuck is she doing here?" She could almost hear Artie yelling without the surveillance aid she had planted there.

She didn't get up, reasonably secure with Harris. She had gone out of her way to become indispensable. Besides, she had just found another bug in a security surveillance sweep. There was the small matter of it being hers but nevertheless it had rattled Harris sufficiently. She had another in the main meeting room. So she just sat there enjoying the January warm spell.

"I want her out of here!"

"She's our security expert."

"We don't need no fucking 'security' expert—not the likes of her!"

"She owned a respected security company downstate. We're lucky to have someone like her, well able to acquire state-of-the art equipment, knows how to use it all."

"I don't care what the fuck she does—I want her out of here."

"Well, I don't see you're in the position to make that call."

Kendra continued to listen but she knew Artie's opposition to her would only make Harris more determined to keep her. Besides her usefulness to Harris, she was aware a real power struggle between him and Artie would develop. With Artie gone for over a year, Harris's position—and consequently hers—had strengthened. Artie wasn't the top dog any more.

* * *

Artie didn't acquiesce without a fight. He didn't come around when she was there but he showed up on the tapes. He didn't openly confront Harris, just circumvented him. Johnny especially seemed to take a new lease on life, new direction. The others were more subtle but Kendra had the feeling more and more that something was afoot.

The winter storms came, one after another. Groundhog Day with Punxsutawney Phil came, saw no shadow, but he lied. No early spring came but record snows through February until everyone was tired of snow, cold and ice.

"Will winter never end?" Kendra demanded as she examined the slate-gray sky and the few beginning snowflakes.

"Hoosier Hysteria," Linda commented from her perch on top of the file cabinets. "Basketball tourneys and winter snowstorms. Remember the year it took the farmers with their front-end loaders to clear the roads to even get the team out to play?"

"Yes. The post office could take lessons from basketball fans. God forbid anything stop the basketball tournament." She closed the door of the cabin. "I had hoped that warm spell meant winter would be over."

Linda made a snort of disgust. "It's only March."

"Yeah." Kendra paced around the office. The recent ice storm had coated trees, bushes, power wires, everything with ice. While it looked beautiful, like everything was made of crystal, it played havoc with power lines, dead tree limbs and in some spots heavy enough, healthy trees. Now it was melting and mostly gone, roads were clear and the damage being assessed, but meteorologists were predicting falling temperatures and inches of snow in the next couple of days. Harris reported, with some testiness, that he couldn't contact the back gate or the shed on their internal phone system. Kendra suspected a broken line from the ice storm and had sent Johnny up to walk the line.

Kendra had always enjoyed winter. The crisp cold air was energizing, but not this year. This year was one winter too long. She hated waiting, and that was all she had been doing for the past year. She wanted it over, good or bad. Artie was back now, things would start happening. She had seen how rattled he had been when he saw her there. It would only be a matter of time before he made a mistake.

"Have you heard anything?" Linda asked after a moment.

"Nada. Nothing. But if I were a gambling person, I would be betting on something happening soon." She shook her head. "Nothing I can put my finger on, just—just something." She picked up some orders and dropped them in the basket. She was restless. The lull before the storm? "Artie's been out for a couple of months and he's done nothing. I don't know; it's just too quiet. God, I hate waiting."

"Be careful what you wish for," Linda warned. "You know things can change pretty quick sometimes."

"Can't be quick enough as far as I'm concerned," Kendra groused.

* * *

The dream started like always, the phone call from her dad. First thing in the morning in Indiana meant predawn hours in California. Her dad never did remember the time difference.

"Honey, I've got bad news."

"What's wrong? Are you all right?"

"No, it's not me. I'm fine." He took a deep breath. "It's Linda. She's missing."

"Missing? What do you mean she's missing?"

"Sue called me last night, wanted your number, wanted to know how to get hold of you."

"Sue hates my guts. Why would she want to get hold of me?"

"She said she thought you might know where Linda is."

"Where Linda is?" Kendra repeated. "How the hell should I know? Linda threw me out, decided to stick it out with that bastard of a husband of hers."

Her dad drew a deep breath. "Well, evidently she changed her mind. According to Sue, at least. She was planning on leaving him. Now no one knows where she is. Sue thinks if she's anywhere, she's with you."

Kendra sat down on the bed, her mind racing. Linda gone? Missing? "Did you give Sue my number? Never mind, do you have hers?"

* * *

Kendra was suddenly wide awake, just as awake as that phone call had awakened her eight years ago. She looked around the darkened, chilled room. She'd have to go downstairs and stoke up the fire. Indiana in March was no warmer than when she was a kid, and the woodstove in this old house would never pass for central heat. Everyone was tired of winter but spring still seemed far away.

As she swung out of bed, she reached for her robe and stepped into her slippers. She glanced at the cell phone she used as a clock, alarm, answering machine, everything. The red light was blinking. Someone had called.

She caught the voice mail as she stumbled down the stairs. It was Travis. Her first impulse was annoyance. Travis knew better than to call her and then the thought occurred to her that something was wrong. Without listening to the voice mail, she called back.

"Travis? Kendra here. Sorry I slept through the phone." Turning on the lights, she headed for the woodstove. "Why are you calling me anyway? I told you not to call unless it was a dire emergency."

"Kendra, I've got bad news. I thought you'd want to know."

Kendra stopped in the middle of the room. Her father's words. "Spill it," she said tersely.

"Robin's missing. She didn't show up for work yesterday. No one's seen her since Friday night. Her cell phone isn't answering."

The news didn't register immediately, and Kendra couldn't find her voice to say anything. If she thought Robin didn't mean anything to her anymore, the lurch in her stomach told her differently.

"They haven't released it yet on the news. We got called in yesterday to check the security at the house. Mike got a little more information from his buddies at the news station. The station hasn't had contact with her since Saturday morning. She talked to her producer, said she had a new lead she was going to check out."

Kendra found her voice. "New lead? On what?"

"Something she was working on. If she told them, they weren't saying."

"The house, was there a break-in?" Impossible, she thought. That system was secure. She knew that for a fact, because Abatis had put in the system, *she* had put in the system. And she certainly had tested it often enough.

"No signs of a break-in, system was on. Once they got in, everything looked like she had just left."

Kendra absently nodded. "What about her car? Do they have it?"

"I don't know."

Kendra took a deep calming breath. Surely she was jumping to conclusions. A lot of things could have happened. She could have left a message and it got dropped. She could have gone out of town and just hadn't made it back. Weather was good but there was a storm to the west, too far to affect them yet but it was coming. Car accident?

"Anyone check the hospitals?"

"I don't know. I suppose."

There was a long pause as Kendra thought of all the things that could have possibly happened.

"I thought, I wondered," Travis fumbled. "I mean, when you were here at Christmas, did you see her?"

"She was at Ellen's Christmas party."

"Did you—I mean, did you talk?"

"Small talk," Kendra said. *I warned her about Artie getting out.*

"I thought—well, I know you two were working on something together a while back. I thought maybe she was meeting you about something."

"No, I burned that bridge last year." What was she anyway, she thought callously. A magnet? Someone goes missing and people assume they're coming to me? Linda. Robin. She stopped. What if she *was* the link? The last thing she needed right now was the police sniffing around.

"I thought—hoped maybe—"

"Not me," Kendra said flatly.

There was a heavy sigh on the other end of the line. "I thought you'd want to know."

"Yes, I do. I appreciate it, Travis. If you hear anything else let me know." Kendra shivered in the morning chill, at least she told herself it was just the chill of the room. "Give me a call if you hear anything more. But Travis…"

"Yes?"

"Keep it quiet. I don't want my name connected with Robin's if it can be avoided."

Travis sighed heavily. "All right. I don't understand, Kendra, but all right. I'll let you know what I hear. But," she paused, fumbled with the words, "you think it could be anything to do with what whatever you're doing?"

God, what a loaded question, Kendra thought. "I don't know, I hope not," she answered honestly.

"And you don't know anything?" Travis pressed.

"Now what the hell is that supposed to mean?"

There was a long silence. "You and Robin, you were both working on something together. I sorta got the idea maybe you still were. You just needed to make it look like you dumped her so you set that scene up with Stella." She paused but Kendra didn't say anything. "I thought maybe you'd know something."

"I don't know anything, Travis, other than what you just told me." Kendra drew a deep breath. "And if I did, I'd be telling someone."

"Really?" The relief in Travis's voice was all too apparent.

"Really," Kendra said firmly as she picked her words carefully. "Robin and I may have had a falling out, a big one, but that doesn't mean I want anything to happen to her or any harm to come to her."

"Oh, God, you don't know how I've worried about this, I've been up all night, pacing the floor. You've changed so much in the past year, and have come up with such weird ideas and withdrawn so much. I knew you liked Robin, really liked her, but then the way you just dumped her. You just don't do that, Kendra, that's not you. Or at least not the you, you used to be. I just knew you couldn't be involved in anything to do with her disappearing."

So if you knew, why were you up all night pacing? As Travis babbled on, Kendra considered how much she might have changed that Travis would even consider the idea, much less be up all night worrying, whether Kendra might be involved in Robin's disappearance.

Kendra put the phone in her pocket as she knelt in front of the stove. Fire was down low. She pulled some from the wood box, watching it catch, all the time thinking of Robin, how she looked in the firelight, how intent she was when she had some information, how intense she was in all her passions.

She knew Robin was still working on the militia story. She had hoped when she told her Artie was getting out, she would at least be more cautious. Artie wasn't the type to forget about her.

Between the dream and the phone call, sleep wasn't just elusive, it was plum out of the question. She went to the kitchen to fill the kettle and brought it back to the woodstove.

"Trouble in paradise?" Linda asked.

"Where the hell is paradise?"

Linda shrugged her shoulders but said nothing from her seat on top of the bookcase. She drew up one leg and wrapped her arms around it, laid her head on her knee.

"Travis called," Kendra answered her as she stared at the teakettle. "She told me Robin's missing."

"You think she came here?"

Kendra shook her head again. "No." She reconsidered. If Robin had a new lead, then perhaps. "I don't know. I told her months ago to stay the hell away. Not that it would have done any good if she thought she could gain some information."

"Do you think she did?"

Kendra gave a cynical laugh that faded quickly in the warming room. "I don't know. I warned her at Christmas about Artie getting out. I hoped she took me seriously." When there was no response, she turned around. The room was empty, and she was alone.

The teakettle began to whistle. She took it off quickly, removed it to the kitchen and wrapped it in the tea cozy that would keep it warm for hours. She poured the water in the mug with the tea bag, added the sugar.

She came back to the living room, sat down on the couch, pulled the blanket down off the back and wrapped it around her. The only light was the glow from the woodstove as she wrapped her hands around the hot mug. This whole deal was getting ugly. If she were in her right mind, she'd call the cops and bail out. But that would mean giving up her idea of getting Artie. She wasn't ready to do that. Not yet.

Where could Robin be? And what would have possessed her to go somewhere without telling anyone? Well, that was a stupid question. Robin would go wherever to get information. What information would lure her out? Artie was out of sight, relatively calm as a matter of fact. Did it even have anything to do with Artie, or the MMU? Was she working on anything else? She had warned Robin, and she wasn't likely to take chances. Calculated risks, yes, but she would have had to believe she was safe. So what could have tempted her?

If they didn't know where her car was, then had she just gone off somewhere? But why wouldn't she have told someone? Or had she been in an accident and just hadn't been found yet? Weather had improved, but it was still a possibility. That would be preferable, but in her bones, Kendra knew that wasn't the case.

Three days now. Not good.

Surely she wouldn't have come here, would she?

The question lingered, so by the time the sun came up and before others would be out and about, Kendra slipped off and "walked the line." Ostensibly she was checking for any security break from the last storm that had come through.

She did find one, a downed limb so soaked with wet melting snow that it took down part of the fence. From there, she checked out the far storage shed. Claudia had built it out of sight in a hollow, not wanting to spoil the view or the illusion that campers were miles from civilization. As Kendra came down through the trees, she blessed every hour she and Linda had gone mushroom hunting in the spring. They knew all the hollows and gullies like their own backyard.

"We did have a grand time, didn't we?"

"Yes," Kendra said shortly as she slipped in the melting snow and mud and landed on her butt. "Just great." She sat there a minute to catch her breath. "Just like old times." She closed her eyes, remembering.

Yes, they did have great times, climbing hill and dale in the warm spring, mushroom hunting. She pulled herself up. Now she was hunting something else.

Lots of tracks, she considered as she came down along the side, trying to stay in the grasses. Looks like pickup trucks. Unusual but not suspicious. A familiar truck using the back gate wouldn't warrant anyone's attention. Even before she got out of the tree line, she could hear shouting and the shed door swung open to bang against the wall. She ducked back into the brush, scrambling for cover.

Harris was rushing out the door, about as angry as she had ever seen him. Right behind him was Artie who grabbed his arm and turned him around.

"Look here, old man! You're already in it. Unless you plan on going to the Feds. And I don't suggest you do that."

Kendra pushed back into the brush more and when she slipped and sat down again, she didn't try to get up, just pulled the brush over in front of her.

Harris shook off Artie's grip. "I didn't bargain for any of this! It's one thing to plan and be prepared! You're planning a whole different scenario."

"Nothing's going to happen," Artie countered. "We just intend to be ready when they make their move. We're being prepared. And like you've said all along, it's only a matter of time."

The argument went back and forth. Kendra stilled, afraid to move as the calm morning air carried the words uphill. Their voices dropped and she couldn't hear. What she wouldn't have given right then for her listening devices, but she could only see Artie's back and the expression on Harris's face. Harris was being persuaded. He didn't look happy about it but he finally nodded.

Not a good sign. Harris was the voice of sanity. She watched as Artie gestured, pointing back to the main cabin, pointing over to his house across the fields. He looked at his watch then up the hill. Kendra froze, hoping that her dark clothing blended in enough with the brush and the mud. When he turned away, she was not sure she could move.

Harris got into his pickup and Artie went to open the gate. As they went in front of the building, Kendra forced herself to move, to cover the thirty feet or so to down behind the building. She could hear Harris's diesel slide in the mud and knew she had just a few minutes. A quick scan of the building through the back window revealed nothing except stacks of red and yellow bags against the wall.

She heard the gate clang shut and quickly moved back up the hill. If Harris was going to the main building, she had barely enough time to cut over the hill and make it back before he drove around. But at least she had seen enough to know there was no one in the shed.

"What do you think?" Linda asked as Kendra crossed the fence into Skyler's field and raced down the fencerow.

"No idea, but I would guess something's getting ready to happen."

"What are you doing to do?"

Kendra shook her head. She had no idea. Right now the thing was for her to be back someplace she was supposed to be before Harris got back. The whole dynamics of the organization had just changed, and she didn't like it one bit.

She was just crossing the compound, noticing the delivery truck there. She was caught off guard when her arm was grabbed.

"Hey, Mac!" Stockton caught her arm and steered her toward a fuel truck. He had invoices in hand and he was pulling her toward the delivery truck.

Kendra let out a yell and jerked her arm away, almost striking him. He backed up, spread his hands out, palms up, as he stood between her and the cabin. "Sorry. Didn't mean to startle you. Just wanted to catch you before they started unloading in case this wasn't for us." He handed over the invoices. "You know anything about this?"

From the corner of her eye, she saw Harris pull in and get out of his truck. "When the hell did I become the warehouse clerk as well?" she growled as she took the invoices out of his hand, flipping through the pages, making a show of being there just in case Harris questioned.

"Since you're the only one who could find anything."

Kendra flipped through the paperwork. Nitro methane? Diesel fuel? Who the hell ordered that? And why? She looked up at the fuel truck, waiting to unload. "Wait here."

Invoices in hand, she wasn't sure whether tackling Harris was a good idea. What was it her dad always said for the ball games? The best defense is a good offense? She caught him just as he stepped up on the small porch and just as Johnny came out the door.

"Harris. What the hell is this?"

Harris turned to look at her with her handful of papers and then at the delivery truck.

"Don't want to accept it if it's not ours. Nitro methane. Came in with the diesel fuel. I've got no records of ordering it."

Johnny stepped forward, reaching for the invoices. Kendra evaded his hand, still watching Harris who was looking increasingly puzzled, as if he couldn't shift gears fast enough.

"For the motorcycle races," Johnny said quickly.

Harris turned to him in slow motion, as if he didn't understand. Kendra watched Harris nod slowly, but faint bewilderment remained. She could read him well enough to know that he knew nothing about it at all.

"Awfully early delivery for races that won't be held for months," Kendra pointed out.

"Wanted to get it on the grounds, so there wasn't any last-minute foul-ups like last year." Johnny's answer was awfully quick, Kendra thought as she glanced at him then back at Harris.

She couldn't recall any foul-ups last year, well no more than usual. Paperwork had been so badly organized she had stepped in, and the races were right after she came aboard. It might be a reasonable explanation, and she would have accepted it if she trusted Johnny. She waited to see Harris's response.

He nodded slowly. "Go ahead and accept it."

"Are you sure?"

"Of course, I'm sure," he snapped at her suddenly. "You think I don't know what's going on around here, that I don't know what's been ordered?"

Kendra bit back her sharp retort. He looked like a man who had just seen a door close in his face.

"I'll take care of it," Johnny quickly stepped in. "I know where it's supposed to be stored. It doesn't go down here but up at the far end." He took the invoices out of her hand and pushed between them to step off the porch and head for the truck.

Kendra wasn't sure how to feel, relieved that her name wouldn't be signing for them, frustrated because she didn't know what it was for. She turned back to look at Harris who stood poised at the door.

Harris watched Johnny leave, then looked back at Kendra before he went into the cabin. She took that to mean she was to follow him and she did. She shut the door firmly behind her. Harris suddenly looked aged and she wondered just how old he really was. She saw no sense in avoiding the issue.

"What's going on, Harris?"

He moved behind the desk and picked up papers. He looked at them for a minute and then seemed to pull himself together. He looked up at her, a remote expression in his hazel eyes. "Nothing. I just didn't expect the fuel to come so early."

Before Kendra could say anything, he went on. "Looks like you've been out this morning. Something going on?" He looked at her muddy boots and pants.

"Went up the hill," Kendra said evenly. If he wasn't going to speak of it, then she wasn't either. "Phone line's broken somewhere along the line to the back gate. I went off without any wire, came back before I got too far."

Harris shook his head. "Let it go. I'll send Johnny down the line after he gets back. I need you to stay up here."

"Is there another project coming up?"

He stopped as he searched the desk, as if looking for something. "I want you to do a sweep today," he said finally.

"I just did one."

He looked up at her in sudden anger. "Then do another one. You do everything on such a damn tight schedule around here, it's too damn predictable. I want another one, and I want it done today."

"Yes, sir," Kendra agreed. "Anything else?"

"I want those," he stopped again. "Expenditure reports," he finally said.

Like the ones I just turned in, Kendra refrained from saying.

"Very well." She stood there, waiting, she didn't even know what for but she remained still.

"Well, are you waiting on?" he demanded angrily. "Go on, get out of here."

She left.

She saw Stockton at the other cabin as she crossed the compound to her own. He started to move and she shook her head. She didn't want to talk to him. She wanted to know where Artie was, what was going on. And she wanted to know where the hell Robin was.

She went through the motions of working, did another sweep of the compound, fuming because it kept her tied down. When she went into the conference room, she was even more pissed because there were papers pulled out of the file, strewn all across the table. She hated it when they left stuff like that for her to clean up, like she was some secretary.

She pulled together the packets of emergency management for Warren County. They outlined emergency contact numbers, the emergency roads, hospitals designated to handle emergencies of any sort. Everything one would need to know. She expected that, it was their home county, but then there were maps for Lafayette, Logansport and Indianapolis too, all cities on the rivers, all within a sixty-mile radius. Flood patterns, she supposed, preparing for spring floods. The Eel, Little Pine, the Wildcat, all creeks but pretty substantial waterways for flooding, then the White River all flowing into the Wabash River, all prone to flooding. Then there were the emergency centers at Indy, Methodist Hospital, the main emergency hospital for the Indianapolis area. There was even a map of the power stations. She stacked them all neatly in the center of the table. The one-hundred and five-hundred-year floods seemed to be coming more frequently.

She was just finishing up when Clyde came in. "What the hell are you doing here?" he demanded roughly.

"A sweep," she spit back, not in such a good humor herself. "And I'd really like to know what the hell got Harris's panties in a wad that he wants another one? Not like I haven't done one lately. Bad enough to be doing all this that I don't have to clean up all your paperwork too."

He turned to the table, startled, but she cut him off.

"Oh, I didn't throw anything away about all your flooding plans. It's all there, neatly stacked. Don't you be getting in an uproar too! I've just about had it with all of you."

He looked over the table and drew a deep breath. "Sorry about that, Mac." He backed down a bit. "If we'd known you'd been doing a sweep, we'd have everything packed up."

Mollified by the apology, Kendra wondered if she was just imagining too much. Or maybe her temper had gotten out of hand. "No problem," she said gruffly. "I'm done here anyway."

God, I must have sounded bad if Clyde's apologizing, she thought as she went back to her cabin.

"What were those anyway?" Linda asked as Kendra printed off the expenditure reports.

"Just maps of Indy, roads there. Using the arena as command headquarters. Worst-case scenario. At least that's what I guessed. It was prominently marked."

"Hope nothing happens while the games are on."

"Hardly. Never floods then, just blizzards. Maybe they should do plans for a blizzard instead. More practical this time of year."

As long as Harris wanted the reports again, she took the opportunity to flip through them. She knew she didn't order the fuel. She really didn't think that Harris did. So who had? She really wished she had been able to get hold of those papers a bit longer to read them thoroughly instead of just a cursory glance.

Harris wasn't around when she left the reports in his office and she didn't much care. As far as she was concerned it had been a bad day from start. When she got back to her house, it didn't get much better.

Travis called.

"I'm giving you a head's up," she said. "There's starting to be questions about Robin, official questions. Police came around to the office today, wanted to know about the security system. Who put it in, all the records."

"And Mike shared them, I assume."

"Well, yes. But other things came up."

"Like?"

"That you and Robin had been working on something together."

Kendra flinched. This was about the last thing she needed. And at the same time, there was nothing to hide. "Okay," she said guardedly.

"I imagine you'll be getting a call in the next day or so." Travis paused. "I'm sorry."

"For what? You were asked, you told them. There's nothing to hide, Travis."

"It just looks strange," Travis said slowly. "I know you said you had to take care of something, and I know that you said you'd be out of pocket for a time, but that's been over a year now, almost a year and a half. You've not gone and done anything to get into any sort of trouble and hiding out, are you?"

"No, Travis," Kendra said in her most reassuring voice as she considered possibilities. *At least not yet.* "There're simply some things that I need to take care of, some things that are long overdue and taking longer than I had originally planned."

"Kendra, what's going on? You've dropped out before, but never anything like this. And now Robin's disappeared." She trailed off.

Kendra said nothing as she debated whether to say anything. Her heavy breathing filled the silence.

"We're just concerned about you," Travis started again in a quiet voice.

"We?" Kendra cut in sharply, already thinking of the ripples of information out about her.

"Peg, me. Even Mike. We don't want anything to happen to you. You're important to us. Whatever you're doing, whatever you feel like you've got to do, we're with you. We just want you back." She paused.

Kendra said nothing, abashed at Travis and Peg's concern. In so many ways, she had taken them for granted and to learn that they were worried about her made her feel strange. "I want to come back too, Travis," she said quietly. "But I need to finish this."

"Kendra." Travis sounded as strained as she could. "We'll stand by you. We'll do anything we can do but we can't cover for you."

Kendra caught her breath, shocked to realize that they thought she might have done something illegal. She was speechless for a moment and to her chagrin, Travis seemed to take that as acknowledgment that she had.

"We'll help any way we can, but we can't do anything illegal."

"Travis," she said bluntly, "are you thinking I had anything to do with Robin's disappearance?"

"No." But the answer was slow in coming and Travis didn't sound certain. Kendra waited. "It's just that Robin's been working on that militia thing and then all of a sudden you started acting weird, talking to all those right-wingers. Damn, Kendra, you've always been apolitical—and if there were any leanings, I would have pegged you for a progressive. Then suddenly you're talking about government conspiracies and survival techniques and all that shit!"

"That might be," Kendra said in a quiet voice that covered how Travis's doubt hurt her, "but that doesn't mean I had anything to do with or know anything about Robin's disappearance. Now whether you believe me or not, I can't do anything about."

"I believe you," Travis said quickly, too quickly. "I'm sorry, Kendra. This just has us all shook up. First you being weird, now Robin gone."

Kendra pulled her thoughts together. Had she changed that much? Maybe so. "I'll tell you what," she said finally. "I'll be on the lookout to see if I hear anything. And I'll call the cops and talk to them. You got the name of whoever came by?"

"Yeah. He left his card."

Kendra took the name and number down, balancing what she would and wouldn't say. She knew nothing about Robin's disappearance? Did she have suspicions? Well yes, but nothing to prove. But the feeling of déjà vu persisted.

She broke the connection and went to the kitchen. She knew she had changed, but not necessarily in a bad way. She had done it deliberately and with forethought, but Travis's comments were a dash of ice water.

"Problems, Sunshine?"

Kendra shook her head. How could she explain to Linda that her feelings had been hurt. Or that she was worried about Robin. Was it just coincidence that Robin was following a new lead at the same time Kendra felt that something strange was going on here? And then last of all, Robin was the second woman connected with her to have disappeared. That just didn't look good.

"Everyone's upset about Robin's disappearance. Suddenly everyone's looking at me differently."

"You didn't think they would?"

"I guess I didn't think they'd look at me at all."

"Out of sight, out of mind?"

Kendra shrugged. "Something like that."

"That puts a different slant on it," Linda observed. "What are you going to do?"

"I guess I'll drive down to Carmel and talk to the police." Kendra frowned, wondering what the weather report was and if she would have time to get back before that storm moved in.

"Is that wise?"

"Well, I sure don't want them showing up here."

* * *

Kendra walked out of the police station, wondering. They hadn't asked the questions she had expected, sticking mainly to the security system, what problems they were having and how she had solved it. Trouble was, Kendra wasn't sure that she had fixed it at all. The false alarms had just stopped. And she admitted she and Robin had gone out for a while and then that ended. The breakup had been over a year before. Except for running into her at a Christmas party, she hadn't spoken to her. Somehow questions about Artie hadn't come up, and if they suspected the militia, they were keeping it under wraps. And she couldn't ask. The police seemed satisfied to leave it there. If they thought of anything else, she was sure they'd get in touch.

She stopped at Abatis where there was a noticeable pall. Having a highly visible client disappear wasn't exactly good for business. Or maybe it was because they had the same question as Travis: was Kendra involved? For the first time, Kendra felt uncertain, wondering if she had made a mistake in going after Artie. Then she shut the thought off. She had invested too much. And besides, she had done nothing wrong.

"You've been gone going on two years," Mike said. "If this doesn't end soon, we're going to need to formalize something." He met her gaze, still looking like the relaxed sales manager he was. There was just something different now. He wasn't leaning back in his chair like he always had, but sitting up, businesslike.

Kendra nodded. "Let it ride until spring," she said. "One way or another, it'll be done." She hoped. The timing was purely a guess on her part.

He had a speculative look and for a moment she was afraid he was going to force the issue but he finally nodded. "Spring."

Kendra drove back to Walton's Corner. Why had she thought she could step out of the picture and it would all be the same when she returned?

"You can't go home again," Linda observed from the passenger seat.

"And where's home?" Kendra sighed as she wondered how many bridges she had burnt. Now she wasn't tiptoeing around just the militia, but the police too.

* * *

Coming back to the farm felt different. Something had shifted. Now this house felt more like home than Abatis did. She wasn't sure she liked that. This was supposed to be a temporary thing. Come back, find out what happened to Linda, and then leave again. She wasn't supposed to settle in, get comfortable.

She turned the television on to catch the news as she cooked supper. She wondered how they were going to explain Robin's absence, but that was covered by the simple announcement that she was off on assignment. The police had indirectly told Kendra to keep quiet. She wondered how long it would be before they would put together her nosing around Artie and Robin investigating the MMU. Time might be running out.

She made the mental note to move all the information she had gathered to the shelter. The laptop, the notes, the cell phone, none of it needed to be left in the house for anyone to find, police or militia. She wanted it kept safe. Right after supper, then she could catch up on the tapes.

* * *

"That's the plan," Johnny was saying as the mic picked up his conversation.

Kendra frowned as she listened to the tape late that night. She wished she could have had a wider range, catch the conversations in the hallway, but she was lucky to have this.

"Kill two birds with one stone."

That was one of the Collins boys, they sounded so much alike that Kendra couldn't always tell them apart. And she wasn't interested so much in who said what but what was said.

"You think she'll bite?"

"Well, look at it this way: either way, it'll tell us something. No more of this fence-sitting. And then we'll know."

Kendra's interest heightened. She had no doubt they were talking about her. She had spent the past year walking the fine line being in the militia without doing anything, assuming they were doing something. She had managed to not do anything illegal, right down Harris's line. Sounded like things were beginning to change; it wasn't going to be Harris's way anymore.

"You think she saw the maps?"

"Oh, sure, she saw them. Whether she put it together or not, well, that's the question. She was pretty pissed that day."

"What about? You think—"

"No idea. But I guess we'll find out soon. Get the map?"

"Yeah, here. Then let's go."

The tape clicked off and Kendra drummed her fingers on the table.

"You wanted things to start happening," Linda pointed out.

Kendra felt the hollow part of her that used to be her stomach. "Yeah," she agreed absently as her mind raced trying to fill in the blanks. There were too many. But she was going to be presented with a choice shortly.

"What are you going to do?"

"Depends," she answered. "But I suspect I'll find out soon enough."

"Kendra, you don't have to go that route. There's still time to get out."

"No," Kendra said with some resignation. "I think I've passed that point. Unless I want to give up the idea of getting Artie. And I'm not ready to do that." *And now there's the possibility, faint as it is, that Robin might be involved.*

"Kendra." Linda used that warning tone when Kendra was being obstinate.

Kendra looked up at the wavering image. "I don't think there's a way out, Linda. Only a way through."

"Damn it!" And Linda disappeared.

* * *

"Where the hell have you been?" Stockton grabbed Kendra as soon as she came into the compound.

"What!" Kendra jerked away, turning on him, fists clenched. She didn't like being grabbed and Stockton seemed to be making a habit of it.

Stockton released her, backed up, his hands spread. "Whoa! Sorry. I didn't mean any harm!"

"Then keep your blipping hands off me!" She stepped back, still prepared. She'd had a restless night, waking up frequently and working out various scenarios in her head, none of them good. "What the hell's got you wound up?"

"Something's going on. Harris is in a foul mood; he was looking for you yesterday, pissed that he couldn't find you."

"I don't answer to him," she snapped. She looked up at Harris's cabin, then back to Stockton who was watching her curiously. "What'd he want?"

"He didn't say. Wanted us to send you up there when we saw you."

Kendra searched Stockton's face as she wondered whether he was warning her or setting her up. She dropped off her tool bag at her workshop and set off for Harris's cabin. She had no idea what she was walking into and was even less sure what she was going to do about it. This playing by ear was wearing on the nerves.

You wanted things to start happening, Linda reminded her. *What are you going to do?*

"How the hell should I know?" Kendra growled in annoyance. "Why don't you be helpful sometime and tell me answers instead of just so many freaking questions?"

Oh, aren't we in a nasty mood. One would think that you might be concerned about this woman.

"Oh, shove it, Linda. If you're not going to help then at least stay out of the way."

Kendra went up the two steps quickly and crossed the porch, her boot heels loud and nasty. She gave a brief knock on the wooden door before she went in. "You wanted to see me?"

She should have waited and listened, she realized as soon as she walked in. Harris and Johnny had their heads together and both men jerked around to look at her. "Stockton said you were looking for me."

"Yeah, I was." Harris looked at Johnny. "You need to go take care of this right now, but carefully. Don't make a bad situation worse."

Johnny nodded and then went past Kendra out the door. She turned back to Harris, who went around and sat at the desk.

"Where'd you go yesterday?"

Uninvited, Kendra sat in the chair at the front of the desk. "Had business back home. I've still got an interest in Abatis. Something came up."

"Involving the police?"

Kendra raised her eyebrows in surprise. Had she been followed? Or was it just coincidence? She gave Harris a speculative look, wondering just how she was supposed to react. Surprised? Insulted? Annoyed?

"Well, as a matter of fact, yes." She tried to keep her tone casual. "There was an incident at one of the houses we secure. I signed off on it. They had a few questions. I thought it might be better if I went to them rather than them coming to visit me."

"Visit you! Here?" Harris sat up abruptly, his eyes narrowing.

Kendra gave a shrug. "Wasn't anything I wanted. So why were you looking for me? Something going on here?" If she hoped by passing her police visit off as a normal run-of-the-mill thing, she could change his focus, she was mistaken.

"They didn't ask where you are now, what you're doing?"

"I got tired of the rat race, dropped out." She gave him a surprised look. "People do it all the time."

"When they can afford to?"

Kendra chuckled. "Sometimes they can't afford not to." She waited a minute, hoping she had stalled all his questions. "So what's going on here?"

"What do you mean? 'What's going on here'?"

"You don't usually keep track of my comings and goings so much, or go in a tailspin if I'm not around."

"You usually tell me when you're out of pocket."

"You were hardly in the mood the other day or I might have mentioned it. As it was, you were nowhere around when I dropped off the reports."

He made his hands into a steeple, rested them against his lips as he contemplated her. Kendra said nothing, not wanting to push. It might be too much to think he'd tell her everything, considering the way Artie felt about her, but she might learn something.

"Artie's in a tailspin about that reporter again," Harris said finally. "The one whose opinion drives him wild. She had a piece last week about militia units again."

"Any woman with an opinion drives him wild," Kendra responded. She thought about Robin's recent pieces. "Which piece? The one on the planned march on Washington?"

Harris gave her a startled look. "You saw that? You watch her?"

"Occasionally. It pays to hear what she knows," Kendra tossed off in spite of the fact the news wasn't reassuring. And it didn't explain anything about whatever Artie had dragged Harris into. "She can be pretty impressive. And she doesn't give up. A certain amount of charm, I'll admit, but not a lady to back down."

"No." He sank back in the chair, convulsively making his hand into a fist and releasing it, again and again. "She's persistent."

Kendra swallowed her amusement. Robin had told her about her attempt at an interview with Harris. At one of the rallies Robin had stalked him, trying for an interview and he had ended up hiding in the john, a fact that he found more than slightly infuriating. Hiding in the men's john from a woman. Undignified. She had forced him to do that!

"You make it sound like you've met her, had dealings," he said after a moment. "I mean, other than just seeing her on the tube, but in real life, up close and personal?"

Kendra tried not to think just how up close and personal she had seen her. "Installed a security system for her. Lady was a pain in the butt, had us out there time after time, a regular tyrant when it comes to her ass on the line. Got to see her in action. That's one determined lady."

She waited but Harris said nothing. He was frowning, staring at the desk, apparently lost in thought. "So," she said finally when it was apparent he wasn't going to say anything else. "Was that all you wanted?"

He looked up at her in surprise. "Yes. Just do me a favor and don't disappear again like that. Looks bad to some people."

Oh really? She gave a smile as she got up to leave. "I didn't know I was so essential but I'll try not to upset anyone."

What the hell was that about? Linda asked as soon as Kendra got to her cabin.

"I don't know—except I get the impression he's being pulled into something he doesn't want to be." She buried her face in her hands. If Artie was in a snit over Robin, did that mean he had done something? Or was planning to? Or what? And what was the deal with Harris?

It didn't take long to find out.

* * *

She was just settling in to watch the game on Saturday, big bowl of popcorn, tall glass of iced tea, when there was a soft knock at her door. She was cautious when she pulled back the curtain to look out.

"Harris!" She unlocked the door. "What are you doing here?"

"Get your coat," he said as he glanced around, looking behind him even. "You gotta come with me, Mac. I gotta talk to somebody."

"Well, if it's just talk, come on in. I can turn off the game."

"No. You gotta come with me."

Not good, not good, not good her logic was telling her. "Let me just shut this down."

"No, leave it on. That way if anyone comes by, they won't think you've disappeared again."

"No one comes by," she protested but left the television on and grabbed her coat. "What's going on?"

"You'll see," he commented as he took off toward the campground.

But will I like it? Kendra wondered what she might be walking into.

"The only reason I'm doing this is because Artie hates your guts. So unless you're really deeper than what I give you credit for, you're not aiding and abetting him."

"Not hardly," she could agree.

"Not that I think you're on the up and up. I've just never been able to figure out what you're after. So I'll take what I can."

"What the hell are you talking about?" She noticed that he had kept to the trees and was going into the side of the campground, not that anyone was likely to see them. Most people in the area would be watching the ball game. Even the police said the crime rate went down during game time.

"If I'm wrong," he was muttering as they approached one of the more isolated cabins.

Kendra refrained from speaking, uncertain as to what was going on. Clearly Harris felt the same about her. Half of her was excited that she was finally going to get to the heart of something, and at the same time, more than a little apprehensive. She had never taken Harris for the violent sort, not that she thought he was incapable, just one of the less trigger-happy members.

She followed him up the porch and was surprised to see a padlock on the door. She said nothing as he unlocked it.

"Go on in," he said as he pushed the door open.

Still apprehensive, Kendra slid by him. A quick look around the room revealed a bed, a fireplace, table and chairs and across the room, someone standing against the wall. Her heart lurched as she recognized Robin. Robin without her makeup which made her a pale imitation of the woman who appeared on television, with her hair combed back instead of wisps around her face, Robin in faded jeans and a flannel shirt over a T-shirt. Hardly the polished woman now, which just might save her from being recognized.

"What's going on?" She whirled back to the door, fearing a trap, but Harris had slipped inside and was leaning against the closed door.

"Seems we have an intruder."

"I was looking for a phone!" Robin stepped forward.

Harris looked from one woman to the other. "She says she was looking for some land her real estate agent recommended. She said she was supposed to meet her out here."

"My car's in the ditch out there. You can go see for yourself!" Harris ignored her and so Kendra did also.

"Well." Kendra bought some time as she thought quickly. "Logans have their place up for sale. I suppose if you came across the creek, turned the wrong way, you'd end up here." She waited to see if he bought this.

He nodded. "Forgot about that," he said finally. "I suppose it's possible." He looked from one woman to the other. "She came in the back road, actually the one you insisted that we needed a wire on when everyone else said that no one would ever come in that way."

Oh, great, Kendra thought. So she's captured because of my devising. "Can't be too careful," she said instead. She began to breathe easier. "I take it you don't believe her story of looking at a place to buy in this neck of the woods?"

Harris gave a noncommittal shrug. "Maybe, maybe not. She doesn't look the outdoors type. Not exactly the weather to go looking for land."

"Depends," Kendra pointed out. "Get to see more problems in weather like this. Things get hidden in nice weather. Certainly you get to see what the roads are like." She gave a small smile. "So it could be real easy to get lost. You make one wrong turn and by the time you realize you're not where you're supposed to be, you're confused. City folks still picture roads laid out on a grid, and since we've got the creek to contend with and the preserves, well, there's no such thing as a grid."

"You're presenting her argument."

Kendra pursed her lips. "It could be the truth."

"You think that it might really have been a mistake, she made a wrong turn?"

Kendra considered the question carefully. "I have no idea. I don't have enough information."

"Actually, I thought you might know her."

"What's that supposed to mean?" Kendra demanded. Slow down, calm down, she told herself.

"We've had a leak for some time, I knew that. I thought it might be you."

"What the hell are you talking about? If you'll recall, I'm the one who showed you the bug."

Harris nodded. "That's true. Which made you pretty much a prime candidate until I did some testing of my own."

"What are you talking about?"

"Some of the misinformation I fed to you."

"Didn't go anywhere, did it?"

Reluctantly Harris shook his head. "No, it didn't. So either you figured it was a trap or you just didn't talk." He stepped into the room but stayed between both women and the door.

"And then, you were just too open about going to the police. Unless you're incredibly stupid. And I don't think you are."

"I suppose that's a backhanded compliment."

"Like I said coming over, you're here for something. I don't know what but it's not because you think the world's coming to an end or you think the government's going to collapse." He looked from one to the other. "And then an intruder shows up." He took a step forward. "And not just any intruder."

Robin pressed back against the wall and said nothing.

"So what's that got to do with me?" Kendra demanded.

"Maybe nothing. Maybe everything. That's what I want to know."

"If you think I had anything to do with her being here, you're mistaken."

He kept looking from one to the other of them.

"She didn't," Robin put in.

"Well, I'd expect you to say that," he commented.

Kendra took a different tact. "What's Artie dragging you into, Harris?"

"Nothing." He looked back at Robin. "I think this is Robin Slusher. She says she's not but I don't believe her." He turned back Kendra. "What do you think?"

"I don't think it makes a damn bit of difference whether she is or not. If she's an intruder, you call the local law and have them deal with it. You don't lock her up and take care of it yourself."

"You would say that."

"And three months ago, you would have said the same thing. Trespassing, breaking and entering, whatever. You would have called the sheriff right off. So what's going on that you're not now?"

"Nothing's going on."

"You're a liar," she said with cold deliberateness.

He stepped up to her, in her face. "I think you're protecting her." He poked his finger at her shoulder. "I don't know what your goal is, but you're not using me."

Kendra didn't yield. "I'm not the one using you. And if I'm protecting anything, I'm protecting the unit, something you seem to have forgotten."

"What do you mean?"

"You're planning on turning her over to Jeffers, aren't you?" *My God, he really has lost charge if he's pandering to Jeffers.*

"What if I am?" Harris drew back as soon as he said it. This was something Kendra wasn't supposed to know and Kendra relished the confirmation.

"You know the man goes crazy about that reporter. So you pass her off as Slusher and get all the brownie points, never mind you'll be an accessory to whatever he does. You know and I know what he does when he goes off half-cocked. I heard about the last time he beat up Sue. She was in the hospital for weeks. He's erratic and he's going to take you down with him. You're risking having your group torn apart again because he goes loony over some reporter. And if that isn't bad enough, you have to clean up the mess when he turns on the television next week and sees Slusher and goes crazy all over again. What's that going to do to the cohesive, *respectable* unit that you've spent these past two years building up? Jeffers is as crazy as a loon; and you'd be a damn fool for pandering to him and throwing away all the creditability and respect you've built up."

Not the way to get ahead, Kendra thought when she was done, calling the commander a damned fool.

He hit her, and it took all her control not to hit him back. He knocked her to the floor and she sat there and looked up at him. "You can take it out on me all you want, Harris," she spit out, dropping any semblance of respect. "You know I'm right. Your failure. Another failed mission."

He stared at her a minute, his fist clenched, his jaw working, and Kendra didn't move. Just when she thought that she had gambled and lost, he rushed out of the room, slamming the door behind him.

Kendra leaned back against the wall and closed her eyes. She flexed her jaw where he had hit her, deciding that it was only bruised. Not a good mark on the commander's record, to hit a subordinate. Maybe that's what put him out of the army. She opened her eyes to see Robin squatting right in front of her. "Are you all right?" Robin's voice was steady even if her face was white.

Kendra began to move, see if there was more damage. "I think so." Kendra got to her feet, rubbed her shoulder where she had hit the wall. "Now tell me what the hell happened. What are you doing here anyway?" Kendra dropped her voice, not knowing where Harris had gone. For all she knew, he was standing outside the door. "I told you to stay away from here."

"Yes," Robin answered back in a matching quiet voice as she stood up.

"I hope you know you're in a heap of trouble."

"Are you going to help me?"

There it was, a simple direct question. That was Robin's trademark, no bullshit, just straight to the heart of the matter. "Any reason why I should?"

"You used me."

"Well, if that isn't the pot calling the kettle black, I don't know what is."

Robin looked away. Kendra sat down at the table, wondering what she was going to do. Robin appearing had not been in her game plan. It was enough she was going to go up against Artie, kill him if she could, destroy him if she couldn't. She didn't need to play rescue heroics for a reporter. Especially when she'd been told to stay out.

Robin came over and sat across the table from her, saying nothing. At least, Kendra thought, she knew enough to keep quiet.

Robin showing up was unnerving. Call it her investigation, or luck or just intuition; she was always at the right spot at the right time. So what if now was the right spot, the right time? What was happening?

"What are you going to do?" Robin finally asked.

Kendra shook her head. She didn't need this. "Nothing I can do," she said simply. "If it was up to me, I'd have called the sheriff and have you busted for trespassing. The land was clearly posted."

"And I'd have you on the evening news."

Kendra shrugged. "Well, I'm not in charge. So I guess that explains why you'll be staying here."

Robin looked back at her with dawning disbelief. "Kendra." Robin's voice caught as she held her hand out. "You can't be part of this. I know you think Artie killed his wife, but there's no proof. You don't even know for sure she's dead."

"I know," Kendra said flatly.

"There wasn't any body found," Robin protested. "He wasn't here. There was never any evidence—"

"Evidence!" Kendra exploded as she leaped to her feet and leaned on her arms across the table. "Evidence! And I suppose when he stalked you, there was lots of evidence he meant you harm! Enough so you had no problem getting a restraining order."

"He never made any direct threats." Robin pulled back, away from Kendra.

"Oh, indeed. But it was threat enough for you to run right out and get a security system. On what evidence, Robin?"

Robin made no reply, refused to drop her gaze.

"Besides," Kendra went on. "What makes you think I could even get you off the compound at this point?" Not likely, she considered, not without tipping Harris off. Circumstances would be so much better if she knew exactly where he stood.

"Kendra, I can't believe you're part of this," Robin said in a low voice.

"Part of what? Being prepared for survival?"

"Something more than that is going on. I've been hearing things. There's something in the works, something they're hoping will draw national attention."

Kendra had heard that too. She was the one who sat underground and listened to all those tapes. The little boys had so many plans, so many ideas, grandiose. Big splash. Big names for themselves. Have people come flooding to their cause.

"It's just talk."

"Are you so sure?"

Big enough to crash the system. Kendra remembered the comment on the tape. Okay, what system? Internet? None of them were computer geeks enough to hack into it. Power system? The power grid came down from the north and that would be hard to pull off in this weather. The safety guards were up for winter storms, ice storms. Besides that wouldn't highlight the government's failings.

"Kendra, I don't believe you've bought into all this. I know what you came here for but there's something else going on."

Kendra said nothing. *Big enough for national attention.* Okay, what would bring more than fifteen minutes of fame? Depends on the news day. Disasters? Bombings got mentioned but no long-run story. Shootings, callous as it sounded, Kendra decided, were getting too common to generate the headlines they used to.

"Kendra, I saw something." The intensity showed in Robin's face. Footsteps on the porch made rush her words. "Please, check out that warehouse. Even if you're not part of it, you can't just stand by and let something happen."

Kendra stepped away from the table as Harris came in. Damn her, she thought coldly. Why'd she have to drop in now and screw everything up? Just when things were falling into place.

Harris looked from one woman to the other. "I think," he said carefully and deliberately, "we can go now, Mac." He waited at the open door.

"What are you going to do with her?" Even if Kendra was pissed at Robin, she didn't want anything to happen to her. Harris wasn't a fool and while he was paranoid, he wasn't a criminal. At least she didn't think so.

"Nothing. At least for the time being."

"I don't want to be a party to her being hurt," Kendra warned.

"You already are," Harris came back with. "You've seen her. You know she's here." He locked the door and turned on her. "Now we're the only two who know she's here, so if she disappears, I'm going to know you've done something."

"You mean your conversation with Johnny yesterday had nothing to do with her?"

His chin came up and he glared. "No, that was something else."

"You know if Johnny knows, Artie's going to know."

"Johnny doesn't know," Harris repeated. He stepped off the porch.

Kendra hesitated, loathe to leave Robin, not really trusting Harris. "God," she muttered, "I wish I could be in two places."

I'm here. In the campground, I can do this.

Kendra shivered. Seeing, speaking to Linda, that might be in her mind. Sometimes she still wasn't sure. Depending on her to guard Robin? She didn't see she had much choice.

"Are you coming?"

Kendra stepped off the porch, unsteady, as uncertain as she ever had been.

"Don't call me a liar again." Harris was casual as they walked back across the campground.

"You hit me again and you'll regret it."

* * *

She paced around her living room, furious with Robin for showing up, furious with her for interfering, furious with herself for her hesitation as to what to do. If she "rescued" Robin, let her go, tipped off the cops, anything, she'd lose her opportunity to get Artie, maybe forever. If she didn't...Harris was still in charge. He might be a lot of things, but she didn't think he'd hurt her.

Yet she couldn't ignore Robin's warning about the shed in the back. She knew that was the crux of it anyway. Artie and Harris had been there the other day.

She finally just gave in. She grabbed her jacket and went out the back. She could do a quick check of the shed, be reassured there was nothing there, Robin was just imagining things and then go back to her plans.

The grounds were empty but there had been activity. She went around the corner, checked the doors. Good old-fashioned padlock. She walked carefully around the building. There should be a window to the rear. Dirty but she wiped it clean, at least clean enough to see through.

The interior was dim. Sunlight drifted weakly through the high windows and she could see what looked like a fourteen-foot rental truck. The back door was lifted and she could see the bags stacked. Horse feed? Maybe they were unloading? She didn't recall any rental crossing her desk. And the horse feed? No horses. And besides the bag color didn't look right but it looked familiar.

Then she heard voices, carried by the wind.

"Any suspicions?"

"Nah, I don't think so. He's so hot about that trespasser he isn't thinking about anything else. But I tell you when the old dyke brought in those invoices, I could have dropped through the floor."

"Trespasser?"

"Yeah, the day the diesel fuel came in. I told you about that, that I found her back here, peering in the windows. When was it? The day it started snowing?"

"No, you didn't tell me. Who was it?"

"Some city slicker who got lost, said she was looking for some land for sale, her real estate agent sent her out here." There was a pause. "You really think we're going to be able to pull it off this year? Thought so two years ago when, well, you know."

"Yeah," came the slow distracted reply. "May have worked out for the best, this year may be even better. You sure this trespasser didn't see anything?"

"Don't matter if she did. Harris still got her locked up. He thinks I don't know, but I saw him. She ain't telling nobody. Whether she saw anything or not."

"I might have to go see this one."

Voices were getting closer and Kendra cautiously started back up the hill, picking out the thick brush to use as cover. She saw Artie and Johnny come around the corner but they were simply doing a walk around, they weren't looking up the hill. She moved cautiously, trying to be careful. Her foot hit a wet spot, and slipped. Her other leg collapsed under her and she went down. Just as she thought she was going to slide all the way down, something, someone grabbed her, jerked her into the bushes, an arm around her waist, a big hand over her mouth.

She struggled instinctively and this voice in her ear spoke harshly. "Be still. Keep quiet or he'll be on us both."

The enemy of my enemy is my friend.

Kendra was still, flat on her back, her leg twisted under her and looking up into Stockton's face. "Quiet?" She nodded. Cautiously he removed his hand from over her mouth. "Up the far side," he whispered, pointing across the gully. "Before they come out."

Wordlessly, they crawled through the briers and down further into the gully and up the other side. They came out in a small flat area cut off from the main part of the camp. Kendra remembered it. It was part of the campground but without going through the gullies, she would have to cross over the fence and cross the neighbor's field to get back.

"What the hell?" she said, turning on Stockton.

"Shut up, voices carry from up here," he said in a low voice. "I don't know what you're doing here, McKenna, but you're going to get yourself killed."

"What the hell is going on?"

"I don't know but it's a sure thing Harris has lost control of the group, if not completely at least a good part of it. And that's not a good thing, certainly not for you."

"I can take care of myself."

"And not for Slusher," he went on, speaking right over her words. "If Jeffers finds her here, he'll go crazy."

Kendra caught her words somehow not even surprised that he knew who Robin was. "Who are you?"

He shook his head. "You can move around better than I can. You need to get her out of here. Now."

"That's easier said than done."

They could hear voices down below, the door closing.

"Do it. Find a way. Now. He'll kill her, or at least make her wish that he would."

Kendra glared at him but she couldn't come up with an argument. "What's he planning?"

Stockton shook his head. "I don't know. That's what I'm trying to find out, but I can't do both."

Kendra was already thinking of what she could do. If Harris was gone, well, she could get Robin out but where to? And how to do it without having to give up her goal. And the cold realization was that Linda's release could not be bought by putting another woman in the grave. "I'll get her out," she said flatly. "And what are you going to do?"

"He's mad—crazy. I need to see what he's planning, how far along, get it stopped."

They both turned at the sound down the hill. Diesel engine. They fell flat to look down through the brush. A pickup was pulling in, went right up to the door. They watched as one of the Collins boys turned it, backed it up to the open doors.

Both Kendra and Stockton moved away from the edge of the hill before they got up. Stockton turned to Kendra. "Get her out of here. I'll find out about that."

"And take all the glory?" Kendra rasped.

"Oh, you'll get your chance," he said cryptically. He looked back over the hillside.

"They're going to be tied up here for a while but he's going to want to check that woman out. You need to get her out of here now, while he's involved here. I don't think you'll get another chance." He turned around. "You know how to get back to the main buildings from here?"

"In my sleep," Kendra said angrily. She didn't like what was happening, too many unknowns, but unfortunately, she believed Stockton's assessment regarding Robin's safety.

CHAPTER FIFTEEN

"What now?" Robin leaped to her feet as the door burst open. She backed away at the sight of a mud-splattered Kendra. "What happened? What's going on?"

"Time for you to leave." Kendra grabbed Robin's sweatshirt off the foot of the bed and threw it at her. "Better put this on, it's beginning to snow." She looked around the room to see if there was anything else of Robin's to take.

Robin pulled the sweatshirt over her head. "What happened? You finally come to your senses?"

"Cut the chatter, we need to get out of here." Kendra grabbed Robin's hand and held it, fingers interlaced, pulling her along as they went through the workroom then pushed her to one side as she opened the outer door. She scanned the compound for anyone who might be around. Spitting snow showers were turning into a steady downfall; the weatherman must have been right for a change. With luck, everyone would be preparing to be snowed in and no one would be here to notice. Harris was the only one who might show up. She didn't know where he was off to, but she had the firm idea Johnny and Artie would be coming shortly. Right now, the compound seemed deserted.

She pulled Robin out and they crossed the yard and cut between the buildings. She was doing fine until Robin realized they weren't going for any of the vehicles or in the direction of either drive.

"Wait a minute!" Robin jerked her hand free and stopped at the edge of hillside. "Where are you taking me anyway?"

"Someplace safe." Kendra turned, scanning behind Robin looking for anyone who might drop in. She didn't know for sure if or when Artie and Johnny would come but she wanted to be out of reach when he did.

"And where is that? And why should I believe you? For all I know you've become as crazy as the rest of these jerks. What are you planning on doing? Taking me into the woods and kill me?"

Kendra jerked around at the bluntness of the question, shocked that Robin would even think that of her. These days in the compound must have given Robin a very good idea of how high the stakes were.

"It's a thought," she said angrily. "I've been working on this, planning it for a whole fucking year and you drop in and screw up the whole thing." She took tighter hold of Robin's arm and turned back, starting up the hill, through the trees, grabbing hold of the smaller ones to steady herself against sliding in the mud and Robin's holding back. "I'm putting you someplace out of the way so you can stay out of trouble."

"All you have to do is let me go. I can make it back to the car."

"Fuck that idea. If you don't run into Harris going one way, you'll run into Artie and Johnny the other way. And frankly, at this point, I couldn't say which one would be worse. I'm just hoping we miss them going this way. Besides you said your car was in the ditch. Was that a lie too? Now stop dragging your feet and get your butt in gear."

She didn't let go of Robin's wrist as they made it up the hill, went across the small clearing and then down the other side. It was snowing more heavily now, which Kendra took as a good sign. The snow would cover their tracks but she'd have to be careful going back. Maybe for a change, a full-blown winter storm would blow in and protect them.

When she reached the clearing, she damned herself for not checking this back entrance to the bunker. She hadn't risked digging it up. The entrances all worked from the inside, so hopefully this one would work from out here. She did a small war dance where she knew the cover would be. When she felt the control, she dropped to her knees, pulling Robin down with her, pulling the knife out of her pocket.

"What are you doing?" Robin shouted, jerking free and leaping to her feet. Kendra lunged after her, catching her ankle and pulling her down. Robin fell, landing hard, as Kendra went up her, hand over hand, until she caught her by the shoulders.

"Will you calm down?" The wind had picked up and she had to raise her voice. "I'm not going to do anything to hurt you."

"No, you're just going to lock me up someplace else!"

"Someplace where you're going to be safe!"

"Just get me out of here!"

"I can't, damn it. Not right now; not when I don't know where everyone's at."

"What are you going to do?"

"Neutralize you—at least for a while." She got off the woman, and hauled her to her feet. She pulled her back to the original spot. "On your knees," she ordered, and she shoved Robin down and picked up the knife.

Robin still pulled back, lifting her arms defensively, but Kendra paid her no mind as she plunged the knife into the ground. She pulled it out, plunged it in again. This time the knife blade hit metal. "Good. Great."

Carefully, she felt around with the knife blade, cutting through the sod and pulling it up. Robin fell silent, watching her with wide eyes. "You'll be safe here," she said, struggling for breath as she pulled back the frozen sod. "It's an old bomb shelter. No one will even know you're here. You'll be safe." Kendra rubbed off the dirt below the frost line to uncover what looked like a manhole cover. She swept it clean, uncovered the pad and punched in a number. She gave a grunt of satisfaction when it clicked and she turned the handle and pulled it up.

She turned back to Robin who looked from the hole in the ground to her and then back. "Great," she said to Robin's uncomprehending face. "Now, I need you to drop down there."

"Are you crazy? You expect me to drop into some hole in the ground? What's down there anyway?"

"Everything you might need," Kendra said impatiently as she scanned the open area. That was the bad thing about this entrance, but the snow was coming down at a steady rate and the entrance would soon be covered. "Hurry up before someone comes along. It's only an eight-foot drop; shouldn't give you any trouble with as tall as you are."

"You want me to just drop in some deep dark hole in the ground?"

"Yes." Her mind was racing as to what to do for the next step when she had a sudden idea. "But first give me your shirt and your pants. And shoes."

"My God, Kendra. I'll freeze!"

"It's warm down there. There's food, clothing, everything you need."

Robin still hesitated.

"Robin, we're running out of time."

"No, not until you explain."

"There's no time. You're going to have to trust me." She looked around again. By now, surely Artie and Johnny had reached the cabin. She was going to have to get ugly. "Look, you can take them off and hand them over, or I can take them. I don't care if they're torn or you get hurt in the process." She paused and Robin didn't move. "You know I'll do it."

Robin glared at her for a moment but she took the shirt off and handed it to Kendra. She shivered in the building snow, then unfastened her pants and took them off.

"That's better. Now sit on the edge and turn around and just drop down. I know you've got the strength in your arms."

"And what then?" Robin took the position Kendra demanded on the side of the hole in the ground. "You going to push me down there?"

"If I have to," Kendra warned. Robin still hesitated, looked up at Kendra in disbelief. When Kendra moved toward her, she turned around, supporting herself on her arms. Kendra knelt down in front of her.

"Look," she said in a kinder voice, "you'll find everything you need down there. I'll be back as quick as I can. I just want you in a safe spot. And no one's going to find you here."

"That's what I'm afraid of."

"I promise," Kendra offered to her. "I will be back. You will be safe. Just let go, drop down. The lights should come on. You'll be in a hallway, but you can find everything you need. I won't be gone long."

"I don't have any choice, do I?"

"You haven't for a while."

Robin dropped and Kendra heard a cry of surprise she thought. She leaned over to see Robin's white face in the fading light. "Lights will come on shortly. Just sit tight. I promise, I'll be back for you."

Then she pulled the cover back over, locked it down and replaced the sod. She stamped it down firmly, brushed back the tall grasses and snow so it wasn't so apparent. More slowly now, she rolled up Robin's clothing and stuffed them under her jacket. The first part was done. Now for the rest.

* * *

Kendra had calmed down considerably by the time she returned to the shelter. Johnny and Artie weren't around that she could see. She didn't know where they were; it was enough she knew where they weren't. Robin was safe. Robin might be angry with her, but she could deal with that. Kendra hadn't run into Harris, and Artie was dealing with whatever he was doing. She would have felt better if she knew where Stockton was but she figured he was quite capable of taking care of himself. Kendra could relax a little.

She'd had the time to check her surroundings, to make sure she wasn't followed. The snow covered the back entrance to the shelter. She had the time to work her way around to the hidden entrance at the front. It would have been so much easier if she could have taken Robin in this way, less frightening for her.

The hallway was dark when she opened the door and went down the stairs. "What the—Damn!" Some part of the system must have failed. Lights should be on. The temperature was cool but not cold, the air was fresh so that part was working. She heard sobbing and she quickly locked the door behind her and hurried down the hall, lights coming on as she passed through.

Robin had pushed herself against the curve of the wall, one hand over her right knee, her other hand clenched into a fist. As soon as the light came on, she raised her arm to cover her face.

"Robin?"

At the sound of Kendra's voice, Robin quickly wiped away tears and struggled to her feet, moving away from Kendra. "Don't touch me," she said hoarsely.

"What are you still doing here? Why didn't you go down the hallway?"

When Kendra took another step toward her, Robin forced herself to her feet, bracing herself against the wall, biting her lip with pain. Her hands flat against the wall, she moved away. "What made you come back?" she demanded. "Want to make sure the job was complete?"

"Complete?" Kendra repeated stupidly. "What are you talking about? I told you I'd be back."

Robin's expression didn't change. Kendra wasn't even sure Robin heard her or at least let her words register. She looked behind Kendra from one side of the hall to the other where the hall opened into rooms. She brought her gaze back to Kendra. "I won't go easy, I promise you. I told you I wasn't a piece of fluff."

She thinks you're going to kill her, Linda said in Kendra's ear.

"I'm not going to kill her," Kendra snapped but she saw the sudden panic cross Robin's face. With sudden hindsight, she considered her rushing in, mud-splotched as she was, still filled with adrenaline from Stockton's warning, pulling Robin out of there. She closed her eyes briefly. She hadn't had time to explain much of anything. And the bonds of trust they had once upon a time evidently didn't exist anymore. Robin saw her as a stranger.

"Robin," she said in a quieter tone, more soothing. She took care not to make any move. "I'm not going to hurt you."

Robin shivered. She had to feel trapped, Kendra realized with new insight.

"Lights were supposed to come one when you moved," she explained as she began to unbutton her flannel shirt. "The same for the heat. If you didn't move, it shut down."

As Robin watched with wide eyes, Kendra took off her shirt. "What happened to your knee? Did you land on it badly or did it get hurt when I tackled you up top?" She shook out the shirt.

"When I landed," Robin said reluctantly.

"And then you didn't move around." She took a step forward.

"The lights didn't come on." Robin leaned back from her but she didn't move.

"I'm sorry I took so long to get back. Did you think I wasn't coming?"

"I didn't know," Robin whispered. "I didn't know what to hope for."

"There were clothes available." Kendra was close enough now to touch Robin. "You must be cold. Let me put my shirt around you." She was relieved when Robin let her drape the shirt over the T-shirt. "I don't know why the lights didn't come on. They might have if you had moved further down the hall but you didn't know that." She slid her arm around Robin's shoulders. Robin shivered convulsively.

"It was dark," Robin said finally. "I couldn't see."

Kendra nodded. "So you couldn't see that there was nothing threatening here."

"Being locked underground isn't threatening?"

"Not if it's a spot where you can be safe," Kendra answered. She cautiously took a step forward and although Robin tensed, there was no place she could go. "I'm not going to hurt you," Kendra repeated in what she hoped was a soothing voice. Robin wasn't this frightened of her when she was in the compound, when she was locked up. "What did you do to your knee?"

"If you wanted me to be safe, you'd let me go."

"I can't be sure you'd be safe," Kendra said reasonably. "Artie stalked you when you were at work, when you were at home. And I suspect he'll be looking for you now. So you need to be hidden, and I know you'll be safe here."

"There's lots of places I'd be safe," Robin spit back. "You could take me to the police station, to the hospital."

"There wasn't time." She took a step and brought Robin with her. "Let's go sit down, Robin. I've got clothes for you. You've got to be chilled. And you probably need to get off that leg."

The pain and uncertainty was still in Robin's eyes, but the panic seemed to be gone. Now that there was light, the rooms were getting warmer, she began to recover her equilibrium.

"What happened to your knee?" Kendra started down the short hallway, bringing Robin with her. She hoped that normal, casual conversation would reassure Robin, ease her fears. She could feel her tension, feel her trembling. In spite of her resistance, Robin took a few steps with Kendra.

"I landed badly."

Kendra turned around and drew Robin into what served as the living room. Robin tried not to lean on her but the leg would take no weight. "So, tell me what to do about the knee? This must have happened once or twice before this. What works?" Kendra asked lightly as they moved toward the couch.

"Usually ice and ibuprofen."

"I think that can be managed." As Robin sat down on the couch, Kendra reached for the sweatshirt and pants laid across the back. "Here, put this on. You'll feel better." She pulled the storage table over for Robin to prop her leg up. "Let me see."

"I did what you asked," she said as she felt Robin's knee. She wasn't an expert but nothing felt broken. "I checked out the warehouse. Yes, something's going on."

Robin sat up, her interest diverted. "What did you see?"

"Not enough to tell me anything." She refrained from mentioning Stockton. "Johnny spilled the beans to Artie about you, so I decided it was time to get you out of there." She got to her feet. "Doesn't feel like anything's out of place with the knee. You probably twisted it when you landed." She retreated to the open kitchen just across the hall and pulled the first-aid kit out of the cabinet.

When she returned with the bottle of water, the ibuprofen and the chemical ice bag, Robin had pulled on the sweatpants. "I'm surprised that knee never gave you grief with your running."

"It did occasionally." Robin took the pills as Kendra snapped the ice pack and laid it on Robin's knee.

"You need to eat something with those? I can fix you something, unless you think I might poison you." The words came out a little more caustically than she had wanted but on second thought, she didn't like how Robin had acted toward her. All right, she wasn't the person she had been, but that didn't mean she was going to murder her.

Robin looked up at her then looked away. "That would be nice, something to eat, I mean, not the poison."

"Okay." Kendra retreated again to the kitchen and started pulling things out.

"What is this place?" Robin called as she sat up and looked around at the open living room, open to the kitchen split by a hall.

"An old bomb shelter."

"You put it in? You think it's going to get that bad?" Robin managed to get to her feet and moved to the kitchen. The high seats weren't exactly comfortable but she propped up her leg.

"Hardly. It's been here since the sixties." She pulled rice, canned meat, vegetables from the cabinet.

"Looks like it's been updated some." Robin looked around, still avoiding looking at Kendra. "You seem to have had this all planned out."

Kendra shook her head. "Not hardly but you know what they say about the best laid plans."

"Yes," Robin agreed drily with a glance at Kendra. Her voice sounded more normal now. "I seem to be on familiar terms with that lately."

Kendra decided to change the subject. "Previous owners put it in during the bomb scares of the sixties. When we bought it, well, my dad was always paranoid. I'm not sure he would ever have put one in but as long as it was here, he kept it up. And it's come in handy. Not big by today's prepper's standards but adequate. There's the bathroom, shower, bedrooms. I'll show you how everything works."

By moving cautiously and reassuringly, Kendra was able to settle Robin. Or perhaps, she told herself, Robin was merely acting to put her at ease, so she had some leverage.

By unspoken agreement they didn't talk about anything that had put them both there. Safe subjects consisted of Robin's knee, Kendra's cooking and the bomb shelter.

Kendra sat across the bar and watched Robin eat. There were so many questions she wanted to ask, but Robin looked so tired with dark circles under her eyes; she looked drawn and haggard. For right now, it was enough that they were both safe, at least for a little while. For the moment, she realized with a sense of pleasure, she had Robin to herself and there was no one and nothing else to worry about.

"Get a good night's sleep," Kendra suggested when she settled Robin into one of the bedrooms. "Things'll look better in the morning."

"Probably," Robin agreed.

Kendra stretched out on the couch in the living room, right outside the room she had given to Robin. She hoped that the storm would keep everyone inside. It would be suspicious if she wasn't at home but she was gambling that no one would check. She wanted to have Robin settled before she had to leave her. And she would have to leave her, sooner or later. Robin did get up once, came to the door.

"Did you need something?" Kendra quickly sat up.

Robin started and drew back into the bedroom. "No," she said quickly. "Just—just restless."

"I can imagine." Kendra considered how on-guard Robin would have been during the past few nights. "It's all right, you're safe. You can sleep sound."

Robin went back to bed and Kendra settled back down, turning over, trying to find a comfortable position and turn off her mind enough to sleep. The truck, being unloaded? Or loaded? With what? And this had been planned two years ago, before he got sent up. But this was better? Questions went around and round, not yielding any answers.

"Figure anything out?" Linda asked quietly. She was sitting on the back of the couch, looking down at Kendra.

Kendra shook her head as she looked upward. "No. And now I really wonder what the hell Stockton is doing here? Tailing Artie, I would guess. Or the unit itself. I don't know. Every time I think I'm getting close, I just find more questions."

"You'll figure it out, I'm sure. You always liked puzzles." And then she faded out.

"You talk in your sleep," Robin announced the next morning when Kendra served her up oatmeal with dried fruit, orange juice. She had already set the bread machine to making new bread and the aroma filled the small area.

"Really? What'd I say?"

"Couldn't understand, just mumbling." Robin chased the cranberries around in the oatmeal. "How long are you going to keep me locked up in here?"

"I'm not keeping you locked up in here. You're just safer here."

"For how long?"

"I don't know—until the storm blows out for one."

"Storm?"

In a pique, Kendra went to the back door and threw it open. She took Robin up the ramp and around the spring where snow had already blown in around the sheltering wall. She pointed outside where the snow was coming down so heavily they couldn't even see the trees. "I'm not keeping you prisoner—this storm is. Now you want to take it up with Mother Nature?"

Robin looked out at the snow, the wind howling through the stone shelter. Whatever she thought, she finally shook her head and turned back. Kendra followed her down the ramp, closing the door behind her.

"As soon as it blows out, settles down, we'll get out of here," Kendra promised. "Right now, the storm is just as much a danger as any person here."

Robin nodded, seemingly resigned. Kendra was reassured and began to breathe easier. She had no desire to put Robin in danger, the whole purpose of putting her here, as long as she was here, was to keep her safe.

Kendra spent the rest of the day showing Robin all the details of the shelter so she could be there alone. Robin nodded, asked the proper questions, seemed most agreeable and cooperative. In between explanations, Robin spent time on the couch, her leg propped up with ice twenty minutes on, twenty minutes off, chewing ibuprofen every four hours. She didn't seem to want to talk so Kendra left her alone, put a movie in the player and went back to her own puzzles. When Kendra went to the bathroom, she didn't give a second thought about leaving Robin alone.

As soon as Kendra heard the muffled slam, she knew exactly what had happened. She hadn't locked the door; she was stupid for relaxing around Robin, thinking that the woman understood that she was in here for safety and should remain. Kendra came out of the bathroom and sprinted down the hallway, grabbing her coat and the second one as she went out the door.

The snow had lessened, not by a lot but some. Robin probably thought it was stopping but Kendra had followed weather reports. This was just between bands of snow.

There was no sound except for the wind, nothing to see but white. Beautiful, Kendra would have thought under other circumstances. Soft, wet flakes that quickly covered her coat, her face. She stumbled through the snow, not daring to call out. Damn that woman, Kendra thought. She's going to get herself killed. No idea where she is. No coat. Stupid, stupid, stupid.

She caught sight of her running across the field toward the woods. Either her knee had a massive improvement or she had exaggerated how bad it was. No matter what the case, she had managed to take Kendra off guard.

By the time Kendra had raced across the field, swept clear of snow by the wind, Robin was already in the woods. She had to slow down then, picking her ways through trees and brush, drifts that hid low spots and gullies. While the trees had blocked a good deal of the snow from the previous storm, they had also blocked the wind from blowing it clear.

Kendra caught up close enough to call to her. "Robin, don't. You'll only get hurt."

Robin looked back over her shoulder, white-faced, and then she turned and dodged quickly through the trees. They were moving downhill now and the ground was slick. Warmer temperatures had made the ground soft and the snow on top first melted and then coated wet soggy ground. Kendra slid, catching hold of trees to keep from falling. The snow that made it through the trees now consisted of large wet soggy flakes. Kendra redoubled her pace when she realized that Robin was heading for the creek. She could hear the water now.

Her heart almost stopped when she saw Robin at the water's edge. She knew what it looked like, snow-covered ice that appeared solid, but looks were deceptive. The warmer temperatures and rains upstream would have thinned the ice. Ice along the creek banks might be solid enough to bear Robin's weight, but ice in the middle would be thin. The water was deep in the center, much deeper than what it appeared to be. Even in good weather, this wasn't the place to cross.

"Robin, don't!"

Robin hesitated and for a moment Kendra thought she would catch up with her. The snow was coming down heavily again, and directly across the creek lights came on at the Pattersons' as night fell. Robin looked up and down the banks and then tentatively took a step onto a log extending out into the ice.

Kendra stopped, realizing that her chase was only forcing Robin to continue and going into the water was dangerous. She leaned against a tree, out of breath. Robin had already taken several steps, balancing on the wet log.

"Robin, don't," Kendra pleaded. "The ice, it's not strong enough to hold you. The weather's been too warm. Flooding has broken it up. It won't hold you." She leaned against the tree, out of breath herself. "Please, don't."

Robin looked back at her then turned to look across the creek. Kendra could just imagine her thinking all she'd have to do was go up the slight slope and across the field to the house with the evening lights just coming on. She'd be safe.

"Robin," Kendra repeated. "Don't do it. The water's deeper than it looks. I can't swim. You go in and I can't do anything to save you." She buried her face against her arm. "Please don't." She heard the crack of ice and a splash.

"Kendra!"

Kendra scrambled through the remaining trees and over a fallen log as Robin turned and reached out for her. Robin slid in the mud under the ice and then just when Kendra thought she missed her, she took hold of Robin's icy hand.

"I'm stuck!" Robin cried.

Kendra wrapped her arm around a tree so she wouldn't slide into the water or have Robin pull her in.

"Don't let me go!"

"I've got you, just hold on, come on. You can do it."

* * *

They made their way back to the shelter, Kendra half dragging, half carrying the partially soaked Robin through the heavy snow. Robin was now shivering uncontrollably. To Kendra's shock she discovered she had left the door open in the spring house, but to her relief, there were no tracks around the door. Hopefully no one would be out and about in this storm and she would gamble the hideaway as still secure. The snow was coming down harder now, and she breathed a sigh of relief that any tracks they made would soon be covered.

"Cold, so cold." Robin muttered as Kendra took her directly to the bedroom and ripped back the covers. She quickly stripped off the cold wet clothing from her, picked her up and put her into the bed, covered her. She went to the kitchen, threw a blanket in the dryer and put the heating pads into the microwave.

She went back to check on Robin as she stripped off her cold clothing and tossed them in a pile in the corner. She grabbed a robe as she went by her room. She went back to the kitchen, turned on the stove; Robin needed something hot in her as well as around her.

She pulled the fleece blanket from the dryer, went back to the bedroom and pulled back the covers, enveloping Robin in them. Robin had her arms draped around herself, lying on her side, her legs drawn up and she was shaking. Kendra wrapped the fleece around her, tucking it in under her and then re-covered her.

"Oh, God, that feels good."

"I'll be right back."

When she returned with the heating pads, she put one at Robin's belly, folding her arms around it and then the other behind her knees. She sat for a moment, brushing back Robin's hair, seeing her color, so waxen. When she heard the chime in the kitchen, she rushed there.

Hot chocolate in a thermal mug. She set it on the side table. "Are you warmer?"

Robin nodded, even as she shivered.

Kendra helped her sit up, keeping the covers around her, so she could drink. Robin leaned against her. The intimacy of their bodies pressed together warmed Kendra more than any blankets. Warmed her enough that she thought maybe she needed to lie Robin back down underneath the covers. And she did make the attempt, but Robin wouldn't let go. She started shivering again.

So Kendra lay down beside her, feeling Robin wrap around her, shimmying her legs between Kendra's heavier warmer ones. Kendra pulled the covers over both of them. "Warmer now?"

Robin nodded but didn't say anything.

Kendra entwined her arms around her, shaken to realize the risk Robin had taken to escape her. She forgot her anger with Robin's interference; she was only doing what she had set out to do. Wasn't that what Kendra had admired in her, her drive, her determination. And what had she become if Robin had to take such a risk to escape her?

She held Robin against her and stared into the darkness. She'd never meant to become someone her friends couldn't trust. In her efforts to avenge one loss, had she almost caused another?

She brushed back Robin's hair, tucked the blanket around them both. She just wanted to touch her, hold her, to assure herself Robin was safe. She laid her cheek against Robin's hair. "Oh, honey," she said softly without even expecting an answer, "why'd you run?"

"Because." Robin's voice was muffled from under covers, against Kendra's shoulder.

Kendra pushed her back so she could see Robin's face. "Without a coat? In this weather? Do you even know where you are?"

Color was coming back into Robin's face. She looked more normal now, resolved and defiant. "I didn't know if I'd have another opportunity. I thought surely I could find a house where I could pound on the door."

"In this weather? At night? You probably would have been met with a shotgun."

"That might be better than what I was facing here."

Kendra stared at her, speechless. She remembered how angry she had been to see Robin in the compound, not afraid for her but really pissed at her interference, when she had been told to stay away. She remembered her rough handling of Robin, even dragging her to the bunker. "I kept telling you I wasn't going to hurt you," she protested finally, but even to her ears it was a weak protest.

"I didn't believe you," Robin said flatly. "You're not the same person. You looked and treated me like a stranger, like an enemy."

"It was safer." Kendra couldn't deny Robin's viewpoint.

"For who?" Robin retorted. "You or me?" Even though she was angry, she didn't move from the warmth of Kendra's arms.

"For both of us." Kendra reached out to brush Robin's cheek and caught herself before she touched. "And now?" she asked tentatively.

"I don't know." Robin shivered and looked away. "You sounded sincere when you pleaded for me not to go out on the ice." She shivered again. "But I still don't understand."

"You know why."

"But to—"

Kendra interrupted her. "Later. When you're warm. When you're rested." This time she did touch Robin, stroke her cheek. "I'll explain."

"Promise?"

Kendra nodded, relieved Robin didn't pull away from her. She closed her eyes and wrapped her arms around the woman, a feeling of relief going through her. She had built up so many barriers over the past year. Letting someone in would be difficult.

Right now, all that mattered was that Robin was safe, they were both safe, and there would be time for explanations. She felt Robin relax as she warmed up.

"Kendra," Robin said in a drowsy voice. "Just one thing I want to know now."

"Hmmm?"

"Where'd the other woman go? And who was she?"

"What other woman?"

"The woman who helped you pull me out."

Kendra lifted her head. "There wasn't any other woman there. I was alone."

Robin pushed back, looked up into Kendra's face. "No. There was a woman behind you, holding on to you, looked like by your coattails so you wouldn't fall as you pulled me up. I know I wasn't seeing things."

Kendra searched Robin's face but she was convinced Robin was telling the truth. "What did she look like?" she asked quietly.

"I really couldn't see, but she didn't have a coat on, just jeans and looked like a western-style shirt. All I could see was a dark-haired woman, her arms around you, holding on. Then when you pulled me up, when you wrapped the coat around me, I didn't see her. I thought maybe she went to get help. Where did she go?"

Kendra shook her head. "There wasn't anyone there, Robin."

"But I know I saw someone!"

"Shadows," Kendra said but she didn't believe what she was saying. "Through the trees. The snow. There was no way you could see clearly."

"I know what I saw." Robin came back into Kendra's arms. "Wasn't any shadow."

Kendra slid her arms about Robin but she was no longer sleepy. "Go to sleep, Robin. We're safe here for the moment."

Long after Robin was asleep, Kendra lay awake. They were safe, for the moment, but this job she had started wasn't complete. Not by a long shot. She was going to have to do something. She would have to come up with some idea to draw them off, get Robin out of here safely. The waiting time was over.

CHAPTER SIXTEEN

"I'm sorry it's come to this," Linda said from the backseat later that night.

Kendra backed the Jeep out from behind her house. It was still snowing heavily and this needed to be done now so snow would cover their tracks. "Well, if you've got any better ideas, now's the time to share them. I'm fresh out."

"You sure you can do this?"

"No." Kendra tried not to think about it lest she lose her nerve. Planning, that was what she liked, and while she was good at that, she wasn't always so good with improvising on the fly. However, she was running out of ideas. And time. And options.

The snow was blinding, so she could barely see where she was driving. Good, it would be easy to explain a missed turn, especially if the driver wasn't familiar with the road. That would add to the idea of Stockton and Robin in the Jeep. Plus Robin's clothes, her shoes and shirt. Hoped it would work at least.

"A shame after you spent all the time hunting old Nellybelle down," Linda commented.

"And the fortune I put into her getting her running again." Kendra took the road along the edge of the valley. She had thought about just running off the road here, there was a drop-off and the Jeep would roll. But then there would be the search for the driver. There were no houses along this stretch but still. She finally rejected the idea, realizing she was just hoping to have Nellybelle back again, one more time. No, the sharp right turn onto the old iron single lane bridge would be better. Going too fast, unfamiliar with the road, the sharp turn, hit the brakes, a skid off the road, down the embankment and into the creek. If she could survive the crash.

"Don't panic," Linda said. "Hit the brake, slide."

"Yeah, you were the daredevil driver, not me."

"Just do what I tell you."

"Yeah, first of all, don't panic."

The snow was coming straight into the windshield. The wipers could barely keep it clean. If she wasn't careful, she'd have a wreck for true and that would really screw the plans. Ahh, the "No Trespassing" sign on the Simons' place. Amazing how much longer the distance seems when you can't see. Just as well she had driven this road every day for years. Warning sign for curve. What an understatement. The gate to the Phillipses' place. Accelerate. Her hand on the door handle. Hit the brake. Feel that back fishtail, come around.

Slow motion and yet so fast, then she realized she had done a one eighty, turned completely around. Not in the plan, damn it! And then the back went over the edge, before the bridge instead of the far side—the wrong side! And stopped.

She fell back in the seat with a jar. Stopped. What the hell? She looked out the door window to see a slender tree right there at her. Shit! Just her luck to be caught by a tree.

"Get out," Linda ordered. "Now. Not stable. Now. Move!"

"I'm moving, I'm moving, I'm moving!" Kendra unsnapped her seat belt, crawled across the seats to the passenger door. She felt the vehicle rock. "Oh, God, just get me out of this mess and I'll never ask anything again."

She almost fell out the door as the Jeep rocked and then, just as she threw herself to the ground almost under the bridge abutment, she heard the sharp snap of the slender tree, and the Jeep slid down, caught, and then rolled down into the river.

Kendra grabbed the guard railing and held on, burying her face in her arms, breathing in great gasps. She lay there a minute, wiggling toes, flexing her feet, her ankles. She felt like she was in one piece. Didn't go the way she planned, but maybe…

"You all right?"

"I think I wet my pants."

"Hope not. It'll be a cold walk."

Shakily, Kendra got to her feet. She stood there, trying to pull herself together. Then she pulled the flashlight out of her pocket. It took three tries to get the damn thing to come on before she could flash it down the hill.

Nellybelle lay in the water, driver's side down in the center of the creek, the deeper water. The driver's door had sprung open. It was a horrible sight.

With luck, any kind at all, there wouldn't be anyone out on the road tonight. Probably midmorning before someone would see it. Snow would cover so much. She was shaking, not just from the cold. She was not cut out for this line of work.

If she went by the road, it was three and a half miles. If she cut across the fields along the creek and then went straight up the hill, it was half that. She glanced at the snow. If she didn't get lost, if she didn't freeze. If she didn't fall in the creek and freeze herself. Or slip on the hill and break a leg.

"Get a grip!" Linda said sharply. "Stop thinking of the things that could happen! You always did think of the worst possibilities! Everything's worked so far, hasn't it?"

"Easy for you to say," Kendra groused. "You're not sitting in there listening to them plan something 'really really big' that'll get everyone's attention and wondering if you're going to end up in jail or dead."

"Been there, done that," Linda retorted.

"Shit!" Kendra remembered who she was talking to. "No offense meant, dear heart, but I'm really not ready to join you."

CHAPTER SEVENTEEN

She worked on getting up a good head of steam as she walked over to the campground the next morning. She hadn't made any plans, just figured on winging it. She did better that way as long as she had the story firmly in her head. She didn't have to fake being irritable. She had thought she'd never get warm after she reached the house; and if she was cold, she couldn't sleep. Now she was sore; her shoulder was bruised. She must have landed on it when she came out of the Jeep. Besides that, she was pissed, pissed she had to put Nellybelle in the creek, that neither she nor Linda could come up with any other idea.

The only reassuring thought she had was that Robin was tucked away, safe and sound. And unable to do anything to interfere. Kendra knew Robin would be angry about being left out, locked up, but she would deal with her later. She just hoped that the note she had left explaining that she had to do something during the storm would buy Robin's understanding long enough for Kendra to figure out the next step to take.

She stomped up on the porch, kicking snow off her boots. There was smoke coming from the chimney so she guessed this is where everyone would be. She jerked open the door and went down the hall to see a bunch of the guys gathered around in front of the fireplace, huddled together. The tension in the room was tangible.

"Hey!" she said sharply. "Any of you yahoos come over and get my Jeep because your sorry-ass vehicles didn't start last night?"

She expected some reaction but not all of them jerking around, the scrape of the chairs on the concrete floor. They looked at her like she had materialized right in front of them.

"What the hell are you talking about?"

"My Jeep's missing," she spit out. "Figured I'd better check here before I reported it stolen."

"Who the hell would steal your Jeep?" Johnny sneered.

"Well, maybe someone merely 'borrowed' it because their sorry excuse for a pickup wouldn't start," Kendra came back with a returning sneer. Johnny's vehicle was forever dying on him and leaving him stranded.

This time she saw the exchanged looks. "What's going on? Is something wrong?"

"When'd the Jeep go missing?"

"Sometime last night after I got home. Had to be someone from over here, wasn't like anyone would come in from the road on the other side."

More looks.

"You leave the keys in it?"

"What kind of fool do you think I am? I'm not that damned trusting."

"Hot-wired." Steve and Harris exchanged glances.

"Well, if you guys didn't take it, then I need to call the sheriff and report it stolen." She turned to go.

"No!" Three of them were quick and she turned around to look at them.

Harris waved her to a seat. "Stockton's missing."

"Missing!" Kendra didn't have to fake her surprise, her shock. "What do you mean missing? He's not just out on some fool assignment you sent him on?" *Or he did stumble into something.* What else could possibly go wrong?

Harris shook his head. "So's the woman, that woman who's not a reporter."

"Shit!" At least in this company, Kendra could release her shock and frustration explosively. "What the hell is going on?"

Harris looked more than a little haggard himself, she noted.

And then as she thought of the ramifications, she felt a piece of ice. If Stockton was missing, he must have found something at the shed. Or somewhere. Who was he anyway? And then she remembered, he had vouched for her. If something happened to him, would that drag her in? Harris was already suspicious. With a sinking feeling, she considered Robin could be in that shelter for a long time, a long, long time if Kendra didn't make it back. Kendra had locked her in.

* * *

Kendra walked back to her house, her mind reeling. She didn't dare go to the shelter in case they followed or watched her. Stockton? There had always been something about him that set off her warning signals but nothing had become apparent. Obviously, though, there were a lot of things she may not have been privy to in the day-to-day gossip.

In many ways, it was a stroke of luck. Harris's theory was that Stockton and Robin got away together, Stockton hot-wired the Jeep and stole it to get away. So don't report the Jeep as stolen, not yet. Later. But they needed time to do some searching themselves. And Kendra, she was to go home, go back to bed, sleep late. Putter around with whatever you do. Don't discover the Jeep missing. It wouldn't be strange if she didn't go outside. The storm had been bad, there was no reason to go outside if you didn't have to. Just sit tight.

Kendra agreed. She could do that. She knew that sooner or later, someone would discover the Jeep in the creek. Sheriff's department should come out and check to see if she were all right. Then she could report it stolen. Yes, that would still work with her plans. Robin would still be safe, probably pissed if it were a while before Kendra could get back as soon as she had promised, but yes, it was workable.

"Told you it would work out," Linda said as she crossed the back lot.

"I've still got a bad feeling about this," Kendra groused. "Just bad, bad, bad."

She heard something as she went up the back step to the small porch. She jerked around, searching the fields. Clear and cold, and nothing. She looked all around, her nerves stretched taut. Nothing. She gave a nervous laugh. "Jumping at the wind. What next?"

There was a moan, closer. No mistaking it this time. She slowly turned, looking at the immediate area, the clean snow. And then she saw this mound behind the bushes, against the house.

No, no, no, her internal voice muttered in disbelief but her mind was sharp and clear. Kneeling, she dusted off the snow. Stockton. Right at her back door. She brushed off more snow. He was cold, past shivering, but he was still breathing. She pulled him up by his arm and then she saw red, bright red over dark red, down his jacket and shirt. But he was still breathing. She looked around again, for anyone who might be watching. She needed to get him out of sight.

Not gentle, wondering if she was doing him more damage than helping, she got him under the arms and dragged him inside. She closed the door, locked it. What else could go wrong?

She tore open his jacket and cringed at the blood. Her medical knowledge was pretty limited but this didn't look survivable. Maybe the cold slowed the bleeding down, maybe if she got the ambulance here right away, but the snow, were the roads open? She started to get up and he grabbed her wrist. She yelped in shock. She didn't think he could even move. He pulled her down to him.

"Slusher?"

"Safe," she answered, her heart pounding.

He swallowed. "Good." He gathered his strength.

"Don't talk," she said. "Let me call—"

"No. No time. Listen. Look in belt. Call them. Something big planned. Bad. Killing." He looked up at her but his eyes were already glazing. "Bombing. Crowd. VIP."

Kendra frowned, trying to make sense of what he was saying. Was he getting carried away with all those wild stories? But he was shot and probably not exaggerating. "Hold on," she assured him. He wouldn't let go of her wrist.

"Trust no one."

Oh, God, did he know about her? Had he said something?

"Gotta stop…" and then he was gone.

Kendra clenched her jaw. This was unreal. His hand relaxed and he released her wrist.

She stared at him trying to put it all together. There was a dead man lying on her kitchen floor. And he died trying to tell her about a bombing. A crowd? Where? When? Damn, if he was going tell her this, couldn't he have given her a few more details!

His belt. With hands she was barely able to get to function, she unfastened and pulled off his belt. A slit, a business card. Nothing but a phone number, but it must be important if it was hidden.

Jerkily she got to her feet, absently seeing blood across her kitchen floor. She made it to the bathroom and threw up. *How do cops deal with this?* she thought as she heaved what seemed like everything she had eaten for the past week.

She leaned against the bathroom door. A bad dream, she considered. A terribly bad dream, she thought as she looked at the card again. But when she went back to the kitchen, he was still there.

* * *

Someone was pounding on the front door. She put the mop in the bucket of soapy water and picked up the towel to dry her hands as she went through the house.

"Calvin!" She opened the door to see the uniformed bulk that just about filled her doorway. Behind him she could see blue skies and a brightness off the snow that was blinding.

"Ms. McKenna." The man in the tan shirt with the bulky sheepskin-lined jacket looked at her in some surprise. "Are you all right?"

"Well, yes," she said uncertainly. "A little put out by the storm but…" She shrugged and spread her hands. "You going around and checking on all us folks who live alone? I don't think I'm old enough yet to qualify as a senior citizen."

His eyes roamed the room and he stood uncertainly, hooking his thumbs into his belt. "Have you been out at all?"

"Well no, not since I got home last night. Looked like it was going to be a bad blow and the weather reports didn't sound promising. I just holed up for the night."

"Did you hear anything?"

Kendra shook her head. "Wind whistling bothers me, so I put my headset on and listened to music." She was suddenly conscious of the cold coming in the door. "Well, come on, don't want all this heat to escape and drive up my heating bill."

He stepped into the living room.

"What's going on?"

He gave a small cough and looked back at her. "You own a green Jeep Cherokee?"

"Well, yeah. You know that, Calvin. Old Nellybelle. The one I owned in high school. Found her, bought her back and restored her." She still felt so proud of managing to do that.

"And where is she?" he asked cautiously, but even as she knew what was coming, Kendra noticed he had given Nellybelle the feminine designation.

"Parked in the shed, of course. You don't think I'd leave her out on a night like last night. She'd get cold."

"Can we go out and see her?"

Kendra gave him what she hoped was a puzzled look. "Sure, but I don't see why? Let me get my jacket."

She walked back into the kitchen, tossed the towel on the table as she gave the room a quick look over. She picked up her jacket off the hook by the back door and turned to see Calvin at the door also looking over the kitchen. She shrugged apologetically. "Storms make me feel hemmed in. I clean when I get nervous."

He nodded. "Wife does the same thing."

They went back through the house and out the front door. His patrol car was parked by the barn and it was a short walk to the shed. The weather this morning was clear, cold. Sound traveled but all she could hear was the crackling of his patrol radio and the crunch of snow.

"Door's open," Kendra muttered when she got close to the shed. "Now I know I closed that."

The empty space was still a shock even if she already knew the Jeep was gone.

"It's gone!" She turned back to Calvin. "Nellybelle's gone!" And she felt afresh all the shock and anger and loss. That part she didn't have to fake. Much to her dismay, she felt tears, and she angrily rubbed them away and then thought maybe that was a good thing.

Calvin walked around the shed, noticing the old pickup truck parked in the next bay. "You leave the keys in it, Ms. McKenna?"

"Well, no. I realize I'm not in the city anymore, but some habit's die hard."

He nodded. A lot of folks still left their keys in their vehicles. He looked in the cab of the pickup where the keys were in that ignition.

"You got them?"

Oh, shit, did I leave them in the ignition? Kendra thought in a panic. She put her hands in her pocket and breathed a sigh of relief. She pulled them out and held them up. She must have automatically done that when she hung over the edge.

"Strange," Calvin commented as he came back to stare down at the dirt floor where the Jeep had been parked. "Keys in the pickup, but the Jeep is gone."

Kendra gave an uneasy laugh. "Calvin, if you had the choice between the two, which one would you take?"

He gave a snort. "Well, got a point there."

"But God," Kendra moaned. "Nellybelle stolen." She thought she was going to cry. "After all my work." She moaned again and then she brightened, turning to Calvin. "Could someone just have taken her for a joyride, do you think she can be found?"

Grasping at straws, she knew. But that seemed like the thing to do.

"I don't think so, Ms. McKenna," Calvin said uneasily.

"Calvin, you could at least call me Kendra. It's not like we don't know each other."

"Yes, ma'am." He stepped back as if unsure how she might react. "I'm afraid I've got more bad news for you," he said cautiously. "We've already found Nellybelle—your Jeep."

"Found her?" She looked at his face and threw herself in to whatever relief she thought he should see. "Someone just took her out and she's in a ditch—she's wrecked isn't she? How bad? I've fixed her up once, I can do it twice." She reached out and took hold of his arm.

He was shaking his head. "I don't think so, Ms. McKenna." He paused. "Someone going across the bridge at Piper's Mill saw her in the middle of the creek."

"Piper's Mill?" That was farther down the creek, three miles down from where she had put her in. Kendra's breath really caught and she didn't have to fake the stunned look. "In the creek?"

"Yes, ma'am. We're searching to see where she went in." In the background, the crackling of his radio seemed loud. "Are you sure didn't loan her out? You know, tell someone they could borrow it if they needed it. Someone might have been desperate in last night's storm if they had an emergency."

Kendra shook her head, numbly. The creek must have been more flooded than what she thought, and she had a moment's true panic as she thought anew of Robin going out on that ice. "No," she said. *Robin's safe at the shelter; I pulled her off the ice, out of the water.* "No," she repeated coming back to the present. "I don't loan my vehicles. And besides, I was in the house. Anyone I knew would have knocked on the door."

"But you had the headphones on."

Kendra shook her head. "If anyone was close enough that I'd loan them Nellybelle, they'd know where to get into the house. They would have gotten my attention." She turned back to him. "You're sure?"

"Yes, ma'am. I'm sorry."

He did look sorry; Kendra almost felt guilty for deceiving him. *Trust no one*, Stockton had said.

"Did you find out who took her?" she asked finally. "I mean." She couldn't go on and all she could think of was Stockton in the root cellar, lying on the slab where she had dragged him until she figured out what to do.

"No, ma'am. We didn't find anyone. We don't know if they got out or…" He stopped. "Those warm days produced a lot of flooding before this storm moved in. A lot of water coming downstream. If this had been rain instead of snow, we'd be having a hell of a flood."

"Might anyway," Kendra said automatically, picking up threads of a coherent conversation. "Once all these snows pass." She looked at her empty bay again. "I need to call the insurance company," she said, beginning to think of things she needed to do.

"You got transportation?"

She waved toward the old pickup. "It'll get me into town." She looked up. "My Jeep?"

"We're hauling it out, have to inspect it. You'll need to file a report."

She nodded. "You need anything else?"

"No, ma'am."

"Very good." Kendra turned around and walked back to the house. She needed to figure out what to do next, what was going on.

"That went well. Maybe you need to take up acting in your spare time."

Kendra closed the door and leaned against it. "Who's acting?" She buried her face in her hands and slid down the door, squatting on the floor. She covered her head with her arms. "What am I going to do?" she moaned.

"Now is not the time to panic." Linda sat easily in the wing chair by the window, her legs crossed.

"If not now, when?"

"Well, if Nellybelle washed downstream, that's good. They'll probably find the point of entry at some point but it'll still take time."

"Probably."

"And if they can't find anyone, then they'll be searching. And Harris will be looking but we know who he's looking for. It's perfect."

"Perfect," Kendra repeated.

"Don't panic yet, dear heart. It's not over yet, and you never panic until it's all over."

"I may break that rule."

"Come on. You've got things to do."

"Yeah. Finish mopping the kitchen floor." Kendra put her head back against the door. She took some deep breaths. She could adapt. She could deal with it. She just had a bad moment then. Unbidden, the thought of Robin on the ice came to mind and she pushed it away. Didn't happen. She was there. Robin was safe. She could deal with it. And then unbidden she thought of the body in the root cellar. Well, she would have to do something about that.

First of all, she called Harris. "Sheriff's deputy was just here," she reported. "Looking for my Jeep. Seems they found it in the creek this morning, down by Piper's Mill…Yes, Piper's Mill. No, they didn't find any body and they're looking to see where it went in. Yes, volunteering to help might be to your advantage…I can't. I'm the owner. I need to do other things… Like call the insurance company, get another set of wheels. File a theft report first. Need to go into the sheriff's office." She listened for a moment. "All right. If I hear anything I'll let you know."

She hung up. Okay, that was taken care of. She went back to the kitchen. Finish the floor, give her time to think. Robin was going to be so pissed at her for not getting back but she didn't dare risk it yet. And there were a couple of other things to do. Robin was safe and sound where she was. God, she hoped the woman wasn't claustrophobic. She made her mental list.

Sheriff's office

Insurance office

Rental agency

Call Travis. Maybe. Maybe not. Travis could pick up so much from her voice. She'd need to get a grip before she called her.

Crowded event. What kind of event would pull in a crowd? Just wasn't the season.

And then there was the small matter of the business card resting in her hip pocket. She didn't even want to think about it.

CHAPTER EIGHTEEN

Kendra walked out of the sheriff's office, paperwork in hand, wondering how many laws she was breaking. Falsely reporting a crime. She'd deal with it later. Sometimes procrastination could work to her advantage. She walked up the street to the storefront insurance office. Insurance fraud. Gee, add another one to the list. Maybe she'd better put retaining a lawyer on her list of things to do.

The bells on the door jingled as she went in.

"Good afternoon," the receptionist greeted. "How can we help you today?"

"Shelly in?"

"Ahhh, yes. She's just getting off the phone now. You are?"

"Kendra McKenna."

The short, somewhat plump, little blonde in the black wool pantsuit came around the desk. "Kendra! It's been so long! I'd heard you were back in town but I've been out every time you came in." She hugged her and Kendra hugged her back. She had gone to school with Shelly's daughter; they had been in band together so there had been lots of practice time, carpooling. "What can I do for you?"

"Tell me what I need to do?" She sat down across the desk from Shelly, taking in the cluttered desk and family pictures. "My Jeep was stolen."

"Nellybelle? Oh, I'm so sorry. Now who would steal Nellybelle?"

Kendra shook her head. She hated to deceive her old friend but—no she wouldn't think of that either. "I don't know. And it gets even worse. Sheriff's office found her in the creek this morning."

"Ohhhh." Shelly folded her arms and bowed her head in sympathy. "After all the work you did restoring her. You must be devastated."

Kendra put out her hand and shook her head. "I—I can't even talk about it," she said with perfect honesty. "Just tell me what I have to do."

"Well, let me pull you up." Shelly went back to business. "You kept the receipts for all the restoration, didn't you?"

"Yeah. Even as pictures of the various stages."

"That's good, better than good. Saves a lot of arguments. And you filed a theft report?" Kendra held up the paperwork.

Shelly made the proper concerned noises as she made out the list. More phone calls. Inspector. Yes, there was the rider to cover a rental. Impounded? Investigation? Was it totaled? Any chance of being restored. No idea. Back and forth, with Shelly nodding, making a phone call or two and coming back with information. Kendra could almost convince herself this was just something she really had had no control over. And she needed to keep thinking that.

"Okay," she said, gathering up more papers. She drew a deep breath and shook her head. "A nightmare," she said, "but I'll get through it." She looked up at Shelly. "Now, change of subject. You looked bubbly when I came in. Everything going well for you?"

"Just great," Shelly said with a smile. And she leaned forward conspiratorially. "Brian's coming to visit. And I'm just so excited, I can hardly wait." Her eyes were glowing, but they always glowed when she spoke of her grandson. "He used to spend every summer with me, and it seems like it's been forever since I've seen him. This job just ties him up so much."

"He lives in Texas? Somewhere out west now?" Kendra ventured. She remembered Shelly's pride in Brian. Every time she stopped in to pay insurance over the years she heard more about Brian. And she remembered babysitting for him, or rather, Connie babysitting for her nephew and him being around quite a bit. She remembered him as a cute kid but that was about all.

"Not Texas. South Dakota. Oh, we're so proud of him. You know he joined the police force out there, first city and then state." Kendra made appropriate nods at the proper time, the proper response as Shelly bubbled on about how great Brian was. "Now he works for the governor's office, one of the advance men, goes ahead to set up security, check the hotels, all that stuff. Oh, you wouldn't believe all the places he's been; to Brazil for a trade conference, to England for an energy conference."

"Quite a bit of travel for a small-town boy," Kendra said with a smile at Shelly's pride and joy. "So he's getting some time off? I would think he could pick a better time to travel than when we're having spring storms. Or has he been gone so long he's forgotten about them?"

"Oh no, this is business," Shelly gushed on. "Something about the governor coming here. He's a native, grew up in the southern part of the state. He's coming for some conference, and then the basketball finals should be about that time. He might be attending. If his old alma mater makes it that far. Which they probably will. You know what a powerhouse North Central is."

"Probably so," Kendra said with a laugh. "Haven't had a state championship without them since I can't remember when." She shook her head. "So little Brian's done well. Boy, he's got a job these days."

"The news hasn't been released yet," Shelly said in a lower voice, "but I know you won't say anything. I'm just so excited."

Kendra went out of the office, envying Shelly. Kendra was glad to see someone happy, so normally happy, and then she thought about how she was deceiving her. She absently picked up the newspaper and folded it under her arm. She'd read it later, maybe take her mind off things. She still wasn't sure what she was going to do about the call to Travis.

And that other call.

She ended up going to the truck stop. They still had phones available for all the truckers coming through, high traffic, busy. The parking lot was full because parts of the interstate were closed. Truckers filled the lot, their diesels still going because of the cold. The restaurant was full of travelers, milling around, the television screens posting the latest in road conditions. Kids running around. Yes, it was just crowded enough.

She waited until she got the phone in the corner, less chance of being overheard.

"You can do it," Linda said behind her.

"Shut up and go away. I can't do anything with you hanging over my shoulder."

She closed her eyes as she punched in the number. A number. That was all she had. Three rings. She was almost relieved there was no answer. She'd tried. But she knew she would have to try again. Then it was answered on the fifth ring.

"Deacon."

"Who is this?" she asked, not sure at all what she wanted to say, or even who she was talking to.

"Who is *this*?" came back the rough demanding question. "How'd you get this number?"

"From Stockton." If they knew who Stockton was, that was good. If not, then she'd hang up.

"Why isn't he calling?" The tone had changed, not argumentative.

"Because he's dead."

There was shocked silence.

"How'd it happen?"

So this was a possibility, Kendra surmised. "Gunshot." She swallowed, seeing again Stockton on her kitchen floor. She had never been so close to violence. She took a deep breath, calming herself. "Who are you?"

"Who are you?"

"Doesn't matter who I am," she said flatly. Was her voice shaking? "All I know is that Stockton's dead, I don't know who killed him but before he died, he said something big was going to happen, a bombing."

"A bombing? Where? When?"

"No idea."

"Are you with the militia?"

Questions, questions with no answers. She was scared enough to be angry. "Who the hell are you?"

"ATF."

Alcohol, Tobacco, Firearms and Explosives. So they did get someone in, was her first thought.

"Now who are you?"

"Doesn't matter," she said. Oh, God, she was in way over her head. "He was what, an infiltrator? Investigating."

"Yes."

"Okay," she said with a sigh of resignation. "I don't know if he was discovered; I don't know who killed him. But I don't think it was the militia so to speak, not as a group. Harris, he's the commander."

"Yes, we're aware who's who."

Oh, shit, then they've probably got me. "Harris is shaken. I don't think he knows Stockton's dead. He thinks he's taken off with this reporter."

"Slusher."

Kendra's stomach cramped more. She clamped her jaws shut.

"Is she safe?"

She nodded before she realized nodding didn't help. "Yes," she could say with certainty. "A Jeep was stolen; found in the Little Pine this morning. They think they took off in it, something happened."

"But they didn't."

"No." She took a deep breath. "Something's brewing; but I don't think—I don't think it's the militia doing it. I think they're being used."

"Are you a member?"

"Manner of speaking," she hedged. "In it, maybe not with it. Everyone's waiting. Jeffers is supposed—"

"Artie Jeffers?"

"Yes, supposed to be planning something. But I don't know when."

Then came the slow, cautious question she'd been dreading. "Is this Mac?"

She hung up, her heart pounding so much she thought she'd pass out. She stumbled away from the phones, lurched into the wall.

"You all right, ma'am? Bad news?"

She straightened up from the wall. She nodded. She let them lead her to a booth, brought her something to drink. *Great undercover agent I am*, she thought with some clarity. "Thank you."

Hot coffee. She hated coffee. She only drank it at Robin's because, well, because Robin was a damn attractive woman and she didn't want to make a fuss. She thought about it. Stockton told her to get Robin out of there. So he knew who Robin was, in spite of her denials. Was he the one she was going to meet? Damn, she had to get back and talk to that woman.

"Feeling better?" the waitress stopped by with a refill. "You were looking pretty white there."

"Much better." She drew a breath, pulled out the newspaper. Anything to distract herself from Stockton, Robin, Linda. Now the Mideast crisis, that sounded manageable. Ice storm weather. Basketball standings. She calmed. Politics. Hopefuls still flirting around with the possibilities. Presidential elections were drawing out longer and longer. Perkins, native son, was flirting with the possibility, but no declaration yet. Much too soon, his office said. Would be making the decision in the next couple of months. But there was a PAC committee set up, so speculation was there that he would be a candidate. And the declared ones were already gearing up. Perkins could be a strong candidate. There was a short bio attached.

"Good God!"

She pulled money from her pocket and threw it on the table. Her imagination could be working overtime and what if she was wrong. Or worse, what if she were right? She was calling her insurance office even as she went to the truck.

"Let me speak to Shelly?" she demanded. "Kendra, I was in there earlier."

She calmed before Shelly came on the line.

"Kendra, is there something wrong?"

Kendra took a deep breath. "No, just idiots on the road, who can't drive in snow and ice." This lying was just getting easier and easier.

"They can be trying."

"I was just on my way to rent a car or something at least. I couldn't remember the restrictions. And is this something the insurance is billed for or do they reimburse me?"

"Up to midsize, although if you want something else and pay the difference, that's your choice. It's a daily limit. And we get billed and then we'll bill you."

Kendra sighed as if that were her greatest problem. "Okay, I can deal with it. I don't suppose they'll have a Jeep but well, at least I know what's what before I go in. Won't be bumbling around like an idiot." She paused. "You know, it was really good talking to you earlier. Calming. Took my mind of it for a while at least."

"That's what we're here for," Shelly said with her cheerful tone.

"And it was great hearing about Brian. I've been so out of touch I hadn't heard anything—or if I heard, I'd forgotten. The governor's office, you said. What governor? Texas?" She held her breath.

"No, not Texas. Perkins. Governor of South Dakota."

"Boy, we do let the good ones get away, don't we? I was just reading in the paper about him. Quite the mover and the shaker, isn't he?"

"Quite. As you can imagine, we're quite excited."

"I'll bet," Kendra said breathlessly. "To think, small-town boy from Walton's Corner. Really up there with the big boys now, isn't he? Now I can see why you're just ready to bust your buttons. Well, here I am at the rental place. Thanks for the info, Shelly. You take care."

She broke the connection and buried her head on her folded arms across the steering wheel. Way over her head.

CHAPTER NINETEEN

"Where have you been!" Robin almost attacked her as she came down the hallway. "Lock me up in here and say you'll be back shortly and then don't come back in just forever! And this—this crypt! I don't even know the security code to unlock the door! If something happens to you, I'll be in here until God knows when! Or was that the idea, all along?"

Robin would have physically attacked her if Kendra hadn't caught her first, taking hold of her shoulders and shoving her back against the wall. "Locking you in was a damn sight safer than you getting a wild hair and taking off. So I'm here now," she said firmly, calmly. "And now we're going to have a little chitchat."

Robin stared back at her, breathing hard, eyes dilated, suddenly looking more than a little scared. So there was something to break the lady's cool. Kendra could hardly blame her; the idea of spending years down here didn't appeal to her either. Robin was right. If Kendra hadn't come back, Robin had no idea how to get out. And would anyone find her? One more detail to take care of. But right now, there were other matters to deal with.

Somewhere along the drive home, she'd crossed a line. Either she was so frightened it didn't matter anymore, or she had just tucked all that panic away and would deal with it later. Right now, everything was becoming crystal clear and she had the nerve to face down anything and everything. She hoped to all the powers that be that whatever this feeling was, wherever it had come from, it would last long enough.

"This time, you're going to be honest with me," she said in Robin's face, watching her gain some control. Yes, Robin knew more than what she had been saying.

"Like you've been honest with me?" Robin retorted.

"I've been straight with you, Robin, probably more so than you've been with me. I don't like being used, lady, and you've done your share of using."

Robin dropped her eyes but just as quickly looked up. "I told you I was investigating Jeffers."

"And I told you I was tracking him down. Now you tell me just what you were really doing here and how you got in."

"You know all that. I don't know why you're acting so hush-hush now. It's not like there's anyone else here. You told me."

"Me? What the hell are you talking about? I never told you anything!"

Robin said nothing, set her jaw. Kendra jerked her away from the wall and shook her, thoroughly angry now and with a new feeling of fear. "Who told you? Only the locals and hunters use that back way."

Robin brought up her hands to Kendra's arms to stop her. "All right, you didn't," she finally got out. Kendra stopped. "Whoever you had call me told me where to go."

Kendra let her go so suddenly Robin sagged back against the wall. "What the hell are you talking about?" she repeated. "I didn't have anyone call you! You think I'm crazy? I told you from the beginning to stay out of here." She stared at Robin, wondering if she was lying, was protecting someone but Robin's eyes widened as comprehension sank in.

Robin swallowed, her hand to her throat. "She said you were in trouble, needed to get some information out about an infiltrator." She pressed herself against the wall, away from Kendra.

Kendra looked into Robin's eyes. The Greeks thought that the eyes were the windows of the soul. What kind of soul did Robin have? How far would she go for a story? No, she said that she came because whoever called her said Kendra was in trouble. Concern? Or a lead for her story? "Stockton," she said woodenly.

Robin shook her head. "She didn't name names, said it was too dangerous, but this Stockton, he's the infiltrator?"

Kendra closed her eyes, trying to take in this new information. "Not anymore. He's dead."

"Dead?" Robin's eyes widened until she looked like one of the characters in a Japanese graphic novel. She reached out for Kendra but stopped before she actually touched her.

"Dead." A shock, Kendra decided as Robin's hand dropped. Did Robin really think these boys were all talk? At least someone was playing for keeps. The question was who. "And I guess the last thing he did was cover your ass by convincing me to get you out of there." She took a breath, still wondering. "I don't like being used. I don't like being deceived."

"Who killed him?"

Even though Kendra wasn't blocking her way, Robin hadn't moved away from the wall, as if she needed it for support.

"Well, I know I didn't." She looked Robin up and down. "And I don't think you did." *Only because you were locked up.* "And that's about all I know, so your guess is as good as mine. Maybe better since someone lured you here."

"Dead." Robin stared at the floor, her face paling. She looked up suddenly at Kendra. "Who was he working for?"

"ATF." Kendra turned and walked down the hall to the living room.

Robin followed her, grabbed her arm. "You've got to let me out of here! I've got to—"

Kendra jerked away from Robin's touch, turning on her with immediate heated anger. "Like hell I do! You're staying put."

Robin stepped back from her and Kendra took a deep breath, calming herself. No, she didn't think Robin was involved but she was certainly unpredictable.

"Harris thinks you and Stockton went off together. Right now, the creek is being dragged for your bodies. They don't know Stockton is dead and they don't know anything about you. So you're staying here, out of sight, so they stay unaware."

Robin took this in. Kendra could almost see the wheels turning. "Are you sure Stockton's—"

"Dead? Quite sure." Kendra calmed herself, the image of Stockton laid out on a slab cooling her considerably.

"What are you going to do?"

Kendra shook her head. "But I know what you're going to do." She looked up at Robin. "You're going to tell me everything you know, everything this woman told you, and everything you surmised."

"And if I don't?"

"Then I'll go back to my original plan of getting Jeffers. And if I get killed in the process, then I guess you've got enough food and supplies here to last for about the next ten years at least. Give you time to learn to cook." She gave Robin a frosty look. "Be one of our little local mysteries as to your disappearance. Maybe you can become a ghost."

Oh, please! Linda said inside her head.

"You wouldn't."

Kendra leaned forward, narrowed her eyes. "Wanna bet?"

Robin gave her a long look and then she slowly shook her head. "No." She waved to the living room. "Can we at least sit down? I've been working on this for a long time."

Actually, Kendra thought as she listened to Robin's summation, she understood it pretty well. Her research indicated that Artie hadn't been working on the pipeline. He was the suspect in several robberies, never on home ground, usually with other loosely-linked politically-aligned groups. While the robberies weren't large enough to garner out-of-the-area attention, they kept him going, buying what he needed, and bringing a wage back home. Working for the pipeline was a great cover story. Other than that, Kendra had learned almost as much as Robin by infiltrating the group.

As they sat across the counter from each other, Kendra began to relax. In spite of everything swirling around her, she was as comfortable as she had been in months. She remembered how they used to talk, and how Robin had felt in her arms two nights before.

Kendra thought of all the times she had spent with her, the games, the dinners. It seemed like a lifetime ago, happening to some other person. Would she ever be able to go back to being that person?

"How'd you find out all this?" she asked when Robin finished.

"Investigation on some of the groups out west. Southern Poverty Law Center keeps track," Robin admitted. "There was one reference to an unknown person. The name didn't match but, well, it sounded like Artie so I just took that hunch and played it out. It pretty much fit."

Kendra had calmed down considerably. What Robin had told her explained a few things. There was nothing there about Linda, but there was definitely enough about Artie to indicate he had the violence, the wherewithal to kill someone. This wasn't a spur-of-the-moment thing. This was something Artie had been planning for some time. She traced her finger in circles on the counter.

"I can't believe someone just called you up and lured you out here."

"She said you were in trouble."

Kendra looked up at her in puzzled disbelief. Could Robin mean what it sounded like, that Kendra in trouble was enough of a lure? She shook the thought off. "Didn't it even occur to you that—not to belittle your skills any—someone might be setting you up?"

"It did, but I guess I wasn't thinking clearly."

Kendra digested that and then put the thought aside. As intriguing as the thought might be, there were a few other pressing matters that if she didn't take care of, she'd never have the opportunity to figure out what Robin really meant. "Tell me what this woman said."

Robin shrugged. "She called the station."

"Not your cell phone?" Robin shook her head. "I would have given your cell number."

"I asked about that, she said she lost it." Robin gave Kendra a look that said she hadn't lost her senses completely. "I wasn't there the first time she called and she wouldn't leave a number. They gave her a time I'd be back, and she called."

"What'd she say?"

"She was a friend of yours from here, that you couldn't call but you needed to see me."

"And you didn't think that was strange?"

"She said you'd found out something important, would be a big story for me."

"She got your buttons right," Kendra commented. Robin fell silent and Kendra was immediately sorry. What did she expect? Robin was a reporter. "Sorry," she said in a brief apology. Nothing would be gained snipping at each other. "What else?"

Robin looked away. "Said that you were sorry for being so ugly, that you wanted to be able to tell me that."

"And you believed her?"

Robin gave a small shrug. "It seemed reasonable," she offered without looking at Kendra. "You were ugly, you seemed rather conciliatory at Christmas. Sounded like something you might mention to a friend."

"A friend. Who have I got here I'd consider a friend?" She sat back, thinking. If she would have said anything to anyone, it would have been Betty Lou but she knew that she hadn't mentioned anything about Robin. And as for her being ugly, well, with her mood for the past few months, describing her as ugly at any point by any number of people would be accurate.

"But you did find out something important, didn't you?" Robin asked cautiously. "Something big."

Kendra frowned, as she thought of all the pieces she had. "Oh, yeah. Big pieces. I'm just not sure how they go together." She began to tick them off. "I thought Stockton was investigating weapon stockpiling but then he said something about a bombing."

"Said?"

Kendra nodded, still thinking aloud. "Artie had been in and out. I thought he was avoiding me but maybe it was something else. And then in the past couple of weeks, there was a lot of excitement. Comments like 'this was even better, make an impact. Something looked possible but it wasn't nailed down.'"

She frowned, didn't like the way this was shaping up. For all the times she wished things would happen, this was moving too quickly.

"And what have you put together?" Robin asked.

Kendra looked up, not sure she wanted to share anything. *Trust no one*, Stockton had said. Did that include Robin? "Artie's got people listening to him, Harris is losing influence. I don't think he knows what's going on anymore."

"Is that good or bad?"

Kendra frowned and sat back in the chair. "Bad, I think. Artie is always egging him on, wanting something to happen. Harris's 'be prepared' philosophy drives Artie crazy. He wants some action. Harris considered Artie capable of doing something but he thought he had him contained."

"He know anything about Linda?"

Kendra shook her head. She was stymied.

"You said he put Sue in the hospital."

Kendra nodded. "Yeah, that tarnished him a little, cracked his reputation. But not enough for anyone to think of him doing anything truly awful. After all, gotta keep the little woman in line." She finished up bitterly. "And Sue's had a mouth on her that would drive anyone to desperate measures." She looked up suddenly. "Not that I'm condoning it. She's manipulative bitch." She had a sudden thought. *Just how manipulative?*

Robin looked away, drummed her fingers on the counter. Finally she asked. "Does he know about this place?"

Kendra shook her head. "No, I don't think so. My dad was a paranoid individual. This was here when he bought the place, and he forbade any mention of it. After all, if World War Three started, he didn't want the neighborhood crowding to get in. Maybe the old-timers knew about it, but I suspect it's been pretty well forgotten. Why? Do you think I'd put you in a spot where he could find you?"

"But Linda knew about it?"

Kendra gave a rueful smile. "Yeah. We had her mother's cabins and this to hide in." She gazed at the counter and for the moment she could think of other times down here. Abruptly she came back to the present. "Why?"

"I just wondered if she was trying to get away from him, why she didn't hide here. I mean, when you searched for her, you did check here, didn't you?"

"Of course. It was my first thought. And I could tell that she had been here off and on but not within the time frame."

She could see the indecision on Robin's face. "What?"

Robin looked down at her clasped hands. "I wasn't sure if you were coming back, or when. So I searched the place, thought surely you must have left something for me as to how to get out of here."

"And?" She looked around at all the kitchen cabinets, the storage areas. "You have been pretty neat. I hadn't noticed."

"Well, you've been distracted," Robin said. "I've had time to kill." She took a deep breath. "I found something."

Kendra merely tilted her head but said nothing.

Without another word, Robin got up and went to the room already designated as hers. She came back with a box. "I found this." She slid it across the bar to Kendra. "I couldn't figure out a combination."

Kendra twirled the numbers, a date. The lock clicked open. She opened the box. There was a packet of letters; she flipped through them. There were several she had sent from California, gambling that Linda would pick up the mail and not Artie. Then there were some others, in Linda's writing. She picked up the one note in an envelope and unfolded it, ignoring Robin.

"I'm so sorry I didn't go with you that day, Kendra. It was my mistake. You were right. I should have gone. I thought I could manage. I thought Artie would calm down after you were gone and I could leave then. You might as well be living around the corner. He's unreasonable about you; even after all this time. Now I'm afraid to leave. He would know that I would go to you, no matter where you were. And he would hunt us both down. I can't live like that; I can't put you in that danger.

"I know you won't sell your farm as long as I am here and I know that Artie won't let it go until there is nothing here to remind him of you."

There was a break, some space, and then her writing picked up again.

"Sunshine, I've got to leave. He's never been violent before but now he's gotten in with some people with some extreme views. I don't know what he's capable of anymore. I'm afraid it's only a matter of time before something really bad happens and I don't want to be part of it. I won't be able to go to you or contact you, at least not for a while. By now, he's totally convinced himself that we've been secret lovers all this time, and there is no reasoning with him. I don't dare take a chance of leading him to you. The way he talks, he might try to kill us both and I want to keep you safe.

"I'm so sorry you got dragged into this, Sunshine. You know that was never my intent. And as much as I hate to say it, I'm so sorry you didn't shoot him that day. If you had, so much grief would have been prevented. But now, I'm so glad you got away and have had your life. If we never meet again, please remember me with love and kindness and please forgive me.

"All my love, now and always—forever—Linda."

The note ended there. Stunned, Kendra folded it.

"Oh, Linda," she moaned, and she put her fist to her forehead. "Why didn't you tell me!"

Only silence answered her.

She sat up, knowing Linda wouldn't answer her this time. Her grief, her anger settled in her with a coldness that froze out all other feeling. For several minutes, she saw nothing, felt nothing and then she came to her decision and knew what she was going to do. Like Harris said, the system was broken. The guilty walked around free.

"Kendra," Robin said cautiously. "Are you all right?" Robin reached across the counter to lay her hand on Kendra's arm.

Kendra jerked away and looked up at her with a cold remoteness. "I'm fine," she said in emotionless tones. "Thank you for bringing this to my attention. I appreciate it." She efficiently folded up the letters, the other paperwork and put them back in the box. She slammed the lid and twirled the dial to lock it again.

Robin was looking at her strangely. "What—was it—did Linda leave word for you?"

"Yes." Her answer was short and clipped, cold even to her ears.

"What did she tell you?" Robin asked cautiously. She still had her arm stretched across the table, reaching for Kendra even though she had pulled away from her grasp.

"That bastard put her through hell because he thought she and I were secret lovers all those years."

Robin withdrew her arm. "But you didn't see her. Did you?"

"No, I stayed away because I thought my being out of the picture kept her safe." She pushed away from the bar and got to her feet. "It would have been better if I had come around. At least then, she might have been able to get away if I was there to help her."

"You don't know that," Robin said in a placating tone. "It might have set him off worse."

"Worse?" Kendra snorted. She charged back at the bar at Robin and even though there was a two-foot barrier between them, Robin drew back. "What in hell could have been worse?" Kendra demanded, leaning over the bar.

"Linda wouldn't have liked it if you were hurt," Robin said in a calming voice. "You know that. Linda probably even told you that."

Kendra glared at Robin but she made no argument because Robin was right. "Yes, that's what she's been telling me."

"Telling you?" Robin repeated in a startled voice.

"Yes," Kendra burst out with, throwing all discretion to the winds. "All along. She wants justice. She wants retribution. But she wants me to be safe. As if that matters!" She glared at Robin, clenching her hands. If she could just do something right now, if she could lay her hands on Artie right now, he'd tell her.

Robin had a look of disbelief and then she took a calming breath. "What are you going to do?" she asked in the voice one speaks with to hysterical people or to people who have a different reality.

"I'm going to make the bastard tell me what he did to her."

"Okay." Robin drew and let out a slow breath. "Well, you're not going to rush out tonight and do it, are you?"

"Don't be patronizing," Kendra snapped. "You know he's not here. But I tell you, if it weren't for you, I'd be at the compound waiting for him when he came in."

"Well, then, you've still got time to plan, don't you?" Robin came back and settled at the bar. "Do you know what's he's planning? How far along the plans are?"

Such reasonable questions, Kendra thought. There was nothing she could do right now except plan and speculate, although she didn't want to do that. Now she felt such a clarity of purpose. Every doubt had been cast out, every argument presented to counter her decision was eliminated, evaporated. She knew what she was going to do, no matter what the cost, and she was determined. No one was going to talk her out of it.

"No."

"No, what? You don't have time? You don't know what he's planning?" Robin cautiously laid her hand over Kendra's clenched fists. "Kendra, this man is dangerous. You need to be careful."

Kendra didn't pull away from Robin's touch but she said nothing, her mind going at a furious pace. What would he have done? What was he going to do?

"Do you think he killed Stockton?"

Of course, she realized. "Possibly," she said. "Probably." They had both been at the storage shed in the back. Where did Stockton say he was going when he told her to get Robin out of there? He was off to find out what Artie was up to, and the next time she saw him, he had been shot. Still, that was over a twelve-hour period. He could have gone lots of places, seen several people in that time. And Artie was conspicuously absent when she had told Harris about the missing Jeep. Was he lying too, going through the motions of looking for Stockton and Robin when he knew Stockton was out of the picture?

"And you're convinced he killed Linda?" Robin's quiet insistent voice brought her back to the present.

"Yes."

"On what evidence?"

Would this woman ever stop asking questions? Kendra didn't bother answering. She unlocked the small box and flung it open. She pulled the letter out and tossed it over.

As Robin pulled it out of the envelope, she got up and went to the kitchen. There was enough food for Robin for a few days, but she had no clear idea how long she might have to remain here. At least she seemed to understand now why she was here. She checked the cabinets, her mind now functioning pragmatically. Frequent trips here might be dangerous. She took stock of the canned goods. The woman couldn't cook but she could operate a can opener and the microwave. The meals might not fit her sophisticated taste but she wouldn't starve. As soon as Kendra could manage it, she'd get her out of here.

She returned to the bar. Robin had finished the letter, it lying to one side, and she was going through the box. She held up a picture, looked at it curiously.

"Is this Linda?"

Kendra took the picture. "Yeah. Last fireworks we went to. One of the ball games down at Indy." She handed it back.

Robin swallowed. "Ahh, this looks like the woman who was holding on to you the other night when you pulled me out of the water. The one I asked you about."

Kendra shook her head. "I told you there wasn't anyone with me."

"But I saw her."

Kendra looked at her in surprise. No one else had ever seen Linda, at least not that they had mentioned to her. "Really?" She caught herself before she told Robin she had been seeing things. Such statements had always infuriated her. Besides, wasn't this some sort of validation? "There was no one there," she repeated.

"You said," Robin started out then stopped. "You said before, that Linda said."

Kendra watched Robin's confusion, understanding it perfectly.

"You talk to her? She talks to you?" Robin finally said lamely.

Kendra reluctantly nodded. "Suppose it will help me with an insanity plea?" Kendra asked drily as she thought of all the crimes she had committed in the last thirty-six hours.

Robin stared at the picture, glancing at Kendra. "I don't know." Then as if she realized what Kendra had said. "What have you done?"

"Well, I made it look like you and Stockton stole my Jeep. Reported it stolen."

"Anything else?"

"Asks the kidnapped victim?"

Robin shrugged. "Well, once you explained it." Robin trailed off. "What are you going to do?"

Kendra shook her head. She didn't have concrete plans about Artie, and if she did, she was even less sure about sharing them with Robin. "Cook dinner," she answered instead, with the thought that food might get Robin's mind off her. And from the brightened look on Robin's face, the distraction seemed to work. "I assume you haven't eaten."

"Well. I found the peanut butter."

"Come on in the kitchen. You're getting a cooking lesson. Then I've got to get back to the house. I can only be missing for so long."

CHAPTER TWENTY

Kendra sat on the couch watching the flames in the woodstove, brooding again. Robin was set for a bit but Kendra had the feeling it wouldn't be long. A surprise that she had seen Linda. But who would lure her here? She remembered the taped conversation with Johnny and Clyde or was it Steve? Anyway— would she bite? She'd thought it was about her. What if it was about Robin? But Robin said a woman called. Kendra picked up the phone.

"Hey, Frog. This is Kendra. Glad I caught you at home. I guess it takes a snowstorm to keep you at home?"

"Keep them women away," Frog said with a laugh. "Heard you lost your Jeep. Sorry about that, Miss Kendra. I know you put a store of time in fixing that up."

"Ahhh, well." Kendra was still sometimes surprised how fast gossip could travel, even with storms like these. "Got a question for you, Frog. You said that day that Linda canceled, you were up at Sue's mama's place? Was Sue there?"

"Yeah, I do believe she was. You know, that was before she married up with Artie."

"Yes," Kendra cut him off before he went into one of his stories. "Did you tell her that Linda canceled?"

"Yes, ma'am. Really surprised me, upset me a bit 'cause I was a'counting on that money. She asked what was wrong, and I told her."

"Uh-huh." She nodded as Frog went on to talk but she was only half listening. So Sue knew.

Wonder if Sue called Artie and he came back? she mused as she hung up. And probably she could be described to anyone she'd had contact with over the past few months as 'ugly' and it would be believed. Robin just had more reason than most.

More pieces of the puzzle. How to fit them together.

"What do you think?" Linda asked.

"I don't know," Kendra said slowly, "but I think I've got all the pieces."

"And how do they go together?"

Kendra shook her head as she turned on the television, needing to catch the evening news and local weather report. The bitter weather was very helpful for her cold storage problem, and she really wanted to know how long it was going to last. And she still needed to put pieces of the puzzle together.

"And right on schedule, the winter storm comes in to attend the state finals. But the weather won't stop the record crowds from coming to the semi-finals of the state high school basketball tournament, maybe keep them from going home. It wouldn't be the first time the attending crowd stayed in the coliseum after the game, although now with the hotels attached, it's not quite as rustic."

"More snow expected?"

"Not so much, but bitter cold."

Kendra turned around to watch the commentators. Bitter cold, that was good. A crowd. Of course, the teams in the state championships were vying for the top state ratings, more chest thumping. Both of them win their afternoon games. They were in different tiers, so it would make one hell of a final game.

She stopped. Basketball final? Record crowd? Bomb the state championships? But a VIP, Stockton said. Perkins, she realized. He was a presidential contender. There would be national media attention just for him. Oh, no, no, no.

And it was in Indianapolis, the state capital. It would make a huge impact. Maybe it would be large enough to bring the state system down just with the sheer number of casualties and the amount of damage.

Without even turning the television off, she grabbed her coat. All she could think of now was Artie's love-hate relationship with basketball.

The ground was so frozen there was good traction, but the air burned her lungs as she circled around the campground and went across Shelby's field. She recalled how crowded those games were, the stands would be packed, the final four schools as well as everyone else who followed the games. She could remember the gas explosion they'd had years before at the end of an ice skating show. That had banned gas used at the concessions, but it meant that everything had to be trucked in. So there would be a lot of rental trucks as concessions trucked in food, drinks. Not everything would be marked well. And it was always so chaotic. How close would the truck even need to be?

She crossed through the fence, went to the edge of the hill overlooking the storage shed. She couldn't see the doors from this side, so she was going to have to go down. She slid, lurched, stumbled from tree to tree as she went down and ended up running into the back of the shed, hoping that no one was there. She rubbed off the window with the back of her arm.

It was even worse. The truck was gone.

CHAPTER TWENTY-ONE

Kendra listened to the ringing phone. "Damn it, Travis, answer it! This is not the time to leave you a message." Kendra paced up and down the drive, glancing around. She didn't want to be overheard on the cell phone but she needed to organize this now.

"Lo!"

"Travis! Thank God. I just about gave up."

"Kendra?"

"I need you to do something for me."

"What time is it?"

"Five—five thirty, something like that."

"In the morning?"

"Well, it's not this dark in the afternoon!" Kendra snapped. Then she caught her self. "Yes, Travis, in the morning. And I know it's Friday and you probably have plans for tonight, but I really need you to do something for me."

"What do you need?"

"Do you remember how to come up to the farm?"

"I think so."

"Do you remember the back way I brought you in? Wait, does your truck have four-wheel? The road is terrible with drifting snow."

"I can do it."

"I need to you to drive up here early tomorrow morning and pick up a hitchhiker."

"What?"

"I need you to pick up someone and take her out of here, take her home. I can't do it and she needs to be gone."

"And she's just going to be waiting on the side of the road?"

"Yes."

"What the hell is going on with you, Kendra?"

"I don't have time to explain. I just need to know if you will do this, without fail."

"Of course I will. You said tomorrow morning."

"Yes."

"And how will I know this person you're palming off on me?"

"Oh, you'll recognize her. And Travis, don't mention this to anyone, not Peg, not anyone."

"All right." She sounded wary. "I assume sooner or later you're going to get around to explaining all this?"

"Soon, I hope. If not, then later. Maybe." *If I live through it.*

She hung up, drew a deep breath. What if she was wrong? Kendra went over and over it again. The fertilizer. The fuel. The city map. The basketball schedule. Steve missing. Clyde missing. Artie always went to the game, would he be able to stay away this year? The idea was just too crazy to be real.

The sports arena. How many people attending the Final Four? Big event for Indiana. Perkins coming? Attending?

Kendra paced through the house, unable to believe, not daring to doubt.

"He always hated the big schools," Linda pointed out.

"Why did Artie kill Stockton?" Kendra asked.

"He discovered the fertilizer. That's what was in those bags. Knew about the fuel. Baker was into cycle racing. Major explosive ingredients."

"In this weather?"

Kendra took a deep breath, glancing at the clock again. Too early to call? She picked up the phone.

Answered on the first ring. "Deacon."

Kendra took a shaky breath. "I think Artie's going to bomb the state championships."

There was a moment's silence. "Are you sure? Hardly political."

"Personal grudge," Kendra said even as she thought how foolish it sounded. "No, I'm not sure. Truck's missing. Collins boys are missing, I think Johnny is too. Artie will probably go down in the morning." She was shaking. "Another thing: Perkins may be attending."

"Perkins? You mean Governor Perkins from South Dakota?"

"He attended North Central. His conference finished up early."

"Jeez." A pause and Kendra wondered if he would believe her. "How do you know this? It's not on his schedule."

"Late change of plans," Kendra said. "He'd left free time if there was a possibility." Did she really want to implicate a proud grandmother of Perkins's advance team? Later. If she had to. Let them check it out. She gave them the information.

* * *

Kendra loaded the Glock and stuck the extra clip in her pocket. She had left letters at the house, signed and sealed, ready to be mailed. Peg, Mike, Travis. They were her family, they deserved to know. Her will was updated, the company was taken care of. All her i's dotted and her t's crossed.

ATF had come in the night before, late at night, and Kendra had laid out all the information she had. Her tapes augmented the tapes they had. The maps had provided additional information. They had left before dawn, taking Stockton, spreading out to contain the campground, to intercept the truck. They had the names, descriptions, Kendra just had to provide a few details that were lacking. She had warned them a head-on assault would play into Harris's hands, convincing him of a government attack and he would resist. Handled carefully, he could be taken. As far as she could tell, he was not a willing part of it, but if pushed into a corner, she didn't know how he would react.

Everything was done, except for Artie.

"It doesn't have to be this way," Linda protested.

"You should have told me." She lifted her foot to the chair seat, wrapped the ankle holster tight, pulled down her pants leg, pulled on her boot.

"I was afraid of what you would do."

"You were right." She checked the revolver, slid the other magazines into her pocket. She really didn't think she would need them but better to be prepared.

"And what are you going to do about Robin?"

"Robin's taken care of. Travis is picking her up and taking her away. She'll get her story, her headline. With good timing, she'll be back there just in time to break the story."

"No."

Kendra turned and Linda was right there in front her. If she had been real, if she had been solid, Kendra would have bumped into her but as it was, they just stood face-to-face.

"Robin could love you; you could love her. Are you just going to throw that away?"

"Robin loves her story, her big opportunity. I was just a means. So now she'll have her story, her opportunity. And I'll have my revenge." She stepped away. Linda was still real enough that she walked around her.

"Are you so sure? Damn, you're just as stubborn as you ever were! Haven't you learned a thing?"

"And what would that be?" Kendra demanded as she put her jacket on, pulling the wristbands tight.

Linda came around in front of her again. "I am gone! I am never coming back! And there is nothing you can do to change that."

"Seems to me you've been back for this past year." Kendra's tone was sharp and crisp.

"It wasn't Artie who kept me here," Linda said in even tones. "And it's not even that my body is out there somewhere in the trees. It's you."

Kendra hesitated, an instance, and then Linda went on.

"I told you to get away, to live your life, to forget about me. You didn't."

"I couldn't."

"You must."

This time Kendra stopped.

"My time is past. I should have gone with you. I shouldn't have married him. I should have, could have, but I didn't. Those are my mistakes, and I lived with them. Don't make them yours."

"You had a hell of a life because of me."

"Damn it, Kendra! That was my choice. Not yours, not your life. My mistakes. Don't compound them by making them yours!"

Kendra went back to checking the house, making sure everything was in place.

"Kendra, let me go. Don't ruin both our lives. Live yours."

Kendra slammed the door behind her and walked out into the cold.

* * *

Artie and Sue were just coming out of the house when she pulled in the driveway blocking their car in.

"Go away, bitch," Artie said without even giving her much of a look as he walked down the sidewalk to the car. "I've got a restraining order on you."

"Do tell." Kendra got out of the vehicle and came around. "Folks around here tell me a restraining order isn't worth the paper it's printed on. Unless you have it with a deputy sheriff attached."

Artie turned to face her as one of his favorite sayings was thrown at him. Sue hesitated at the end of the sidewalk and while Kendra placed her, she didn't look at her.

"Got one handy?" Kendra asked.

"Got them on speed dial." Artie pulled out the cell phone from his pocket.

"Go ahead. I'm sure they'll be along shortly anyway, Artie. I just wanted to get here first. Domestic terrorism is going to be much more important to them than a first wife missing. I want to know where you laid her after you killed her."

"Didn't kill her," he denied. "She left. She find someone better than you, bitch?"

"You laid her in her grave," Kendra said evenly, "after you chased her through the field and caught her in the woods."

He looked startled, looked at Sue and back at Kendra. Then he gave a shaky laugh as he shook his head. "No, she was already gone by the time I got back from my hunting trip."

"Kendra," Sue cut in, stepping forward. "You're wrong. She was already gone when he got here."

"Not when he came back the first time," Kendra answered, "after you called him." She never took her eyes off Artie. "She was packing. She expected to be long gone by the time he came back from his hunting trip, but she got delayed and he came back early." She gave Sue a sideways glance. "Wonder why that happened. I don't suppose you would know anything, would you, Sue?"

Sue turned red in the face. "She was being a coward, sneaking out on him. After all he had done for her, putting up with you. I knew she'd cut out on him sooner or later. When Frog told me she'd canceled the appointment with him, I knew."

"Knew what? That she was leaving him or leaving you?"

There was the crystal clear moment of dead silence and Kendra could hear the sirens in the distance. She had gotten here first but she was going to have to move along soon.

Artie looked confused, like he couldn't grasp what Kendra was saying. "What!" He took a step forward. "What the hell is she talking about, Sue?" He looked from one woman to the other.

"As soon as Frog told her Linda canceled, Sue made tracks over to see her. She could stand for Linda leaving you, but she couldn't stand for her leaving the area. She needed to know if she had a chance."

296 M. E. Logan

"A chance?" He turned to look at Sue. "A chance for what?"

"For them, for Sue to be the significant other in Linda's life. And Linda told her she was leaving. It had taken a while, but she realized she'd made a mistake not leaving with me."

"The hell you say!"

"Yeah," Kendra sneered. "So I guess that's when Sue called you. Thought you'd come back, foil her plans. At least then, she'd still be around. And Sue and Linda could continue to be 'pals'—'buddies.' And you wouldn't be any the wiser."

"You're lying."

"Look at her and tell me that."

He turned to his wife and searched her face but he realized the truth. "You telling me they were lovers?" Sue shook her head, backing up from him as he turned on her. "Her and Linda, all along?"

"No. Linda had too much integrity. She couldn't live a lie. When she realized she'd made a mistake, she was ready to get out. If that meant leaving everything, she was ready to do it."

"You called me," he said to Sue. "You told me she was leaving."

"What else did she say, Artie? What'd she say to inflame you so much that you drove all the way back to confront her?"

"She was cleaning me out, the joint accounts, everything. The farm was going to go into foreclosure. I'd lose everything."

"So you found her packing, getting ready to leave and killed her."

"No!" He turned back to her. "I didn't kill her."

"I think you did."

"You can't prove anything."

"Who said anything about proving?" Kendra retorted. "I know."

"And what do you know, bitch?"

"I know you found her packing. You said it would be a cold day in hell when she left you. You cornered her in the living room, was pushing her to the bedroom. She grabbed one of the logs from beside the stove. Hit you with it."

"Like I said, you've got a vivid imagination." But his voice sounded more strained.

"Yeah, I do." She watched him. He looked a little paler now. "And I imagine you're going to tell me exactly where she is before I leave here."

"Or what?"

"Or you won't be able to answer any questions anymore."

He half turned, his hand reaching behind him.

"He's got a gun!"

Kendra had already pulled hers out. She really didn't care if she killed him but she wanted his answers more. "So do I."

"You had your chance, bitch."

Kendra leveled the revolver. "Sorry I passed on it. Life would have been different."

He must have read something in her face for abruptly he tossed the gun into the snowbank. "You going to shoot an unarmed man?"

Kendra smiled. She was constantly amazed at people who didn't play by the rules but expected everyone else would. "In a heartbeat."

Artie shook his head, his hands up, outstretched, still holding the cell phone. "I didn't kill her," he said suddenly. "You gotta believe me."

"Why?"

"Because it's the truth."

Kendra hesitated for an instant. What if it was?

"I came back early, yes. And yes, she was packing. I'll even own up that I hit her, knocked her across the bed. But she was alive when I left."

"And why should I believe that?"

He took a step forward in protest. "I loved Linda! I had for years! She was the only woman I ever loved. I only wanted to help her but she wouldn't let me! She might have married me but that was only because of her mother. She thought I was a failure, that I hadn't done anything since high school, that I was all hot air, that I never followed through on anything."

Kendra hesitated. Artie's words had the ring of truth in them. What if she were wrong? That still left the question of what had happened. They could hear the sirens coming down the valley road. She heard the cars coming in the gravel drive.

"What's that? What's going on?"

"They stopped the truck, Artie." To her knowledge, they hadn't for sure but they should have and she was gambling that he didn't know. And it gave her immense satisfaction to see that flicker of uncertainty. "They should be raiding the compound about now. It'll just be a matter of time before they're here. But like I said, I wanted to get to you first."

"The truck!" Sue burst out with. "Raid the compound?"

"What, Artie? You keep wifey in the dark?" She glanced from Artie to Sue and saw her horrified look. "Artie packed a truck with explosives, got Johnny and one of the Collins boys to take it to the coliseum. Big bang for the state championships."

"You did what!" Sue took several steps toward him and stopped abruptly at Kendra's movement. "You're fucking crazy!"

"Yes," Kendra agreed. "Probably so."

"You're lying." He looked at Sue. "She's lying, just a crazy dyke who hates me because her girlfriend preferred me."

"Ahh, the other issue," Kendra said, surprised at how calm she was feeling. "Now that is what I wanted to talk to you about before the law got here."

"I guess she really didn't prefer you if she was leaving you. Must have really damaged your ego."

"She never left, Artie. She never got away. And if she was alive when you left, gone when you returned, what happened in between?"

They must have had the same thought at the same time for they both looked at Sue.

"What are you looking at me for?" she protested. "I didn't do anything!" She backed up from both of them.

"You were the only one who knew," Kendra said slowly as she realigned puzzle pieces.

"You said she left with someone," Artie accused. "You said you talked to her. You knew I had hit her." He grabbed Sue by the shoulders even as Kendra heard cars in the driveway, doors open, people getting out. Time seemed to be in slow motion.

"What did you do?" Artie shouted in Sue's face.

"Put the gun down, Kendra," the voice came down from the other side of the car. "We'll take it from here."

She was too intent on Artie and Sue to pay attention. This wasn't supposed to happen this way. Artie was the one who was supposed to have killed her.

"Kendra," came Travis's reasonable voice from somewhere behind her. "Don't do this. Don't be foolish. Put the gun down."

What was Travis doing here? some part of her mind demanded but she was too intent on watching Artie shake Sue. For a small man, he sure had the strength in him as Sue was shaken like a rag doll. She still wanted answers and was still determined to get them.

"What did you do?" Artie screamed.

"It was an accident!" Sue screamed back.

Kendra's jaw dropped. Of all things she had thought. She was frozen, listening.

"I didn't mean to!"

"Son of a bitch!"

Artie became aware of everyone else there, and still holding on to Sue, fell back toward the house. "No, not in this lifetime."

Kendra lost all awareness of everyone, everything, except for Sue. Sue was the one who had the answers. And Artie was pulling her into the house. Nothing could happen, not now, not this close to getting the answers. She dropped the gun and sprinted, just as they reached the door.

She tackled Sue, Artie fell into the house, just as someone tackled her. Not letting go of Sue, she rolled and there was someone pulling them away from the house. Just as she took a deep breath, the house exploded, not even a large explosion, except the propane tank at the back of the house went next.

She felt something hit her back, Sue was under her, and she knew soon she would have the answers one way or another. If she didn't get the answers from Sue, Linda would be able to tell her. In the meantime, she recognized the jacket, the hand around her.

"Travis, I thought you didn't like fireworks."

CHAPTER TWENTY-TWO

"You don't know what it was like!" Travis exclaimed as she recounted the story to Peg and Kendra. "I come down this road, I've been sliding all over. You weren't half kidding when you said the roads were bad. If it wasn't snow and ice, it was mud and ice and someplaces just plain mud, which was worse than the ice. And I see her just sitting on the side of the road on the little bridge abutment. Cool as could be, as if she just knew I'd be along and she didn't have to worry about anyone else coming along.

"And I just about lose it when I see who it is! I mean this woman's been missing for days. They keep saying that she's off on assignment, but we know different, that she can't be reached. That her people are getting worried. That maybe something's happened. And here I go down the road and she's just sitting there waiting for me to pick her up."

Travis's face glowed with excitement. Kendra moved carefully in her hospital bed. A broken arm, concussion. She'd been lucky. She turned to reach for the glass of water but Peg was there first, handing it to her. She sipped through the straw, looking up, catching Mike's eye from his seat on the foot of the bed. Then they all turned back to Travis.

"So I stop and she just gets in, slides in, and I'm just speechless. She looks at me and says 'Hello Travis,' and I feel great that she recognizes me much less remembers my name. 'I understand that you're supposed to take me home and I'm not supposed to give you any trouble.'

"Yes, ma'am, I say. That's about all I can say. So we start down the road, and I don't know where in hell he came from but this deputy sheriff shoots by me like I'm standing still. And then we get up to the turnoff and there's police cars all over the place. We're being directed one way and she's saying no, grabbing my arm and practically crawling over me to the window.

"We need to go there, she says. You've got to. Kendra's down there. She may need us. I swear, Kendra, that's what she said." She looked at Kendra as if offering the excuse.

"I told you to take her home."

"Christ Almighty, Kendra, the woman's a reporter and a determined one. Let me tell you, don't stand between that woman and a story."

"Yes, I know," Kendra said with a sigh. "I know." *And it was Robin's luck to be where the real story was.* She paused a moment. "Go on."

"So we go on and there's all these black vans and people with jackets that have FBI on the back and ATF and HOMELAND SECURITY. The place is just crawling with them, and she's out of the truck and we see you holding that gun on Artie and Sue. God, I thought you were going to get killed for sure if you didn't put that gun down."

Kendra sighed and put her head back. Yes, she had thought so too. She had thought she would have a bit more time; she had thought Artie would confess. She just wanted answers. The answers she got weren't the ones she expected.

She still had memories of the detective coming in.

"I suppose you want to know," he said. Kendra didn't even remember his name. She had been in a fog, emotional and physical.

"It'd be nice," she had said. She had no clear idea how big her legal problems were but it would all be worth it if she had her answers.

"Sue confessed. She actually seemed relieved. She had gone back after Artie left. She said that Linda was woozy, but getting up and continuing to pack. She was pissed because she knew Sue had called Artie. She wanted Sue to leave, took hold of her arm and pushed her to the door. Sue was crying, went to hug her and Linda pushed her away. Sue blew up, pushed her back. Linda fell, hit her head on the cast-iron stove there."

Kendra was staring at the ceiling, still listening to Travis. So many things she was wrong about. Artie hadn't killed Linda; he thought he was a failure because Linda was leaving. That was when he said she could come to me forever if that was what she wanted. But he left her alive.

Sue was the manipulative one, playing on his fears of failure. So he planned something big to show he wasn't. The planning, the acquisition of materials. He came close, save for Stockton. And her.

He'd booby-trapped the house, knowing they would search it. He just hadn't planned on having to retreat. But surely he knew that going back in, Kendra considered. Maybe he thought he'd fail at that too.

And Kendra had pulled Sue back to save her, by then realizing her role in Linda's death. She still wanted answers.

Harris, yeah, she had thought he was harmless. And he was unless he thought he was cornered. All those Feds coming in must have been his worst nightmare. At least he wasn't killed. He might even escape jail time.

And then there was Robin. Who wanted the story, bad enough that Sue could call and pretend to be Kendra's friend, and lure her in. From what the detective gathered, Sue thought that Kendra wouldn't rest until she knew what happened to Linda. That was certainly dead-on. And if another woman linked with Kendra disappeared, well, it might look like she was the killer.

Mistakes. Miscalculations. Fate. Kendra was supposed to go back to California and never show her face again in

Walton's Corner. She hadn't counted on Kendra's dad getting sick and Kendra moving back to Indiana. Artie was supposed to move on with his life but he kept going over and over his last conversations with Linda. Sooner or later he was going to mention it to someone so Sue married him. Wasn't hard, he just wanted to be bossed around, wasn't much success unless someone told him what to do. Then he goes off half-cocked, gets with this survivalist group and thinks he can bring down the government, overload the system. Be a big man again.

Well, Robin got her story, came close to being a big part of it. National coverage, nice little video of Kendra being the mad deranged dyke, Travis being the big hero.

And what did Kendra get? She had managed to destroy almost everything she had built over the years. And what did she have to show for it?

She looked around the room. At some point while she had been listening but not hearing Travis's story Betty Lou had come in. She was sitting beside the bed, reached over and patted Kendra on the leg, gave her a smile.

Betty Lou, Peg, Travis, Mike. They were standing beside her. Friends who were there when it counted. Friends she hadn't expected to be there. Maybe that was something.

CHAPTER TWENTY-THREE

Kendra walked up the slope to where the police had gathered. How many times had they searched Artie's land, Linda's land, and found nothing? Because Linda had been buried on Kendra's land.

The digging was almost complete by the time Kendra got there. Wasn't a bad place, Kendra thought as she looked around. On a slope, overlooking the valley, the creek down below. Pretty nice actually. Just not known, not where people could go and mourn her.

She got up to the group and they parted to let her through. She stood at the foot and watched as they uncovered what remained, mostly skeleton. Would this bring her peace, Kendra thought. Artie was dead, not by her hand, and not for lack of wanting him to die, but certainly by the seeds he had sown. His plans for revenge had been thwarted too. Close call. The truck almost made it to the sports arena and it would have caused mass destruction.

There was little left in the grave for identification but one of the forensic people picked up something, metal. It looked familiar. Kendra leaned over him.

"May I?" she asked politely. He glanced at the person in charge and then handed it up to her.

A belt buckle with a turquoise stone. A Christmas gift she had given Linda so many years ago.

Kendra nodded and handed it back.

Someone moved in to stand beside her, suggest she leave now, let them take care of the details.

She really didn't want to stay anyway. This wasn't Linda, this was just bones and remains and, and what? She turned to go back down the slope and stopped.

Robin was down there, standing before the camera, giving a report on the latest story, perhaps the last story on Artie Jeffers. She had got quite a bit of mileage out this, might take her to the big time. Kendra didn't know how she felt, didn't know if she had been used or been the user.

Walking down, she had to pass Robin. She couldn't avoid her. She really didn't know what she felt, only that she was terribly conscious of her, her voice, her bearing, her intensity.

She was almost past her when she heard the report end.

"Kendra."

"No comment," she said automatically. It wasn't the first time she had been approached by reporters. Linda was buried on her land, they had been supposed lovers, she had searched for Linda for years, now all public knowledge.

"Kendra." Robin had made it up beside her now.

"No comment," Kendra repeated.

Robin caught her arm, made her turn around. "I'm not being a reporter now," she said. "I just want to talk to you."

Kendra turned. She wasn't angry. She felt nothing at all except a profound tiredness. "Not a reporter?" She frowned and looked at Robin curiously. "I can't imagine that; I didn't think you had any other existence."

"Kendra, we need to talk about what happened."

"What? We both got what we wanted. You got your story and I found Linda. What else is there to talk about?"

"Something else happened, something between us?"

"Did it?" She searched Robin's face. "I don't know that. I know I thought so at the time, but you were just a reporter looking for a story."

Robin dropped her arm. "I wasn't always a reporter."

"You could have fooled me. But then, that's what you were doing, wasn't it?"

She turned away, walked past the house. She didn't even want to go in anymore. Travis was waiting in the drive to take her back to Carmel, to pick up the pieces.

She got into the new Jeep, Nellybelle II. "Let's go," she said to no one in particular. "I'm tired. I've seen enough for today."

CHAPTER TWENTY-FOUR

"Are you going to let them in?" Linda was sitting by the fireplace.

Kendra picked up her glass and examined the contents before she finished the whiskey. "I don't think so." She could hear the murmuring at the front door via the speaker but it was too much effort to move. She just wanted to sit there, let the world spin by.

"Are you sure she's in there?"

"I think so. Can't really tell, this damn house, you can't see a damn thing." That sounded like Travis.

"Didn't you have a key? You were looked after it for over a year!"

"She rekeyed the locks."

"All of them?"

"Maybe…" That voice went away.

Kendra continued to sit there. She wasn't concerned about them getting in. Actually, she hadn't been concerned about much lately. She had stopped going into work. They had managed to do without her for this long. She really felt unnecessary. Superfluous. The legal issues? She had gotten a lawyer. Correction, Peg had gotten her a lawyer. He'd advised her to keep a low profile. That certainly was not a problem.

She laid her head back on the back of the chair and closed her eyes. She had plotted to kill someone. And with cold deliberate planning, she had taken two years out of her life to work toward that goal. She would have succeeded too except for a twist of circumstances. Maybe he did deserve it. After all, he had organized a massive terrorist act. So she was a hero for all the wrong reasons.

She heard the back door to the garage open. Travis must have gone over the fence. She heard her stumble over something in the garage but it wasn't worth getting up for. Sooner or later, they would come in. Now, or later, what difference did it make?

Travis opened the side door. She could hear the murmurs of their voices. Peg, Travis, Betty Lou and Robin. Surprised they didn't bring the lawyer, the therapist, whoever. They'd been trying for a couple of weeks now.

The four of them came traipsing down the hallway.

"So this is where you've been hiding," this brash voice came.

Kendra turned her head, opened her eyes. Betty Lou stood there, hands on hips, looking at her, shaking her head.

"If you don't look a mess," Betty Lou announced. She marched to the kitchen. "Where's that coffeepot? I know you must have one."

"She hates coffee," Robin said.

"Well, too bad." Betty Lou rummaged through the cabinets. "She's got to have one for company. Ahh, here it is. Here, Peg, you make the coffee. I've got another little cure for her."

Robin came around to take the glass out of Kendra's hand. "Kendra, come on, sit up. You've got to get off this pity pot. You're not doing yourself or anyone else any good."

"Travis, go start the shower."

A cold glass was put in Kendra's hand. "Bottoms up," Betty Lou announced.

"What's that?" Robin asked of the creamed-coffee colored liquid.

Kendra obediently drank it, not really caring what it might be.

"Coke and milk. Old staff sergeant I knew swore by it. Said it wasn't any worse than a root beer float and sobered her up every time."

Almost immediately Kendra bolted for the bathroom.

"Still works," Betty Lou commented.

"She can't go on like this," Robin said.

* * *

A shower, a change of clothes, some sleep made Kendra feel something, just not necessarily good.

"I was so wrong," she said as she stared at the plate of food Betty Lou sat down in front of her.

"Welcome to the human race," Peg said.

She looked up at the women surrounding the table. "I was so convinced Artie did it."

"You and most of Walton's Corner," said Betty Lou. "No one ever suspected Sue could even do something like that."

"Well, it did sound like an accident," Travis put in.

"Which never would have happened if she hadn't called Artie."

"She was always jealous of you, Kendra. She thought she was more suited to be with Linda. She was more the outdoors type, could keep up with Linda." She shook her head. "Big strapping farm girl, wasn't anything on the farm she couldn't do."

Kendra shook her head. That didn't excuse her actions.

"Look," Robin said sharply. "You can wallow all you want but look at what you did. You solved a murder. You thwarted a bombing that even could have killed a future president. You saved how many lives. You had the wrong theory but you did an awful lot of right things."

Kendra wasn't mollified.

"You saved me," Robin added.

Kendra grunted. "Now I'm not so sure Artie would have done anything more than try to scare you into silence."

"I don't scare easy."

Kendra shrugged. "Well, you got your story."

"Yes," Robin repeated with a frown, "I got my story."

"What are you going to do now?" Peg asked Kendra.

Kendra shook her head. "I don't know. I've got a pile of legal bills. I don't think they're charging me with anything. My attorney thinks there's a deal in the works." She glanced at Robin. "But that's off the record."

"Well, of course," Robin bristled. And there were a few moments of strained silence.

"Anyway," Kendra picked up the conversation. "I don't know what I'm going to do." She looked around the house. "I'm putting the house up for sale. Mike made me an offer for my half of Abatis but I haven't decided."

"Why don't you get away for a bit?" Peg asked. "Change of scenery."

"Like I've got the money to go somewhere?"

Talk went back and forth as they finished dinner and did the dishes. By the time they left, Kendra was thinking again, maybe functioning. Maybe not, she thought as the last one left.

She walked back into the living room.

"You've got friends," Linda commented.

Kendra glanced at the faint image by the fireplace. "I thought you were going to be gone, once I found you."

"Got a few things still left to get settled."

"Like what?" Kendra picked up the bottle of Maker's Mark that Peg hadn't found from beside the chair and tucked in against the side table. She held it up to see the level and was seriously considering having an after dinner drink when the doorbell rang.

Someone probably forgot something, she thought as she turned toward the front door. She stopped when she saw that it was Robin. "Might as well get it over with," she muttered as she walked toward the door.

"Forget something?" she greeted.

"Maybe," Robin said cautiously as she stood there. When Kendra didn't invite her in, she finally ventured again. "Can we talk?"

Kendra shrugged and turned back into the house. Robin followed her into the dining room where Kendra picked up the bottle from the dining room table and put it away in the cabinet. Maybe not today, not now at least. Later maybe.

"You weren't just a story," Robin said abruptly. "All right, at the first, the very first, I saw that we could help each other, so maybe you were. But that changed."

"Okay, so it changed." Kendra could admit that. At least, it had for her. She had thought it had for Robin, but she had been wrong on so many things.

"Are you going to tell me that I was anything more than a source of information for you to go after Artie in the beginning?"

After some hesitation, Kendra shook her head. "No. You had the knack of digging out information and I wanted to know how you did it. Pure and simple."

Robin took a deep breath and plunged on. "Look, Kendra, we started out using each other, but something happened along the way. I thought there was some caring involved. And then you shut me out."

Kendra set her jaw. She had cared, but she cared more about getting Artie, just like Robin cared more about her story.

"We had some good times," Robin said slowly as she searched Kendra's face. "At least I thought they were good times. Weren't they?"

"Yes," Kendra admitted reluctantly. Good times that made her ache with the memories, good times that made her wonder if she had made the right decision in dumping Robin.

"I didn't discover that until after you were gone. And then no one was telling me anything."

"I thought you didn't want anyone in your life."

Robin shrugged. "I thought that was what I wanted." She hesitated. "Maybe you weren't the only one who discovered she was wrong about a few things."

Kendra's heart leaped in hope but then she caught herself. She had made so many bad decisions in the past year. She didn't know what to say now.

"I'd like to see if there's anything there," Robin said slowly. "Without any excuse of a story or any distractions in the way. Just us. If you're interested."

Yes! came this voice behind her. She could feel Linda's urging. *Seize the day.*

"What did you have in mind?"

"You need to get away from here for a while, sort things out. I have a condo in Sarasota. It makes a great getaway." She came closer to take Kendra's hands in hers.

Kendra was uncertain. Was Robin offering her space? Or was she inviting her along?

"We'd have time to talk," Robin continued. "Without distractions. Nothing except sand and surf. We can see if there's anything there for us." She still held Kendra's hands, but she didn't come any closer.

Kendra swallowed the lump in her throat. She would have hesitated more except for the hard push between her shoulder blades that propelled her right up against Robin.

Robin blinked in surprise, started to step back but Kendra caught her, an arm around her shoulders.

"That might be possible," she agreed. "If you're sure."

Robin nodded. "I'm sure."

Robin felt so good against her. Kendra couldn't believe this was happening. "Sure there's not a human interest angle in it for you?"

"Oh, yeah," Robin countered. "I think it might even be a real big story." She moved closer. "But this one's off the record." She turned her face up to Kendra's, pulled her toward her. "Completely off the record."

Bella Books, Inc.

Women. Books. Even Better Together.

P.O. Box 10543
Tallahassee, FL 32302

Phone: 800-729-4992
www.bellabooks.com